PRAISE FOR YVETTE MA

"Start this engrossing, mesmerizing and loving book and you won't
want to put it down. From the first page, I was transported into Yvette
Manessis Corporon's layered story of resilience and strength. She
writes with heart and soul and offers unforgettable characters, rich
in history and mythology. A page turner to the very end. *Daughter
of Ruins* would make for an excellent screen adaptation—listen up
Hollywood!"

—ADAM GLASSMAN, *OPRAH DAILY*

"A moving and transporting novel about the possibilities of friendship and fulfillment amidst deep loss. *Daughter of Ruins* explores
the harm caused not just by forces of nature but by damaged souls.
A testament to the magic and love that women constantly create
in ordinary days and despite extraordinary circumstances."

—MARJAN KAMALI, BESTSELLING AUTHOR OF
THE LION WOMEN OF TEHRAN

"The word is spellbinding! Yvette Manessis Corporon makes history
feel intimate in this sweeping novel, which goes beyond the Greece
you've seen in tourist photos and into the country's tumultuous 20th
century. Demetria, who has an artist's spirit in a time and place that
finds such things impractical, finds out what it means to forge her
own path. You will be cheering her on."

—ELENA NICOLAOU, TODAY.COM,
FOR *DAUGHTER OF RUINS*

"*Daughter of Ruins* paints a vivid, heartfelt depiction of three very
different women who fight to take control of their destinies after
suffering devastations, injustices, and circumstances beyond their
own dominion. Through beautiful writing and perfectly rendered

nods to mythology, we journey to a conclusion that truly brings to life the strength of these enduring women."

—JENNI L. WALSH, *USA TODAY*
BESTSELLING AUTHOR OF *UNSINKABLE*

"A sumptuous feast of love and history, *Daughter of Ruins* is Corporon's most robust and poetic offering to date. With lush language and arresting backdrops, the myth and magic of women bound by tenacity and threatened by circumstance and war, is as enriching as it is unforgettable."

—RACHEL MCMILLAN,
AUTHOR OF *THE MOZART CODE*

"An epic, transportive saga complete with vibrant settings, rich mythology and storytelling, and unforgettable heroines—compelling, immerse, and deeply satisfying."

—LEE KELLY, AUTHOR OF *THE STARLETS*
AND *THE ANTIQUITY AFFAIR*

"Corporon brings to light a little-known part of European history with her fluid prose, attention to detail, and character-driven narrative."

—*HISTORICAL NOVEL SOCIETY* FOR
WHERE THE WANDERING ENDS

"Written with a perceptive eye, *Where the Wandering Ends* considers the challenges faced by people during wartime and highlights the determination to survive despite painful circumstances. Corfu's beauty, which Corporon describes in sumptuous detail, is juxtaposed against the turbulence and devastation caused by war. Fascinating historical facts and references to mythological Greek tales intertwine with moving scenes, tension-building plot points and surprising revelations to create a powerful, soaring story. This is a spectacular novel about the enduring devotion of family and the steadfast loyalty between friends."

"Love, hope, courage, and survival thread their way through this magically crafted story combining history and mythology. This story stays with me—the love and sacrifice of mothers, promises made by children, unbearable loss, and dreams cast aside but never forgotten."

"From maestro winds to fried smelt, from Mother Nyx to the Ionian Sea, and from ouzo to olive trees, this book hums with the tantalizing spirit of Greece. Leaning into 20th century Greek history—including a pivotal storyline including Britain's Prince Philip, and his mother, Princess Alice of Greece—author Yvette Manessis Corporon, herself a first-generation Greek-American, takes us past the Second World War, through the bloody civil war of the late 1940s, and through the difficult years in the conflict's aftermath, all through the eyes of a few families from the island of Corfu whose lives intersect through the years. A sweeping, multigenerational story of love, loss and sacrifice, *Where the Wandering Ends* is a beautiful journey through time in a war-ravaged, picturesque land of royalty, ruin, and hope."

"Set on the romantic island of Corfu, *Where the Wandering Ends* is a powerful, emotional tale of recent history, showing the disruption of lives during the Greek civil war, not only to the simple Corfiots but also to the Greek royal family who called Corfu their home."

—RHYS BOWEN, *NEW YORK TIMES* BESTSELLING
AUTHOR OF THE ROYAL SPYNESS AND MOLLY
MURPHY HISTORICAL MYSTERIES AND INTER-
NATIONAL BESTSELLER *THE VENICE SKETCHBOOK*

"In her latest novel, *Where the Wandering Ends*, Yvette Manessis Corporon takes readers to the Greek isle of Corfu, a stunning locale where the sun-drenched cliffs meet the shimmering blue of the Ionian Sea. There, a sweeping family saga unfolds over multiple generations, filled with war, love, loss, and ultimately redemption. Corporon tells a transportive story filled with pathos and longing, a tale of homecoming, woven with beautiful threads from history, mythology, and the indelible truths and wisdom of the human heart."

—ALLISON PATAKI, *NEW YORK TIMES* BEST-
SELLING AUTHOR OF *THE MAGNIFICENT
LIVES OF MARJORIE POST*

"A soul-stirring tale of love, loss, friendship, family, and fate set amid the ravages of war, *Where the Wandering Ends* is especially relevant today. Yvette Manessis Corporon writes with grace and crystalline clarity about what matters most: the transcendent resilience of the human spirit."

—CHRISTOPHER ANDERSEN,
#1 *NEW YORK TIMES* BESTSELLING AUTHOR

"Emotive, transportive, and gorgeously rendered, this novel plumbs the depths of how we find our way back from great heartache and loss. Heartbreaking one moment and utterly life-affirming the next, *Where the Wandering Ends* will open your eyes to a moment in history that should not be forgotten."

"Yvette Corporon takes her place among the best of historical fiction with this evocative, sometimes mystical, novel. Filled with characters you'll come to love, hard-won faith, dreams lost and found, and settings that will take your breath, this story follows the complex and winding ways that life endures in the aftermath of war. From the hillsides of Corfu to the streets of NYC, *Where the Wandering Ends* is a sensitive celebration of unconditional love."

"A vibrant tale of family, love and loss, and the hope of new beginnings. Corporon's research is impeccable as she lays Greece's rich and storied history before readers, providing the perfect backdrop for her multigenerational story. *Where the Wandering Ends* truly brings readers to the heart of Greece in a story that is as sweeping as a saga and yet as intimate as a mother's love. I enjoyed it immensely."

daughter

of

ruins

ALSO BY YVETTE MANESSIS CORPORON

Where the Wandering Ends

When the Cypress Whispers

Something Beautiful Happened

daughter

of

ruins

a novel

YVETTE MANESSIS CORPORON

HARPER MUSE

Daughter of Ruins

Published by Harper Muse, an imprint of HarperCollins Focus LLC.

This book is a work of fiction. The characters, incidents, and dialogue are drawn from the author's imagination and are not to be construed as real. Any resemblance to actual events or persons, living or dead, is entirely coincidental.

Any internet addresses (websites, blogs, etc.) in this book are offered as a resource. They are not intended in any way to be or imply an endorsement by HarperCollins Focus LLC, nor does HarperCollins Focus LLC vouch for the content of these sites for the life of this book.

Library of Congress Cataloging-in-Publication Data

Names: Corporon, Yvette Manessis, author.
Title: Daughter of ruins : a novel / Yvette Manessis Corporon.
Description: Nashville : Harper Muse, 2024. | Summary: "A sweeping story that follows a Greek woman through the mid-twentieth century as she reconciles her family's troubled past and forges a path all of her own"—Provided by publisher.
Identifiers: LCCN 2024022216 (print) | LCCN 2024022217 (ebook) | ISBN 9781400236114 (paperback) | ISBN 9781400236121 (epub) | ISBN 9781400236138
Subjects: LCGFT: Novels.
Classification: LCC PS3603.O7713 D38 2024 (print) | LCC PS3603.O7713 (ebook) | DDC 813/.6—dc23/eng/20240513
LC record available at https://lccn.loc.gov/2024022216
LC ebook record available at https://lccn.loc.gov/2024022217

Printed in the United States of America

24 25 26 27 28 LBC 5 4 3 2 1

For my husband, Dave.

I am not an angel and do not pretend to be. That is not one of my roles. But I am not the devil either. I am a woman and a serious artist, and I would like so to be judged.

—Maria Callas

Prologue

Dear Mama,

    Today I am so excited. Baba and I are going to visit Thea Olga. It has been so long since I've seen her. I'm ten years old now, old enough to take the bus alone, but Baba won't let me so I begged and begged for him to take me. I think he agreed to get me to stop asking. I can't wait to see her and the sacred snakes! I get so excited each time I see them, especially when Olga places one in my hands. I will say a special prayer for you, like I always do. Maybe you will come visit me one day like the snakes do. That would make me so happy.

Your daughter,

Demitra

DEMITRA GLANCED AT the clock and smiled. She still had enough time to send the letter before they left to catch the bus. She looked out the window and saw *Baba* at the well scrubbing his hands.

She slipped to the outdoor kitchen and grabbed a book of matches Baba kept in a jar beside the kindling. Placing the letter between her lips, she struck the red-tipped match against the striker and inhaled the smoke and sulfur. She held up the burning match, then took the paper from between her lips with her other hand and touched it to the fire.

Her eyes widened as the paper erupted in flame, her gaze following the smoke as it drifted up to the sky. Distracted by the dancing smoke, she waited a bit too long before dropping the burning paper, watching as it floated to the ground. She brought her finger to her mouth to soothe the sting where the heat singed her.

Demitra was three when Mama died in America and Baba returned here to Cephalonia to raise her. Demitra's fragmented reminiscences of Mama were more feelings than actual memories, since she'd lost her at an age when memories are as easily made as they are lost. The security of her small hand in Mama's, the sanctuary of sleeping tucked within the curve of her body, the wave of warmth and love a mother's mere smile can elicit.

She was unsure if the hazy, disconnected moments she coveted were even true memories at all. Perhaps they were a daughter's wishes floating up to the heavens, like the smoke of the letters she began composing to Mama before she could write, when her letters were nothing more than a child's hopeful drawings—a stick-figure family of three, a crudely drawn heart tossed into the evening fire when Baba was not looking.

As hard as she tried and did her best to focus and concentrate to conjure Mama, Demitra could not remember what Mama looked like, only what she felt like. Soft. Warm. Safe. She wanted to believe she might one day recall her face, that a personification of her existed, yet Mama was always somehow out of reach, like a magnificent oasis in the distance of a dream.

She searched for her night and day, staring at her own image in the mirror for hours sometimes, hoping she might recognize at least a piece of her mother. Did Mama share her dark eyes flecked with brilliant gold? Did Mama's hair cascade in a torrent of curls, unruly and wild, as if the River Styx itself flowed down her back? And like Demitra, had Mama dreamed of a life beyond the stifling confines of her village?

"I hope my note finds you, Mama," she whispered as she knelt, reaching out her hands to sift through the pile of ashes, all that remained of the dozens of letters she had written these past several weeks. "I hope I find you."

BABA SHUFFLED ALONG behind her, dragging his feet as he smoked cigarettes one after the other, while Demitra raced ahead. The walk was short from the bus stop to the church where they would meet Olga, but to Demitra it felt like an eternity.

Olga had explained the legend of the snakes of Panagia to her years ago. The story dated back centuries to when pirates once invaded Cephalonia. Knowing the invaders were coming, the nuns of the monastery locked themselves inside the church and prayed for the Virgin Mother to save them. When the pirates finally broke down the door, they entered the room to find the nuns gone. Only the snakes were left behind, slithering across the floor and marked with the shape of a cross between their eyes.

Every year since then, the blessed snakes of Panagia have returned each August in preparation for the Ascension of the Virgin Mary on August 15. They made their presence known by appearing in the church, slithering across the altar and icons, and allowing the faithful to hold them and pray with them. And each year after August 15, the snakes disappeared again until the following August, when they came again to bless the faithful.

Demitra spotted Olga pacing the courtyard the moment they walked through the gate leading to the church.

"Thea Olga!" Demitra shouted as she ran into the arms of her aunt. Instantly she was enveloped in the woman's black robes, smelling of incense and soap.

"Hello, my sweet girl." The nun held Demitra tight, kissing the top of her head.

"Hello, Pericles." She greeted Baba with a kiss on both cheeks. He nodded in return.

"Thea Olga, I've been dreaming of this since last year. Can I please hold a snake again? I promise to be gentle." The words spilled out of Demitra's mouth as she scanned the grounds of the churchyard while holding Olga's hand and pulling her toward the church entrance.

The nun looked down at her niece, her usual bright smile replaced by pursed lips. The black fabric of her habit obscured her hair and rested low on her brow. Olga's deep brown eyes, usually so clear, were red-tinged. Her skin, typically sun-kissed from working in the garden, had a gray pallor, her face lined with wisdom and with worry.

"Demitra." Olga spoke softly, kindly.

Demitra continued to tug her toward the church entrance. "I promise to be gentle. I'm not afraid of them, not at all."

"Demitra, listen to me." The nun stopped and knelt in front of the child.

Demitra paused, still giddy with the excitement of spotting her first snake, her eyes darting about the grounds.

"They are not here," Olga said. "They have not come."

Demitra looked at her aunt and tilted her head, confused by her words. Even Baba inched closer from the edge of the courtyard where he was smoking a cigarette.

"What do you mean?" Demitra asked. "Who is not here?"

"The snakes." Olga spoke slowly and gently, as if the tone of her voice might somehow temper the implications of her message. "They haven't been seen, and tomorrow is Panagia's. They always come at least a week before, but they have not come."

Demitra's brow furrowed as she contemplated her aunt's words. "What does that mean?"

"This has never happened before," the nun responded, her voice a mere whisper.

Baba flicked his cigarette to the ground and stomped it out with his foot. He walked toward his sister and daughter. "But what do you think it means?"

Olga scanned the ground one last time. Nothing but dirt and grass and rocks all around them.

"It's an omen." Olga did not whisper this time. Taking Demitra's hand in her own, she led the child toward the edge of the churchyard, overlooking the lush green hills below. "They are sending us a message with their absence. I don't know what it is or what it means. But I fear they are trying to warn us of something."

Although she felt the flush of her cheeks and the sting in her eyes, Demitra promised herself she would not cry. As disappointed as she was, she vowed she would find another way to get a message to Mama.

Squeezing Olga's hand, she noticed for the first time the slight tremble in her aunt's touch. "It's all right, Thea Olga." Demitra leaned in and hugged her. "I'm sure everything will be all right."

Taking both of Demitra's hands in her own, Olga raised them to her lips and kissed Demitra's knuckles. She remained silent rather than frighten the child or speak words that were untrue, which would have been a sin.

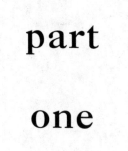

part

one

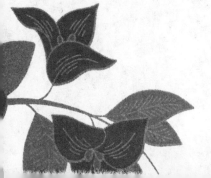

Chapter One

Cephalonia, Greece

1943

THE SNAKES WERE right.

There was reason to worry. Just as Olga feared, the disappearance of the snakes was indeed an omen, ushering in years of devastation and destruction on Cephalonia, across Greece, and around the world.

We are the lucky ones, the residents of Cephalonia thought at first, confident that their patron saint, Gerasimos, and the snakes of Panagia had once again performed miracles, protecting the islanders from harm in the early days of the war when the Italians occupied the island. But as the years passed and the civility of the Italian soldiers gave way to the bloodthirst of the Germans, it was evident that even beautiful Cephalonia was not immune to the horrors of war.

At first the islanders feared and resented the occupying Italian soldiers who descended upon the island by the thousands. But soon the Italians and the villagers found themselves coexisting, as they learned that occupier and occupied were more alike than different.

For thirteen-year-old Demitra, life under Italian occupation went on as it had before. Her days were filled with school and chores around the house. Mr. Stafanotithes, the schoolteacher, was a kindly man who helped fuel Demitra's passion for mythology by allowing her to borrow his personal copies of works like the *Odyssey*, *Medea*, and the *Oresteia*.

Just last year when Demitra turned twelve, Baba announced that money was tight and Demitra was old enough for the cooking, cleaning, and other house chores to fall to her. She heeded Baba's orders and came straight home after school, passing the hours after her chores were finished by losing herself in the ancient myths, enthralled by their tales of love, betrayal, and revenge. She spent hours reading her favorite stories and then attempting to draw them, translating her favorite scenes to the page in her own way. What had begun as a lonely child's attempt to communicate with her lost mother, the crudely drawn pictures of hearts and flowers and stick-figure images of a family, developed over time into a hobby and then a passion.

Each day, after finishing her lessons and then her chores, Demitra filled the quiet, lonely afternoons with her sketch pad and pencils, bringing to life on the page the friends and companions she longed for and prayed might one day appear. She was tempted to show Baba her sketches but thought better of it, deciding her art would be her secret, just as he had his.

Demitra could never claim that Baba was unkind to her. He kept to himself, going about his day, working any odd jobs he could find, and providing for her all the things one might need to survive. But surviving and thriving were two very different things. The house never lacked firewood or food. The well provided more than enough water for drinking and cooking. And each year Baba commissioned two new dresses from the local seamstress, as well as new shoes from the cobbler.

"She's a girl, not a feral cat," Olga would scold him each time she saw her brother, reminding him that young girls need more than food and water and firewood to survive.

One spring day in 1943 a slight breeze filled the air, carrying the scent of burning kitchen fires across the island. Demitra watched as the tall, slim cypress trees swayed back and forth as if dancing to music only they could hear. She glanced up at the majestic spears towering above, dreaming that they were not trees but skyscrapers like the ones in America, where she had been born. Lost in her thoughts, Demitra imagined what her life might have been like if Baba had stayed in America, if she had been raised there, among tall buildings and beautifully dressed women like those in the magazines that Areti, the kindly woman at the *periptero*, allowed her to leaf through even though Demitra had no money to pay.

Her daydreaming was interrupted by a sound she was not accustomed to hearing in the quiet of the village—a woman's voice, boisterous and unbridled. A laugh like that seemed out of place in this time of uncertainty with talk of tensions between the occupying Italian forces and the Germans. It was a time when friends and neighbors went about their daily chores as quickly and as quietly as possible before retreating again behind closed doors and drawn curtains.

"Come straight home." Baba's warning rang in her ears. And yet, curiosity got the best of her. Demitra diverted from the path and followed the sound of the woman's laughter toward the bluff overlooking the beach.

She had seen the Italian soldiers in town a handful of times. They were always in uniform, always polite and surprisingly friendly, buying bread or unloading supplies at the port. She had never seen them like this. A dozen of them were down on the beach, shirtless and glistening with sea and sweat. With the soldiers were several women, beautiful with curled hair and painted lips. They, too, ran toward the surf and then into the arms of the young men, who twirled them around and around, laughing and singing before falling into the arms of the next one in line for a dance.

Demitra watched in wonder, feeling butterflies in her belly as she gazed at them. She counted three women on the beach, each clad in a beautiful dress with a bold color and pattern. A raven-haired woman sat beside a soldier on a blanket, lifting the hem of her dress just above her knee. She unhooked her stocking and peeled it off with the tips of her fingers. She batted her kohl-lined eyes at her companion before tossing her stocking into the air, then tilting her head back and laughing before jumping up and running toward the surf, kicking and splashing at the men as she lifted her face toward the sun.

Then Demitra heard the same laugh that first caught her attention and called her to the bluff. She scanned the beach but could not place her at first. Finally she spotted the woman as she sprang out from inside a changing closet, followed by a young soldier with crimson lipstick marks visible on his mouth and cheek.

Unlike the other women's, her hair was yellow, a shade so pale it looked like the silk of September corn. She wore it short, hanging just past her chin, curled in the American style. The blonde woman ran toward the surf, splashing the young man who chased her into the water and then picked her up, flinging her over his shoulder effortlessly as the butcher might carry a baby lamb.

He carried her back to the blanket and placed her down gently. She smiled up at him, reaching her red-tipped fingers around his neck. She then pulled him toward her, falling back on the blanket, his mouth on hers.

Demitra inched closer to the edge of the bluff. As she did, she stumbled on the stones, dislodging a few that tumbled down to the beach below. Hearing the rustling, the soldier sat up and looked toward her.

"*Chi e la?*" he shouted in Italian. His blonde companion sat up as well, placing her hand over her eyes to block the sun.

"*E una ragazza,*" she announced as she spotted Demitra.

Frozen now with fear and shame, Demitra stayed rooted to the ground, unsure of what to do.

The soldier stood and took a few steps closer as the blonde woman remained on the blanket.

"*Ciao, bella!*" the soldier shouted and waved to her. He removed his cap and bowed, revealing a shock of red hair. Demitra had never seen red hair before and wondered if the soldier had dyed it.

The woman stood and ran over to the soldier, who placed his cap back on his head. She wrapped one arm around his waist and waved the other frantically in the air toward Demitra.

"*Ciao, bella.*" She smiled broadly. "*Bellisima.*" The woman then brought her fingers to her lips and blew Demitra a kiss.

Demitra felt the heat of her face and imagined the flush on her cheeks matching the red of the soldier's hair. A tenuous smile crossed her mouth as a mix of embarrassment and excitement whirled inside her. Still seated on the ground, she lifted her hand slowly and waved back.

The blonde woman smiled again, winking at Demitra before turning away, running again toward the surf with her soldier in pursuit.

That day was the first of Demitra's many visits to the bluff and into the world of the young women the Italian army imported, along with food and wine and supplies, to keep the regiment satiated.

For weeks, a rare excitement filled Demitra's world as she stopped by the beach on her way home after school to bask in the laughter and levity of the young, beautiful women and their soldiers. Each time, she sat on the ground beneath the towering olive tree, wedging herself between the massive roots that perforated the ground, imagining what it would be like to peel off her own stockings and run along the shoreline, laughing and twirling among them with unbridled abandon.

The first surprise came after a month of visits. At first she thought it was a trinket left behind, perhaps fallen from a pocket or lost in the entangled limbs of an afternoon tryst. As she kneeled to take her place on the ground, she spotted a tube of lipstick propped against the olive tree. She reached over and opened the tube, twisted and watched in awe as the cherry-red wax emerged.

She had never seen a tube of lipstick before and had certainly never held one. She looked around to see if perhaps the owner was nearby, but she was alone. After glancing around one more time, Demitra touched the lipstick to her mouth, running the tube across her top and bottom lip. With no mirror she had no way of seeing what she looked like, but knowing the color was there lifted her spirits and put a smile on her face.

She sat and watched, scanning the beach for the blonde woman. Demitra knew now that her name was Elena. She had heard "*Elena!*" shouted countless times by then in loud, boisterous laughter and in soft, urgent moans. She spotted her that day as she emerged from the changing closet, hand in hand with a young soldier who looked to be only a few years older than Demitra. Elena glanced up and smiled as her eyes landed on Demitra. She waved and shouted, "*Bellisima!*" as she traced her fingers across her lips and smiled.

Demitra understood at once. This was a gift. She clutched the lipstick tightly in her hand as excitement swelled in her chest.

The summer months brought an unprecedented heat wave and unexpected adventure as Elena continued to leave surprises for her new friend. First Demitra found the lipstick, then days later, the remnants of a perfume bottle. And Demitra found ways to reciprocate, leaving clusters of wildflowers or a piece of sea glass for Elena.

Fall approached and as the heat of summer broke, so did the dream that Cephalonia was immune to the horrors of war. Demitra had overheard Baba speaking with the men at the *kafeneio* who worried what it meant for the islanders that the Italians had surrendered to the Germans, whose crisp uniforms, guttural language, and penchant for cruelty changed the fabric of the island.

She climbed to the bluff once more, wrapping a shawl across her shoulders against the crisp breeze as she took her place on the ground between the roots of the olive tree. Down below on the sand, the soldiers appeared more subdued than usual. Instead of singing and dancing, they huddled together, deep in conversation as the women listened and appeared to comfort them.

Elena lay on a blanket stroking the hair of a young man as he rested his head in her lap. She glanced up toward the bluff, smiling as she spotted Demitra but making no effort to greet her as she usually did, instead quickly turning her attention back to the soldier.

There was no way of knowing that mid-September afternoon in 1943, as Demitra watched Elena and the young men on the beach, that it would be their final goodbye.

"Don't go out today," Baba warned as he left for work the following morning. "There's talk of problems with the Germans and the Italians. I don't know what it means, but it's better for you to stay home."

Baba had never learned the secret of her afternoons on the bluff. It wasn't like she was lying to him, she reasoned. He never asked where she had been or how she spent her days. He always asked the same question as he walked in the door each evening:

"What's for supper?" There was no need for any more questions, or any more answers.

As she approached the bluff that crisp September day, she should have sensed something was wrong. No chatter of conversations carried on the breeze; no hint of smoke from a bonfire or notes of an old favorite song filled the air. As she neared her spot by the tree, Demitra was met with nothing but silence.

She shivered as she walked closer to the edge, unsure if it was the breeze or perhaps a premonition of what was to come. When she reached the olive tree, she glanced down at the beach and saw nothing but sand and surf below.

Then she heard the commotion of urgent conversation farther down the way, not in Greek or Italian but the guttural language of German soldiers.

She inched forward, making sure to stay hidden, tucked behind the trees. And then she spotted them, unsure of what she saw at first, not believing it to be true. Stumbling back, she found herself on the ground among the roots and rocks and dirt.

It can't be true, she thought. *It can't be.* She shuffled ahead again, this time on her hands and knees, closer to the edge, certain her eyes had been playing tricks on her, yet fearing they had not.

A second glance down the beach confirmed her fears.

Just beyond the changing room where she had first laid eyes on Elena, Demitra saw the Germans walking back and forth along the sand, shouting and pointing their guns at a handful of Italian soldiers. She could not make out what they were doing at first, but then she looked closer at the mounds piled up on the beach— bodies dressed in the uniforms of the Italian soldiers.

As the Germans pointed their guns and shouted, the young men who had run and played and laughed as they carried Elena and her friends over their shoulders were now carrying the bodies of their fallen brothers. One by one they lifted lifeless bodies and carried them to a barge in the water where they piled them on top of each other.

She watched as one of the soldiers walked to the pile and removed his hat as he bowed his head. Even from the distance, she could clearly see the shock of red hair as he knelt.

A German soldier walked behind him, hit him with the butt of his rifle, and shouted. The soldier staggered a moment and then stood. He reached down and lifted the body of his friend over his shoulder and placed him on the death pile.

Demitra felt the hot, wet sting of tears streaming down her face and the urgent need to leave that place. She stood and ran the entire way home.

NEWS OF THE Acqui Division Massacre spread quickly across the island. Demitra caught fragments of whispered conversations as she went about her chores in town. But it wasn't until she lingered behind the well next to the kafeneio where several of the village men were gathered that she overheard the full extent of the Germans' atrocities.

"Those animals killed seven thousand of those young men."

"It was supposed to be a civil surrender." Another man spat in disgust as he spoke. "But the Italians refused to give up their arms so the Germans retaliated by shooting them five at a time."

"Even those who were left behind were not spared." Demitra recognized Baba's voice. "Those bastards promised the survivors safe passage home to bury their dead, only to blow up the barges."

Demitra never told Baba about her visits to the bluff while the soldiers were alive, and she never mentioned what she saw in the aftermath of the massacre either. She, like Baba, had her own secrets that haunted her.

✺

THE SKY ABOVE was a cloudless, brilliant blue that mid-November morning as Demitra left her home for the thirty-minute walk up the mountain to Elena's house. All across the village giant tarps were laid out beneath olive trees in preparation for the harvest. She stepped gingerly as she walked among the ancient trees whose roots protruded from the earth and whose gnarled branches hung heavy with fruit.

At last she reached the clearing where the ground was covered with wildflowers, and a dozen or so sheep grazed as their shepherd napped in the sun. Demitra continued along, farther up the mountain, until at last she spotted the small house in the distance. It was a simple village home, like so many others, that had been built with nothing more than raw determination, mud, and stones. A small garden out back burst from the ground as white sheets swayed on the laundry line next to a pale yellow dress Demitra recognized from happier times on the beach.

The other women had gone back to Italy in the aftermath of the massacre, but Elena did not join them. The story of the blonde *poutana* was fodder for the island gossip mill, the villagers whispering and snickering about the Italian prostitute who came to service the young men and then stayed to entertain their ghosts.

Demitra walked to the door and stood there, breathing deeply a few times before she finally summoned the courage to knock. They had never been face-to-face before and Demitra did not know what to say or how to act. She only knew she needed to be there, to bring the woman this gift. She hesitated a moment, then reached her hand out and rapped her knuckles against the door three times. Demitra leaned in, attempting to peer through the window, but it was covered in yellowed newspaper.

She waited for several minutes in silence.

"Elena?" Demitra called out, tentative at first and then finding her voice. "Elena?" she called again, but there was no reply from within the house, nothing but the sound of the breeze rattling the leaves of the olive trees and the occasional crow of a far-off rooster. Demitra waited a few more moments before bending down and slipping her gift under the door. She placed her hand against the wood one more time, leaned in, and whispered, "I hope you like it," before turning to walk home.

She should have been halfway down the mountainside by then, but the pomegranate tree just beyond the clearing next to Elena's house proved too tempting a detour. She had been so excited by the idea of meeting Elena that morning that she'd raced out the door the moment Baba was out of sight, forgetting to make her own breakfast after preparing his.

She promised herself she would remember this spot. Here, the fruit was plentiful, hidden away from the foot traffic of the villagers. The pomegranate tree was a short distance from the house, affording a perfect view of the front door should Elena arrive home while Demitra was near. She reached up and plucked a few of the red orbs from their branches. They were dense and heavy, which made Demitra smile as her mouth watered. The fruit inside would be juicy and sweet. She placed the scarlet treasures in her pocket, excited to bring them home to Baba.

Of all the fruits, Baba loved pomegranates most. Demitra recalled a time when she was ten or so, and a neighbor brought over a basket of giant pomegranates from her tree. After Baba had soaked himself in drink, he was unusually chatty that night, sitting back and sipping his whisky and popping the tiny seeds into his mouth one after another. As he filled his glass for the third time, Baba began to recount the story of Hades and Persephone to her, slurring his words as he drained his glass.

"And so, because she had eaten six tiny seeds at Hades's table, Persephone was bound to spend six months of the year with Hades in the underworld as her mother, Demeter, the goddess of the harvest, mourned and cried and refused to allow any crops to grow on earth until her daughter was returned."

Demitra smiled again at the memory of Baba slurring his way through the myth. As much as she loved to read and learn about ancient myths, the story of Persephone, and how she longed for her mother, always moved Demitra in a way the others did not.

After she plucked one final pomegranate from the tree, Demitra glanced up and saw it. She dropped the fruit and it tumbled to the ground. But Demitra paid no mind to the pomegranate as she sat in the dirt, never taking her eyes off the white stream of smoke now rising from the chimney.

The reality washed over her in a wave of disappointment as she struggled to catch her breath. Elena was inside and had been the entire time.

Chapter Two

Cephalonia, Greece

1943

THAT MORNING INSIDE the house, Elena had pulled the quilt over the bed and tidied up the dishes from her simple breakfast of hard-boiled eggs and orange slices. Each day was the same. She would make a fire and then settle into her chair, a blanket draped across her shoulders and lap, and spend the afternoons, often well into the evening, staring into the blaze.

Within the frenetic dance of the darting flames, Elena watched transfixed and transported as scenes of her life played out. Between the flames she saw images of herself as a young girl, the lonely childhood among the pleasure houses of Sicily, where her mother and the other women did their best collectively to raise her in between entertaining their clients. There, in the thick smoke rising and swirling up the chimney, images of her school years played out like a newsreel on a cinema screen.

She could see herself as clearly as if it were yesterday, sitting alone in the back row of the school, the other children forbidden from sitting with her or playing with her. Among the orange embers burning themselves out until they were nothing more than dead black lumps, she saw the moment she realized what she was, what she had been destined to be.

Elena was nineteen years old and filled with dreams and possibility when she splurged her savings on a beautiful black dress, cut elegantly like the ones worn by women who worked in the bank. And that day, as she sat straight in her chair in her tasteful dress, the employment officer announced that no one would ever hire a woman like her.

It did not matter that she carried herself with the refined elegance she'd studied on the screen of the American films she devoured in the cinema. It did not matter that she was a virgin who attended Mass each Sunday and sometimes during the week as well. Her fate had been decided by where she was born and to whom.

Elena closed her eyes and replayed that afternoon in her mind like she had countless times before. She had left the employment office in tears, returned to the pleasure house, and told her mother what happened. Elena sat on the bed and cried, watching as her mother wrapped the black dress in tissue paper before tucking it away in the back of her closet. Elena's mother then took her by the hand and led her downstairs to the salon where she sold her daughter's virtue to the highest bidder.

Also in the darting flames Elena saw glimpses of her life in Cephalonia before the day that devastated them all. She wondered and dreamed endlessly about the boys who had in her arms imagined themselves men. Hers had been the last hands to caress their cheeks, to stroke their hair. She had been their last embrace, their final kiss. And she could not help but wonder, could not help but hope and pray that in some way the finality of it all made it somehow matter. For them and for her.

She focused on the flames, desperate to see those images of happier times replayed before her again. All she had left were the images embellished in her mind and in the fire.

They were all gone now. She had no proof that their time together had happened, that it had mattered. That *she* had mattered.

But the young girl from the bluff had been a witness to it all. Elena had been so excited when she spotted the girl coming up the path toward her door this morning. Elena glanced at herself in the mirror, tidying her hair and pinching her pale cheeks to bring some color and life to her complexion, readying herself to open the door and welcome the girl inside.

As she lunged toward the door, Elena stopped herself. She felt the cool metal of the doorknob in her hand and easily could have turned it. With one swift movement she could have ushered the girl inside and reminisced together about the handsome young men and the laughter and the songs.

Then more memories came rushing back to Elena, the whispers and the stares of the women in town. The way they pointed at her as they held tight to their children, warning their sons to stay away from women like her, warning their daughters to keep their distance. She remembered the pain of what it was to be an innocent young girl so unfairly branded and judged. And she took pity on the young girl who knew loneliness as well as she did.

Releasing her fingers from the doorknob, Elena turned and walked away from the door. She dragged the chair farther into the recesses of the room, away from the light and the window, and sat down and listened as the girl knocked and called her name.

When she was certain the girl had left, Elena finally stood. Wrapping her shawl around her shoulders, she walked over to see what the girl had slipped under the door. She unwrapped the paper, her once perfectly manicured fingernails now chipped and jagged as they slipped under the wrapping to reveal what was inside.

"Ohh." She sighed as the paper fell away. Instinctively she drew her hands to her mouth, dropped the paper, and watched as it drifted to the floor. She stood motionless, staring down at the gift.

It was a drawing, a black-and-white pencil drawing of Elena on the beach. Her head was tipped back, her eyes wide and bright as a young soldier held her in his arms as if twirling her in time to the music. The fine details, the glint in her eyes, the laughter in his, were all drawn in black and white. The only color on the page was the crimson of her lips, the imprint of her lipstick on his cheek, and the red of her fingernails, which she ran through his dark hair.

Elena smiled as she recognized the familiar stain of her lipstick on the page.

Taking the drawing in her hand, she sat back down in the chair, where she spent the rest of the afternoon gazing at a drawing made by a young girl whose name she did not know and yet who managed to capture a fleeting moment in time when Elena's existence had mattered.

Chapter Three

Cephalonia, Greece

1948

Dear Mama,

It's been years since I last wrote to you. I'm eighteen now, no longer a child, and I know I don't need to send you messages in smoke and ash for you to be with me. I now understand that you are always with me. But today is a special day and I felt the need to tell you about it myself, to feel you close to me. Today, Baba is getting married.

Her name is Stella. The villagers joked that her mama fainted when Baba asked for her hand in marriage, that Stella's parents never imagined marrying her off at this age. And to be honest, I never imagined Baba marrying either.

It feels good to write to you again, Mama. I no longer believe in the myths and fairy tales like when I was a child. But I still believe in you.

With love, your daughter,

Demitra

DESPITE THE FACT that both the bride and groom were of a certain age and that everyone, including the bride, understood this was a marriage of convenience, the wedding itself was a celebratory affair. Typically, the marriage of a couple advanced in years would merit a small church ceremony and simple luncheon. But Stella's parents, who had resigned themselves long ago to their only child dying as a childless spinster, viewed the occasion as nothing less than a miracle worthy of slaughtering a lamb and hiring the best musicians on the island.

Many in the village whispered that Stella, with thick, unfortunate ankles, was well past the age of conceiving a child, but her mother, Martha, refused to give up hope of becoming a *yia-yia*. Martha prayed incessantly to Saint Gerasimos, the island's patron saint, to cure her thirty-seven-year-old daughter's womb of the ravages of age and see fit to grow a child inside her.

Martha had but one request for the quiet widower who asked for her daughter's hand. She begged him to delay the wedding until after October 20, the feast day of Saint Gerasimos. It was only after mother and daughter made a pilgrimage to the saint's church in Lixouri—where Stella was made to lie on the ground as the procession carrying the saint's relics passed over her—that the bride's mother deemed her daughter ready to perform her sacred duties as a wife.

Wearing wedding crowns joined by a ribbon, Stella and Pericles walked three times around the altar that afternoon as the priest joined them in holy matrimony. The bride wore a simple dress of beige cotton, which her mother had embellished by embroidering tiny gold flowers along the neckline and hem. Her hair was pinned up off her face and adorned with a cluster of white stephanotis.

"Really, she would be better served to wear her hair down to hide those wrinkles and that lazy eye," Andriana, a sharp-nosed distant cousin of Stella's, muttered. As the bride and groom emerged from the church to a shower of rice, Demitra made certain to aim her generous portion of rice not at the bride and Baba but straight down Andriana's back.

The luncheon was held in the town square under the fading afternoon light with the Ionian Sea glistening in the distance. It seemed as if everyone from the neighboring villages came out to enjoy the festivities. Even those who had not attended the church service could not resist a free meal of lamb and a chance to witness and gossip as the curmudgeonly old widower and the woman he saved from spinsterhood began their new life together.

"We'll leave in an hour," Olga said as she took a glass of wine from Demitra's hand, wagging her finger and shaking her head at her niece.

Demitra nodded. "I'll be ready."

Olga began to walk away, but Demitra called to her. "Olga."

The nun turned. "Yes, child?"

"Why do you think he did it?" Demitra finally found the nerve to ask the question that had been gnawing at her since Baba came home several weeks ago and broke the traditional silence of dinnertime to announce that he would be marrying Stella.

Olga took a moment, breathing in deeply as if measuring the significance of her words.

"I know it seems new and strange, but I pray it will be a new beginning for you all. I hope she brings your father some joy and comfort." Olga then took Demitra's hand in her own and squeezed. "And I pray she is a kind soul who will bring you comfort and joy as well."

Yes, but why now? Demitra could not get the question out of her head. All those years when she was a child, when he could have used the help of a wife and companion to help care for her and raise her, he never mentioned marriage. Demitra was no longer a child and could take care of herself and her father and the house as well. It made no sense. Then again, not much about her father, his life and choices, made much sense to her.

The drone of the bouzouki music picked up. Stella made her way from greeting a group of well-wishers to where Olga and Demitra were standing.

"I hope you are enjoying yourselves." Stella smiled at them both.

"Yes. Very much," Olga replied. "I don't think the village has seen an event like this in years. Everyone is having a wonderful time. Your parents are most gracious hosts, and you are a lovely bride." The nun turned her attention to her niece. "Demitra, please make sure you are ready. We can't miss the bus." Olga smiled at the bride one last time before walking toward the other side of the *plateia* where Father Emanuel was chatting with several villagers.

"Where are you going?" Stella asked Demitra as she filled two glasses with wine and handed one to her, winking conspiratorially.

"I'm spending the night at the monastery with Thea Olga."

"Why?"

"I was told it's the right thing to do since it's your wedding night."

"Is it what you want?" Stella asked, the sincerity of her words evident in her kind eyes. "There's no need for you to leave."

"That's not what your mother said," Demitra replied. "And I don't mind, really."

"My mother?" Stella's eyes narrowed as she leaned in closer to Demitra. "What does my mother have to do with where you are staying?"

"She came to the house a few days ago when Baba was at work. I made her a cup of tea, and she gave me an envelope with bus fare, saying it was only proper to leave you alone on your wedding night."

"Oh, that woman." Stella huffed, scanning the room until she found her mother holding court among the yia-yias of the town, no doubt dreaming of the moment she might join their ranks.

"She means well. But from the moment I said yes to your father, she has thought of nothing but holding a grandchild in her arms." Stella shook her head. "And you're a little too old to be bounced on her knee." She gently poked Demitra in the ribs, dissolving them both into giggles.

Demitra caught her breath and looked up at the woman who had with three turns around the altar become her stepmother. There was a gentleness about her and sincerity in her eyes, despite what that horrid Andriana claimed.

"Why did you say yes?" The words escaped Demitra's mouth before she could stop them. "I'm— I did not mean to . . ." Her face flushed red.

"No, that's all right." Stella lifted her hand into the air as if to wave away any perceived misunderstanding. "It's a fair question, and I've wondered many times what you must think of this." She glanced away, her mouth pinched, eyes narrowed, but then she looked back at Demitra with a warm smile.

"I know your father is not much for words. I know he loses himself in his memories and in the bottle, Demitra. We all find ways to cope, to try to help us forget our pain sometimes . . ." She leaned in and took Demitra's hand in her own. "But that's all right. I tend to talk a lot, in case you haven't noticed already." Stella shrugged.

A chuckle escaped Demitra's lips as she brought her hands to her face, attempting to regain some composure.

"Oh, I see you've noticed." Stella cocked an eyebrow at her, and they both laughed again. They composed themselves, but in that moment, Demitra sensed a shift. In that moment of shared conspiratorial laughter, Demitra understood that Stella could be more than just her father's wife.

"So why did I say yes?" Stella continued, glancing up at the star-filled sky and pausing a moment, collecting her thoughts before turning once again to Demitra. "I've never been someone who dreamed of a husband. I've never had fairy-tale visions of being someone's wife. But I've always wanted a child, Demitra." She lifted Demitra's chin with a finger, smiling dreamingly as she spoke.

"I've always prayed that God would answer my prayer and help me become a mother one day. One by one the years slipped away and so did my prospects of ever finding a husband, of having a child. And then a few months ago I ran into your father in the church where he was painting the wall around the cemetery. We talked for a few moments, and I thought nothing of it—until he came to my house a week later to ask if I would marry him. I was surprised at first, but then I realized it made perfect sense.

"We're all missing something in our lives. Companionship, comfort, someone to talk to, someone to listen to us, and somewhere to belong. We can all help one another, your father, and me, and you. You're practically a grown woman and I would never try or pretend to be your mother. But I can be a lot of things. I can be someone to talk to and someone to listen to you. And someone who is there, so you know you are not alone. Because I don't want to be alone anymore either."

Demitra wanted to say so much in that moment, but words escaped her. As she scoured her thoughts to find the right response, Stella seemed to find the words for her.

"I know you had a family once, Demitra, and a mother who no doubt loved you so very much. I know I can never replace her, but I can be something else for you, a new beginning. Look around. I bet most of the women here despise their husbands, forced into marriages they had no choice in. No one forced me. This is my choice, and I choose you. I choose you as my family. Let's lean on each other and help each other find our way? Ok?" She reached her hands out to Demitra, who offered hers in return. They stood there in the middle of the reception understanding that with three turns around the altar, they, too, had been bound to each other.

The pace of the music changed, and Baba tipped his glass and bowed his head to the bouzouki player, who responded with a nod. Each chord became more melodramatic and soulful than the last, each note seemingly summoning Baba to the dance floor.

Half-drained ouzo glass in hand, shirt unbuttoned now to his navel, he placed the glass on the ground, lifted his arms, and snapped his fingers as he closed his eyes and began to feel the music. He twirled and spun as the melody changed, bending down in rhythm, slapping the floor with his hand and standing back up again, eyes closed, head tilted back as if he was in his own world, dancing to a song whose words only he could hear.

Dusk settled across the island, and Demitra watched, transfixed, as her father danced a *zeibekiko* while the lone bouzouki player strummed his mournful lament. It was as if all the passion, emotions, and even the stories he'd kept locked away from her all these years were on full display for the entire wedding party to witness. *How can he bare his soul to an entire village and still feel like a stranger to his own daughter?*

"He's a fine dancer," Stella said as she leaned over and filled their glasses with more wine.

"Yes. He is." Demitra scanned the plateia, making sure Olga was nowhere in sight before bringing the glass to her lips. Confusion and hurt were etched on her face as she watched her father dance.

"You know, it's like this for men." Stella's gentle demeanor matched the tone of her carefully chosen words. "Sometimes the things they can't or won't speak about are expressed only through their dance."

"Even today, even on your wedding day, did you notice that he didn't dance earlier with everyone else? Only now, alone," Demitra said, never taking her eyes off him.

"There's a reason your father only dances the zeibekiko, Demitra." Stella spoke softly, her words barely audible above the music. Demitra inched closer, and Stella smiled at her, as if confirming that this would be the first of many secrets shared between them.

"It's a dance that originated on the battlefield, a soldier's mournful dance for a fallen comrade. It's a dance of feeling, of inexplicable emotion, of allowing their movements to speak for them, to express the things men can't bring themselves to say out loud. I don't pretend to know a lot about men, but I do know this: a man will say things in dance he could never bring himself to say with words." Stella turned again to face Demitra.

"Some men keep their pain bottled up, hidden from the world, and the world rewards them for it, calling them brave, stoic, strong. When men express their pain, it's seen as beautiful, poetic." She paused a moment, frustration evident on her face as she finished her thought. "Heroic. And yet, when women express pain, we are seen as weak. Weak in character and weak in strength." She exhaled deeply, leaning in closer until their faces were inches apart. "But you and I know the truth, don't we? We are nothing of the sort. We are stronger than they would like to believe and in ways they can't even begin to imagine."

Demitra nodded, blinking in rapid succession. She opened her mouth to reply, to agree with her new stepmother and to ask why it was this way, but before she could get the words out of her mouth, she was interrupted by Irene, the wife of Nektarios, the village baker. While her husband was well regarded for his baking skills, Irene was known for being the town gossip and know-it-all. She marched over to where Demitra and Stella were standing. In one hand she held a platter of honey-soaked baklava and in the other she gripped her son, Niko, her fingers wrapped viselike around his wrist.

"What a beautiful wedding," Irene gushed. "We are so happy for you all." Her steely gaze fixed not on the bride but on Demitra. "Isn't that right, Niko?"

Niko was silent.

"Isn't that right, Niko?" Irene repeated, digging her elbow into her son's side.

"Yes," Niko replied, keeping his eyes cemented to the floor.

"Demitra, make sure you stop by the bakery this week. I'd love to send you home with some treats to celebrate." Irene leaned closer to Demitra as she spoke. It took all of Demitra's willpower to keep from wiping away the spray of saliva she felt land on her cheek.

"I will." She forced a smile.

"Wonderful. Niko will make sure you get the freshest bread and pitas. Won't you, Niko?" Again her elbow landed with precision on his rib cage. "Niko will take the very best care of you, no matter how busy we are. Right, Niko?"

"Yes, Mama," he mumbled, this time daring to look up at Demitra, who met his eyes and never once looked away.

Across the room the music stopped as Baba finished his dance. He glanced over to where Demitra, Stella, Niko, and Irene were gathered before draining his glass and walking over to join Nektarios and the other men.

"We look forward to seeing you at the bakery," Irene said before leading Niko away.

"What was that all about?" Demitra whispered.

"I may be new to all of this, but I'm not stupid. And neither are you." Stella shot Demitra a knowing look.

"You don't think . . ." She didn't want to say the words out loud. Demitra always knew this time would come. And now it made perfect sense. She was eighteen, the age when most girls had already been betrothed. Baba had never once mentioned the idea of marriage to her. But then again, he rarely said much to her beyond asking what was for dinner.

Just as Demitra lifted her wineglass to her lips, Olga appeared at her side.

"All right. That's enough." Olga reached out and took the glass from Demitra's hand.

"Congratulations, my dear Stella, and welcome to the family." Olga leaned in and kissed Stella on each cheek. "Come, Demitra. It's time to go."

DEMITRA WOKE WITH the sun the next morning. She always slept well at the convent. How was it that there the stillness and quiet were comforting while at home she found them suffocating?

Breakfast was the same as always in the convent—a cup of chamomile tea that the nuns picked and dried from the mountainside and sweetened with honey harvested from their own hives. There were also hard-boiled eggs and savory biscuits. The existence of a second tin, filled with sweet biscuits, was never discussed out loud.

The other nuns had come and gone before sunrise, off to their morning chores, leaving Demitra and Olga alone in the kitchen.

"I'm going to be like you. I'm never going to get married," Demitra said as she added another teaspoon of honey to her tea.

"Why would you say that?" Olga wiped her hands on her apron and walked to sit beside her niece, winking as she placed a sweet biscuit before her.

"I don't want a husband." Demitra dunked the biscuit in her tea. "I got the feeling yesterday that Baba and Nektarios have come to some sort of agreement about me and Niko. But I have no interest in being a baker's wife, or anyone's wife." She took a bite, lingering a moment as the softened biscuit with hints of clove, orange, and nutmeg melted on her tongue. She closed her eyes, savoring each note and sensation. "Oh, these are my favorite."

"Maybe if you marry the baker, you can ask for the recipe." Olga flashed a mischievous grin.

As she reached for another biscuit, Demitra waved her cloth napkin at Olga. "Very funny. Who knew nuns could have such a sense of humor?"

"Ah, you'd be surprised," Olga said. "But don't change the subject. And don't close yourself off to love, Demitra."

"Why? You've never been in love, and you've done just fine."

"Don't be so certain." Olga's raised eyebrow was partially obscured by her habit.

Demitra's eyes widened. "What do you mean?"

"I know what it is to be in love, Demitra." Her eyes softened as a smile formed on her lips. The creases around her eyes deepened as her smile broadened at the memory.

"You were in love?" Demitra put down her cup, pulling her chair closer to Olga. "With a man?"

"Of course, with a man. What did you think, with a goat?" Olga chuckled, the sound resembling more of a snort, which sent them both into giggles. "Don't look so surprised," she scolded even as she smiled. "I was young once too. I know what it is to fall in love, and I also know what it is to have your heart broken."

Demitra's mouth was agape. "Why didn't you tell me?"

"You never asked."

"I'm asking now," Demitra said, leaning closer. "Tell me."

"All right then." Olga smiled and sighed. She closed her eyes for a moment as if to conjure memories long ago tucked away. "I was younger than you, about fourteen years old, when I fell in love. He was my neighbor. We promised ourselves to each other and we were engaged. Our family did not have money for a dowry, but your father was in America at the time, and he promised to send money, so the betrothal went forward.

"His name was Marco. And like so many men—then and now—he left to find work in America with a promise that he would return for me, and we would be married. It was only supposed to be a year, just one year of separation and savings, and he was to return to me." She smiled at the memory, a distant, fleeting moment in time that even now, even so many years later and after so much pain, could summon the youthful feelings of being in love and hopeful. And then, as suddenly as it had appeared, her smile dissolved.

"What happened? How did you end up . . ." Demitra paused. "I mean—"

Olga put her hand up. "It's all right." She looked off across the kitchen toward the window and the garden beyond, as if the scenes of her life were playing out again among the lemon and apple trees.

"He said he loved me, but in the end he loved his new life in America more. He never came back." She turned to face Demitra, her eyes red and glassy even now, a lifetime later.

"Did you ever hear from him?"

"No. Not a word. Only once did he write about me to his parents. He told them I was released from our betrothal." She lifted her teacup to her lips, blowing on the hot liquid before taking a small sip. She set the cup down once again in its saucer and straightened the napkin on her lap. When she glanced up again, she smiled sadly as her gaze landed on Demitra.

"He released me from our promise, from our bond, but how do you release your heart?" She glanced down again at the golden liquid inside her cup. "We made a promise to each other, and I could not see my way past it. I overheard my parents talking about how they would never find another man to take me, now that I had been tainted."

"Tainted?"

"I had given my heart to him, even though I had not yet given my body. For me it was one and the same. And it was this way for the rest of the village as well. I knew I had done nothing improper, but who would believe me? Imaginations and innuendo can be a dangerous thing for anyone, Demitra. Even more so for a girl who has nothing to her name, whose most valuable . . ." She inhaled deeply and then exhaled a long, slow breath as she contemplated her words.

"No. Whose only assets in life are her virtue and reputation." She lifted the cup to her mouth again and sipped before continuing. "I knew then that I would never marry and never allow myself to love another man. In my mind and heart, I had already committed myself to him. And in my dreams, I had not only envisioned our life together; I had lived it. In my dreams I experienced our wedding day. I saw the home we would make together, the children we would raise. And, yes, in my dreams I saw our life together as man and wife. While everyone around me cried and cursed and asked how God could be so cruel, I knew they were wrong. Because I realized then that my dreams were a gift from God, that God had allowed me to experience in sleep what I would never have the chance to live in the light of day. In my dreams I had experienced a true love, a pure love. And I realized it was enough for me."

"But why?" Demitra leaned across the table. "You were so young. You could have found another man to love."

"What other man? There were no other men to love, even if I had wanted to. All the men had gone. They left one after the other for America, for work and new opportunities. But even if the village had been filled with men, the choice was mine. I didn't want another man. I knew even then that once a heart is broken, it is forever changed. You are forever changed by the knowledge that the person you love and trust most can change their mind and hurt you in such a way.

"No. I had a pure love once, Demitra. And for me, that was enough. I decided I would devote myself and my life to Christ. It's the circle of life, Demitra. This is God's promise to us. Even in our darkest hours, God will always provide a new path, a new beginning, to remind us that there is always new life after death. Never forget this, Demitra. Even when the world seems so dark that you think you will never find your way, God brings the dawn, and with it, the light shines on a new path. The light of a new dawn will always pierce the darkness."

Demitra took a few moments before she could respond. "I had no idea. Does everyone in this family have secrets? Does everyone have a lost love they keep hidden and locked away?"

"No, it's not the same. Your father never talks about the past because he was so deeply wounded by what happened. He never shared the full story with anyone, not even me. I tried. When he returned from the United States to Cephalonia with you, he was a broken man. So broken he could not even stay in our family's home in Sami. He left it all behind and said he wanted a fresh start. He found your house in Argostoli, and at first he barely ate, barely slept. I left the convent for a while to help him and to care for you." She placed her hand on Demitra's shoulder. Demitra leaned in, her cheek against Olga's skin.

"Day and night I tried. I was patient, allowing him the space to grieve. But he never talked about it. He never talked about her. Not to me. Not to anyone. All he would say was *'I lost her, Olga.'* And nothing more. None of us knew your mother. All we knew was that they met and married in America and they had you, this precious child.

"The pain was too much for him to relive, Demitra. He never discussed her or how she was lost—perhaps a sudden illness that took her from him, from you, so cruelly and unexpectedly. So many of us tried to convince him to let us help. I asked if he would allow me to bring you here, to raise you with the sisters as we have done with so many children before. But he would not hear of it. He would not even let me finish. He was determined to do it his way. So he raised you himself and did the best he could, all while keeping his memories of your mother locked tightly away."

"I wish I had clearer memories of her, Olga," Demitra said. "I've tried so hard to remember her. Sometimes I think I do. Sometimes I think I can see her clearly in my mind. But then the picture fades before I can be certain. There's one thing I do remember—her laughter, this sweet sound, a soft giggle that echoes in my mind. Even as I struggle to remember her face, I hear her laughter so clearly sometimes and I know that she, that we, were happy once."

"Memories are a precious gift, and it seems so unfair for you to have none of your mother. Hold tight to the sound of her laughter in your heart."

"Do you remember the book of myths you gave me when I was about seven?"

"Yes. I do. You always had a passion for those stories. I remember you curled up in your bed reading them over and over again."

"They were more than stories to me," Demitra said. "I would read those myths and wonder if they held the secret to Mama's true identity, to mine. Was she a goddess, an ethereal, magical creature, like in the myths? Had Mama visited Baba under cover of darkness, the way Cupid visited Psyche? Had she tried in vain to keep their perfect love hidden, keeping her identity secret, even from her one true love? Did Baba bring me back to Cephalonia to keep me safe, to hide me from the jealous gods?"

She stood, clearing the table and taking her teacup to the sink. She gazed out the window toward the garden and lifted her face to the warmth of the sun. After a moment she turned toward Olga.

The older nun smiled then and said, "You are not wrong, my dear. Of course she was magical. After all, she created you."

Chapter Four

Karditsa, Greece

1921

Look at this one!" Maria raised her arm high into the air, clutching the large potato she had just dug up with her spoon. "Mama will be so happy. Look, it's as big as my hand! It's big enough to feed all of us."

She smiled broadly as she wiped away the caked earth that clung to the potato before she slipped it into her basket. The soil beneath her feet was dry and cracked. It had not rained in months and the ground, which was typically arid and rocky, was as hard as stone. The metal spoon she had used to scrape and dig for something Mama could boil into soup had become bent and tarnished.

The drought had taken a toll on all the families in the village over the past year. While the harsh climate, scorching summers, and bitterly cold winters had always made life difficult in the mountainous villages of Thessaly, the people had always been able to cobble together meals from their livestock and gardens. But with no rain for the past seven months, the depleted ground produced only a fraction of the crops they needed to survive, and certainly not enough to stock up for the unforgiving winter months.

Mama had joked just days before, telling her girls that when potatoes were first introduced to Greece by Governor Kapodistrias in the mid-1800s, Greeks all across the country were wary of the foreign crop, refusing to eat it, let alone plant it and contaminate their gardens. In Karditsa the priest had gone so far as to warn the villagers against the evils of the foreign enticement, cautioning the men to refrain from planting it. And under no circumstances, he insisted, should they allow their wives to cook with it. He claimed the potato was the very apple the serpent had used to tempt Eve.

"Now look at us," Mama had said, shaking her head as she ladled thin potato soup into their bowls for dinner yet again. *"What was sinful then is our salvation now."* She'd laughed a hearty belly laugh then in the way of the village women. Mama, impoverished and uneducated like the generations before her, always found ways to joke and tease about misfortunes rather than spill tears over things that were beyond their control.

Maria stood, arching her back and letting out a deep yawn. Her long black hair, which Mama had so carefully plaited and coiled around her head this morning, was now an unruly mess, dotted with leaves and twigs. Her blouse and skirt, which this morning smelled of mountain air and lavender water, were now soaked through with perspiration and spotted with filth.

Maria squinted and lifted her blackened fingers toward the sky, stretching her body toward the heavens under the noontime sun. In this bright light her eyes glowed with flecks of amber and gold. She closed her eyes against the brightness, an image of Mama immediately coming to mind and bringing a smile to Maria's face. It was as if she could see and hear her clear as day.

"I'm a poor woman with nothing of worth to my name," Mama always said. *"I have no jewels to drape over you or gold coins to fill your pockets, but I have given you the one thing of worth I have; I've given*

you my golden eyes. The eyes I inherited from my mother and her mother before her. Because you, my darling child, are more precious to me than the finest or rarest gems. You are my treasure."

Maria smiled at the memory and lifted the basket into her arms, excited to share these treasures with Mama.

"We should go," Maria said, turning to her sister, Paraskevi, who was still down on her knees digging in the unforgiving ground. At fifteen Paraskevi was a tiny slip of a girl, petite and slim with a birdlike fragility about her and eyes as dark as a bitter cup of coffee. Mama always said that while she had inherited Baba's sable eyes, her youngest child's golden virtue was in her kindness and gentle spirit.

Paraskevi stood, shaking her skirt and sending bits of dirt and caked mud flying.

"At least we have enough for soup," Maria said, peering into the basket where the fruits of their morning labor were collected. Five potatoes, three onions, a handful of black-eyed peas, and two limp zucchini. "Mama will be so happy." She placed the basket on her head as the sisters began the trek down the mountain toward their village and home.

After walking thirty minutes through the thickest part of the forest, they came to the fresh spring where they'd left their water jug earlier this morning before making the journey up the mountain to forage for food. One of the girls' many daily chores was to gather fresh drinking water from the village spring.

While Paraskevi groused and moaned and dragged her feet each time it was her turn, Mama never had to ask Maria to fetch the water twice. Maria loved going to the spring where she would meet with the other girls of the village to chat and gossip. Besides church, the spring was the only place a young girl was allowed to venture alone.

The moment she spotted Maria and Paraskevi, Anastasia raced over from where she was washing laundry in the pool beneath the waterspout.

"Did you hear?" Anastasia was exploding with nervous energy.

"Hear what?" the sisters asked in unison as Maria set down the basket and began to rinse the vegetables one by one in the cool water. Paraskevi reached for their jug, waiting for her sister to finish before she could fill the container with water.

"About Voula?" Anastasia's cheeks were flushed, the words tumbling out of her mouth faster than the running spring.

"Are you going to tell us what happened, or are we waiting here for the spring to run dry?" Maria asked, placing her hands on her hips and pursing her lips.

Paraskevi shot her sister an annoyed look. "Stop it," she said before turning her attention back to Anastasia. "What happened?"

"Well . . ." Anastasia leaned in closer to the sisters. "She's going to America!"

Maria dropped the potato she'd been rinsing as if she had just pulled it out of the fire with her bare hands. It fell with a splash into the soapy water basin beneath the spring where Anastasia had been washing her clothes.

"Yes." Anastasia nodded, speaking so quickly her words were a jumble. "She got the news today, but it's not what you think." Her eyes widened. "Her family isn't going with her."

"What on earth are you talking about? What do you mean her family isn't going?" Maria's dismissive tone dripped with annoyance. "Like they're going to send a young girl off to America by herself when they won't even let us go to the periptero alone."

"Be quiet, Maria." Paraskevi swatted her hand at her sister. "Let her speak."

Maria folded her arms across her chest and rolled her eyes. "Well, speak then."

Anastasia shook her head at Maria, then turned to face Paraskevi. "She's getting married!"

"Married?" Paraskevi asked. "But to who?"

"That's just it. She doesn't know. A man in Thessaloniki sent her photo to someone in America, and they received a letter today. He found her a husband in America. Her uncle in New York sent money for the dowry."

Maria's mouth fell open at the news. She turned to glance at Paraskevi, whose lower lip was trembling.

"I'm so sorry," Maria said, reaching out and taking Paraskevi's hand in her own.

Paraskevi and Voula were the best of friends. Born two days apart, the girls had been inseparable since Mama and Voula's mother stood side by side at the altar holding their baby girls as the priest performed the forty-day blessing on the newborns.

"But she's my age. She's only fifteen," Paraskevi said as she looked up at Maria, her eyes glistening.

"Yes," Maria said, her tone softer, understanding that Paraskevi's heart was breaking at the news. "Voula's the oldest of five. All girls. I heard Mama talking with Voula's mother the other day. Voula's mother was crying, saying there wasn't enough food to feed them all. She told Mama she had not eaten in two days, just so she could feed her girls."

No one spoke a word or reacted to this news. The same story had played out in house after house across the village these past few years. Maria recalled all the times these past several weeks that Mama insisted she was not hungry, even as her empty stomach rumbled.

Rustling sounded at the other end of the clearing, and the girls looked up. Voula was walking to the spring, balancing a water jug on her head. Even from across the clearing, her face looked red, her eyes swollen. All three girls ran to her, enveloping her in their arms.

"I don't want to go. I don't want this." She sobbed in the arms of her friends.

The girls did their best to comfort and soothe Voula, despite their own tears. They all sat together on a patch of grass blanketed by tiny blue forget-me-nots, a tangle of arms and legs as they continued to hold Voula close.

"A few months ago, a man came to visit," Voula said. "Baba told me he was an old friend from Thessaloniki and he was going to take my photo. Baba said he wanted to give the photo to Mama as a gift. He said it was a surprise, and we would give her the photo on her name day." She bit her lip and shook her head at the memory. Her breathing was rapid and shallow, her words slipping out between sobs.

"Baba lied to me. The photo was not for Mama. The man was a marriage broker. He sent my photo to America and a man in a place called Tarpon Springs picked me. I'm leaving on a ship from Piraeus next week to go to America and get married."

Maria's stomach lurched, a wave of nausea overtaking her body. She turned away and retched. She clutched her stomach, willing herself not to be sick.

"Maria!" Paraskevi shouted. "You're white as a ghost. Are you all right?"

"You don't look well," Voula echoed as she wiped her own tears with the back of her hand.

"This man . . ." Maria's voice was barely a whisper. "Was he short with a thick mustache and oil-slicked hair?"

Voula's eyes widened. She took Maria's hand in her own.

"Yes," she said. "And he smelled—"

"Like stale cigars and whisky."

"He took your photo?" Paraskevi asked, panic rising in her voice.

Maria bit her lip and closed her eyes. "Yes," she whispered.

The girls gasped collectively, wailing and moaning, their lament song carried on the breeze across the forest and the mountain toward the heavens above.

Maria breathed deeply in and out a few times before she was able to form the words. "Baba told me the same thing, that it was a present for Mama. For her name day." She paused, thinking back to that day, how happy she felt to be doing something so special for Mama. Her stomach lurched again at the betrayal.

"He said he wanted to surprise her and that I shouldn't tell anyone, not even you." She turned to Paraskevi. "He said there was only enough money for one photo this time. He said this was my turn . . . and that one day you would have your turn as well."

Paraskevi threw herself to the ground, a low moan escaping her lips.

Maria lowered herself to sit beside her sister and rubbed her back, attempting to console her, even as she felt bile rising in her throat. Suddenly she stood, panic and fear overtaking her.

"Mama . . . ," she said, reaching her hand out to her sister with urgency. "Mama— We have go. We have to go find Mama."

Hand in hand the sisters ran all the way home, forgetting the vegetables and water at the spring. They had only one thing on their mind; they needed to get to Mama. Mama would know what to do. Mama would have the answer. Mama would make everything better, as she always had.

Minutes later as they rounded the corner from the plateia toward the house, they heard the screams and wails piercing the afternoon stillness.

"No!" Mama cried from somewhere inside the house. The sound was primal, animalistic.

"Be quiet, Aphrodite!" Baba shouted. "Stop your dramatics. The entire village can hear you. It's our only option and it's done. Accept it."

"No! Please, please." Her scream was high-pitched and desperate. "Please, I beg of you. Don't take my child. You cannot take my child."

Chapter Five

Cephalonia, Greece

1952

FROM THE DAY Baba married Stella, conversation and kindness replaced the quiet at home. It was not that Baba himself changed; he remained a gruff man of few words and even fewer outward emotions. But that no longer mattered because Stella's light and laughter were enough to fill the space of their home and lives.

Stella was at once a companion and coconspirator, always mindful of her husband's wishes, yet always strategically and carefully advocating for Demitra. She knew what it was to be lonely and what it was to dream of a life beyond the confines of her parental home.

Nearly a year after the wedding, when Demitra's brother was born, the house had come alive with new possibility.

"You must name him Gerasimos," Martha announced moments after his birth as she placed the freshly swaddled child into the arms of his mother.

"I think it's only fitting." Stella beamed, sitting back on the bed as Martha dabbed at her forehead with a wet cloth.

The arrival of baby Gerasimos at once brought joy and laughter into the house. It also brought the constant presence of Martha, who could not stand to be away from her grandson for even a moment.

"I waited all of my fifty-six years to hold a grandchild in my arms," she announced to anyone and everyone. *"I'm not going to wait a moment longer to enjoy him."*

Shortly after Gerasimos was born, Martha found her husband cold and lifeless in the marital bed they had shared for forty years. As the family grieved the loss of a kind and gentle man, everyone in the village remarked what a blessing it was that he had danced at his daughter's wedding and held his grandson before God called him home.

No longer having a husband to tend to, there was nothing and no one to keep Martha away. It had never occurred to Demitra that a house once too quiet could ever become too loud or too full. With Stella and a new baby brother at home, not to mention the constant presence of Yia-yia Martha, another shift came to Demitra's life. With more people in the house, there was actually less work for Demitra and more time for her to lose herself in what had grown over the years from a hobby to a passion: her art.

"I got you a gift," Stella announced just after they celebrated Gerasimos's second birthday. "I saved all year and went to town to buy him a soccer ball. While I was there, I spotted something special, something for you. I thought you might like these," she said as she placed the gift in Demitra's hands.

Demitra felt a sting in her eyes the moment she opened the box and peered inside. "Oh, Stella," she cried. It was a box of pencils, at least two dozen of them, each a different shade of the rainbow.

"Look"—Stella lifted the blue pencil from the box and held it up to the sky—"they're soft, and you can blend the color with your fingers if you like. And you see this little string? You can peel it back and the layers of paper will fall away so you have a new tip. You never need to worry about finding a pencil sharpener. And here"—she reached into the box and pulled out a pad of paper—"a new pad for you, so you can focus on what you love and create magic with your hands."

Demitra placed the box on the table and then ran to Stella, wrapping her arms around her. "Thank you." She cried as she hugged her tighter. "Thank you."

With encouragement from Stella, Demitra began to spend more time in the yard drawing at a table in the shade of the olive tree. That was where Baba found her one Sunday afternoon. She had spent the morning capturing the light as it filtered through the trees, playing with tones of green and blue, rubbing the pencil marks until her fingers were raw, layering the colors to get the perfect hue on the paper. She was so engrossed in her drawing that she did not notice Baba until he sat down beside her.

"Baba," she said with a start. "I didn't realize you were home." She began to gather her pencils. She had never discussed her passion for drawing with him before, and he had never asked. "I was just taking a little break while Gerasimos is napping and the laundry is drying on the line." She glanced over to the garden where the sheets she and Stella had washed and hung on the line after breakfast were billowing on the breeze.

"What's this?" he asked, leaning closer to examine her pad. He stared at the drawing for a few moments in silence.

She felt a flash of heat in her chest and neck working its way up to her cheeks.

"I tried to draw the olive tree. It's not very good, I know." She shook her head now, knowing she was rambling, unable to harness her nerves.

She turned to face him, watching as he continued to study the drawing.

"Imagine if I could be an artist one day." She blurted the words before she had a chance to think them through.

He reached into his pocket and pulled out his tobacco and paper, then focused on rolling a cigarette. He placed the cigarette between his lips and struck a match, then took a deep, long drag. After he sat back, slowly exhaling a thin stream of smoke, he finally spoke.

"Imaginations are for fools or the wealthy. We are neither."

She blinked rapidly, willing the sting of tears to go away, angry with herself for being disappointed and hurt by his response. She had learned long ago never to expect anything from him so she was never disappointed.

"Nektarios and his family are coming for dinner tomorrow," Baba said. "Stop wasting your time on useless scribbles. Stella is spoiling you. It's time you apply yourself in the kitchen, where it matters. Where you can be useful to your husband's family."

She knew what he expected of her, that marriage and mother-hood were her predestined fate. But even so, she finally spoke out loud the words that had been fermenting in her mind for years.

"But I don't want that." There, she had said it. It was done. Her innermost thoughts unleashed into the world like a river rushing over its banks, no longer able to be contained.

His eyes narrowed as he leaned forward across the table toward her.

"You don't want what?"

She sat up straighter in her chair, summoning her voice and her courage. "I don't want to get married, to stay here in this village forever." There was no turning back now. She sat up even taller. "I don't want that life."

He leaned back in his chair again, running his hands through his hair, which over the past year had become generously streaked with gray.

"They'll be here at eight," he said. "You're twenty-two years old, old enough. It's past time that you were married."

Her voice was shaking now. "Old enough? I've watched you all these years; I've seen the pain caused by your marriage to my mother. Why would I want that? Why would I want something that could hurt me as much as her death hurt you? You never even shared her with me, and suddenly I'm old enough? When will I be old enough for you to tell me about my mother or why you never speak of her? It's like I lost her twice, Baba. She was taken from me twice. Once when she died and then again when you withheld her from me."

"Don't speak of things you know nothing about." He focused on his cigarette, turning it this way and that, examining the ashes as he flicked them into the dirt, never once looking at her.

"I don't know anything because you never told me. We've lived side by side in this house all these years, and you have never once spoken to me about her. You never told me what she was like, what she wanted. You never asked what I wanted. I don't want to get married. Maybe what I want doesn't exist here. Maybe it's in America, where I was born, where my mother is buried. Where we were happy." She closed her eyes for a moment, conjuring her mother's laugh, the soft tone and timbre of her giggle, the only fragment of Mama that lived concretely in her memory. The memory infused her with strength.

"I don't want to stay in this village for my entire life, married to someone I don't love."

He said nothing but glanced at her as if she were an insignificant inconvenience, a fly to be swatted away, a dead bird in the road to be stepped over. He stood then and walked away from her, out of the courtyard and toward town.

Trapped. She felt like an animal trapped in a snare, unable to escape her fate. She was nothing more than a possession to him, a piece of property to be sold or bartered.

As a child she had believed her existence was a myth, that she had been born of magic, her loneliness serving a greater purpose—to keep her hidden away and safe, a daughter of the divine. But with each year that passed, her childhood dreams and fantasies had been slowly stripped away, revealing the bitter truth.

There was no magic. There was no beauty. There was only one reality.

She had the misfortune of being born a girl.

DEMITRA WOKE THE next morning before the sun. It had been a night of fitful sleep as she replayed the conversation with Baba in her head. What she wrestled with in the light of day had crystalized with uncertain clarity in the dead of night.

"He can't move on with me here." Her existence was a reminder of a past he had tried so hard to lock away and forget. To move on with his life, he needed Demitra to move on from him.

Unable to sleep, Demitra grabbed her sketch pad and pencils. It was still dark out and she knew she could make it to the bluff just in time to watch the sunrise. She wanted to study the light, the way the colors pierced the black and bled out across the sky. She was unsure if she could capture such beauty on the page, but she wanted to try.

"Why are you up so early?" Stella asked as she shuffled to the kitchen.

"I'm going to the bluff to draw the sunrise. I'll be home later."

"Nektarios, Irene, and Niko are coming for supper tonight."

Demitra took a few steps closer to Stella, watching as she opened the coffee tin and spooned dark grounds into the *briki* before placing it over the fire. The aroma of fresh-brewed coffee filled the air.

"I'll need your help preparing, all right?" Her words conveyed her husband's wishes, yet her eyes and tone appeared soft, apologetic.

"This is about me and Niko. That's why he wants me here, isn't it?" Niko was a few years older than Demitra and had always struck her as rather quiet and shy.

Stella said nothing as she stirred the coffee, then pulled it off the fire just before it boiled over.

"I'm not interested, Stella. You know that," Demitra said as she gathered her pencils and pad.

"Yes, I know," Stella said as she poured the coffee into a demitasse. "But your father and Nektarios have other ideas. They see the practicality of it. Nektarios's business is growing. The bakery is busy and there's talk of the family opening a restaurant. A group of Italians wants to build a hotel on the island, and they approached Nektarios and Irene about running it. Your father sees this as an opportunity for you, a way to give you security."

"My father never asked what *I* needed."

"Please, don't shut yourself off without giving Niko a chance. Keep an open mind."

Demitra grabbed an apple from a bowl on the counter and put it in her pocket. "You told me you were happy even when everyone around you pitied you. No one forced you to marry when you didn't want to. Why is that too much for me to ask as well?"

"I know. And I'm sorry, but these are your father's wishes, and we must respect them," Stella replied, then brought the cup to her lips and took a sip. "You won't be the first woman to marry a man she doesn't love. And you won't be the last. No one wants you to be unhappy. Just keep your eyes and mind open to the possibility that this could be a good option for you, that you could eventually find love in this match."

"Even if it's not for my husband."

"Yes, even if it's not for your husband," Stella replied, her voice filled equally with conviction and melancholy, the tone of a woman who had given up on one dream to salvage another.

"I'll be home in time to help you, but I make no promises about Niko," Demitra said as she headed toward the door, sketchbook under her arm. Stella exhaled in relief before she shut the door behind her.

It was still dark as Demitra set out on the path to the bluff. She took the apple from her apron pocket and sank her teeth in with a hearty crunch. The fruit was tart and crisp, just the way she liked it.

When she reached her destination, she sat on the ground and leaned against the trunk of the ancient olive tree where she had spent so many hours watching Elena and the Italian soldiers. She opened her pad on her lap and took her pencil in hand, preparing to study the view and sketch. The first light of the day pierced the dark sky, and she lifted her pencil to capture the image as she continued staring out over the horizon.

With a few delicate strokes, her pencil skimmed the paper, barely leaving its mark, and the awakening horizon before her began to emerge on the page. As the day dawned, the light instilled new confidence in Demitra. With each passing moment her strokes grew more certain, more precise. She focused on the sea, challenging herself to capture the way dawn's first light appeared to breathe life into the black water, transforming it first to a molten silver as the tide swelled and flowed, then to a mirror reflecting the majestic reds and rusts and blues as the sunrise bled across the sky.

She was so caught up in the beauty and splendor before her, so intent on translating it to the page, that she ignored the sound at first, thinking it was nothing more than a bird or animal in the distance. But then she heard it again, a low moan. She glanced across the beach and up and down the pathway and saw nothing.

A few moments later, the sound came again. It was a mournful and guttural wail, nearly secreted between the lapping waves of the incoming tide. As the day fully dawned and the final remnants of darkness lifted to reveal the sea and the beach below her, it revealed something else to Demitra as well.

Elena.

Shoulders hunched forward, she was wrapped in a shawl and seated on a large piece of driftwood on the sand, gazing out to the sea. Even from behind she seemed merely a shade of the beautiful, vibrant young woman who had caught Demitra's attention nine years before, the woman who had danced and laughed and loved on this very beach. Only the faded dress, which now hung from her emaciated frame, invoked the memory of who she once was.

Demitra had seen her only a handful of times since the day she made the journey up the mountain and slipped the portrait under her door. On the rare occasion that Demitra spotted Elena in the village, she always smiled and kept her distance, hopeful that Elena might smile back at her again, the way she had so long ago. But now each time they crossed paths, Demitra felt her heart sink as Elena averted her eyes and hurried off, away from her. Even after all these years, seeing Elena still stirred an unmatched excitement in her, as if spotting a mythical creature in the wild, like a winged Pegasus or a wild woodland nymph, something to be admired and revered carefully and quietly from afar so as not to scare her off.

As the sun slowly rose against the impossibly blue sky, Demitra watched Elena stand, slip off her dress, and walk into the sea. She set aside her pad to get a better look, wondering if Elena's intent was to swim or drown, but then Elena began washing herself.

Frenetically, she rubbed her hands up and down her arms and chest and all over her body as she dunked herself in and out of the sea. As she washed, even as the tide continued breaking against her sunken frame, even from the distance of the bluff, her trembling convulsions and the sound of her crying were clear.

When she was finished, Elena turned and walked back to the beach. She reached down to retrieve her dress, wrapped herself in it, and began the long walk home.

Demitra sat motionless, watching until Elena disappeared from view. Then she looked down at her pad, at the pencil strokes she had made a short while ago, and stared at them as if she was uncertain how they had appeared. She turned the pad over to a new blank page and closed her eyes for a moment, conjuring the image in her head. Then Demitra opened her eyes, lifted her hand to bring pencil to paper, and began transcribing the vision in her mind onto the page.

AS EXPECTED, NEKTARIOS, Irene, and Niko arrived that evening for dinner promptly at eight. Martha, who could not bear to stay away, made a moussaka for the occasion.

"She can brag all she wants about her pitas, but everyone knows my moussaka is the best," Martha said as she placed the platter on the table before their guests arrived. "The secret is . . ." She looked around the room where Stella sat at the table drying freshly washed glasses as Baba read the newspaper and Demitra prepared a plate of feta and olives.

"There's no one here to steal your secret, Mama," Stella said, glancing over at Demitra, who instantly turned her back and covered her mouth to hide her giggles.

"Well . . ." Martha pursed her lips at her daughter and then continued, "The secret is, of course, to cut the eggplant ever so thin and then sweat them with a generous sprinkle of salt. Now, you must be sure to wipe the eggplants dry before—"

The knock at the door interrupted Martha's story.

"I'll get it," she said, walking toward the door as she straightened her dress and smoothed her hair with her hands. "And I'll finish telling you about the moussaka recipe later," she announced. "I'm sure Irene will ask me once she tastes it, but no matter what that woman says or how she asks, I simply will not tell her."

"Open the door, Mama," Stella snapped at her mother.

Demitra walked over to where Gerasimos was playing on the floor and scooped him into her arms, tickling him as he erupted into a fit of giggles.

"I see what you're doing," Stella whispered, rising to greet her guests. "Don't use my baby as a shield."

Demitra laughed, hiding her face in Gerasimos's neck.

Irene entered first, carrying a basket piled high with a variety of baked goods, followed by Nektarios, who had combed and Brylcreemed his hair to slick perfection. Niko trailed his father. At twenty-four years old, Niko was only a couple of years older than Demitra. But with his slouched shoulders, unkempt hair, and eyes that seemed permanently affixed to the floor, he had always seemed younger to Demitra. He was taller now and his shoulders were broader as well. A dark shadow of stubble covered his upper lip and chin. As she watched him make his way across the room, Niko seemed to be a walking paradox—the body of a man with the uncertain demeanor of a child.

"So lovely to see you," Stella greeted everyone as they arrived. "Come, let's sit outside." She ushered their guests to the patio where the table was set with small plates of olives, cheese, stuffed grape leaves, and home-cured salami. A carafe of homemade wine and a bottle of ouzo sat at the center of the wooden table, flanked by small, boldly colored glasses. The delicate plates, painted with yellow roses, and the glasses had been part of Stella's dowry.

"Please, enjoy. It's bedtime for this little man." Stella smiled as she took Gerasimos from Demitra's arms and disappeared into the house.

Without her little brother to hide behind, Demitra took a seat at the far end of the table.

"I hear the bakery is going well," Pericles said as he filled his and Nektarios's glasses with wine.

"Yes, thank God," Nektarios replied. "After so many years of devastation, I pray our luck has finally turned around."

"So it's the Italians who came back?" Pericles asked.

"Yes. Imagine that. A few men were called back before the surrender . . ." His voice trailed off before he drained his glass. "Then they came back after the Germans left to investigate the murders. Every morning they stopped in to get something to eat."

Stella came back outside to join the group. She walked to the far end of the table and smiled at Demitra, opening her eyes wide and mouthing, "*Smile*," when no one was looking.

"They especially loved my spanakopita and meat pitas—said they were the best they ever had," Irene chimed in. "That there's nothing like them across the Ionian or even back in Italy."

"Oh, is that what they said?" Martha dabbed at her mouth with her napkin while Demitra and Stella each bit their lips and stole knowing glances at each other.

"Through the years we've become quite friendly with the families. They all have fond memories of our island and their time here. Arturo was a captain. I remember him from the occupation. Always a decent man, a gentleman, even then." Nektarios paused for a moment. "Especially then." The entire table nodded in agreement, everyone remembering well the civility of the Italians and then the inhumanity of the Germans.

"He's come back several times and brought his partners and their wives and children. They have wonderful boys who are Niko's age and they have become great friends too. Isn't that right, Niko?" Nektarios lifted his glass toward his son.

Niko glanced at his father from under a canopy of dark hair and lashes before looking away again.

"They want to invest here, and with us. They have plans to build a hotel and market it to other Italians," Nektarios continued.

"That's incredible news," Baba said.

"Congratulations. It seems we have much to celebrate, don't we?" Stella stood and began to serve the moussaka.

"Excuse me." Irene smiled as she stood and walked into the house. She emerged a moment later with a plate piled high with her meat pitas. "You simply must try this new recipe of mine. I've perfected it and the Italians say this dish alone will bring boatloads of tourists to Cephalonia." She reached across the table and placed a generous portion on everyone's plate.

Martha's nostrils flared and her mouth formed a tight line as she watched Irene.

"What about you, Niko?" Stella asked, diverting attention away from her mother's tantrum. "How are you enjoying working at the bakery? It must be an exciting time with so much happening for your family."

Niko said nothing.

"Come on, Niko." His mother inched closer to him and placed her hand on his arm. "Our host asked you a question."

Demitra glanced at Niko from across the table. She had seen him on occasion at the bakery, but rarely had they spoken more than a passing hello. He always seemed so focused on his work with an intensity she could relate to; it was how she felt when she was drawing. Here, away from the ovens and flour and yeast, he seemed out of sorts, lost.

"Niko." Irene reached out and placed her hand on his arm.

"For the love of God, answer the woman!" Nektarios bellowed as he lifted his glass to his lips. His booming voice startled Niko, who sat up straighter in his chair.

Niko lifted his eyes and looked at his father. Finally, he spoke.

"I can tell you this," he said as his eyes drifted downward again, focusing on the floor. "I don't like waking up in the middle of the night."

"Oh, it's not that bad." Irene waved away his complaint as she lifted a forkful of the moussaka to her mouth.

Martha watched her, unblinking. After a few moments, Irene smiled and dug her fork into Martha's moussaka again as Martha sat back in her chair, a satisfied grin across her face.

"Yes. Waking up isn't so hard for you because you don't have to do it," Nektarios said to his wife. "Niko and I get in early and do the heavy lifting, the work that needs to be done before dawn in order to have the breads and pitas ready for breakfast. Irene comes in after sunrise, but she stays later than we do. After all, she is far lovelier than we are and much better with the customers." He laughed as he reached over and refilled his glass, then topped off Baba's as well, although his was still nearly full.

"I hated getting up in the middle of the night at first also, but now there's something I rather like about waking up before the day has started, while everyone else is asleep. We have the island to ourselves, at least for a few hours, don't we, Niko?" Nektarios gulped his drink as he glanced at his son.

"Well, I don't like waking up in the dark, but I do like baking. I really do." Niko kept his eyes downcast even as a small smile appeared on his face. "I like to mix things together in just the right way, just the right amount, not too much and not too little, and bake it at just the right temperature. It changes the ingredients and makes them something new. When you look at each ingredient you think they are one thing, but together they make something you never thought they could be." His eyes darted across the table to Martha and then to his mother and his father. Finally, his gaze rested on Demitra. "It's almost like magic."

"Like art . . . ," Demitra said, not realizing she had spoken the words out loud, then wishing she could take them back.

Niko sat up straighter in his chair. "Yes. Exactly." A small smile appeared on his face before averting his gaze to the floor again. "For me, baking is art."

Demitra could feel the eyes of Stella and Martha burning into her. She used all of her willpower to keep from turning toward them. She knew what they were thinking, what everyone was thinking.

Demitra's quiet contemplation was interrupted by Martha's booming voice. "Demitra is an artist. Aren't you, Demitra?"

She turned her head to face Martha, raising her hand in protest. "I wouldn't call myself an artist, really." She chewed at the inside of her cheek, fidgeting in her chair. "I like to draw, but I'm not an artist. Not by any means."

"Well, that's not true at all. I've seen you sitting out here for hours hunched over that pad of yours." With a loud moan Martha lifted herself from her seat and walked back into the house. She emerged moments later holding Demitra's sketch pad in triumph.

"I told you. See, it's all right here. You two have so much in common," she said as she waved Demitra's pad in the air. "Both artists."

Demitra simmered with embarrassment and rage.

"No, please." She jumped up from her seat. "Please, that's not really ready for anyone to see," she pleaded as she lunged toward Martha with her arms outstretched. "Please. Can I have that back? They're just doodles, really."

"Come on, Demitra, you spend hours and hours out here over this pad. There must be something you can show us. Don't be shy now." Martha laughed as she licked her finger and began flipping through the pages. "Here. What's this?" she asked as she held up the pad for all to see. It was the sketch from earlier that morning as the sun rose, the one Demitra had been working on just before she spotted Elena.

Demitra lunged toward Martha and snatched the pad from her hands, folding over the page, revealing the unfinished sketch of the sunrise over the water. She held it up and showed it to everyone. Her hands trembled as she held the sketchbook, her fingers turning white from clutching the page so tightly.

"I told you I'm not a real artist. This was my attempt to capture the sunrise. I spent all morning out there. And look, not very much to look at, is it?"

All eyes were on the page as they took in Demitra's work. It was nothing more than a crudely shaded sketch of the sea and sky with no depth and no detail. Nothing that would stand out in any way to reveal any talent.

Irene pursed her lips. "Well, I can teach you to cook."

Demitra tucked the pad under her arm and started to clear the table, eager to end this conversation. She grabbed a few of the empty glasses and took them inside, placing them on the counter by the sink. She stopped a moment to listen to the conversation outside, making certain they were fully engrossed.

"That was delicious. Martha, what's your secret?" Nektarios asked.

"My secret?" Martha laughed. "Well, if I tell you my secret, then you'll need to hire me to work with you in your new restaurant."

As the conversation continued outside, Demitra scanned the room, making sure she was alone. She flipped open the pad, turning to the sketch of the sea that she had just shown everyone. She sucked in her cheeks and then exhaled as she turned the page one more time, smiling as she gazed down on the drawing she had spent the entire day working on.

Chapter Six

Karditsa, Greece

1921

T HE ENTIRE VILLAGE came out to say goodbye and wish the girls well on their journey to America. Although Voula's four sisters were there to see her off, her mama stayed home behind closed doors and windows that were shuttered to the light.

"It's a black day that I lose my child, and I won't allow the sun to see my face," she wailed from inside the house.

Maria held tight to Mama's and Paraskevi's hands as she walked from the house to the plateia. Baba had gone ahead, claiming the crying had given him a headache. Maria did her best to tamp down the feeling of dread as she walked through the door of her childhood home, wondering if it was the last time she would cross its threshold. The tears fell freely as she walked, and she was unwilling to release the hands of her sister or Mama, unsure if she would ever again have the comfort of holding their hands in hers.

"I feel like Iphigenia walking to the sacrifice," Maria whispered as they walked farther into town.

"And perhaps, like Clytemnestra, I will kill your father," Mama whispered slowly and deliberately, turning her head to face her daughter. Her eyes were black, glazed over.

"I'll be all right." Maria smiled at Mama, squeezing her hand, attempting to calm her. She wasn't sure if that was Mama's village humor or if she was truly capable of such a thing.

"When I get to America, I will find a way to save money and send it to you." Maria squeezed Mama's hand tighter as they approached the bus stop.

Mama hugged her daughter one final time and then collapsed to the ground in a heap of tears as Maria stepped onto the bus. The village women all rushed to help Paraskevi pull Mama up to sit on the low wall and fanned her face as someone ran to fetch her a cool drink of water.

"Everyone for Athens on board!" the bus driver shouted as Maria lurched from her seat to go back outside to check on Mama. The driver stuck his arm out, blocking her path as he honked his horn. "Last call for Athens." With similar scenes playing out all along his route, the driver needed to stick to his schedule; otherwise they would never make the connection in Athens to the bus that would take the brides to Piraeus, where they would board the ship to America.

Maria had no choice but to take her seat. She leaned against the window, placing her hand and forehead on it as the bus pulled away. Voula sat beside her, holding her hand as their tears slid down their cheeks. Maria watched as Mama, Paraskevi, and their friends and family waved white handkerchiefs and leaned on one another for support. As the bus took them farther and farther from the village, the images grew smaller until they were no more than a memory.

Baba was seated at the kafeneio before the bus even pulled away.

Chapter Seven

Cephalonia, Greece

1952

Iт had been nearly a month since Demitra spotted Elena on the beach crying that day. She had not seen her since, yet Elena was never far from Demitra's mind. *How lonely she must be with no one to keep her company and no one to talk to. How does she manage to pay her rent and buy her supplies? Why does she run away from me like a scared animal?* The questions swirled in her mind and fueled her curiosity to a fever pitch.

Each day since she'd watched Elena crying on the beach, Demitra had hidden away to work on her portrait in private. Finally, it was ready. She waited until the afternoon when most of the village took their afternoon siestas to steal away to Elena's house again.

Demitra had not returned since that day nine years ago, after the Acqui Division Massacre, when she slipped her first portrait under Elena's door. Everything was so different now. The tiny home was alive with plants and color. The stone and stucco facade, once brown and gray and drab, had been painted a pristine white and accented with cheerful blue shutters. The door had been painted blue to match and was flanked by two large clay pots containing lush, fragrant basil plants.

As she approached the door, Demitra glanced up at the chimney where a steady stream of white smoke wafted toward the clouds.

A tentative smile crossed her lips. There was no question today; Elena was home. Demitra felt her stomach lurch with excitement and trepidation. Yes, she was home, but Demitra understood there was no guarantee she would open the door and invite her inside.

With the portrait wrapped in paper and secured under her arm, Demitra sucked in a deep breath and walked closer to the door. The newspapers that covered the windows the last time she was there had been replaced by lace curtains. Demitra peeked through the window, hoping to catch a glimpse of Elena inside before she knocked on the door and made her presence known. She inched closer, narrowing her eyes and squinting through the delicate holes in the fabric.

At once she brought her hands to her mouth, unsure if she had screamed out loud or only in her head. She stumbled back, knocking into the basil plant before steadying herself and attempting to catch her breath. She shook her head, uncertain if what she'd seen could possibly be real. Stepping forward and squinting again through the tiny holes of the curtain, she bit her lip. No, she had not imagined it.

There, seated in a chair beside the fire, was Niko.

Demitra steadied herself against the freshly whitewashed wall. She placed her forehead on the glass and watched him as he sat there staring into the fire. He was motionless, slumped in the chair, his shoulders hunched forward just as he had remained for most of the night at dinner in her yard. Just as she had remembered him in school. Detached, disinterested.

She stood there for a few moments trying to wrap her head around what he might be doing in Elena's house, what his presence could possibly mean. Her internal dialogue was interrupted by movement from the far side of the room where a bed was positioned against the wall, half obscured by a blanket draped across a line.

Nektarios. He was shirtless, his hair in disarray, his hands zipping his pants as he walked toward Niko. Elena followed him, tying a pale pink robe at her waist. Her face was emotionless, her eyes blank, cold.

The window was cracked just enough for Demitra to hear as Nektarios spoke, motioning for Niko to get up.

"It's your turn, son."

Niko remained in the chair, staring into the fire. He made no attempt to move.

Nektarios took another step toward him, his mouth drawn in a tight line, his hands clenched into fists at his sides.

"I said get up. It's your turn."

"No. No, thank you." Niko stood and turned to face Elena. "It was nice to see you again," he said before turning toward the door.

"Where are you going?" Nektarios demanded, physically placing himself between Niko and the door.

Niko turned to face his father. "Home. I don't want this."

Elena clutched her robe as she inched back toward the bed.

"No?" Nektarios shouted as he lunged forward and grabbed Niko by the collar. "What kind of man are you? You're not a man. You're nothing!" He raised his hand and slapped Niko across the face.

Demitra flinched and covered her mouth with her hand. Niko stumbled backward and then stood, leaning into the table as he steadied himself. He did not cower. He stood there expressionless.

"I brought you here to become a man, and you're not leaving until you do. You won't embarrass me again. It's time for you to grow up and act like a son of mine should act."

"But I'm not like you," Niko replied, his tone even, composed, unlike the rage simmering in his father's expression.

Nektarios took two steps toward Niko, raised his hand, and slapped him again. The sound, the crack of his hand across Niko's cheek, reverberated through the air.

Niko said nothing for a moment, then he looked past his father to Elena.

"I'm very sorry, but I would like to go home now."

Niko turned and took two steps toward the door. Before he could take a third, Nektarios lunged at him, grabbed him by the collar, and pulled him back.

"I didn't say you could leave! You're not leaving here until you become a man." He held tight and shook Niko, who did his best to remain standing.

Niko yanked free and faced his father.

"I am a man," he said as he stared into his father's black eyes.

"No, that's not what our Italian friends told me. You're not a man. You're an embarrassment. You dare embarrass me at this important moment when our lives and our future are on the line. Those boys went back and told their fathers what happened when you came here, when Arturo paid for you all to come here. They told their fathers that you refused, that you left before it was your turn. How does that reflect on me? On us? Do you think they'll do business with a family whose son is soft? Do you think they'll invest their money with a man who can't even manage his own son?"

"I just want to go home."

"You don't go home until I say so."

Elena, arms wrapped around her body, walked toward the men. She reached her hand toward Nektarios and stroked his arm.

"Please, let him be. Another time when he is ready. I'll be here. Let him take a little time. It's no harm."

Nektarios turned to face her. The slap across her face was swift and hard and sent Elena reeling against the wall with a thud.

"Don't tell me how to be a father. You stick with what you know. Keep your mouth closed and your legs open." He walked toward her and shoved her back toward the wall. She fell to the floor in a heap. A moan escaped her lips.

Niko ran past his father to her side.

"Are you all right?" he asked as he knelt beside Elena, pulling her robe closed where it had fallen open to expose her breast.

"I-I'm f-fine." Elena's voice trembled. "It's all right, really." A slight smile crossed her face, but her eyes fluttered as she breathed in and out slowly, pain etched across her face. The mark of a hand covered her cheek in red and purple.

"Your mother coddled you from the day you were born!" Nektarios's voice boomed, his face crimson. "She's the one who made you this way. Weak!" He took a step closer to Niko and kicked him as he said the word. "Soft!"

Niko curled into a ball beside Elena but said nothing.

Nektarios then reached down and pulled Niko up by his shirt collar. They stood nose to nose. Niko, expressionless, stared into the cold, black eyes of his father.

"I've worked too hard for too long to have you jeopardize it all." Nektarios spat at the floor, never taking his eyes off his son. "You and your mother. Both of you!" He placed his hands on Niko's shoulders again and pushed him.

Niko stumbled and fell to the floor beside the table. The sight of his son, lying on the floor and writhing in pain, seemed to incite a new rage in Nektarios.

He took three steps toward Niko and kicked him again.

Outside the window Demitra gasped at the cruelty and clutched her own gut as Niko lay in a fetal position and moaned on the ground.

"Look at you! Nothing but a worthless heap. It's your mother's fault. She knows how to make bread and pies. She has no idea what it takes to make a man!"

Elena coughed from where she was still lying on the floor. She raised her hand to her mouth, and when she held it out, her fingers were stained with mucus and blood.

Her coughing seemed to remind Nektarios she was there.

He stormed over to where she was lying on her side.

"Get up," he commanded.

Elena rolled to her side and placed her hands on the floor. She pushed herself up and swayed, unsteady on her feet, leaving a bloody handprint on the floor.

"Your mother doesn't know what it takes to make a man, but I do," Nektarios hissed at Niko while towering over Elena. She inched away from him, pressing her back against the wall, her chin held high.

"What are you doing?" Niko yelled as he attempted to stand. He winced with the pain and stumbled forward on his hands and knees.

"What am I doing? Showing you what a man looks like, even though you will never be one." Nektarios tugged at Elena's robe. She turned her head away from him but said nothing as her robe fell open and he pinned her against the wall, his forearm under her neck.

Niko stood, leaning against the table. He grabbed his side and took another step toward his father and Elena. He opened his mouth to speak, but Elena raised her hand at him and shook her head. *"Please. I'm OK."* She mouthed the words as a tear slid down her face. *"Please. Just go."*

Niko shook his head. "Leave her alone," he said, mustering his strength as he took two steps toward them.

"No, Niko. Please. Just go." Elena spoke now, her voice cracking with emotion, her words no more than a whisper. "Please, go."

Nektarios turned to see Niko was standing a few feet from him. He released Elena and turned toward Niko. Lurching forward, he grabbed Niko by the collar again and shook him with all his might. Niko fell to the floor again and did not get back up.

Nektarios stood there, poised and ready, fists raised, but Niko made no attempt to get up. After a few moments, Nektarios turned his back on his son and walked over to Elena.

"Get in there," he growled as he tugged her arm and tossed her on the bed as if she were a sack of flour at the bakery.

Demitra looked away. She could not bear to watch another moment. She slid to the ground, holding her head in her hands and crying quietly for all Niko and Elena endured at the hands of that man, that monster.

She was unsure how much time had passed before she heard the sound of shuffling from inside the house. She stood and looked in the window again. Nektarios was lying on the bed. He appeared to be asleep, his chest rising and falling under the thin blanket. Beside him, Elena was still.

Demitra scanned the living room and spotted Niko leaning on the edge of the table. Beside him a chair had toppled to the floor. Demitra watched as he reached down and placed the chair upright, then tucked it into its proper place. On the table a vase of vibrant pink roses had been knocked over in the scuffle. One by one he placed each stem back into the vase. Once finished, he lifted the vase to his face and inhaled, closing his eyes to take in the scent before placing the vase back down on the table. He untucked his shirt and used it to wipe the table clean before walking toward the door.

Before she could hide, the door opened. Demitra turned and came face-to-face with Niko. He walked out slowly with a slight limp and closed the door behind him.

They locked eyes. His were red and swollen; hers brimmed with tears. They said nothing for what seemed like an eternity but was no more than mere moments.

"Niko." Demitra broke the silence. She took a step toward him and then stopped, unsure if she should comfort him or walk away and try to forget what she had witnessed.

He looked at her, expressionless. If he was surprised to see her standing there, he did not show it. His face showed no emotion at all.

"I'm so sorry," she said, still rooted in place.

"So am I," he said, clutching his side as he started to walk away, his steps slow.

She took two steps toward him. "What can I do? How can I help you?"

He stopped and smiled at her then, blood visible on his teeth. "There is nothing you can do. But thank you." After a few steps more, he turned back to face her. "You shouldn't be here. Don't let him see you."

Demitra watched as he walked away. She was a mix of so many emotions, but above all, she felt pity. In all the years she had prayed and wished her life was different—that she had a mother, that Baba would show her some kindness, pay more attention to her— she had never known physical cruelty. It was now clear that Niko had, and that this was not the first time.

She stayed there for a moment, replaying his words in her mind. *"You shouldn't be here. Don't let him see you."*

The urgency hit her at once. With the portrait tucked under her arm, Demitra made her way down the hill toward the pomegranate tree. There, she knew she could remain out of view as she watched the front door.

A short while later, Nektarios emerged. He lit a cigarette as he stepped away from the house and walked toward home. His shirt was once again tucked into his pants, his hair combed into place.

She waited until he was out of sight before she dared approach the house again. Her legs were still shaky as she inched toward the window. She leaned close and glanced through the glass.

Still clad in her robe, Elena now sat in the chair staring into the fire. Demitra was tempted to pound on the door and shout for her, but the gnawing in her stomach told her not to. She remembered the last time she was here, how Elena chose to stay hidden, even as Demitra knocked and called her name. How Elena had darted away from her in town, like a scared, startled animal, desperate to hide. Demitra tried to push those memories from her mind.

She turned toward the door, reached her trembling hand forward, and grasped the doorknob, tempted to turn it and burst inside. But she didn't. They were women and, as such, in control of few things in their lives. For Elena, even fewer. The precious, intimate pieces of themselves that women held sacred were the very things Elena sold in order to survive. Perhaps the very thing Elena treasured above all else was the only thing she had left that afternoon: the privacy and sanctity of her home. Who was Demitra to burst through the door and take that away? Demitra released the doorknob and turned once more toward the window.

She glanced into the room through the veil of the lace curtain. She had not noticed it before, but there, tacked to the wall above the table, was the drawing of Elena she had slipped under the door years before. Demitra placed her hand on the wooden window frame and leaned her head against the cool glass.

"I'm so sorry," she whispered. She dug her hand into the pocket of her apron and felt the sharp tip of a pencil. She took it out and held it up, regarding it for a moment. She knew who she was, what she was. She had little to her name and no power to change anything about her own circumstances let alone anyone else's. But as she regarded the pencil in her hand, then glanced back into Elena's house and saw her portrait tacked on the wall, Demitra knew if she had any power, she held it there, in her fingers.

I'm so sorry, she scrawled across the top of the wrapping, careful not to press too hard, careful not to damage what the paper held within. Her hands trembled as she slipped the package under the door, then she turned to make the journey home.

Chapter Eight

Cephalonia, Greece

1952

ELENA WAITED UNTIL she was certain he was gone. It took all the strength left in her battered body, but she managed to drag herself from the bed to the chair. There was not an inch of her that did not ache.

She sat there as the afternoon light faded into silver-gray dusk and the last of the fire's orange embers faded to black. Without the heat from the fire, the room had cooled considerably, and she shivered in her thin robe. Finally, she stood, a moan escaping her lips as she grabbed the chair for support. Her cheek was hot and tender where he had struck her, and her head throbbed. She raised her hand to the back of her head and felt a bump, her hair matted with blood.

She'd intended to drink some water and perhaps eat a crust of yesterday's bread, then make her way back to the bed. The pounding in her head seemed to have gotten louder and a distinct ringing filled her ears. Sleep was the only thing she wanted, to drift away and dream, to be transported to a world where she could be what she intended, where she could escape the reality of how cruel men could be.

She took a step toward the kitchen and then turned, spotting the paper out of the corner of her eye. She knew what it was instantly.

The girl had come again.

A sharp pain tore through her body as she bent to pick it up, the throbbing in her head intensifying. She placed the package on the table, the words *I'm so sorry* written across the top. She pulled her hand away as if the letters burned to the touch. Slowly and carefully, she unwrapped the package. Elena traced the outline of the paper with her finger, a swell of emotion working its way from her belly to her throat and ultimately her eyes.

She stared down at the image. She had not been alone that morning on the beach. The girl had been there too.

That morning, as the island slept in the darkness before dawn, was the first time she had experienced his cruelty. She met him in the bakery storage shed as he had requested, as they had arranged. One of the Italian officers made the introduction when he visited the island a few weeks before, so she had not thought twice about her safety or his intentions. The Italians had treated her with nothing but kindness, as had the handful of islanders she'd entertained. She had no reason to fear or believe he would be unkind.

She remembered smiling as he walked in the door and she greeted him with a kiss. He reciprocated by pushing her against the wall and wrapping his hands around her neck. When he was finished, there were no kind words, no caress, no thank-you. He tossed the money at her without even glancing her way. She'd felt discarded. Used. Like a piece of trash.

She had composed herself and stumbled to the beach to wash the stain of him from her body. She soon learned that even the sea was powerless to do so.

As she stared down at the picture before her, Elena cried at the beauty of it, of what the girl had captured. She had seen it all, and yet she also managed to see past it. The tears came faster. She cried not only for what the girl had seen and captured with her pencil, but also for what she had seen and left off the page.

Elena traced her finger along the pencil strokes. It was a portrait of Elena standing in the sea with the wind in her hair, surrounded by the swirling tide as the sun's rays streamed down on her between the storm clouds swirling above. Her arms were outstretched as she tilted her head back, her face lifted toward the heavens.

She did not even know the girl's name, yet the girl from the bluff was the only person who had seen Elena for who she truly was.

I'm so sorry, she had written on the paper.

The girl had come again. The girl was there. Today. The reality hit her then, panic and bile rising in her throat. What did the girl see?

In all these years Elena had never allowed hate to seep into her heart. She had learned years before that hate, like regret or hope, was useless for someone in her position. But now, it was done. For the first time in her life, Elena understood what it was to hate.

She despised Nektarios with every fiber of her being. Not only for how he had hurt her and Niko; she hated him for what he had done to the girl. The thought of her witnessing his cruelty, that he might have taken her innocence, was too much to bear.

"I'm sorry too. I'm so sorry," Elena whispered into the air.

She placed the portrait on the table and turned to get a drink of water. Her head throbbed harder, and her throat burned. She took a step away from the table and felt unsteady, as if the floor had shifted beneath her. She reached her hand out to grasp the table, and the room seemed to spin all around her. She tried to steady herself, but she grasped at nothing but air.

And then the darkness crept in.

Chapter Nine

Cephalonia, Greece

1952

DEMITRA NEVER INTENDED to tell anyone what she'd witnessed at Elena's. As she walked through the door of her home late that afternoon, Martha looked up from where she sat at the table mending Baba's shirt while Gerasimos snacked on a bowl of potatoes mashed with milk and fresh-churned butter. When Martha's eyes fell on Demitra, she seemed to immediately sense something was wrong.

"Stella!" Martha shouted as she stood and scooped Gerasimos into her arms. "Stella, come inside."

"What is it, Mama?" Stella asked as she walked in the door, her basket overflowing with freshly picked vegetables from the garden.

Martha said nothing but motioned toward Demitra, who was removing her shoes near the door. Stella hurried to her side.

"Are you all right?" She placed her hand on Demitra's forehead.

"You look like a ghost, like someone scared the life out of you," Martha said as she sent Gerasimos off to play.

"I just don't feel well," Demitra replied. Despite her best efforts to stay composed, her voice was shaky.

Stella and Martha exchanged a glance and sprang into action. Within moments Stella had Demitra changed into a freshly laundered nightshirt and tucked in bed with a hot cup of tea.

As she sat in bed sipping the tea, Demitra heard rustling and clucking from the chicken coop and then the sound of the axe coming down. The house was soon filled with the comforting aroma of chicken soup simmering on the stove.

She wanted desperately to sleep, to rest and wake clearheaded. But each time Demitra closed her eyes, the images replayed in her mind. Nektarios striking Elena, then tossing her on the bed like a rag doll. Niko, bloodied and broken, slowly limping away. *"Don't let him see you."*

Her mind raced with questions, yet there seemed to be no answers.

When the soup was ready, Martha carried a steaming bowl into her bedroom and sat at the foot of her bed, making sure Demitra ate.

"My soup always works wonders. It's better than any medicine those fancy doctors give you. I should bottle it and sell it. That would show Irene." She smiled haughtily as she leaned forward to see that Demitra had drained the bowl of its last drop.

Demitra lay back on the bed, closed her eyes, and thought about the day's events. Finally, after what seemed like an eternity, sleep overtook her. It was a fitful, restless sleep, filled with fractured dreams and visions.

Demitra woke to the distant crow of a rooster and the pale light of the new day filtering through the window. She was disoriented and unsettled, remembering fragments of her dreams. It had been so long since she'd dreamed of Mama, but Mama came to her last night as she slept.

She knew I needed her, even after all these years.

Rolling over in bed, she brought the blanket to her chin and closed her eyes, summoning the hazy vision of her dream. Mama beside her, comforting Demitra, holding her and telling her that she loved her. She tried with all her might to focus on Mama, to somehow crystalize the blurry mirage, but it was no use. Even with the dream so fresh in her mind, Mama's face was distorted and just out of reach. Even so, an overwhelming feeling soothed Demitra. Although she could not see Mama clearly, she could feel her. She'd felt safe. Warm. Loved.

In an instant the memory of what she'd witnessed at Elena's house came flooding back. Demitra fell back on the pillow in confusion and despair.

A short while later, the rumbling of her belly interrupted her thoughts. She sat up again and inhaled, the smell of a fire and the fragrant aroma of freshly brewed coffee thick in the air. She reached for her sweater and shuffled to the door, emerging from her room to find Baba reading the paper and Stella and Martha sorting beans at the table while Gerasimos made a game of flicking them across the room, much to his mother and grandmother's feigned despair.

"There she is." Stella jumped up to greet her. She placed her hand on Demitra's forehead. "You're not warm. And your color is better."

"So much better," Martha chimed in. "See? I told you my soup works miracles. Ha, whoever heard of a meat pie curing a fever or a headache?" She reached across the table to slice a piece of freshly baked bread. She slathered it with a generous spoonful of butter and then drizzled honey on top before setting it on a plate on the table for Demitra.

Demitra devoured it.

Baba folded the paper and placed it on the table. He stood, grabbed his fisherman's cap, and headed for the door.

"I may be late tonight, so don't wait for me for dinner. I'm helping the doctor build a new office. We were supposed to start yesterday, but he was delayed with an emergency."

"An emergency? What happened?" Stella asked.

"When Manoli went yesterday to collect his rent from the poutana, he found her collapsed on the floor."

Demitra stopped midbite and looked up at her father. Her eyes were wide, unblinking, yet she said nothing.

"Is she sick?" Stella asked as she reached for another slice of bread and slathered it with butter and honey.

"He said it looked like she had been beaten. Not surprising in her line of work." Baba spoke of Elena completely devoid of emotion, as if he were discussing a fish caught in a net.

Demitra looked at her father and could barely form the words. "Do they know who did it?"

"No, and they won't. A woman like that won't tell. It's to be expected anyway. I'm just surprised it hasn't happened sooner." He grabbed his hat and was out the door in an instant.

"That poor woman. Can you imagine what it must be like to live like that, at the whim and mercy of men?" Stella shook her head as she gathered the day's laundry before heading to the well.

Demitra let out a nervous laugh and shook her head at the irony of Stella's statement. Instantly she regretted allowing her emotions to get the best of her in such a public way.

"Those must have been some very vivid dreams you had last night," Stella said as she sorted the items for the wash. "You tossed and turned for half the night."

"What do you mean?"

"I wanted to be sure you didn't spike a fever, so I came to check on you a few times. You were fitful, talking in your sleep. But when I touched your cheek, you placed your hand on mine and held it there for a moment. Then you settled down and slept finally."

Martha raised her eyebrow with no hint of irony or joking. "It was the soup. I told you."

Demitra and Stella stole a glance, each doing their best to tamp down their laughter. Then Demitra's mind replayed the fractured dreams from her restless night.

"That was you last night in my room?"

"Of course it was me." Stella smiled as she balanced the laundry basket on one hip.

Martha snorted as she hiked up her skirt to scratch her knee. "Who else would it be? Do you think Queen Frederica left King Paul at the palace to come pay you a visit?"

Stella exhaled and rolled her eyes at her mother's dramatics. She placed the laundry basket on the floor and took a few steps toward Demitra.

"I just wanted to make sure you were all right. I'm worried about you."

"Thank you. I'm fine." Demitra did her best to sound convincing, even as she fidgeted in her chair.

"Go on, that laundry isn't going to wash itself," Martha commanded with a wave of her handkerchief. "Do you want your husband to come home to wet underpants? You'd better get out there and get started on that wash."

Stella glared at her mother, then grabbed the laundry basket and stomped out to the well with an exasperated *humph*. As soon as she was out the door, Martha turned her attention to Demitra.

"These old eyes of mine are not what they used to be, Demitra, but I can still see clearly enough to know you are not fine." Martha sat in the chair across the table from Demitra. The older woman moved in a way Demitra had not experienced before. Soft yet deliberate, unlike the bombastic, larger-than-life pronouncements and gestures that usually accompanied her presence.

"What happened yesterday?" Martha's voice was calm, as was her demeanor.

Demitra stared at her wide-eyed. She said nothing but felt heat creep into her neck and cheeks.

Martha leaned into the table, her palms flat against the wood she had polished just yesterday with a cloth soaked in olive oil. Her voice was steady and just above a whisper, a volume Demitra did not realize she was capable of.

"I know you know that woman, Demitra. I saw your sketch when I flipped through your pad that day we had dinner with Niko's family. I know I have a big mouth and I sometimes say too much. But I also know when to hold secrets close. I said nothing that night and pretended I didn't see your picture, but I did see it. And I kept your secret this entire time." She paused a moment, looking around, ensuring they were still alone. "I also know when keeping secrets can be dangerous and damaging. So I will ask you again. What happened?"

Demitra shook her head and a tear slipped from her eye. She did not respond at first.

"It's not what you think." The words were out of her mouth before Demitra could stop herself. It was too late now. She had cracked open the door ever so slightly, and Martha was sure to barrel through with full force.

Martha tilted her head and took a deep breath, as if willing herself to stay calm and composed. "I need you to tell me. You were there with her, weren't you? Who hurt her? Did anyone hurt you?"

Demitra bit her lip and glanced down at the floor. She said nothing.

"The sun is strong and there's a brisk breeze. I imagine the clothes will be dry in no time. Gerasimos should be up from his nap soon," Stella said as she came back inside carrying the empty basket. Scanning the room, she seemed to sense the tension.

Stella set the basket on the floor and walked over to the table, where she placed her hands on Demitra's shoulders.

"She won't stop until she knows you are all right. Believe me, she's as stubborn as they come. I remember quite well what it was like attempting to keep secrets from her when I was younger. In this case, I must tell you I agree with her. I won't stop asking until I know you are all right." Stella smiled at her. "We both saw your face yesterday, and it's the same now. Something is haunting you." Stella sat in the chair beside her and took her hand. "Your father's not here. It's just us now. You can tell us."

Demitra looked away.

"Did that boy do something to you? Did Niko do anything to you?" An urgency filled Martha's voice, an undercurrent of fear mixed with rage. "I swear if anyone hurt you, they will have me to answer to."

Demitra was a swirl of emotions, but even so, something dawned on her in that moment. How many times had she prayed that her mother would be there to comfort her and protect her and to confide in? In all those years of yearning and praying, Demitra had been so focused on mourning the mother she had lost that she had not taken the time to recognize the beauty and magnitude of the mothers who had been found.

In that moment Demitra knew she had to tell Stella and Martha the truth.

"I was there . . . ," she began, her voice tentative.

Stella squeezed her hand, and Martha reached out, taking the other.

"You can tell us. And we'll find a way to help you, no matter what," Stella assured her.

Demitra gathered her thoughts, and as she opened her mouth to speak, she felt a release.

"Her name is Elena. I saw her on the beach and drew a picture of her. I wanted to give it to her, a gift. I was going to place it under her door and leave. It was just a drawing and nothing more, but then I looked in the window and I saw them."

Stella and Martha leaned in closer. Martha opened her mouth to speak, but Stella shook her head, allowing Demitra the space to continue with her story in her own way at her own pace. After a moment's breath, she did just that.

Demitra closed her eyes and breathed in deeply before finally saying their names out loud. "Niko and Nektarios."

"They were there together?" Stella brought her knuckle to her mouth as Martha digested the news in shocked silence, her eyes seeming to double in size.

"Yes." Demitra nodded. "Nektarios tried to force Niko to be with Elena, but Niko refused. He hurt them both. He hit them both. And then he hurt Elena in more ways . . ." She looked up at Stella, unable to say the words out loud.

Stella nodded in understanding. "Oh, my poor girl. My poor, poor girl."

Martha said nothing as she sat and listened, taking in Demitra's story, digesting each word. Her silence did not go unnoticed. Demitra glanced over at her, anxiety and trepidation coursing through her as Martha remained uncharacteristically silent.

"Niko saw me there as he was leaving. It's not his fault. He didn't do anything wrong. My heart broke for him."

"We have to tell your father," Stella replied.

At last, Martha spoke. "No, we don't. You'll do nothing of the sort."

The pronouncement startled Demitra and Stella.

"You'll say nothing to your father. What good would that do? To have your father confront Nektarios? About what? Grown men visiting a prostitute? A father introducing his son to a pleasure house? A man taking out his anger on a helpless girl? Such things have been going on since the beginning of time and will continue until the end of time."

She slammed her hand on the table and stood, pacing the room as she pursed her lips and shook her head. "What good would come from confronting Nektarios?" Martha continued, walking back and forth as she sorted through her thoughts.

"No, that would only backfire. He would insist on going through with the betrothal and wedding to save face and to save his family's reputation. Nektarios was trouble when he was a boy, and he is trouble now."

As she paced back and forth, the quiet restraint she had shown earlier was long gone. Once again Martha was infused with the passion and fire her late husband had lovingly and laughingly referred to as a mix of ambrosia, vinegar, and donkey urine coursing through her veins.

And then, as suddenly as Martha had jolted up, she stopped dead in her tracks, a wide grin unfurling across her face.

"Well, I remember when Irene's father could not afford shoes, let alone a dowry. Actually, there are a few more things she would like to forget that I would be more than happy to remind her of." The sly grin was replaced by a broad, confident, gloating smile.

Demitra blinked several times, trying to understand what Martha was saying.

Placing her hands on the back of a chair, Martha leaned in toward Demitra, lifted one hand, and wagged her index finger.

"I know it may seem sometimes that we women are powerless, but that's not true, Demitra. It's not true at all," Martha said, speaking slowly and deliberately. "Never forget that as women we are the ones who give life and sustain it. We are the ones who make a home, who make a family. Without us there is nothing but empty walls, empty space. I know you know this. You lived it for your entire childhood. But look around you now. Look at Stella and Gerasimos and me. Look how different life is now that your father welcomed Stella into your home. Let men think they hold all the power because we know the truth. We are the ones who give life and bring life. There is nothing more powerful or important." Martha reached over and patted Demitra's cheek.

"Men think they hold the power, but we are the power, Demitra. And we bring the magic and the love." She released her grip on the chair and headed toward the door.

"Where are you going?" Stella called after her.

"To see an old friend," Martha called over her shoulder as she hurried out the door. "No granddaughter of mine will reduce herself to joining a family like that."

"What do you think she's going to do?" Demitra asked as she turned to face Stella.

"I don't know, but I haven't seen her move so quickly since she dragged me by the arm and made me lie down in the dirt for the saint to bless my lady parts." Stella smiled at the memory. "I may not know what she's up to, but I do know this." She reached across the table and placed her hands on Demitra's face. "God help anyone who stands in the way of what that woman thinks is best for her family."

In that moment Demitra sent up a prayer of thanks. Her crudely drawn pictures sent to the heavens in ash and smoke had not been in vain.

MARTHA RETURNED A few hours later with a basket of bread and baked goods and a giant smile on her face.

"It's done," she said as she placed the basket on the counter.

"What's done?" Stella asked, eyeing her mother.

"There will be no betrothal, no wedding. It's done."

"How did you manage that?" Stella asked as she glanced over to where Demitra was sitting, staring out the window.

"Remember I told you we knew each other when we were girls? Well, I recalled stumbling upon a scene myself just about twenty-five years ago. Irene was with one of the local fishermen on his boat. I wasn't the only one who spotted them—the fisherman's wife did too. Soon after the wife paid a visit to Irene's parents, Irene and Nektarios announced their engagement. Even then, Nektarios had a reputation for cruelty. He was always the boy to shoot arrows at frogs and salamanders. It's not a marriage either of them wanted, but it was a way for her parents to save face, and her dowry, although it was not much, paid off Nektarios's father's gambling debts. They were married and their son, Niko, arrived just six months later." She raised an eyebrow. "He was quite chubby and healthy for such a premature birth."

"But how did you convince her?" Stella asked.

"I reminded Irene that my math is better than hers. And now that Niko is known all across the island for his baking success, the old fisherman who lives in poverty may be interested to know that the child with the uncanny resemblance to him will soon be worth much more than the three snappers that drunkard pulls in with his nets, when he's not too hungover to cast them, that is."

"You did not!" Stella gasped, her mouth wide.

"I did, and I'm proud of it. Our girl is too good for that family."

"What about Baba?" Demitra asked.

"Don't you worry. I'll take care of everything," Martha said as she leaned in and kissed Demitra on the forehead.

Martha sat and pulled the baked goods from the bag she'd brought home from the bakery. She lifted a piece of pita to her mouth and took a bite.

"Dry. So very dry," she said as she wrinkled her nose and tossed the pita back on her plate.

❁

THAT NIGHT OVER dinner, Martha broke the news to Baba that she had paid a visit to the bakery and returned with more than dry baked goods.

"Irene was a mess when I saw her." Martha wrung her napkin in her hand as she spoke.

Stella and Demitra said nothing.

"What do you mean?" Baba asked.

"I'm afraid the news is not good. Niko is brilliant is some areas, the way he remembers every detail of a recipe—he never needs to write anything down; it's a blessing and a gift. But there were concerns when he was young, and the teacher told Irene and Nektarios they should see a doctor. But of course they were too stubborn for that and decided to pull him out of school instead.

"Well, their pride and stubbornness caught up with them. Just a few months ago, when they were in Athens visiting family, Niko fell and sprained his ankle badly. In the hospital a doctor noticed his behavior and asked if he could run a few tests. They just got the full report back, and it's not good. Physically he's fine, but Niko has the mind and maturity of a ten-year-old and the doctors say that will never change."

Baba shook his head yet said nothing as he lifted his glass to his lips.

Martha went on. "Thank God we found out now, and only after I forced it out of her. She's always been a terrible liar, ever since we were girls. And to think she would try to keep this a secret." Martha clucked her tongue and shook her head as she held her glass out to Baba. He poured a small portion and attempted to pull the whisky bottle away, but Martha shook her glass at him until he poured her a bit more. Satisfied, she smiled and took a deep sip before continuing.

"To think she would try to marry him off, knowing what the doctors said. Can you imagine such a thing? I told her she should be ashamed of herself, that the first thing she should have done was to race over here to tell you herself." She raised her glass toward Baba.

"Thank God we found out before it was too late. God bless him, the poor thing." She shook her head and made the sign of the cross three times. "He seems like a nice boy, and I wish him well. But what kind of marriage would that be? What kind of children would they have—if they could have any at all." She shook her head again and clucked her tongue before draining her glass.

Baba set his fork down and leaned back in his chair, the full implications of Martha's report slowly sinking in. He glanced across the table at Demitra, who met his gaze. She did her very best to keep her expression neutral, knowing better than to reveal the joy she felt upon hearing the news.

"Well, that's not the only news I had today." Martha stole a glance at Demitra and winked as Baba got up from the table to open a fresh bottle of whisky. "I had a letter from my sister, Soula, in Kerkyra. Well, she has a little restaurant in Ipsos. Her daughter, Sophia, has a little girl, Kiki. Anyway, the family restaurant is doing very well now that a new hotel opened just down the beach. Between the restaurant and little Kiki—and, of course, Soula would like more grandchildren—they don't know how they'll manage. Soula is desperate to find someone they can trust to help."

Baba said nothing as he continued eating his meal and listening to Martha.

"They need someone to help with the cooking and Kiki—and, God willing, a new baby when the time comes. It's been so hard for Soula since her husband, God rest his soul, was murdered by the Communists during the Civil War. She said after the war so many families left for America that there's barely anyone left to work. This restaurant is the only hope she has of feeding her family, and they've been given a second chance, but what good is that if

Soula drops dead from exhaustion while stirring her pots?" She looked over at Baba as she wrung her napkin in her hands.

"I don't know how they will manage or what will become of my poor sister. I wish there was some way we could help them—someone we could send to her."

"You're certain they could use the help?" Baba asked, glancing from Martha to Stella.

"I'm certain of it. I don't know how else they'll manage, honestly. Soula's a wonderful cook, and the restaurant has the potential to change their lives, but they just can't manage it all."

"What about Demitra?" Baba asked, placing his fork down on his plate.

A broad smile crossed Martha's face, and she brought her hands together in prayer. "Oh, God bless you. Demitra would be a godsend."

Demitra's mouth fell open at the mention of her name.

"We never announced the betrothal publicly," Baba said, leaning back in his chair. "It would be a way to get her away from Niko without a hint of scandal. Who could say anything negative about a girl going to help a family member in need?"

"That's a brilliant idea." Stella's fork fell to her plate with a clang. "Of course, I'll miss Demitra, but I'd do anything for Thea Soula. Demitra would be such a blessing for them." She reached under the table and took Demitra's hand in hers, squeezing tight.

"Well then, there's only one more person to ask," Martha announced as she dabbed at her mouth with her napkin. "Demitra, would you be willing to go to Kerkyra for a bit to help my sister and her family? She's a very good cook, although not as good as me, of course." Martha reached her arm out across the table and took Demitra's hand, a broad, hopeful smile on her face. "You would be doing our family a great service."

"Maybe now you'll stop wasting time with your stupid pictures and focus on learning some useful skills," Baba said as he lit his cigarette.

Demitra felt her stomach seize at his words. Her visceral reaction was to push back, to tell him how wrong he was, that her art was not a waste of time but something meaningful and significant. She wanted to tell him what it meant to Elena, how she'd tacked the portrait to the wall and kept it there for years. But she thought better of it. She was finally getting the chance to leave this place, to experience life away from these four walls, away from his judgment and austerity.

Demitra smiled and nodded, squeezing Stella's hand under the table and silently saying a prayer of thanks.

Smiling gratefully at Martha, she said, "Of course I'll go to Kerkyra. Anything to help my family."

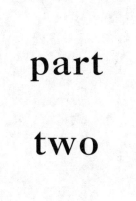

part

two

Chapter Ten

Megali Hellas Ship

1921

TWO HUNDRED PICTURE brides boarded the *Megali Hellas* as the ocean liner prepared to leave Piraeus bound for New York City that clear July morning.

Overwhelmed with sadness, fear, and anxiety at the unknown stretching before them like the seemingly endless ocean, Maria and Voula clung to each other as the ship began its two-week journey from Piraeus, Greece, to New York. They shared a small third-class cabin, consisting of two bunk beds and a washbasin, with two other girls.

Anna was an eighteen-year-old seamstress from Nafpaktos whose mother had died five years before.

"My father sent my photo to the marriage broker the day my sister turned fourteen, saying she was old enough to take my place and care for the house and other children," Anna explained.

One less mouth to feed, Maria thought, repeating the story she heard over and over again.

"This is Anastasios. He's from Evia," Anna said, holding up the black-and-white photo of the man she had been promised to. He looked to be around thirty years old with a slim build and bright eyes. "We are to live in Milwaukee where he works in a restaurant. He's handsome, don't you think?"

"Yes, very," Maria replied. "I'm going to Milwaukee also." She managed to muster a smile and pulled out the photo of her intended. "His name is Pericles."

"Oh, how wonderful." Anna clapped. "Thank the Lord we will be together. Maybe our husbands know each other. Maybe we will live near each other and can spend time together when the men are at work. Wouldn't that be so wonderful?" A hopeful smile appeared on her face.

"Yes," Maria agreed, smiling back, a small sense of relief washing over her. At least she would not be alone on the journey to Milwaukee. And hopefully, as Anna said, their intended husbands would know each other. She hoped Milwaukee might be like the village at home, where she found companionship in the other women, the way the women and girls gathered at the spring.

At twenty-five, their other roommate, Athena, was one of the oldest brides on board. Quiet and shy, Athena was one of the few girls who did not voice her concern or fear at what the future held. One night, about a week into the journey, Maria glanced down from her bunk as Athena was dressing for bed and spotted yellow-and-purple bruises along her back and up and down her legs. Athena turned and caught Maria's eye as she stared at the bruises.

"I'm so sorry," Maria said, averting her eyes. She felt bad having been caught staring, and yet her embarrassment was insignificant. All that mattered was one thing. "Are you all right?"

Athena smiled hesitantly. It was the first time Maria had seen her smile since they boarded the ship a full week before.

"His name is Marko," Athena said as she reached into her satchel and handed Maria a photo. He was stocky with a full mustache and bright eyes. "He's a farmer in Kansas. The priest in our village made the arrangements." Athena paused, as if weighing her words. "He knew I needed to get away. He knew how bad things were for me at home. He wrote to a priest he knows in Kansas, and they sent out my photo and found a farmer who needs a wife. His wife died in childbirth and his daughter is now a year old."

"Will you marry in New York or in Kansas?" Maria asked, handing back the photo.

"Oh no." Athena shook her head as she lifted her hand, a thin band of gold on her finger. "We're already married."

Maria's brows knotted in confusion. "You're married? But how?"

"My priest performed the ceremony in our village. I held his photo and the priest in Kansas did the same."

"Congratulations. May God bless your marriage." Maria did her best to sound upbeat. These were strange and difficult times, but she had never heard of such a thing. "I hope you'll be very happy."

"Thank you," Athena said as she climbed into her bunk. "I don't know if I'll be happy." She pulled the blanket up to her chin. "But I know I'll be happier."

Each night dinner was served in the communal dining room where the rations of meat, potatoes, and bread were meager, yet more nutritious and filling than what most passengers had eaten these past few years.

On the final night of their voyage, Voula climbed into bed with Maria, as she had most nights on the journey. The friends held tight to each other as the ship rocked slightly, crossing over from the Atlantic into New York Harbor. They said nothing as they held each other in the darkness, Voula's head resting on Maria's shoulder. Tomorrow, they would go their separate ways and begin their lives as wives and *Amerikanides*.

"Maybe they'll be good men. And maybe we'll be happy," Maria whispered into the darkness as she stroked Voula's hair.

"Yes. Maybe they will be," Voula replied softly, her tears falling into Maria's hair.

They lay there in silence, comforted by the warmth of the familiar body beside them, knowing that after tomorrow they would be sharing their beds with strangers.

In the darkness of the overnight hours, the usual quiet of the third-class cabins was disrupted by intermittent sobs reverberating down the corridors as the picture brides shared their final night together. From somewhere down the hall, the gentle strum of a mandolin filled the night air, accompanied by the melodic, emotional voice of a young woman singing. It was the lament song they heard many times on the passage as the women gathered on the deck, finding comfort and companionship in one another and their shared journey to the unknown.

How can I leave my village, my home?
I don't want to leave the mountains and the sea and the village
*   that I love.*
Please don't make me leave. Please don't send me away.
I want to be here with you, Mama.
To grow old with you, to take care of you in your time of need.
I don't want to be a wife to a stranger.
I don't want to live in a strange land.
I want to sit with you as you plait my hair and tell me the stories
*   of your youth.*
Please, Mama, please tell him not to send me away.
How will I live without your guiding hand, your gentle touch?
Please, Mama, please tell him not to send me away from you.

Maria closed her eyes and tried to tamp down her anxiety at what lay ahead. Instead, she focused her energy on Mama, conjuring her face, envisioning her smiling down, her golden eyes shining, before she finally drifted off to a fitful sleep.

Chapter Eleven

Corfu, Greece

1952

As she stared out from the deck of the ferry, Demitra thought the scene before her could not be real, that she must be dreaming. Martha had spent the past several weeks preparing her for the trip, educating her on each of the family members as well as the rich and colorful history of Corfu. Even so, she was ill-prepared for the vista before her as the sickle-shaped island revealed itself in exquisite detail.

Demitra gazed out across the water, marveling at the kaleidoscope of reds and rusts and amber-hued buildings, churches, and steeples, seemingly held back from falling into the Ionian by a massive seawall. *How is this magic possible?* She took in the golden glow of the island in the breathtaking moments at the cusp of dusk. The sea and land alike shimmered with ethereal light, as if they were on fire and dipped in gold.

Would it be possible to replicate the beauty before her on paper with her pencils? She would try, but even though she had improved as an artist, she doubted she could do this magnificent scene justice. It was as if this palette, these colors and tones, were reserved for enchanted beings, not for the hands of mere mortals.

At the southern tip of the island stood the old Venetian fort of Corfu, a hulking structure of rock and stone and earth that jutted out into the sea. Atop the remnants of the ancient fort, a single massive cross stood sentinel.

"*Saint Spyridon stood on top of the mountain and raised his arms as the Ottoman invaders approached Corfu in the summer of 1716,*" Martha had explained. "*As the saint commanded the seas, a massive storm formed, swallowing the invaders and tossing their ships against the rocks, saving Corfu and her people. Corfiots placed the cross atop the fort to honor Saint Spyridon and remind all who pass that he is always watching over them. They love and revere their saint the way we do our beloved Saint Gerasimos.*"

Above the fort and rooftops, swarms of swallows flew, soaring over the city and then diving below in unison, as if welcoming Demitra with their frenetic ballet.

"Demitra! Demitra!" called someone from somewhere in the crowd that had gathered on the dock to greet the ferry. As she scanned the group, Demitra locked eyes with the young woman calling her name. She looked to be in her early twenties with glowing olive skin and shiny black hair that she wore straight and to her shoulders. She held the hand of her daughter, who looked to be about four years old and had the same shiny black hair as her mother, hers tied in pigtails with bright pink ribbon.

"Demitra!" the woman yelled again and then leaned over and nudged her daughter. "Go on, there she is." The girl smiled and raised her arm to wave.

"Demitra. It's you, isn't it?" the woman asked as she made her way through the crowd. "I'm Sophia, if you haven't guessed already." She laughed. "And this is Kiki." The little girl smiled shyly as she shifted her weight from one foot to the other.

"Hello. It's so nice to meet you both," Demitra said as she set her suitcase on the ground and leaned in, kissing them both on each cheek.

"How was the trip? You must be famished. Oh, I'm so glad you're here. You have no idea how happy I was when my mother told me you'd be coming. Things have been so difficult since Baba was killed."

"I'm terribly sorry. Martha told me about the tragedy."

"Yes . . . It's been six years now, and it still does not seem real." She reached out and squeezed Demitra's hand. "It was devastating. At first I thought there was no way we would survive. Our hearts were broken. We were broken. And we needed a way to earn a living, to support us, all of us.

"When the new hotel opened, we knew Saint Spyridon had heard our prayers. Now the problem is that we have too much work and can't manage it all on our own, and there is no way my stubborn mother would ever agree to hire a stranger. She's convinced anyone outside the family will steal from her. I hired the nicest Albanian girl a few months ago, but she lasted only two weeks before Mama drove her away. When Martha called with the news that your engagement was broken and asked if you could come here to escape village gossip, well, it was the lifeline we've been praying for." She smiled and hugged Demitra.

Men think they hold the power, but we are the power, Demitra. And we bring the magic and the love." Demitra smiled as Martha's words echoed in her mind.

"Come." Sophia took Demitra by the hand. "The bus stop is right over here. It's about thirty minutes north to Ipsos. Our place is right in town, right on the shore."

Sophia paid the fare, dropping her drachmas into the bucket, and they took their seats on the bus. Sophia opened her purse and pulled out a package wrapped in a dish towel.

"Here. I thought you might be hungry. I know I am. *Boureki.* Chicken pie. My mother made it."

"Thank you. I didn't realize how hungry I am. I was so nervous and excited that I haven't eaten much these past few days." Demitra took a piece of pita and brought it to her mouth. The phyllo was perfectly baked and crispy. The filling of chicken, rice, and dill was creamy and savory perfection.

Sophia handed a piece to Kiki and took the last piece for herself.

"My mother's boureki is really something special, and she's not shy about telling anyone either. Since you've spent quite a bit of time with my aunt Martha these past few years, I'm sure you'll see that they have a lot in common."

Demitra laughed, instantly bringing her hand to cover her full mouth.

"I see you know what I mean." Sophia winked as she took a bite of her pita.

Demitra gazed out the window as the bus wound its way up the coast. So much of the island reminded her of Cephalonia, yet Kerkyra was infused with a different energy; already she could feel the difference. She had no doubt the island was magnificent with its natural beauty. At first glance one might see the verdant hills and crystal-clear water and nothing more.

Yet the more Demitra digested her new surroundings, the more she noticed the imperfections. The dark moss that clung to the seawall and coated seemingly every surface like a persistent shadow, the cracks and decay and peeling paint pocking and disfiguring the ornate architecture. All along the journey, beside tidy homes adorned with brightly painted shutters, potted plants, and flowers were structures reduced to rubble by the German and Allied bombings of World War II. Children ran and played, laughing and climbing atop the ruins, reminders of Corfu's complicated and often painful past. Here, beauty and decay, brilliant light and darkness, and even antiquity and modern life all coexisted in a way that made the island at once achingly beautiful and heartbreak-ingly tragic.

Demitra spotted Soula as the bus came to a stop in Ipsos. She didn't need Sophia to point her out. Soula stood there dressed in widow's black, a large figure of a woman with the same dark black hair as Sophia, yet hers was liberally streaked with white and pulled into a bun, her flowered apron covered in a white dusting of flour.

"There you are! There you are, my beauties!" Soula shouted as she bent to envelop Kiki in her arms. She gave the child a hug and kiss and then fixed her gaze on Sophia. "Go lie down. You look tired and pale. I told you the trip would be too much for you, but no, you always know what's best. You don't listen."

"Mama, I'm fine," Sophia insisted.

"How do you expect Saint Spyridon to help put a baby in your belly if you're always running around like a chicken with its head cut off?" Soula scolded, waving her arms in the air. She pursed her lips and exhaled before turning to regard Demitra.

"Well now." She reached her arms out and took Demitra's hands in her own as she looked her up and down. "Just look at you." She sighed, toggling her head. "A bit skinny, sure. But that doesn't matter. It's that boy's loss, I tell you. Did he really think he could find someone better?"

Demitra knew better than to correct Soula or take offense. Instead, she said what was expected of her. "It's so nice to see you, Thea Soula. I'm so happy to be here with you."

"Oh, child, I'm the one who's happy. Come," Soula said as she slipped her arm through Demitra's.

Arm in arm they walked along the shore as the beach of Ipsos curved toward the mountains and Kiki skipped ahead. It was a short distance to the restaurant, which was tucked into the hillside overlooking the sea in the center of town.

"Sit," Soula commanded as they reached the patio. The restaurant was small and tidy with a large patio out front facing the sea. The patio was crowded with a dozen tables, each decorated with a tiny vase stuffed with delicate wildflowers. Colorful pots overflowing with thyme, rosemary, dill, basil, and tomatoes lined the space, infusing the air with the fragrant perfume of the countryside. Sophia took the seat next to Demitra while Kiki ran off to play with a litter of kittens.

Soula returned from the kitchen carrying a platter piled high with pasta, red sauce, and meat. She did not ask if they were hungry before serving up generous helpings on each plate.

"This is our famous Corfiot *pastitsada*," she said as she pushed a plate in front of Demitra, then added a slice of warm bread on top. "Make sure you get the pasta and the sauce and a bit of meat as well. The sauce is the best part, so you have to mop it up with the bread. I promise you, you've never had anything like my pastitsada," Soula insisted as she lifted her chin haughtily.

Despite the fact that she had devoured the boureki on the bus less than an hour before, Demitra found herself famished. She brought the fork to her mouth, closing her eyes and savoring the extraordinary taste. The meat was tender and melted in her mouth. The sauce was savory yet unlike anything she had ever tasted before.

Soula preened as she watched Demitra devour the dish. "It's my special *spetsieriko*, my spice mixture—the nutmeg, cloves, and cinnamon, and of course a few special secret things I don't tell anyone, no matter how much they beg. My recipe has been handed down for generations from when my grandmother worked in the finest homes of Corfu, the noblest families who brought the spetsieriko with them from Venice. They say your pastitsada is good when the aromas are so strong that the cook has to put on a new bra and the sauce is so rich that it will turn a man's mustache red. Well, mine does both," Soula said as she leaned back in her chair, fanning herself with a dish towel.

"And you won't find a more humble chef all across the island." A man's voice came booming from behind Demitra.

Before she could turn to see who it was, Kiki came skipping down the patio. "Baba, Baba!" she cried as she leaped into his arms. Kiki buried her face in his neck, and he kissed the top of her head, then tossed her high above and caught her, her squeals echoing across the patio.

"Stop it now or you'll make her sick all over my floor, and I just mopped this morning," Soula scolded. Yet the smile on her face told a very different story.

Kiki's baba wore a faded black fisherman's cap atop a mop of sun-streaked brown curls and a deeply tanned complexion. He bent forward and tipped his hat toward Soula.

"Yes, Mama," he replied obediently, to the delight of Kiki, who stood on his feet and wrapped her arms around his legs. Kiki laughed even louder as he strode around the patio while she hitched a ride on his feet.

"Demitra, this is my husband, Tino," Sophia said, smiling as Kiki's delighted giggles filled the air.

"Yes, he may look like the husband, but by the way he acts sometimes you might mistake him for another child." Soula snorted.

It seemed that was all the encouragement Tino needed to prove just how juvenile he could act. With Kiki still firmly planted on his feet, he galloped around the patio, braying like a donkey.

"Yes. Jackass. Exactly." Soula chortled even as a broad smile erupted on her face.

Kiki continued to laugh and squeal until her father ended the ride back at the table where he extended his hand to Demitra and bowed deeply.

"Tino," he said. "Welcome, Demitra. I hope your trip was pleasant. How about the pastitsada? It turns my mustache red every time." He winked as Soula placed a heaping plate before him.

"Tino worked on the docks all his life, but since the hotel opened, he's been mostly helping us here in the restaurant," Sophia said.

Tino shoved a forkful of pastitsada into his mouth. "It's more than a hotel, really. Club Mediterranee, they are calling it."

"What's that?" Demitra asked.

"It's either our salvation or a ticket straight to hell, depending on who you ask in town. It's owned by a Frenchman who came to visit and fell in love with Kerkyra before the war. They're bringing in hundreds of tourists by plane and by boat. But it's the oddest thing—he came all the way to Greece to build this paradise, yet it's not even Greek."

"What do you mean it's not Greek?" Soula scolded as she pointed down the beach with her serving spoon. "Look. A Greek beach on a Greek island where they swim in the Greek sea. How can it not be Greek?" She made the sign of the cross in protest of such stupidity.

Tino ignored Soula's dramatics and went on with his story. "My friend Antoni was hired to take the tourists out fishing on his caïque. He sees it every day with his own eyes. The Frenchman brings people here to pretend they're in the South Pacific. They sleep in jungle huts, dress in grass skirts and coconut bikinis, and dance around waving bamboo fronds."

"Here in the cradle of civilization and they pay a Frenchman to live like savages?" Soula huffed. "They should be ashamed of themselves. Haven't you seen them stumbling around town drunk and nearly naked?"

"You don't seem to mind when those drunks are soaking up all the alcohol with the food you are charging them double for." Tino waved his fork at her. "Come on, Soula, those French tourists are a godsend, and you know it. This village has been dying for years, and now business has never been better. You said it yourself."

"Yes, well, it's good for business, but I just wish those women would have some dignity and put some clothes on. The way they stumble around with everything hanging out for everyone to see. It's shameful and uncivilized."

"They're printing money over there, Mama," Sophia added. "As long as they print enough for us, who cares what those crazy foreigners do?"

"You won't be saying that when those women flash their coconuts in your husband's face." Soula snorted as she began clearing the table.

Tino shrugged as an impish grin crossed his face, and Sophia quietly placed her head in her hands.

"Jesus Christ, Virgin Mary, and Saint Spyridon, please help us." The dishes clanged as Soula piled them onto a platter before disappearing into the kitchen.

"Is it really like that, Tino?" Sophia asked, lifting her head again once her mother was gone.

"Yes. It is," he whispered. "Antoni said he's never seen anything like it." Tino craned his neck to make sure Soula was still well out of earshot. "He said it's like spearfishing in a tub."

"What do you mean?"

"The women." He leaned closer and lowered his voice to a whisper. "He said the women are crazy. He's only worked there for a week and has been invited to two huts already, if you know what I mean."

Sophia's mouth dropped open. She reached across the table and grabbed Demitra's hand. "You haven't been here even a day and already we've scandalized you. There's no hope for us, is there?"

"Oh, just great," Tino chimed in. "She'll probably be on the first boat back to Cephalonia."

"Please don't leave us alone with my mother again." Sophia lifted Demitra's hand to her mouth, covering her skin with kisses.

"Yes, please." Tino reached out and grabbed Demitra's other hand and kissed it as well. "Please don't leave us alone with her."

Demitra could no longer contain herself as she threw her head back and laughed freely in a way that surprised her. She could not recall the last time she laughed like this, unfiltered and raw.

"What's so funny?" Soula asked as she returned to the table.

"Oh, I was just being juvenile as always," Tino said and winked at Demitra.

Although she was enjoying herself, the exhaustion and stress of the past few days finally caught up with Demitra, and she let out a long, deep yawn.

"Oh dear. It's been a long day." Sophia stood and yawned herself. "Let's get you home and settled. Shall we?"

"Thea Soula, that was the most delicious meal. Thank you so much for such a warm welcome. I'm looking forward to helping you and learning from you."

"Good night, dear," Soula said as she started to sweep the floor. "I won't wake you in the morning. Sleep as late as you like."

Sophia and Tino exchanged glances, and Sophia did her best to stifle a laugh.

"What is it?" Demitra asked.

"Good luck sleeping past dawn with Soula in the house," Tino muttered.

"He's right. There's nothing quiet about that woman, and I mean *nothing*." Sophia again tried to stifle a laugh as she watched her mother chasing away a salamander with her broom. "Come on, the house is just down the road. It's simple, but it's clean and quite comfortable. You'll be in the house with Mama, and we're just a few doors down."

As Demitra stood, Tino opened his arms wide, and Kiki took that as her cue. She raced across the patio and jumped into her baba's arms. He placed her on his shoulders and then reached down to pick up the suitcase. Together, they walked down the path from the restaurant to the sea toward home.

The sea was still, reflecting the low clouds and full, silver moon. All along the shoreline, the road was dotted with small stores and tavernas, most of them shuttered.

Soon they turned into a back alley and climbed the hill where Soula's house sat behind a small cluster of olive trees. The house itself was small yet meticulously maintained, the entrance marked with two slim cypress trees.

"I'll see you at home, sweetheart. Have a good night, Demitra," Tino said as he placed Kiki back down on the ground, patting her head before she skipped ahead into the house.

Inside, Sophia flicked on a light, illuminating the room. The entranceway was spare, save for a table covered in a white crochet doily and several framed family photos. Sophia led the way toward the back of the house and opened the first of two doors that were side by side across the hall from the small kitchen.

"Here you are," she said as she led the way inside. There was a single bed covered in a white crochet coverlet tucked in the corner beneath two icons nailed to the wall. One was of the Virgin Mary and the other was of Saint Spyridon. A small dresser stood into the corner across from the bed. Atop the dresser was a small vase of wildflowers, the same as those that adorned the tables at the restaurant.

"I picked those for you." Kiki beamed as she pointed to the flowers.

"Well, they are beautiful. Thank you so much." Demitra bent down before Kiki and tapped her nose with her finger. "I can't wait to pick more flowers with you. Do you promise to show me where the best flowers on all of Corfu are?"

Kiki's eyes brightened as her mouth erupted in a smile.

"I know this is not the most exciting village, but I do hope you'll be happy here with us," Sophia said as she peeled back the coverlet and fluffed the pillows. "There aren't many of us left. So many families left during the German Occupation. It was a terrible, terrible time. We thought they'd come back once the Germans surrendered.

"But then, even if they'd wanted to, the Civil War made it even more difficult for people to find their way home. After a while, there wasn't much to come back to. How can you raise a family if there's no one for your children to play with? No prospects for your daughter to marry? Nowhere to find work? It's been so difficult these past few years." Her fingers dipped in and out of the delicate rosette pattern of the coverlet.

"It was the same in Cephalonia," Demitra said as she placed her suitcase on the bed and began to unpack. "I was so lonely growing up. There were no girls my age in the village, and my father was not a man of many words or emotions." She looked over at Sophia, who stopped fussing with the bed and smiled at Demitra. That gentle smile was all the encouragement Demitra needed to continue.

"When I was young I filled my time with imaginary conversations with my mother, and later with books and my drawings. Then Stella came into our lives, and our house became something I never knew it could be."

"Do you know why he waited so long?" Sophia asked, confusion on her face. "Why didn't he marry when you were younger? It must have been so hard for him to raise you alone all those years."

"I don't know. I've wondered that myself so many times. As difficult as he could be sometimes, I pity him. When I was a child I didn't know what it meant to be a family. I didn't know what I was missing all those years that our house was silent and still. But he did. He had a family once and then it was gone. I was too young to remember, but he knew. He knew all along what he'd lost, what was missing from his life."

"And what about the boy? The one you were going to marry."

Demitra shook her head as she sat on the bed beside Sophia. "I was never going to marry him." The words slipped out easily without thought or emotion. "I knew that, even if no one else did."

"Then I'm glad you didn't."

"Me too."

"And I'm glad you're here." Sophia placed her hand on Demitra's.

"Me too." Demitra smiled.

"And me too." Kiki giggled as she did a running leap to get between them on the bed.

SOPHIA WAS RIGHT. It was not the crowing of the roosters from the hillside that woke Demitra the following morning; it was Soula clanging and banging pots and pans even before the sun rose. The woman was as unfiltered and unrestrained in her cooking as she was in conversation.

"Oh dear, did I wake you?" Soula asked as Demitra opened her bedroom door and joined her in the kitchen.

"Can I help?" Demitra asked as she rubbed the sleep out of her eyes.

"No, you sit and have some coffee. You're probably still off from your trip." Soula reached for the briki and poured the thick black liquid into a demitasse cup, then placed it before Demitra on the table.

The coffee was bitter and hot, and Demitra instantly felt more awake with each sip. She sat, watching as Soula cleaned, chopped, sautéed, and roasted a bounty of vegetables into a platter of perfectly seasoned and prepared *briam* before turning her attention to a bowl of octopus in need of tenderizing. Soon the kitchen was flooded with a symphony of savory and delicious aromas, as well as the pink-tinged light of a new day.

"Yia-yia!" Kiki bounded into the kitchen, a jumble of excitement and energy. She hugged her yia-yia and then skipped over to Demitra before climbing into her lap.

"I missed you." The little girl hugged her tight.

Sophia entered behind Kiki carrying a bouquet of freshly cut wildflowers. "We picked these for you this morning. Kiki insisted."

As Demitra finished her coffee, Kiki tugged at her skirt. "Will you play with me?"

"Kiki, let the girl have a minute. I'm sure she's still tired from her trip," Sophia said.

"No, it's fine," Demitra said as she took her cup to the sink and then reached out to take Kiki by the hand, "Let's have an adventure together, shall we?"

Hand in hand Demitra and Kiki walked along the shore, stepping gingerly along the pebble-strewn beach. It was just a short walk to the schoolyard playground where Demitra pushed Kiki on a swing while the little girl reached out her hands to touch the heavens.

They had only been gone for two hours when Demitra wondered how she would fill the rest of the day and keep Kiki entertained. She remembered her own childhood and how she passed the hours by escaping into a world of her own creation.

"Come on." She smiled at Kiki and held out her hand.

"Where are we going?"

"Anywhere your imagination can take you," Demitra said as they skipped together along the shore and back toward the house.

"Wait here. I'll be right back." Demitra planted Kiki in a chair on the patio and ran into the house. She returned with two glasses of lemonade and her sketch pad tucked under her arm. She flipped open the pad, turning page after page, showing her drawings to the delighted Kiki.

Her eyes opened wide in wonder. "Did you really draw these? With your own hands?"

"Yes. I started drawing when I was just about your age. My mama went to heaven, and I missed her terribly. I would draw pictures for her so I could still talk to her. I wanted her to know how much I loved her."

"How could she see your pictures all the way from heaven?" Kiki asked. "That's a very long way." She squinted. "I can't even see the end of the street from here. And heaven is a lot farther away."

"That is a very good question." Demitra leaned in and tapped Kiki on her nose with her finger.

"I would draw a picture—sometimes it was a heart, so she knew I loved her. Sometimes it was our family, so she knew I missed her. But always so she knew I was thinking of her. And then I would take my picture outside and set it on fire, and I knew the smoke would deliver my message all the way up into the sky and all the way up into heaven where she could read it."

"Can I draw a picture?" Kiki asked.

"Of course. Why, I had no idea we had another artist in the family."

Kiki sat up straighter in her chair and seemed to grow three inches at the compliment.

Demitra opened her pad to a blank page and placed it before Kiki. She handed her a sharpened pencil.

"Here you go."

Kiki went to work. She leaned over the pad and drew while Demitra watched. When she was finished, she stood back, allowing

Demitra to examine her work. She'd drawn a heart in the center of the page and a stick figure on each side with their hands extended and crossing in the center of the heart.

"See, that's you." Kiki pointed to one figure. "And that's me," she said as her finger moved along the picture. "And see, that's my heart right here. It's big, so big because you're here." She looked up at Demitra, her long black lashes fluttering.

"It's beautiful." Demitra smiled. "You are quite the artist."

"Can we send it to your mama?" Kiki asked without looking up from her pad. "So she knows you're here with me. And that I'm so happy you are."

"That's a great idea."

Together they walked outside to the front of the house. Standing between the two cypress trees and facing the gentle Ionian, Demitra struck a match and set fire to Kiki's picture letter. She held it for a moment as the flames consumed the paper and then watched as it floated to the ground, reduced to ashes.

They stood side by side, holding hands and gazing up as the white smoke ascended toward the heavens until nothing was left but the memory of a child's wish.

Chapter Twelve

Corfu, Greece

1952

S HE HAD BEEN on Corfu for only four months but already Demitra felt changed. A lightness surrounded her. A hopefulness and joy that can only come after the most difficult times, when you've given up hope and yet found it again in the most surprising way. For Demitra that hope was in this small village whose unexpected rebirth and reawakening seemed to mirror her own.

When Sophia's childhood friend, Angeliki, announced that she would be returning from Athens to marry in the village, it was a cause for celebration up and down the island.

As Angeliki's wedding day approached, the village filled with a buzz of electricity, excitement, and the friends and family who had left in search of a better life. The tavernas and *ouzeries*, which had grown silent since the war, once again came to life with the chatter of families and friends reunited.

In the early afternoon of the wedding day, everyone walked to the bride's house where guests gathered to escort the bride to church. Inside, the house was a cacophony of activity. Violins played as family members and friends streamed in and out to share their well wishes with the bride and her family.

As each person entered the room to greet the bride, they tossed drachmas on the bed to wish her prosperity and sugared almonds to symbolize fertility. Angeliki was a vision in a simple cap-sleeved dress of white lace that cinched at her waist and fell to the floor. Her hair was pulled off her face and fastened at the nape of her neck in a knot.

"Oh, you look so beautiful," Sophia said as she kissed her friend on each cheek.

"You're just in time," Angeliki said. She picked up one of her wedding shoes and turned it over. "This is Demitra, right? The cousin you told me about?" The bride smiled at Demitra as she wrote her name on the sole of her shoe along with the names of the other unmarried girls attending the wedding. The girls whose name were erased from the sole would be the next to get married.

Demitra smiled politely. *No, thank you.*

Outside, a handful of women and young girls dressed in the traditional Corfiot costume waited to escort the bride through the village to the church and into the arms of her soon-to-be husband. The women wore long colorful skirts and white lace blouses topped with the short *pesseli* jackets of red velvet, embroidered in gold thread. On their heads they wore voluminous red headbands woven with crimson flowers and white ribbons.

As the violins played and the villagers came out of their homes to join the wedding procession, Demitra felt an excitement swell in her stomach and chest. It was unlike anything she had ever experienced before. She felt as if she had woken from a deep sleep to find the world had bloomed and come alive in color and song.

The ceremony was beautiful and joyous. Angeliki beamed as she took her fiancé's hand, and with three turns around the altar, wearing crowns of woven stephanotis joined by a white ribbon, Angeliki and Stellios became man and wife.

The joy and love spilled out across the plateia for the reception where everyone gathered under a star-filled sky for dinner and dancing as the smoke and scent of grilled lamb and souvlaki filled the air.

Red-faced and winded, Demitra sank into a chair next to Sophia and Tino after dancing an especially fast *hasapiko* that took her breath away. Tino was savoring a glass of whisky and a cigar when his face brightened.

"Hello, old friend!" he said as he jumped up to hug a dark-haired man who, wearing an impeccably tailored suit, seemed a bit out of place in the sea of moth-eaten jackets, faded shirts, and well-worn suits.

"Hello." The man slapped Tino's back several times as the men embraced.

"I heard you were back on the island," Tino said as he pulled away to regard his friend. "Look at you. Success looks good on you. I hear you've done quite well for yourself. London, isn't it? I always knew you'd make it. But I never imagined you'd come back to our sleepy little island."

"I had to come back. I had unfinished business here, a promise to keep." The man smiled as he turned and bowed his head to the ladies.

"Where are my manners?" Tino placed one arm around Sophia and pulled Kiki close. "Ladies, this is my friend Aleko. We went to school together in Corfu Town, that is, until he went off to a fancy university in London and became a big success. This is my wife, Sophia, and her cousin, Demitra."

Aleko looked down at Demitra and tipped his head toward her. "So lovely to meet you. Demitra, a name befitting such a beautiful young lady."

Demitra felt her face flush at the compliment from this stranger. The words were on her tongue to thank him, yet she was unsure if it was appropriate to say them out loud. She remained silent, anxious about making a mistake in front of such a gentleman.

She glanced up at him. His eyes crinkled in the corners when he smiled, and his teeth were white and straight, unlike those of the villagers who often went their entire lives without the luxury of dental care. His shirt was crisp and starched, perfectly pressed in a way that even the most skilled housewife could never achieve with a home iron heated over a kitchen fire. Perhaps most telling were his hands. Demitra had never seen hands like his. The skin was smooth without even a hint of a scar or callus. He was unadorned of jewelry, save for a simple watch around his wrist.

"I have an early meeting and need to head back to Kerkyra. But I have business nearby, so I'll be spending some time here up north. I'll come by Soula's to see you this week. Goodbye, Tino. Ladies." Aleko nodded toward them and headed across the plateia.

"I can't believe he's back," Tino said as he took a sip of his drink.

"What do you mean?" Sophia asked as she held Kiki's hand and twirled her in time to the music.

"He came from a very poor family, one of the poorest in our school in Corfu Town, and that was saying something," Tino said. "He worked harder than anyone I knew in school and earned a scholarship to Cambridge business school. I heard he did well with real estate investments and settled in London. He always said he would come back, but I never imagined he would. Look at him, though, a man of his word."

The band struck up another joyous hasapiko. The violinist was joined by a clarinet and bouzouki whose moody notes filled the air with traditional village songs. To the guests, they were more than songs; they were the very essence of the island, the music that generations of these families had grown up on, danced to, and celebrated every milestone of life with.

"Come dance with me." Sophia pulled at Tino's sleeve and then motioned toward Kiki and Demitra.

"Well, of course." Demitra stood at once, taking Kiki's hand and leading her to join the circle dance. They kicked their legs in unison and danced around and around as a gentle breeze kissed their skin on a perfect summer night.

DEMITRA HAD SETTLED into a comfortable routine of entertaining Kiki and helping at the restaurant during the week and attending church with Soula on Sunday mornings. After the service they walked together to the periptero for their weekly call to Martha, Stella, and Gerasimos, who would be waiting at their periptero, where Areti, the elderly attendant, always gave them first priority among her Sunday callers. Baba would be in his usual spot across the plateia sipping ouzo and discussing politics with the men.

When the women were all caught up with news and gossip, Demitra and Soula went back home where Soula enjoyed her traditional Sunday afternoon siesta. With Sophia and her family gone to visit Tino's parents each Sunday, Demitra found herself with the entire afternoon ahead of her. Some days she enjoyed walking along the shoreline or lending a hand as the village yia-yias collected greens and chamomile flowers from the fields beyond the beach, but most often she spent this precious time doing what she loved most: drawing.

The Sunday after Angeliki's wedding was no different. Demitra knew exactly how she wanted to spend her day. After grabbing her sketch pad and pencil, she raced out the door.

Dragging a table down the taverna stairs and across the street to the beach would not be an easy task, but Demitra was determined to do so. She placed her pencils and her sketch pad on the table as she began to tug it across the taverna patio. The table was heavier than she'd imagined and she struggled, pushing and pulling with all her might. She made it to the stairs, but with the first step she nearly lost her balance as the table tipped precariously and her pad and pencil tumbled to the ground.

"Hold on there!" A voice came from behind her just as she thought she might fall over. A man approached and steadied the table with one hand and her with the other, placing his arm around her waist.

"What on earth are you doing?" he asked as he pulled the table back to the safety of the patio.

She turned to face him, and a current coursed through her body as her eyes locked with his. Aleko, Tino's friend. She might die of embarrassment right there on the steps of Soula's restaurant.

"Are you all right?" His forehead furrowed.

"Yes. I'm fine," she said, shoving her trembling hands into her pockets. "All good. Thank you." Her words were unconvincing, even to herself.

"Does Tino know you're rearranging the restaurant?" Aleko laughed as he pulled a cigarette from his shirt pocket and placed it between his lips. He then pulled a silver lighter from his jacket and in one swift motion flipped open the top and ran his thumb down the wheel. The air was instantly infused with the acrid scent of lighter fluid and smoke as he lit his cigarette. He inhaled deeply, then leaned his head back as he exhaled a long thin stream of smoke. Demitra had never smoked a cigarette in her life, nor had she ever been tempted to try it, but the combined scent of his lighter and tobacco was somehow intoxicating.

"You're an artist," he said as he placed the cigarette between his lips again and bent down to grab the pencil and sketch pad, which had fallen open to an unfished drawing of Kiki playing with the kittens.

Demitra's face burned with embarrassment. She wanted nothing more than to disappear. She reached out and took the items from him, closing the pad to prevent further humiliation.

"I . . . I like to draw," she replied, struggling to find her words. "But I wouldn't call myself an artist, really. It's just a hobby, a way to pass the time."

"What were you doing with the table?"

"I was trying to drag it across the street so I could draw the restaurant for Soula—to surprise her."

"Ah, I see." His mouth formed a mischievous smile. "Well, Demitra, the artist with the beautiful name from the beautiful island of Cephalonia, let me help you surprise Soula since that good-for-nothing Tino is not here to help you. We can't expect a young lady to be dragging furniture into traffic now, can we?"

Demitra smiled, clutching her pad so tightly that her fingers turned white. Even as she leaned against the wall of the restaurant, she felt unsteady on her feet.

"Where exactly do you want it?" he asked as he lifted the table effortlessly.

She focused all her might on steadying her trembling hand as she pointed to the sidewalk across from the restaurant. "Over there. Please."

He proceeded to carry the table down the stairs to the other side of the street and set it adjacent to the sea. He then walked back to the patio, picked up a chair, and carried it over, tucking it under the table.

"There. Now the artist has the perfect spot to create her magic," he said as he pulled the chair back out from under the table and motioned for her to sit. She felt as if she were floating outside her body as she walked across the street and sat. She placed the pad on the table and looked up at him.

"What time does Soula arrive to open the restaurant on Sundays?"

"Five."

"All right then. Your secret is safe with me. I'll be here at four thirty to put the table back in its place and no one will be the wiser." Without another word he tipped his hat and walked away from her down the beach.

Demitra watched as he got in his car and drove away. She sat in stunned silence, gazing out across the empty street. A few moments later, her trance was finally broken as a stray cat yowled and rubbed itself against her leg.

She took a breath and exhaled, forcing herself back to reality and the task at hand. She opened the pad to a pristine blank page and glanced up to the entrance of the restaurant. Demitra pulled her pencil from her apron pocket and brought the sharpened tip to the paper. She pressed the point to the blank page, willing herself to focus, her hand trembling.

It was still trembling when he returned promptly at four thirty to return the table.

THE RESTAURANT WAS bustling with clients from Club Mediterranee who wanted to explore Corfu beyond the round huts and canteen diners of the resort. Beautiful, tanned young men and women devoured Soula's dishes and filled the air with their melodious chatter as Demitra sat drawing with Kiki at a corner table later that evening while Soula and Sophia managed the kitchen and Tino greeted the guests.

"Might you have room for an old friend?"

Demitra recognized his voice at once. The familiar current raced through her body again, and she looked up to see Aleko standing beside Tino at the patio entrance.

"Hello, welcome." Tino motioned for him to join them.

"So nice to see you again." Aleko nodded toward Kiki and Demitra with no mention of their seeing each other earlier that afternoon. "Demitra, right?" he asked with a sly smile as he sat in the chair next to her.

She nodded, then averted her eyes.

"I had a meeting in town and thought I would stop by for some of Soula's famous cooking," Aleko said.

Tino disappeared into the kitchen. Demitra did her best to focus on Kiki, even as she felt Aleko's eyes boring into her.

"Don't worry, your secret's safe with me," he whispered as he inched closer.

She lifted her head to meet his gaze. His smile was kind and gentle with a hint of mischief.

"I MUST SAY, you've made us proud, my friend. I can't imagine what it must feel like to come back in this way after conquering the world." Tino placed a plate of *pastichio* before Aleko and poured them both a drink.

"It's not that I ever wanted to leave," Aleko said as he devoured the dish. "I had no choice. There was no opportunity for me here, so I had to go and make the opportunity for myself. I knew I would come back one day to change my family's story."

"Cheers to you." Tino raised his glass to Aleko. "Not only have you rewritten your family's story, but you've managed to rewrite ours as well." He glanced up as a group sat down at a table near the front of the restaurant. "Excuse me."

Aleko turned his attention to Demitra, who was finding it increasingly difficult to focus on Kiki and her drawing.

"Teaching the next generation of artists?" he asked.

She met his gaze and lingered.

"Can we send this to your mama when we're finished?" Kiki asked as she drew a cluster of hearts in the sky.

"Sure, Kiki. That's a great idea." Demitra mustered a smile.

"Back in Cephalonia?" Aleko asked as he leaned back in his chair.

"No. My mother died in America. When I was little, I would write letters to her and send them up to heaven by burning them."

"An artist's soul from the start." He smiled at her again, but there was no mischief in his eyes, only warmth.

"Thank you for not mentioning this afternoon," she whispered. "Everyone here has been so kind and made me feel so welcome. It means a lot to me to be able to surprise them, even if it's just a small token."

"They are lucky to have you. I would never get in the way of your surprise."

She felt the tension in her shoulders dissolve at his words.

"Besides, we all have our secrets, don't we?" He winked and smiled slyly, then stood and tipped his hat to her, waving goodbye as he walked out into the night.

Chapter Thirteen

New York

1921

THE NEXT MORNING Maria woke before the sun. She lay there quietly so she wouldn't wake Voula, who was still asleep beside her. At seven o'clock the ship's horn blared, followed by an announcement, but it was not the message anyone had anticipated.

"Attention, passengers," the captain said. "We will not be docking and disembarking in Manhattan today as planned. We are being detained due to recently enacted immigration laws."

A collective gasp and groan sounded up and down the ship from the crowded third-class accommodations to the luxurious suites of first class. The captain went on to explain that Greece had exceeded the newly established immigration quota for July, and no more Greeks would be allowed to enter the country until August 1. For three additional days the *Megali Hellas* and all her passengers would be held off the coast of Atlantic Highlands, New Jersey, until the new monthly quota for Greece went into effect at the stroke of midnight on August 1.

That evening, as they strolled the deck after dinner, Maria heard shouts coming from the second-class deck above.

"Go home, you dirty Greeks! It's your fault we're rotting here on this boat." Even though she did not speak English or understand what the men were shouting, Maria knew enough to realize that it would be best if they remained in their cabin until the ship pulled into New York and they could safely disembark.

LYING IN HER bed, Maria felt the jolt and then vibrations as the ship's engines groaned to life at the stroke of midnight on August 1. As the metallic clang of the lifting anchor echoed in her ear, she knew this would be her final night as Maria, the daughter of Aphrodite and sister of Paraskevi from Karditsa. Each moment the *Megali Hellas* cut through the choppy waters and sailed toward New York Harbor brought her closer to her new reality and identity as the wife of a stranger named Pericles. She was still awake as the sun rose over Manhattan Island and the ship pulled into port just after 6:00 a.m.

Please, please, God. I just want to go home. I just want to go back to my life in Karditsa, she prayed as the other women stirred awake. Wide-eyed and nervous, they packed their belongings and prepared to face their new lives and husbands.

After she made her way to the third-class deck, elbow to elbow with the other anxious brides, Maria leaned against the railing and gazed upon the Manhattan skyline for the first time. It was a wonder, a marvel of steel and glass reaching up to the heavens. The buildings, tall and ornate, looked like works of art. How she wished Mama and Paraskevi were there to see.

"Did you hear what happened?" Koula, a bride from Milos, asked breathlessly as she hurried down the deck, suitcase in hand.

"What is it?" Maria asked, turning her attention from the glittering streets of New York to a red-cheeked and winded Koula.

"There, the ship beside us." She pointed to a black-hulled ship farther down the harbor, its name, *Calabria*, visible on the lifeboats. "One of the deckhands told me they docked right after us this morning, literally two minutes after. But since we got here first, and with the new immigration laws in place, we will be allowed to stay, but the brides on board the *Calabria* will be sent back. He said there are too many Greeks between us and fifty of them will be sent home. Imagine, after all the preparations and dowries, and after two weeks of feeling sick at sea, to be turned around and sent back home." She clucked her tongue as she continued on her way.

Maria gazed at the *Calabria* longingly, watching as clusters of women huddled together on her deck. *If only I could trade places with you*, she thought. *If only I could be sent home too.*

The first- and second-class passengers disembarked while the third-class passengers waited for their turn on deck. Maria marveled at the women and their beautifully tailored traveling outfits and hats as she ran her hands over her best dress, a pale blue smock she had saved in her suitcase for today. At home Mama always made sure her clothes smelled of lavender water and fresh mountain air, but after almost three weeks aboard the ship, nothing about her clothes or her appearance was fresh.

As she gazed at the elegant passengers below, one particularly well-dressed woman caught Maria's eye. Her hair was blonde, almost white, and coiffed into perfect finger waves that fell at the nape of her neck. Her lips were crimson and her dress a pale pink that fell to midcalf. She wore a dizzying number of pearls draped from her collarbone to her waist. The woman looked up, catching Maria's eye. She placed her hand above her forehead to shield her eyes from the sun, her cupid's bow lips parting to reveal a perfect gleaming smile. Maria smiled back. What must it be like to exist in a world where painted lips were a sign of elegance and refinement, not immorality? Her mind drifted as she imagined a life where a woman was valued for her beauty and skill as a conversationalist, not just for keeping house and bearing sons.

The woman's companion followed her gaze up to the third-class deck to Maria.

"Don't waste your charms on the likes of them, my dear. Those savages are the reason we missed the Vanderbilts' party last night," he said as he ushered her away.

Maria watched the exchange, her stomach sinking as the smile disappeared from the woman's face. She did not know what the woman's companion said, but that fact was insignificant. By their demeanor alone, Maria understood perfectly.

She looked up at the skyline again, picturing the woman at home in such a building, maybe even high above on one of the top floors. *I bet she can see all the way back to Greece from there.* Soon Maria's thoughts were interrupted by shouts and commotion coming from the dock below.

Chaos. It looked like chaos as Maria leaned over the railing and scanned the scene on the dock. The prospective grooms were packed shoulder to shoulder looking up at the ship and waving to the women. The men were dressed in their Sunday best, hair slicked back and oiled. Many held flowers and boxes of chocolates as they waved the photos of their brides and shouted their names, scanning the decks for their betrothed.

Ariadne. Daphne. Camilla. The men shouted as the women craned their necks, scouring the docks for the faces that matched their own photos.

"Ladies, my name is Nicole." A tall, well-dressed woman greeted them on the deck in heavily American-accented Greek, clapping her hands to command the attention of the brides. "I'm a volunteer from the Traveler's Aid Society. We are here to help you safely navigate travel through customs into New York and your new lives.

"Once you have been processed through immigration, you will walk out on the dock to meet your groom. Please make sure you match your photo, as there are unsavory and unscrupulous men waiting to take advantage of ladies such as yourselves. I will be here to help, along with my colleagues. You can identify us by our badges. Look for the ribbons pinned to our chests. Now, good luck to you all, and welcome to New York."

"What does she mean by 'unscrupulous men'?" Voula asked, inching closer to Maria.

"One of the ladies in the kitchen warned me," Athena replied. "She said a few months ago a girl from Sparta was approached by a man who claimed he was her fiancé's cousin and had been sent to pick her up. She went with him, and . . ." Athena paused and made the sign of the cross before finishing her story.

"Well, he was not who he said he was. The poor girl was taken and beaten and forced to sell herself to men before she was finally found by the police. They put her on the ship and sent her back to Greece, to her family in Sparta. She tried to kill herself on the voyage back. She cut her wrists and when they found her bleeding, she begged the doctor to let her die. She said death was better than the dishonor she brought her family."

Maria, Voula, and Anna all made the sign of the cross.

Three hours later, the four girls finally made their way through the immigration line. They huddled together as they walked toward the crowd of men, leaning on one another for support and encouragement as they faced the great unknown and the chaos all around them.

"Athena! Athena, is that you?" came a voice from within the throng.

The women turned and watched as the stocky, mustached man from Athena's photo pushed his way through the crowd.

"Athena!" he shouted again as he finally made his way to her. "It's me, Marko." He tipped his hat to her and bowed his head. "These are for you." He smiled as he handed her a bouquet of flowers.

Maria and the other girls stood in place as Athena stepped forward, taking the flowers in her hands.

"Thank you," she said, then she leaned in and kissed him on each cheek. He smiled at her broadly, the edges of his mustache curling up toward his cheeks.

"You are even prettier than your photo," he said, and Athena's face lit up in a smile.

"I left the baby at home with my cousin. I thought it might be nice to have a few days here to get to know each other before we go home," he said. "I never expected you would be delayed like this, but that's all right. You are worth the wait." He bowed his head, then took her hand in his and kissed it.

Athena flushed red. She smiled again at him and nodded before turning to hug each of her roommates.

"May God bless you and keep you safe." She took a deep breath then, as if gathering her courage. "I'm ready," she said, turning back to Marko as he grabbed her suitcase in one hand and slipped his other arm through hers. It was a bold move for a man and woman who had just met, but then again, they were already man and wife in the eyes of God. With her head held high, Athena walked away with her husband toward her new life in America.

Maria silently thanked God that Marko appeared to be a kind man and wished the best for Athena after all she had been through.

Maria was so consumed watching Athena depart that she did not notice the tall, slim man approaching them.

"Excuse me," he said. "Are you Voula?"

Voula spun to face him. "Yes." Her voice was tentative.

"I'm Petro." He bowed his head toward her. "I will be your husband. We will leave for Florida by train tonight, and then travel on to Tarpon Springs where my brothers and I work on the sponge docks."

Voula grabbed Maria's hand and squeezed.

"We are the most successful sponge divers in all of Tarpon Springs," Petro continued, his voice loud and bombastic, as if he intended for all of Manhattan to hear. "We should be going," he said as he picked up her suitcase. "There is a train leaving Pennsylvania Station at 6:00 p.m. We can't miss it. I do very well, but it was rather expensive waiting for you here these extra days."

Voula made no attempt to move. She just stood there, statue still.

Finally, she turned toward Maria, her cheeks tearstained. Voula hugged her old friend as if she might never let go.

"I want to go home," Voula whispered into Maria's ear.

Maria tucked a stray tendril of hair behind Voula's ear.

"It will be all right," she said, trying to convince Voula as much as herself. "Be brave. Be strong and I pray God will bring us together again. Maybe one day we will bring our children home to Karditsa. Maybe they will splash and play in the fresh spring the way we did as children."

Voula was only fifteen, still a child, the same age as Paraskevi. It sent a chill down Maria's spine to imagine her sister handed off to a man like this, a stranger, in exchange for a few hundred drachmas.

"Come, Voula. It's time to go." Petro summoned Voula, waving for her to follow him. He was neither warm nor unkind, simply matter of fact, as if picking up his bride was another chore, another item ordered and delivered.

Voula's lips trembled as she stood there, rooted in place.

"It will be all right," Maria said again.

"I want to go home." Voula's lips trembled.

Maria stepped forward to face Voula and placed her palms on Voula's cheeks, which were hot and wet to the touch.

"This is our home now. We must make the best of it."

"We can't miss this train," Petro said again, a slight edge in his tone. "We have to go." He reached for her elbow to guide her through the crowd, and she reluctantly walked away from Maria and toward her new life in Florida.

Maria watched them go, feeling as if a piece of her was boarding the train to Florida along with Voula. There was nothing left of home now. Only her memories and a photo of Mama she'd found in a drawer and tucked away in her suitcase. She linked her arm with Anna's and offered her a smile.

The crowd had thinned considerably. Only about twenty women remained on the dock, craning their necks in search of the men who would match their photos.

Nicole and the ribboned ladies from the Traveler's Aid Society weaved in and out among them, checking photographs against faces and offering recommendations to any bride and groom who needed help with transportation or lodging.

"Get away from here, you scoundrels! We don't need your kind here." Nicole swatted her papers at a group of men who stood smoking cigarettes and watching the women. They had inched closer, predators stalking their prey.

"I said get out of here! I'll call the police and have you hauled away." Nicole stood with her hands on her hips, as if forming a barrier between her charges and the unsavory characters.

"Excuse me." Maria heard him before she saw him. "Are you Maria?" a man asked as he held out a photo toward her face.

"Yes, I am Maria." She released Anna's arm and stepped forward.

"I am Pericles. I am to be your husband." The man spoke with an awkward formality.

"Hello, Pericles." As she struggled with what to say next, Nicole appeared beside her.

"May I see your identification papers, please?" Nicole was direct, matter of fact as she scanned his documents. "Very well. What are your plans from here? Will you be getting married here in New York?"

"Yes. I spoke to the priest at Saint Nicholas on Cedar Street and he is expecting us. He will marry us today."

Maria felt unsteady on her feet. For weeks she had been preparing herself for the idea of marriage to a man she did not know, and her wedding day was suddenly upon her, scheduled for that very afternoon.

"Very well." Nicole was satisfied with his response. "Good luck to you. May your marriage be blessed."

"Thank you." Pericles nodded toward Nicole. "Maria, Father is expecting us. We can't be late." He motioned for her to come.

"Excuse me, sir," Anna said, taking a step closer to Pericles. "My intended is also from Milwaukee. His name is Anastasios. Perhaps you know him?"

"No. I don't." He looked Anna up and down before turning his attention to Maria once again. "Come on. We need to be on the next bus. We can't keep the priest waiting."

Anna's face crumpled.

"I'm sure he'll be here soon. Don't worry. Everything will be all right." Maria did her best to reassure her, knowing there was no validity to her words. She, like Anna, was powerless to understand what was happening around them and powerless to do anything about it.

"We'll find each other in Milwaukee. I'm sure of it." Maria hugged Anna, who was trembling.

"I don't know what's worse—if he comes, or if he doesn't." Anna's voice was a whisper as she squeezed Maria one last time.

"Maria, we need to go or we'll miss the bus." There was no mistaking the agitation in his voice. Maria said goodbye before falling in step beside the man she had just met, the man who before sunset would be her husband.

The dock was nearly empty with only a dozen or so of the brides left. They stood clustered together, confusion and fear etched on their faces as Maria glanced back one final time.

Nicole and the other Traveler's Aid volunteers stood near them, making note of the late hour. Before she was out of earshot,

Maria heard Nicole say, "Ladies, I am so sorry, but it appears as if your grooms have not come today. Unfortunately, this is not the first time this has happened. With the new immigration laws in place, I'm afraid you will not be allowed entry to the United States without the support of your intended husbands."

A collective gasp rose from the women.

"But what does that mean?" someone asked.

"It means we will escort you to temporary housing as you await passage on a ship that will return you to Greece."

Sorrow filled Maria's heart for the women, but there was nothing she could do for them. She followed Pericles through the crowded sidewalks and whispered a prayer for them and her own unknown future.

Chapter Fourteen

Corfu, Greece

1952

DEMITRA HELD THE phone to her ear and leaned against the periptero wall as Stella chattered away during their weekly phone call the following Sunday. Soula, who had complained incessantly about the heat all morning, fanned herself furiously as she took respite under the shade of a nearby lemon tree.

"Olga came to visit, and she brought biscuits, the ones you like. Oh, they are so delicious. I couldn't stop eating them." Stella prattled on without taking a breath.

"Maybe we should send Irene to the monastery," Martha said in the background. "No doubt that woman could learn a thing or two from the nuns. Maybe another miracle will occur. Maybe the snakes will turn her tasteless cardboard into something edible."

"Mama, please," Stella chided. "Anyway, Gerasimos is growing so fast. Oh, you should see the way he runs around, playing football and hide-and-seek with his friends and learning his letters, so pleased with himself. Oh, Demitra, it's the cutest thing. I wish you were here to see it."

"Me too. I miss him so much, and all of you, of course."

"We miss you too, but we hope you're enjoying your time in Kerkyra."

"How's Baba?"

"Oh, he's the same. He doesn't say much as you know, but if he's not talking, he's not complaining, so that's a good sign. Hold on, Mama wants to say hello."

"Well, I knew it was only a matter of time." Martha began speaking before she brought the telephone to her mouth. "That woman has no shame. None, I tell you."

"What is it?" Demitra asked.

"You know it's to save face. There is nothing but trouble in that house. I mean, it's not the poor boy's fault he was born like that or maybe his mother dropped him when he was a baby, but to pretend everything is fine . . ." Martha clucked her tongue in disgust.

"What are you talking about? What happened?" Demitra asked again.

"Niko is engaged. They just announced his betrothal to a girl from Simi. The nerve of that family! That poor girl doesn't know what she is getting herself into. I heard her family doesn't even have a dowry, but Nektarios is so desperate to put on a show for the Italians that he approached the father, and they made the arrangement."

"Well, I feel sorry for both of them. I'm just glad it's not me. Has anyone seen or heard from Elena?"

"No. She keeps to herself. We never see her in town. Whatever business she got into with Nektarios was swept under the rug and kept quiet. How are things in Kerkyra?"

"They're great. Soula and I are making boureki today."

Soula preened at the mention of her name, emerging from her shady spot under the tree and grabbing the phone from Demitra's hand. "Yes, sister. I'm teaching her everything I know. When I'm done with her, she won't need a dowry. Men will be begging for her hand because of my delicious boureki recipe." She snapped the fan open again and handed the phone back to Demitra before retreating to the shade.

"Ah, don't let her tell you it's her recipe," Martha scolded. "I'm the one who taught her to make boureki, so it's only fitting we give the credit where it belongs. You tell her I said so, Demitra. You tell her you know whose recipe she's using, even if she tries to tell you otherwise."

Demitra did her best to stifle her laugh. She was grateful for the life lessons and laughter the sisters provided.

The women soon said their goodbyes, and Demitra and Soula made the short walk home.

"Enjoy your afternoon, dear," Soula called out as she closed her bedroom door. She yawned loudly as she lowered herself onto the creaky bed for her Sunday siesta.

In her own room Demitra slipped out of the plain brown dress she'd worn for church and opted for the prettiest thing in her limited wardrobe, a pale blue dress with a boat collar that showed off her neckline. Stella once told her the color complemented her olive skin. She took a few extra moments to brush her hair, doing her best to tame her curls as she tucked her hair behind her ears. From the bottom of her suitcase, she fetched the lipstick Elena had given her so long ago and dabbed her finger on it and then on her lips and cheeks, just enough to add a hint of color.

She had no reason to expect Aleko would be there, but as the days passed and Sunday grew nearer, she found herself anxious with the thought that they might cross paths again.

She gave herself one last look in the mirror, then tucked her sketch pad under her arm and wrapped her fingers around the pencils in her dress pocket. It was a gloriously sunny late-summer day and the streets were alive with tourists who had left the resort to explore the town. It seemed everywhere she looked, Demitra spotted young lovers arm in arm, strolling along the beachfront promenade, splashing into the sea, or spilling out of the tavernas, red-cheeked from ouzo and beer.

With each step toward the restaurant, Demitra felt her stomach tighten. She reined in her mind to focus on the task at hand. Today she would make progress on the drawing for Soula, but she felt dizzy with excitement that Aleko might come by again as he had last Sunday. Demitra exhaled as she approached the restaurant entrance to find the patio deserted, save for the kittens, who were chasing one another below the tables.

"I'm being ridiculous," she said aloud to herself. He had given her no indication of anything other than polite conversation and gentility, yet Demitra found her mind wandering and lingering over the small details of their encounters. The way his eyes glinted in the sun, the way he'd said they all have secrets as he leaned in toward her, the sound of his bold laugh. She was drawn to his eyes, excited by the mischief in them, and curious when she'd noticed its absence.

"Ridiculous," Demitra said as she walked to the top of the patio, determined to expel him from her mind. She would concentrate on her drawing for Soula. Demitra was frustrated with herself. She was no longer a child and no longer had the luxury of crafting fairy tales in her mind.

She sat on the patio steps, which afforded her the best view of the entrance without the indignity of trying to drag a table across the street again. Demitra opened her pad and balanced it on her lap. Putting pencil to paper, she began with light feathery strokes but soon found herself distracted. Annoyed with herself, she pushed aside the pad and glanced across the street.

Aleko stood there smoking a cigarette, a big grin on his face as he watched her. Beside him was a chair and an artist's easel set up in perfect position.

She stood, grabbing her pad and pencils, and was halfway to him before she realized what she was doing. And then she was beside him, feeling unsteady on her feet and yet somehow at peace.

"An artist needs an easel," he said as he motioned toward it.

She traced her finger along the wood. It was smooth and pale, a broad, clean surface to work on as she stood facing her subject instead of sitting hunched over in the way that always left her neck and back aching.

"I . . . I don't know what to say," she said. "That's very kind of you. I'll repay you for certain."

"Absolutely not," he said. "Consider it a gift."

"But why?"

He smiled at her then in a way he had not before. "I know what it is to have a passion in your heart but to be told repeatedly to tamp it down. I know what it is to want to soar when others are holding you down. I see this in you."

How was that possible? He didn't know her at all, and yet he saw her with more clarity than anyone ever had before.

"I'd like to think you are right. But you and I both know it's easier from where you stand. It's easy for a man, especially a man of wealth, to tell me to be free. If you haven't noticed, we're not like the French. I can't walk around in skirts and coconuts doing as I wish."

The mischief in his smile made her blush. "You're an artist. So be an artist."

She ruminated on his words. She wanted to believe it was possible, to trust that having faith in herself was enough. But allowing herself the luxury of dreams such as this came with a heavy cost in reality.

"How can I repay you?" was all she could think of to say.

"It's a gift. And it's my pleasure. But you can save me some of Soula's pastitsada. I'll be by tonight."

"I will." Her heart raced at the knowledge that she would see him again.

"The easel folds up and you can keep it hidden, so no one needs to know your secret unless you want them to."

With that he walked over to his car, climbed in, and sped away down the street.

Demitra clamped her pad to the easel and picked up her pencil, uncertain if she would be able to focus. When she put her pencil on the paper, her hand moved with ease, the pencil flowing effortlessly across the page.

NEARLY EVERY TABLE was taken that night by nine. Tino's friend Antoni continued to recommend Soula's authentic Corfiot cuisine to the patrons of Club Mediterranee, and in turn, every night a table in the darkest corner of the restaurant was reserved for Antoni and his latest French companion. Each night was the same. Soula would leave the kitchen to greet him with a warm hug and words of thanks while muttering under her breath about *Galikes poutanes*, French whores. The women simply smiled up at her, their eyes glazed over with wine.

Demitra was clearing tables when she heard Tino's boisterous greeting.

"There you are, Aleko. I was hoping you'd join us, friend."

Once again she felt a tickle in her belly at the sound of his name. She glanced over in his direction and found herself smiling. Aleko looked her way, a broad smile lighting up his face as he spotted her.

Within moments Demitra was at his table with a plate of pastitsada. She placed it before him.

"You remembered." He smiled. "Join me. A shame to eat alone." He motioned to the empty seat beside him.

"I'm sure you'll be fine," she said even as she wondered what it would be like to have the freedom to linger over dinner with him.

"So this is Soula's famous pastitsada," he said as he picked up his fork and dug in. She watched as he took a bite and closed his eyes, savoring the flavors.

"Now this is pastitsada. It reminds me of the way my grandmother and mother made it."

"Soula's very proud of her recipe. She said her great-grandmother learned it working with the finest families in Corfu."

"And this is something Soula speaks of with pride?" he asked, his eyebrows raised.

"Yes, very much so."

"I see," he said before taking another bite. "Our revisionist history strikes again."

"What do you mean?" she asked.

"I mean we tend to whitewash our history sometimes, to make it pretty when the reality was anything but."

"I don't understand." She shifted from one foot to the other.

"There was no employment in the homes of nobility, Demitra. The Venetians brought so much rich culture to Corfu—architecture, music, art, and, yes, pastitsada," he said with a wave of his fork. "But they also brought the feudal system, and if Soula's great-grandmother worked in one of those homes, then she was not merely a chef . . ."

"Well, what was she then?"

"She was a piece of property."

Demitra shook her head, unsure if she'd heard him correctly. "What are you saying?"

"Yes, Demitra. A feudal servant. Property, like my own family. Polite society tends to forget our difficult history. It's easier to gloss over the reality sometimes than to remember what came before."

She opened her mouth to ask more, but before she could summon the words, Tino was upon them.

"How is everything, friend?" Tino asked as he walked up to the table and placed a fresh bottle of beer before Aleko.

"It's excellent," he replied, taking a long, deep drink and stealing another glance at Demitra. "Just excellent."

Chapter Fifteen

Corfu, Greece

1952

AND SO BEGAN Demitra's new Sunday routine. After attending church with Soula and calling home for Martha and Stella to fill her in on the news and gossip of the village, Demitra would grab her sketch pad and head to the beach where Aleko would be waiting for her. Each week he lingered a bit longer, marveling at the progress of her work and offering words of encouragement.

One day, about a month after their first meeting, she held up her drawing to him.

He took the pad in his hands and studied the sketch. It was a beautifully rendered drawing of the restaurant capturing the warmth and welcoming atmosphere Soula so carefully cultivated. At the entrance of the patio, Demitra had sketched the mama cat nursing her kittens. Beyond the tables, a lamb cooked on the spit over coals, and just beyond the patio, in the far distance of the kitchen, was the image of Soula standing guard over a large pot simmering on the stove.

"It's beautiful," Aleko said. "You really captured the spirit of the restaurant."

"Thank you." She blushed.

"It's finished then?"

"Yes."

"Good," he replied as he folded up the easel, then walked to his car, which was parked a few meters down the street. He opened the door and tossed the easel into the back seat before turning back toward her. "How about we go for a ride?" he asked, opening the passenger door.

She paused for a moment, surprised by his request. Instinctively she glanced around, knowing it would be scandalous to be spotted getting in the car with this man to whom she had no familial relation and whom she barely knew. A scan of the beach confirmed that only a handful of French tourists were about.

She started walking toward him.

"Where are we going?" Excitement and fear simultaneously coursed through her chest. She felt as if she was floating on air and also as if she might be sick.

As she approached he leaned in close and whispered, "Every artist needs inspiration."

Demitra slid into the seat and he closed the door behind her. She placed her hand on the door, thinking in a panic that she should not be there, that she should not leave with this man and that she should flee at once. But something kept her rooted as he slid in beside her. She glanced at him and he smiled back. Instantly she felt the tension leave her body, uncoiling like a spring.

"I really shouldn't be here. I should not be doing this," she said, allowing her head to fall back on the leather of the headrest.

"Should I let you out then?" he asked, reaching across her as if to open the door.

"No." She shook her head, her eyes staring at the road before them. "You should drive."

Aleko grinned and sped off down the street. Demitra had never felt more free in her life. She rolled the window down as far as it would go, closed her eyes, and lifted her face into the breeze. There was so much she wanted to say and ask, and yet there was perfection in the silence of the moment.

He drove south along the coast, past the port where Demitra had arrived with such anxiety just months before. As they drove along Garitsa Bay, she gazed out at the imposing old fortress and the expansive Spianada Square. All along the square and streets, café tables were filled with people enjoying their Sunday afternoon.

"It's beautiful here," she said as they drove past an open field where young men played cricket and families picnicked on the grass, cheering them on. The streets were alive with people strolling along the arched porticos of the Liston. Back in Ipsos, the sleepy village seemed to shut down in the afternoon hours, allowing the villagers to rest. But here in the city center, every avenue, lane, and alleyway buzzed with friends and families savoring the energy and light of the historic, magical place.

They drove south past the square and continued along the coast for about twenty minutes before turning off at the village of Gastouri. The car snaked up a steep and twisty mountain road, so narrow in certain areas that only one car at a time was allowed to pass. The view to the valley below was expansive and spectacular.

"We're here," Aleko said as he parked beside a small taverna where a slim elderly woman, dressed from head to toe in black, swept the steps with a broom made from twigs bound together with twine. She smiled a toothless grin as they exited the car.

"Yiasas." Aleko tipped his hat to the woman before turning his attention back to Demitra. "There's something you need to see." He led her across the street, following a tall wall. He stopped when he reached a large metal gate and pulled a key out of his pocket, then turned it in the lock. He looked back over his shoulder and smiled at Demitra before pushing open the gate. "Come on."

"Oh my goodness!" She gasped as if the gate gave her entrée to a world she never could have imagined. The stone path beneath her feet was wide and pale and lined with stately palm trees that swayed in the afternoon breeze. The path sloped upward toward a center garden planted with tall cypress trees that stretched to the pale blue sky.

Beyond the path stood the most magnificent building she had ever laid eyes on. Massive columns lined the entrance on the ground floor just beyond the oval garden. Multiple levels rose above, each patio lined with stone and marble railings, each railing showcasing various sculptures—a book of myths come to life. Everywhere she looked, satyrs and goddesses and nymphs danced, laughed, and watched over them.

The magnificence of the structure was not dulled by the decay and neglect evident in the grayed patina, peeling paint, and cracks visible on every surface. But just as when she laid eyes on the weathered vista of Corfu as she arrived into port for the first time, Demitra saw only the beauty of this place.

"It's stunning."

"Yes," Aleko said. "It is."

"Aleko!" A man waved from a worktable near the building's entrance.

"I'll be just a minute," he said to Demitra as he waved to the man. "Enjoy the grounds and I'll come find you."

She walked ahead, entranced by the beauty all around her. Farther up the path she came upon a staircase adorned with sculptures of the gods and goddesses she had dreamed about so many times.

When she reached the top of the stairs, Demitra found herself in a vast garden. Lush and elegant yet chaotic and overgrown. It was a verdant oasis, dotted all around with sculptures of stark white marble and rich bronze. She walked slowly toward them. There at the edge of the building was a patio paved in salmon-and-white tile, boasting more statues of women lined up one after the other, each adorned in cloaks, hair gathered in floral and laurel wreaths, yet each was unique. She counted nine in total.

"The muses," she whispered aloud. Each statue was imperfect in some way, damaged and decaying, but that only made them more exquisite for all they had weathered and endured.

She paused by the first woman and reached her finger out to touch her. The woman's arms were crossed beneath her cloak, her face turned away as if she were in pain. Demitra touched the smooth white marble perfection of her cheek and then traced along the sculpture to the rippled folds of her cloak, blackened with mold and rough to the touch.

"Melpomene," Aleko said as he appeared beside her. She had been so enraptured by the gardens and sculptures that she hadn't heard him approach. "The muse of tragedy."

"Of course," she said, turning back to the statue, tilting her head as she regarded her.

He inched closer to her as she spoke.

"This place . . ." Her voice drifted off as she scanned the gardens all around them. Trees in full bloom shading sculptures of gods and goddesses and the mortals who lived and died by their whims. "It's so beautiful. The most beautiful place I've ever seen, that I could ever imagine. But there's something else here." She sensed a heaviness amid the beauty. She felt it all around her, permeating the air and soil. "Everything is so lovely, but it seems to be weeping at the same time. How is that?"

"You can feel it too?"

She nodded.

He reached his hand out, delicately placing it on her elbow and guiding her along. "Come."

She did not recoil. The touch was light, and yet something shifted in that moment. It was as if the world opened up to her, a world of possibility.

He led her to a statue at the end of the patio. It was a reclining figure, larger than life, naked, with its arm outstretched toward its leg. A long thin object was held in its hand. He led her around the sculpture to the front of the figure. It was a man, his well-defined muscles conveying his strength, yet the anguished expression on his face revealed vulnerability and pain. He wore a plumed helmet, his face turned up toward the sky.

"Achilles," she said, glancing at the arrow protruding from his ankle.

"Yes." Aleko smiled. "Achilles."

"The moment of his death. When the divine could not save the mortal." She remembered all the nights as a young girl when she imagined she, too, was the child of a divine being and a mortal, hidden away and trapped in a place between this world and the next, praying she, too, might somehow be saved.

"You're right," he said as his fingers lingered over the statue. "There is a sadness here. This palace is the Achilleion, built by Empress Sisi of Austria and dedicated to Achilles. Sisi came here searching for peace after the death of her only son."

"A mourning mother's monument to another lost son."

"Exactly." Aleko reached out to her once more, taking her elbow in his hand. The shift would have been imperceptible to an observer, but she felt the difference, sensing his fingers through the fabric of her dress like electricity on her skin.

They continued walking toward the end of the garden, to a vast terrace overlooking the island below. And there, standing sentinel above it all, was a colossal bronze statue. A warrior. Massive, imposing, rising toward the sky, holding his spear in one hand

and his shield in the other. His stance stoic and strong, a steely expression on his face, his helmet planted firmly on his head, tall and bringing him closer to the heavens.

"Achilles." She turned to Aleko. "The warrior. The hero." She placed her hand over her eyes to shield them from the afternoon sun as she looked up toward the statue's face. "The demigod."

"Yes. This was commissioned by Kaiser Wilhelm of Germany, who lived here after the empress."

"While the mother mourned the human, the emperor glorified the god, the warrior," she said as she regarded the statue, taking in every detail of the massive figure.

"Yes. Exactly." He walked a bit farther to the garden's edge where the large terrace overlooked the island, across the valleys and hills of Corfu, across the water to the mainland beyond. He grabbed the rail and leaned into the view. Demitra stepped closer, feeling the enormity spanning the green valleys and mountains of Corfu to the Ionian shimmering in the distance.

"Thank you," she said as she continued taking in the view. "I've never seen anything like this. I've never experienced anything like this."

He turned to look at her as she kept her gaze fixed on the horizon. "I knew you would love this place. That it would speak to you."

She took a few more moments to soak in the magnificence of the Achilleion, turning again to the soaring statue of Achilles behind her, silhouetted against the sun. Here, high above the villages below, standing in the shadow of the demigod, she felt as if her childhood dreams had at last come true and she had been summoned to Olympus where the gods looked down upon the earth below.

"How are we allowed in here? Do you work here?" she asked.

"I'm hopeful that one day I will have the honor of working here. We are petitioning the government to allow us to develop the Achilleion as a casino."

Her face lit up at the thought. "A casino?"

"Yes. I'm working with a group of investors to help modernize Corfu and turn the island into an international tourist destination. Look at what we managed to do with Club Mediterranee. We've turned the economic disaster of Ipsos and Dassia around in less than a year. Those villages were on the brink of dying, of becoming yet another ghost town on this island, like Peritheia. The entire village is gone. It survived for centuries at the top of a mountain, separated from the rest of the island, enduring the harshest conditions for generations.

"But now in this modern age when we have roads and electricity, and doctors and police are a phone call away—now there's no one left. The promise of an easier and better way of life seduced the villagers of Peritheia and brought them down the mountain one by one. We can't afford another Peritheia. By bringing tourism to the island, we're not only making Corfu an international destination but helping save so many small businesses like Soula's and keep those families from leaving."

"You left," she said, narrowing her eyes as she regarded him.

"Yes. I left to study, to learn the tools I needed and to build the relationships I needed, but I always knew I would come back. This is my home. My family's home. So many people leave to find new opportunities, but I didn't want that. I wanted to create new opportunities here."

"My father left." She trailed her fingers along the railing. "He went to America. And he came back, but not like you." Both Baba and Aleko left their homes and returned; one found meaning and one lost himself along the way.

"What happened? Why did he come back?"

"My mother died. He came home to Cephalonia and raised me there."

"What is he like, your father?"

"Broken." She breathed in the crisp afternoon air and closed her eyes, picturing Baba, a shell of a man, devoid of emotion, clutching a drink in his hand. "Haunted."

"We're all haunted, Demitra. All of us. Show me someone who isn't damaged or haunted in some way. The only difference is what we do with that pain. Do we drown in it, allowing it to pull us down further until we disappear into it? Or do we use that pain, that brokenness, to inspire us?"

She looked at him and nodded, understanding his words were meant for her as much as her father, perhaps even more.

"What about your mother?" he asked. "What was she like?"

She could feel his gaze on her, but she could not bring herself to look at him in this moment.

"I was young when she died. I have vague memories of her, or what I think I remember of her. But I'm not sure, really." She clasped the railing and pitched forward, tempting fate in a way that both exhilarated her and scared her. Demitra had never been the reckless sort, and yet standing there in the shadow of the kaiser's tribute to the demigod, she leaned out as far as she dared, occupying the space between land and air, recalling a time when she'd imagined herself at the crossroads of mortal and immortal, like Achilles.

The image of Empress Sisi's Achilles flashed in her mind, and she leaned back again. "I've felt her presence, though, like she's with me in some way, watching over me. Like a ghost."

"Don't shy away from what haunts you. Embrace it. Just look around you, look at the magnificence of this place, look at what can happen when you face your pain, the very thing that broke your heart, instead of pretending it never existed."

"That's easy for you to say. You're a man. You know it's different for you. You get to decide your future."

"You'd be surprised. It's not always that way. Sometimes we all have to fight for what we want or need." He opened his mouth again as if to share more but then looked down at his watch. "We should go. It's time to get you back."

She nodded, wishing she could linger in this place, with him, longer.

They walked back through the garden and when she reached the muses' patio again, she paused in front of a statute she had not taken time to study earlier. Her white marble cheek was stained, and she wore a far-off expression as she held a lyre against the folds of her cloak.

"Erato," Aleko said, inching closer. She could feel his breath against her neck. "The muse of erotic poetry." He smiled at her and then turned back toward the sculpture.

Demitra felt her face turn crimson and prayed he would not notice.

"How do you know all of this? Did you study mythology or classics?"

"No, I didn't study either, Demitra. I studied how to break the cycle of poverty." He paused, his eyes unblinking and fixed on hers. "And that taught me to ask questions, to learn from the people who have studied, who know more than I ever will, and to do anything in my power to win, to get what I want." He took a step closer to her as he spoke. "Now it's your turn. What do you want?"

She felt a flutter in her stomach.

Her response was visceral. "I want to be an artist."

He smiled at her answer. "Look around you. Look at what moves you, what speaks to you and makes you feel. You chose to come to Corfu. You chose to get in my car and come on an adventure with me today. It's obvious you don't want to be passive in your life. Why are you passive in your art? Why are you spending your time drawing kittens and cafés when you are capable of so much more? Art should invoke passion, make you feel something. Where is the feeling, the passion, the storytelling in your drawing?"

As she gazed up at him, her eyes misted over.

"I'm so sorry. I didn't mean to upset you." He placed his hand on her arm.

"No," she said, shaking her head. "It's all right. You didn't upset me. Not at all." She closed her eyes and saw an image so clearly in her mind, the passion and pride she felt when she peered through the window to see her portrait tacked to Elena's wall. "You reminded me what art is capable of. What I'm capable of."

He placed his hand on the small of her back, guiding her ever so gently across the patio. A flash of electricity jolted through her, making her feel as if every inch of her vibrated with energy and with heat. She wondered if he could feel the shock through the fabric of her dress.

"Good. I'm glad." He gazed down on her, his smile broad and beautiful. "Come, let's get you home before Soula notices I've stolen you away."

"All right," she said, even though she wanted nothing more than to stay with him in this beautiful palace built from the tears of an empress.

Chapter Sixteen

Corfu, Greece

1952

WHEN SUNDAY MORNING at last came again, time seemed to slow. Soula's arthritic knees forced them to walk at a snail's pace. The priest added ten pages of chants and prayers to the liturgy. Martha decided to recount the comings and goings of not only everyone in the village but everyone on all of Cephalonia as well.

At last, after what felt like an eternity, Demitra escorted Soula home.

"Enjoy your rest," Demitra said, doing her best not to appear rushed as she closed the door to Soula's bedroom and raced to her room where she changed into her blue dress, then dabbed her cheeks and lips with the remnants of Elena's lipstick.

She grabbed her bag and raced toward the door, praying he might be waiting for her again, although they had never formally made a plan to meet. Demitra glanced at herself one last time in the mirror and turned the doorknob.

When the door swung open, she stumbled back. Sophia was strolling up the path.

"There you are." Sophia smiled as she walked up the stairs and onto the porch.

Demitra forced a smile as she felt the world close in around her.

"I thought you went to visit Tino's parents. Aren't you going?" Demitra asked, putting every effort into not sounding too eager or too disappointed.

"I sent Tino and Kiki along. I was feeling a little lightheaded earlier, so I slept in and then thought I'd come by to have some tea with you while Mama naps. It's too early to tell for sure, but I think . . ." She smiled, placing her hands on her belly.

"Oh, Sophia." Demitra threw her arms around Sophia, beaming as she hugged her tight. "That's wonderful news. How are you feeling? Can I get you anything?" Excitement and disappointment simultaneously washed over her. There would be no meeting Aleko today, no stolen moments or rendezvous. "I'll fix us some tea." Demitra forced a smile as Sophia took a seat on the porch.

"Hey," Sophia said, grabbing Demitra's arm as she passed. "What's going on?" Her eyes narrowed as she scanned Demitra from head to toe.

"What do you mean?"

"I mean, look at you. You're wearing your good dress, and if I'm not mistaken, that's rouge on your cheeks." She tilted her head as she narrowed her eyes. "And lips." A knowing smile filled her face.

Demitra said nothing, feeling her cheeks grow a deeper shade of red.

"Come on, now." Sophia stood, pulling herself up by the chair railing. "You know you can tell me. What's his name? And how on earth did you manage to find a boyfriend in this town?"

Demitra waved her away with a swat of her hand as she averted her eyes.

"Tell me already. Your secret's safe with me. I won't tell Soula." She glanced around to make sure they were alone. "I won't tell a soul."

"It's nothing." Demitra did her best to appear earnest. "We've just spoken a handful of times."

"For the love of God, woman. I can't take the suspense any longer. Who is it?"

Demitra looked out toward the water, unable to face Sophia's stare as she spoke his name.

"It's Aleko. Tino's friend Aleko."

"Ohh." Sophia slid back down into her chair. "I see now. Very nice. He's quite a catch, that one. Educated and handsome."

Demitra said nothing.

"And rich." Sophia pursed her lips and rubbed her fingers together. "Honestly, he sounds like a better match for you than that baker your father tried tethering you to."

"Anything is better than that." Demitra laughed, allowing her body to relax and leaning closer to whisper, "I don't want Soula or anyone to know. There's nothing to tell them, really. He's just being kind to me."

"There is no such thing as a man just being kind to a pretty, young, *single* woman. He's not stupid, Demitra. He's obviously interested in you, and you would be insane if you were not interested in him." Sophia stood again. "Come here." She summoned Demitra with her finger. "Turn around."

Demitra did as she was told, turning her back to Sophia. Instantly she felt Sophia's fingers in her hair, lifting half off her face, then taking the clip from her own hair and fastening it to Demitra's.

"There." Sophia spun Demitra around. "Much better. You have a beautiful face. Let's show it off, shall we? Go meet your new friend." She winked. "Your secret's safe with me. Only don't forget your cousin when you're a rich lady with a grand house in Corfu Town."

All her life when the subject of marriage came up, Demitra's visceral response had always been the same—disinterest and aversion. But now, as she listened to Sophia prattle on, her reaction was very different. Instead of pushing back at the thought, she allowed her mind to wander, wondering what it would be like to wake up each day in his arms.

"You won't tell?"

"Of course not." She took Demitra's hand in her own, lifting it up to her mouth and kissing it. "I know we are not bonded by blood, but you're our family, Demitra. I'll be forever grateful for the warmth and love you show Kiki and for how happy you've made all of us. I would love for you to stay with us forever, but I want you to be happy, to have your own life. So go." She shooed Demitra away with her hand. "Go meet your friend."

Sophia stared off for a moment, tapping her finger against the chair in careful contemplation. "I'll tell Mama I sent you on an errand, to buy you a bit more time. Just come back by seven to help with the dinner service. I'm so tired lately, no matter how much sleep I get. I really do think I'm pregnant, but I don't want to tell my mother yet. She'll drive me crazy." She groaned as she placed her legs on a stool. "We'll keep each other's secrets."

"Are you sure?" Demitra asked.

"Of course I'm sure, silly. Now go off and have an adventure with your boyfriend. Only, please be careful." She raised her eyebrows and pointed to her belly. "I'm sure you know what I mean."

Demitra's eyes and mouth flew wide.

"Oh, don't play the shocked maiden." Sophia laughed. "But seriously . . . ," she cautioned, raising an eyebrow.

As eager as she was to leave, Demitra hugged Sophia one more time.

"Thank you. Truly, thank you," she said again before turning and walking briskly toward the beach.

❀

THERE WAS NO plan. There was no meeting set in place. There was no guarantee he would be there, yet Demitra's pace quickened as she approached the beach and the spot where he had come to meet her each Sunday for the past month. As she turned the corner and the beach came into view, her heart sank.

How could I be so stupid? she chided herself. *How could I be so bold and dumb?*

She found herself walking up and down the beach several times, watching as the local men entertained their latest conquests. *Kamakia*, Tino had called them with a laugh, saying that picking up drunken, love-starved tourists was like harpooning fish in a barrel for the Greeks.

She sat on a bench facing the sea, losing herself in her thoughts as the tide swelled and crested and then broke on the shore.

Like the current, her emotions roiled and churned and crashed with the realization that she had been wrong. He was not coming.

She resigned herself to walking home, dreaded the thought of confessing to Sophia how wrong she had been, how stupid. She rounded the corner past the taverna and glanced up to see where Soula had tacked her drawing to the olive tree at the entrance. As she continued along the road home, she heard the hum of a car engine and then looked up to see his car pulling up beside her.

"Where are you off to?" Aleko asked, a broad smile on his face. His window was rolled down as he leaned out toward her.

She inhaled sharply, trying her best to appear calm and to regulate her stuttered breathing.

"Hi," she managed to say.

"I planned on getting here earlier but got a bit tied up in town. I was hoping you might still be here and hadn't given up on me."

She was silent, her smile speaking for her.

He got out of the car and walked around to the passenger side door and opened it. "Get in."

They drove north this time, farther up the coast along Corfu's wild and rugged shoreline to the seaside village of Kassiopi, tucked along the horseshoe-shaped harbor in the shadow of the ruins of a medieval castle. They walked the narrow lanes and cobblestone paths toward the sea, reaching the gated entrance to the Church of Panagia Kassopitra.

The church was small with rows of carved wooden chairs on each side of the aisle. The altar was adorned with icons depicting the saints and the Virgin Mary. Aleko reached in his pocket and placed a twenty-pound drachma note in the tray beside the candles. She took a brown tapered candle from the pile and leaned into the trough, lighting the wick with the flame of a burning candle in the sand. She then placed her own candle in the sand and walked over to the icon of Panagia, making the sign of the cross and bending over to kiss the icon.

"What a lovely church," she said as she turned and smiled at him.

She looked around one last time, inhaling deeply as the musty scent of incense and candles soothed her. There was a serenity in the air invoking the warmest reminiscences of a childhood spent praying beside Olga, asking Panagia for a miracle, that Baba might open his heart as well as his vault of memories and share Mama with her.

In this dimly lit church, hundreds of miles away from the house she was raised in, standing beside a man she barely knew, Demitra felt a peace wash over her. She allowed the feeling to settle in, realizing it was more than just the physicality of this place, the candles, the icons, the familiar aromas. She glanced up at Aleko, who caught her eye and winked at her, his lips curling up in a smile.

That was the moment she realized what this feeling was. It was him.

They left the church and turned toward the port, walking along the narrow lanes as women in white kerchiefs shepherded children home for supper and the men seated at the kafeneio smoked cigarettes and sipped ouzo while discussing politics. At last they stopped at a seaside taverna at the edge of the harbor. Aleko pulled her chair out for her, and Demitra glanced over her shoulder, smiling up at him as she took her seat. Above them, tucked away among the olive, pine, and cypress trees covering the cliffs, the neglected ruins of the ancient castle of Kassiopi, so long ago magnificent and imposing, continued to stand watch over the harbor.

"This village . . . ," she said as her eyes wandered across the castle ruins to the hills above and then to the crescent-shaped port where weathered fishing boats bobbed in the water. "It's magical."

"It is," he agreed, leaning back in his chair as he silently regarded her. The intensity of his gaze at once excited and intimidated her.

"We have a church on Cephalonia that reminds me of this one. It's dedicated to Panagia, and once a year a miracle occurs." She blurted this out to break the silence.

"The snakes," he said, his posture relaxed, yet the intensity of his gaze unchanged.

"Yes. The snakes." She nodded eagerly. "My thea Olga is a nun in the monastery. I was there with her in 1940, the summer the snakes didn't come. She knew it was an omen. I only wish others had paid more attention."

"And what good would that have done, Demitra?" Aleko's tone was not harsh, yet it was clear that he disagreed with her assessment. "No one was prepared for the brutality of the war. No one imagined how monstrous Hitler and his Nazis could be. Even if people had paid attention to the warning, to the omen of the snakes, even then I don't think they could have imagined what was to come. Here on Corfu, the entire Jewish community was exterminated. Eighteen hundred of two thousand, gone. The few who made it out of the camps alive, the ones who by some miracle returned to Corfu—no one believed them when they spoke of the horrors they endured. The proof was standing before them like walking corpses, and still no one believed them."

"They took the entire Jewish community, four hundred people, from Cephalonia too," Demitra said as the waiter placed wine and an assortment of appetizers on the table.

"And the Italians . . ." Demitra's voice trailed off at the memory. "The Germans murdered thousands of them." She brought her glass to her lips, closed her eyes, and took a deep sip of wine before revealing what she had never spoken of out loud.

"I saw them that day." She opened her eyes to find a softness in his. It was the encouragement she needed to continue with her story. "I went to the bluff that day to draw, like I had countless times before. I saw the bodies of all those young men piled on the beach, one on top of another, as if they were trash. The soldiers, they were boys merely playing at being men. I watched them day after day on the beach before then, singing, dancing. They were supposed to be going home." Her voice was no more than a whisper. "But they never made it home."

"Oh, Demitra." He sighed. "I'm so sorry."

"I've never told anyone what I saw that day. I thought that maybe if I kept it to myself, if I didn't speak the words out loud, I could somehow convince myself that it never happened. But no matter how hard I try to forget, to imagine it was just a dream, I know the truth."

"You never told anyone what you saw? What happened to you that day?"

She shook her head.

"That's a heavy burden to carry. Secrets take their toll. They eat away at you little by little at first, and then all at once. Why? Why didn't you tell anyone?"

She thought about his question and how she might answer. She was no longer the isolated, lonely little girl conjuring up the ghost of her dead mother for company, and yet there was still so much of herself that she kept locked away, unable or unwilling to share.

"I didn't have anyone to tell." She bit down on her lip and then took a moment to consider what she might say next. "Until now."

They were from different worlds, different lives and experiences. And yet, she saw something in him, something familiar. For all he had—the wealth, the culture, the worldly experience—there was an emptiness that existed in him as well.

"What about you?" She fidgeted with the napkin in her lap. "At the wedding when Tino asked you why you came back, you said you had unfinished business here, a promise to keep. You have all the freedom money can buy; you could go anywhere in the world, and yet you came back here. Why? What was this promise that brought you back?"

Aleko lit a cigarette and exhaled a thin stream of smoke toward the sea. He looked away from Demitra to watch as an elderly fisherman mended his nets on a weather-beaten caïque.

"I wanted to be successful." He sat up straighter. "No . . . I *needed* to be successful. I came from a poor family. I promised my mother when I left that I would come back to take care of her."

There was something in his eyes. Despite his success, despite his wealth, she noticed it each time he mentioned his family.

"This is about more than caring for your mother. I see it in you. I told you something I've never told anyone. Something I carried privately for years. There is something similar in you as well. I know there is." She set down her drink and crossed her arms. "I'll ask you one more time, and I won't ask again after that. What promise brought you back?"

He exhaled in a way that was part breath, part nervous laughter.

"I'll tell you my story, Demitra, but then you have to promise me something."

"What's that?"

"That you'll tell me yours."

"I don't have a story."

"Yes, you do. It's obvious you do."

She could have said so much in that moment. Instead, she chose to nod silently.

It was all the encouragement he needed.

Aleko raised his wineglass to his lips, took a generous sip, and then began his story.

"I made a promise to myself and to my family. We were poor, so poor. My father would take the shoes off his own feet so I could go to school with shoes, so the other children would not make fun of me. My mother would go for days eating mere scraps so she could send me to school fed, so I would not be distracted by the rumble of my belly. My great-great-grandmother, Roula, was a servant for a family in Corfu Town. Count Parlante. His home still stands, just steps from the Liston in the shadow of Saint Spyridon Church. Like all the feudal homes at the time, it was something to behold. Roula was raised in the kitchen beside her mother and then gifted to Count Parlante and his wife on their wedding."

Demitra's eyes widened. "Gifted?"

"Yes. She was given as a gift, a piece of property. People talk about the Venetian era here, and they remember the beauty and the opulence of it with its art and music and architecture. We remember the masks and costumes of Carnivale. We savor the pastitsada and talk about the noble families with their crests and titles and elegant traditions. But there are things we don't talk about, things that don't fit conveniently into the narrative we've crafted.

"The servants were not merely servants, Demitra; they were slaves. Each day, from before sunrise until after the family was asleep, Roula prepared every meal for the family, cleaned, and cared for them, all while raising her son, Stavros, beside her in the confines of that kitchen. She was not an educated woman. She knew nothing about the world outside, and yet she wanted more for her son.

"It took her years, but slowly, over time, she took articles of clothing, pieces of jewelry, silver, small enough and far apart so she didn't arouse suspicion. On his fifteenth birthday, she placed a satchel containing the items in Stavros's hand and told him to leave the only home he had ever known, to forget who he was, where he was born, and to forge a new path and a new identity for himself. She gave him a new name and a new chance at life. She knew no one would ever see him for who he was or what he was capable of; all they would see was his lineage, his bloodline. And she wanted more for her son. She wanted him to have a chance."

"She sent him away?"

"Yes. She drove away her only child. She played the role to perfection, the grieving mother. She told everyone he got sick and died. No one cared; no one bothered to check. No one asked if there had been a funeral. Why would they?

"Stavros did as she instructed. At first he gathered oregano and chamomile and bay leaves and dried and bundled them, the way he'd learned by his mother's side. He began selling his herbs in the market and eventually made a name for himself among the merchants for his fair prices and high quality.

"As time went on, his reputation grew and he reinvented himself as a spice trader, doing business with the finest shops of Corfu. And although it was not her job, three times a day his mother would volunteer to empty the chamber pots, carrying them more than a kilometer each way to dump and clean them in Garitsa Bay, hoping she might catch a glimpse of Stavros doing business among the merchants and shopkeepers. One day she did spot him. She saw her son dressed as a gentleman, negotiating a price for olive oil he had produced on land he had purchased after years of savings, and she knew her sacrifice had been worth it.

"But the story does not end there. I wish it did." He removed another cigarette from its pack and tapped it on the table three times before bringing it to his lips and lighting it. He took a deep, long drag before continuing.

"Stavros found success, married, and had a child. That child was my grandfather. For a while it seemed Stavros had managed to do the impossible, to rewrite his fate. Then one day after closing a deal to provide oregano, chamomile, and olive oil to the spice trade between Corfu and the Asian markets, he was invited to celebrate the closing of the deal with a coffee at the Liston, a celebration of the gentlemen, the businessmen who made Corfu thrive and flourish."

"That's the arched promenade by the cricket fields?"

"Yes," Aleko said. "This was even before the French built the arches. In Venetian times only those noble families whose names were listed in the Libro d'Oro, the Golden Book, were allowed to take their coffee there. Stavros sat there under his assumed name savoring his success, celebrating that he had finally been accepted into business and into society. A rival merchant, a man who owned a large farm on the north side of the island, spotted him and decided to take care of his rival once and for all. He had been watching Stavros for months and felt threatened as this young, hungry businessman encroached on his territory, eating away at his profits.

"Fifteen minutes—Stavros had only fifteen minutes seated in the Liston, sipping a coffee as he celebrated his mother's sacrifice, believing he had done it, that it was possible to create a new life, a new lineage for our family. And then everything changed. The rival merchant alerted the police. There was no record of Stavros or his family in any of the books of nobility at the time. He was discovered to be a fraud, dragged from the square, beaten, and publicly humiliated. Everything he worked for, everything his mother sacrificed for, was gone in an instant.

"Once again he was thrust into poverty and stigmatized as well. He lost more than his fortune that day. It broke him. Stavros had lost his livelihood, his dignity, and he also lost his mind. He became a recluse, abusive, fueled by liquor and rage. And my grandfather, who I loved with all my heart, grew up in the aftermath. The Venetian era ended in 1897 when the French occupation of Corfu began. The French put an end to the feudal era, and even publicly burned the Libro d'Oro in the Liston. But it was too late; our family had once again been thrust into the never-ending cycle of poverty.

"My father did his best to make something of himself, but he died when I was young. My mother was left to care for my grandparents and me on a cleaning woman's salary. My grandfather raised me. He raised me on the stories of his difficult childhood and the abuse he suffered at his father's hands. I made a vow to him that I would make a difference. That not only would I break the cycle of poverty, but I promised I would make our name mean something again, here on Corfu and across Greece.

"My office sits across the street from a building owned by the family of the man who reported Stavros to the police. They now own dozens of buildings across the island. Their name is everywhere. That name is a reminder to me, every time I see it, that I need to prove them wrong." He ran his hand through his hair as he leaned back in his chair and looked at her. "So now you know. There is something powerful that drives me."

"To get back at those who hurt your family?" Demitra asked.

"No. It's not revenge, Demitra. I've read enough mythology to know that never ends well. It's validation I seek. Validation that we deserve to be here, that we deserve a seat at the table, at the Liston or any other place. No one has the right to tell me where I do or don't belong or what I'm capable of. As long as I earn my place at the table."

Wordlessly, he leaned across the table and took both of her hands in his. They sat like that in silence as twilight fell across the port, the sea reflecting the changing light above, like molten silver gently lapping at their feet.

The spell was broken as the waiter returned, clearing dishes from the table.

"We should go," Aleko said. He stood first, then reached his hand out to her.

Demitra took his hand and they walked out to his car. As the sun set beyond the western hills and the day surrendered, succumbing to the night, Demitra allowed herself to do the same.

She placed her hands on his cheeks, the boldness of her gesture surprising her, even more perhaps than him. She pressed her lips against his. It was the briefest kiss, their lips meeting for merely a moment. But in that moment she found what she had been searching for since she was a child. By closing her lips and pressing them against his—this man who was committed to redefining his family's story—she knew she had found the person who would encourage and inspire her to craft her own.

Chapter Seventeen

Corfu, Greece

1952

THE WEEK DRAGGED by endlessly, but when Sunday came again at last, Sophia once more proved to be a savior, providing Demitra with an alibi.

"How lovely of Angeliki and her new husband to invite you to spend the day with them in Kerkyra," Soula said as they walked home from the weekly periptero call to Cephalonia. "I've been thinking how terrible it is that we're all so busy and haven't had the time to show you anything besides the kitchen. Now that the tourist season is ending, I'm sure we'll have more time to show you around."

"That's all right. I'm perfectly happy here with you." Demitra took hold of Soula's arm as they walked. While she felt terrible about lying to Soula, her guilt paled in comparison to the excitement she felt in anticipation of spending another afternoon with Aleko. Unlike the previous weeks when only intuition told her he would be waiting for her, they had parted ways the previous Sunday with a plan.

ALEKO TIPPED HIS hat to her as she slid into the passenger seat of his car. After he took his own seat behind the wheel, he reached his hand out to her across the gear shift. She took his hand in hers and squeezed it. And as he drove off, away from Ipsos, she sat back in the seat, her head resting against the soft leather, her hand resting in his.

"I have a surprise for you," he said, stealing a glance at her as he navigated the road.

"What is it?"

"Well, it wouldn't be a surprise if I told you."

She did not ask again, nor did she say another word while he drove. There was a perfection in the moment as they silently sped away toward an adventure together. It didn't matter where the adventure took her. All she knew was that in his presence, she felt whole, and beside him, she felt at home. The rest was insignificant.

"We're here," he announced a few minutes later as he pulled the car into a small marina.

They walked to the end of the dock and stopped in front of a magnificent boat. It was larger and more modern than the traditional caïques of fishermen, yet it maintained an old-world charm.

She watched as Aleko pulled in the lines and maneuvered the boat out of the harbor toward Garitsa Bay. Once they rounded the old fortress, the lush coastline of Corfu opened up before them like an untold story. There, along the southeastern coast of the island where the land narrowed, the shoreline was a rugged, wild thing of beauty. The tranquil sea stretched out before them, her color ever-changing, from the deep cobalt depths closer to the mainland to the pale turquoise and cerulean waters that disappeared into the many caves carved into the cliffs. Up and down the coast, slim, tall cypress trees stretched upward as if to pierce the cloudless sky above. All along the shore, patches of wildflowers grew, a swirling kaleidoscope come to life.

They passed a pier where a young couple ran hand in hand and then jumped into the sea together, their laughter carrying on the wind. Demitra watched them as they broke through the surface of the water, laughing in delight as they swam back to the dock.

"Just look at them," Demitra said, the longing in her voice dripping from every word. "So free. So beautiful."

"You are beautiful." Aleko reached over and placed his hand on her cheek.

She shook her head, unable to meet his gaze.

Still caressing her cheek, he placed his other hand under her chin and lifted her face until he caught her eyes again.

"Yes, you are beautiful." He leaned in and kissed her softly. "I never noticed before, but when the sun hits your eyes just right, it's like they're made of pure gold."

She blushed as she burrowed into his arms.

"I have another surprise for you," he said. "I want to take you somewhere beautiful and special."

"Where?"

"Paxos." He laughed as he pushed the throttle and sent them speeding toward the open sea.

As they sailed the two-hour journey to Paxos, Demitra was again struck by the natural beauty around her. Similar to Corfu and Cephalonia, Paxos's shoreline was a mixture of pristine beaches lined by jagged cliffs topped with lush trees and flowers. All along the western coast of the island, dazzling grottos and caves filled Demitra's imagination with visions of Calypso and Circe.

"Do you know how Paxos and Antipaxos came to be?" Aleko asked.

"No. Tell me." She laughed as she lifted her face, feeling the warmth of the sun on her skin.

"A long, long time ago, when gods ruled the world, the great god Poseidon spotted the nymph Amphitrite dancing at a wedding," Aleko began. "Poseidon fell madly in love with Amphitrite and knew she was who he wanted by his side for the rest of his days. There was only one problem: Amphitrite knew Poseidon was married, and she refused his advances, wanting nothing to do with the tempestuous god and his complicated life.

"Yet Poseidon would not be deterred. He sent the dolphin god Delphin to her, offering gifts of gold coins and pearls and deep-sea treasures. None of it stirred Amphitrite or changed her mind. When Delphin reported back that Amphitrite would not be swayed by precious gifts, Poseidon fell even deeper in love with her. Eventually Delphin spoke plainly and eloquently to Amphitrite, convincing her of Poseidon's character and devotion.

"'He loves you,' Delphin said. 'He loves you simply and beauti-fully, and he will move heaven and earth and the stars and the sea for you.' Despite all he could offer her, all of the riches and magic he commanded with the sound of his voice or the mere raising of his triton, Amphitrite knew this was by far the most precious gift the god could offer—the only gift that mattered to her. She was so moved by the dolphin god's words that she agreed to go to Poseidon and to love him as he loved her.

"At the sight of Amphitrite riding atop Delphin and returning to him, Poseidon lifted his trident into the air and pierced the southern tip of Kerkyra, breaking off a portion of the island. And that is how Poseidon created Paxos and Antipaxos, the perfect location for him to live and celebrate his love with Amphitrite, away from prying and judgmental and jealous eyes."

When he was finished, he looked at her and smiled.

"Oh, I like that story," Demitra whispered.

The port of Gaios stretched out before them, lined with a dozen or so shops and cafés. Of the few that were open, most sat empty, save for a couple of scattered tables of families sipping their afternoon coffee and elderly men sipping ouzo as they played backgammon or sat staring out at the water, twirling worry beads in their hands.

Aleko maneuvered the boat close to the dock, and an elderly man wearing an apron of starched white, matching his snow-colored mustache and brows, waved to them from where he was wiping down tables outside a small café. The sign above, written in large blue letters, read *Stamatis*. The man put down his rag and scurried toward the dock to greet them.

"Hello!" he said, his smile bright and cheerful. He could have been fifty years old or possibly eighty; Demitra couldn't know for sure.

"I'm Stamatis." He reached his arm out and caught the line Aleko threw to him, then expertly secured the boat with a perfect hitching knot before extending his hand to Demitra. "Welcome to Gaios and to Paxos."

"Thank you," she said as she took his hand and stepped onto the dock. Aleko extended his hand to shake Stamatis's, but instead, the older man grabbed him in a bear hug, slapping his back as if they were old friends.

"Come, please. Stay for lunch," he said as he ushered them to a table facing the water.

Aleko and Demitra glanced at each other and smiled in agreement.

"Polixeni, come, we have guests!" Stamatis shouted toward the restaurant as he pulled a chair out for Demitra to sit.

Almost instantly, a woman—Polixeni most likely—darted out from inside the restaurant. With her silver hair and black dress, the stout woman carried herself with the same frenetic and kind energy as her husband.

"Welcome, welcome!" She echoed her husband's warm sentiments as she placed a basket of freshly baked bread, a small plate of slick green olives, and a bottle of olive oil on the table before them. "I made the bread this morning, and the olives and oil are from our grove. We have bottles and bottles of it if you'd like to take some home with you. Enjoy." She clapped her hands together as she scurried back into the kitchen as quickly as she had come.

Demitra and Aleko lingered over lunch, savoring each dish Stamatis and Polixeni placed before them. Everything from the pita dipped in olive oil to the spanakopita to the meat pie and veal sofrito was superb.

"Please, you must try Polixeni's orange cake. It is truly a marvel," Stamatis said as he placed two demitasses of coffee on the table, along with a generous slice of the cake. The scent of orange mixed with honey and cinnamon made Demitra's mouth water, even though she was uncomfortably full from the meal.

"Yes. Please, enjoy." Polixeni smiled as she glanced at Demitra's ringless finger.

"I hope you will come again," she said after Aleko and Stamatis went to settle the bill inside the restaurant. "Maybe after you are married, you can come and spend a few days with us." Polixeni smiled. "We have beautiful and clean rooms for rent."

Her instincts about Polixeni were correct, yet when she opened her mouth, Demitra only said, "How lovely that would be."

"Sadly, God did not bless us with children. This is the black reality of our lives, the burden God has chosen me to carry. May God bless you and your young man with many children. May your home always be filled with love and laughter."

Demitra's heart broke for this lovely woman and her husband, childless and alone in a fading village. In that moment Demitra felt a shift, as if something long dormant inside her had at last stirred awake. In all the years Stella had extolled the magic and fulfillment of motherhood, Demitra had never shared the innate urge. But now as she gazed up at Aleko while standing with this older woman steeped in longing and regret, Demitra finally understood.

She had never yearned for children before. She had never longed for a husband before. In all the years she'd pined for her mother, in all the years she'd craved the warmth and love of maternal affection, she had never seen herself in that role. She had never imagined that she herself could be the one to fill that void. But as she watched Aleko, she realized that was exactly what she wanted. That was what she craved. While Polixeni prattled on, asking God to bless their union, Demitra remained silent. Because for the first time in her life, she could envision it all.

"There's one little detour we need to make before we head back." Aleko grinned broadly as he and Stamatis rejoined them. "Stamatis has generously offered to show us the best view in all of Paxos before we leave."

"Yes, yes." The old man slapped Aleko on the back as if they were old friends. "You cannot leave our beautiful island without taking in the view of the gods." He turned to face the mountain and pointed up toward a small home, seemingly built into the cliffs.

"Yes! After the wedding you must come and stay," Polixeni insisted. "There," she continued as she pointed up the cliff. "You see the house with the terrace overlooking the orchard and the sea? It has been in our family for years, and now with so many gone to America, it sits there sad and empty, like everything else. Please, promise me you'll come back and stay with us after your wedding. Our home is yours."

The path to the house was something of a daydream. The narrow alleyway behind the port snaked up the hill, overlooking the small harbor and the sea beyond. It was not a steep climb, nor was it a difficult one, but Demitra felt breathless nonetheless. As she looked around her, she marveled at the pristine gardens and orchard.

"You like it?" Polixeni was beside her as Demitra took in the sumptuous landscaping.

"It's magical," Demitra replied.

"The good Lord did not bless us with children, so these are our children." Stamatis beamed as he stretched his hands out, gesturing to the roses, wisteria, bougainvillea, and irises that brought the garden to life. "We spend our days tending to them as if they were our babies—loving them, nurturing them, and whispering to them, and they speak to us as well."

Beyond the flower garden stretched a grove of ancient olive trees, knotted and bent.

"Ah, these olive trees are a wonder. Our family has made the finest olive oil on Paxos for generations," Stamatis said as he showed them around the property. "There was a time when we would sell out each year. The housewives and the tavernas all across the island knew better than to waste their time milling olives. People lined up for our oil, and the sales kept us fed and clothed and warm in the winter. Now there is no one left to buy it, but we still harvest and mill and bottle our green gold. It is our joy. Maybe one day the villagers will return. When they do, I'll be here waiting for them."

The house itself was small and pristine. A dozen cypress trees lined the path toward the home, which was one in a cluster of small homes built in the same clearing. The patio stretched out across the hillside, the view unlike anything Demitra had seen before. From there, high above the harbor and tucked into the hillside among the pines and olives and cypresses with the azure Ionian churning below, Demitra felt as if she were soaring above the clouds, gazing down on the miracle of God's creation.

"My family has lived on this island for generations." Stamatis sighed deeply as he shook his head. "We survived everything and everyone, from the pirates who carried off half the villagers and sold them to slavery to the stand against the Ottomans. But now Polixeni and I find ourselves alone with the chickens and olive grove and our view. Please come back and visit us. We would love for you to be our guests."

They made their way back down the hill and to the dock, and just as he had when they first stepped foot on the island, Stamatis sent Aleko off with a warm bear hug.

"Thank you," he said as he held Aleko in a warm embrace. "God bless you and safe voyage. Please, come back and see us soon. We will be waiting for you."

As they sailed away from Gaios and toward open water, Demitra waved to Stamatis and Polixeni one last time.

"Aleko." She called to him from where she sat on the sideboard, eyes still glued to the figures of Stamatis and Polixeni on the shore. "They're crying. I mean really crying. Look at them. Do you think something's wrong? Should we go back?"

"No. There's nothing wrong."

"But look at them." She craned her neck to keep her gaze on them.

"There's nothing wrong. I promise." He smiled at her as he reached into the basket Polixeni had sent with them and pulled out a piece of the orange cake.

Her eyes narrowed. "What do you mean? How do you know?"

"I bought the olive oil."

"You what?"

"I bought the olive oil. All of it. Hundreds of bottles."

"But why?"

"That wonderful man has been eaten alive with worry and stress. They've been existing on what little they can grow or catch. He said there's no money for anything else and hasn't been for a while. His brother sends money from America sometimes, but it's not enough. He took my hands and kissed them, telling me God must have sent us to them, that our visit was a miracle."

"It was." Demitra wrapped her arms around his neck and kissed him gently. "It was a miracle, because you are a miracle."

She turned her head once again toward shore, watching as the figures grew smaller and eventually out of sight. As the wind whipped through her hair, Demitra looked back upon the raw, natural beauty of Paxos.

"Since that day at Achilleion, I've thought about what you said, about my art. I've thought about what I'd like to draw—*who* I'd like to draw. And I think I found her. I'm going to draw Amphitrite."

"I think that's a perfect choice. And I, for one, can't wait to meet her." In the distance a dolphin sprang up from the sea, forming a perfect arch before it disappeared again beneath the water. "And it looks like I'm not the only one." Aleko laughed.

She inhaled deeply, standing taller as she leaned into the sea spray, gazing upon the island where Poseidon had shared a home and a refuge with his great love, and where Demitra felt that at last, she, too, had found hers.

They reached the marina at dusk, just as the swallows began their evening performance. After securing the boat to the dock, Aleko reached his hand out to guide her ashore.

"No," she said, smiling at him as she drew him toward her, pulling him back onto the boat.

He laughed at her playfulness and then she leaned in, kissing him longer and harder than either expected. He pulled away from her, a question in his expression.

"Yes. I'm sure." She took his hand and led him to the cabin belowdecks.

The rhythm of their bodies moving in unison mimicked the gentle rise and fall of the tide. While her limbs entangled with his, Demitra didn't think about what was expected of her or care about how proper Greek girls should behave. For the first time in her life, Demitra dictated her own story, exactly the way she wanted it.

Chapter Eighteen

Corfu, Greece

1953

NO MATTER HOW she busied herself, the weekdays dragged by torturously as Demitra waited to be reunited with Aleko each Sunday. At first they spent their afternoons exploring Corfu and the neighboring island. As the weeks turned to months and fall turned to winter and winter to spring, their time together evolved into lazy hours spent belowdecks exploring each other.

The arrival of baby Spiro in May was a welcome distraction for Demitra, who threw herself into helping care for the newborn and his sister during the day and taking over Sophia's responsibilities in the restaurant at night. Each day she glanced at her pad and pencils, collecting dust on the bureau, promising herself that once things settled down, she would get to work and bring Amphitrite to life.

As tradition dictated, Sophia rested at home, observing the traditional forty-day isolation period before her son was received publicly for the first time in church.

"How is he? Have you heard from him?" Sophia asked as she sat nursing the baby.

"I told you. He went to London on business. He said he'd be gone a month at least and it's only been two weeks."

"Be sure to tell me the moment he's back," Sophia insisted as she rubbed the baby's back. "We'll come up with a plan so you can escape Soula's prying eyes and spend some time together." Sophia gasped and sat up with a jolt, startling the baby, who began to cry. "Do you think he's buying you a ring?" Her eyes darted around the room, making sure Soula could not hear her. "Is that why he went to London, to buy you a ring?"

Demitra shrugged and smiled. "Let's not get ahead of ourselves. We haven't talked about marriage." She did not want to admit it out loud, but the idea had consumed her thoughts. Her evening childhood dreams of falling asleep in her mother's embrace were now replaced by nightly fantasies of being entangled in Aleko's.

Sophia looked around the room, making sure Soula was not within earshot. "I see the difference in you, Demitra." She smirked, cocking her brow. "I know, because I used to walk around with that very same faraway look on my face. But it's been months now of sneaking around. You can't continue like this unless he makes his intentions clear."

"Don't worry." Demitra did her best to reassure Sophia, even as she blushed. "Before he left for London, he told me he wants to sit down when he returns and have a talk." She shrugged and smiled coyly. "He said he has something to tell me." Her smile widened at the possibilities as she kissed baby Spiro and walked into the kitchen.

TWO WEEKS LATER, the entire family boarded the bus to Corfu Town, where baby Spiro's forty-day celebration was marked with a blessing at the Church of Saint Spyridon.

The spring breeze carried the perfume of wisteria and honey-suckle across the cobblestone lanes of Corfu Town as the hazy smoke of grilled souvlaki and lamb filled the air. It was a rare treat for the family not only to make the trip into town but to dine out at one of the crowded tavernas tucked within the labyrinthine

alleyways of Kerkyra. And although she was known for her thrift-
iness, Soula insisted that her grandson's introduction to the church
be marked in a fine establishment.

After they were seated, Soula stood, glass raised in the air. "To
my first grandson, Spyridon. May God bless him and keep him
safe, and may he live a long, healthy, and prosperous life."

"Amen." Everyone clinked their glasses in unison.

The meal was perfection, from the lemon-doused pork souvlaki
to the feta-, mint-, and rice-stuffed zucchini flowers and the créme
caramel for dessert. Even Soula was left speechless by the delicious
meal and only snickered when she looked over the bill.

"You'd think the portions would be larger for what they
charged."

Tino hoisted Kiki onto his shoulders as they made their way
from the restaurant to Spianada Square, making a show of it as
he weaved in and out of the crowd dramatically. Soula delighted
in pushing her grandson in his pram and beamed with pride
each time someone stopped to admire the baby. Arm in arm,
Sophia and Demitra strolled behind, savoring every moment of
the perfect evening.

The mournful drone of a clarinet filled the air as they approached the gazebo at the center of the square. A lone musician
with leathery skin and a thick black mustache regaled onlookers
with his moody serenade. Demitra and Sophia were so caught up
in the music that they did not notice when Tino darted across the
square.

"Well, hello! Look who it is!" Tino shouted as he waved Demitra
and Sophia over. Soula stood beside him, beaming as a woman
bent over to peer at the sleeping baby.

"Look who I found," Tino cried out as they reached his side.
"Aleko's back."

The familiar tremor ran through Demitra.

"Hello," she said, beaming, mindful of keeping her excitement in check publicly. The same could not be said of Sophia, who practically leaped with delight.

"Welcome back! How wonderful that you are here. We're just so happy that you're back," Sophia said. "Aren't we?" Smiling broadly, she nudged Demitra.

"Yes."

Tino snorted, amused by his wife's enthusiasm. "Well, not only is he back, but he brought a surprise." Tino fanned his arm out toward the woman standing over Spiro's pram.

"This is Alexandra, Aleko's wife. And this is his daughter, Flora. And this is my family." Tino grinned as he made the introductions. "You sly devil," he said as he slapped Aleko on the back. "I didn't even know you had settled down. You never told me you got married."

The world spiraled, tilting and spinning as the blood drained from Demitra's face. She stared at the woman and child before her. *His wife. His daughter.*

How? How was this possible? How could it be true?

Oh dear God. Demitra's legs buckled and she stumbled. At once, Sophia's arm was around her waist, steadying her.

It was a lie. Every moment, every touch, every whisper. Nothing but lies.

I'll never be his wife. He has a wife.

I'll never have his child. He has a child.

"So you've been keeping us secret, have you?" Alexandra teased Aleko from where she stood, still hovering over Spiro's pram.

Flora, a striking child with olive skin, green eyes, and unruly blonde curls, stood between her mother and her father, leaning against Aleko's leg. She looked to be about five years old.

"It's lovely to meet you all and to finally be here," Alexandra said. "Flora and I stayed behind in London while she finished her school semester. I must admit, I wasn't so sure about leaving London at first, and to be honest, I put up quite a stink. Didn't I, dear?" She glanced Aleko's way. He did not meet her eyes as his head sank lower. Alexandra either did not notice or did not care that she did not have her husband's attention.

"I finally see why Aleko was so insistent on coming back. Corfu truly is lovely. We found our dream apartment. I would have preferred to be near the sea, to be honest, but Aleko insisted on the Liston; nothing but the best for our Aleko." While steeped in saccharine, her voice also dripped with sarcasm.

"Please promise me you'll come for dinner once we're settled. You must join us." Her eyes settled on Demitra and narrowed as they seemed to take in every inch of her from head to toe. "Demitra, isn't it? Please, promise me I'll see you again. I would love nothing more than to get to know you better."

She knows. A wave of nausea overtook Demitra. *She knows.* Demitra felt it with every fiber of her being.

Sophia sprang into action. "How gracious of you to offer. We will surely continue this conversation another time. I'm so sorry, but we must be going. We have a bus to catch and it's getting late. Come, Mama, Tino. We don't want to miss the bus." With that, Sophia used all the strength in her body to keep Demitra upright, practically dragging her as they crossed the plateia.

Only when she took her seat beside Sophia on the darkened bus did Demitra allow herself to cry. She stared out the window, watching as the beauty of Corfu Town disappeared into the distance. So, too, did her dream of the life she would have and the family she would love.

"I'm so sorry," Sophia whispered as she stroked Demitra's hair in the dark. "I'm so, so sorry."

There was no quieting the sobs that racked Demitra's body as she lay in bed later that night. As she lay on her side, the sheets soaked with her tears, Demitra pressed her face into her pillow as she dismantled each chapter of the story, their story, that she had written in her imagination these past few months.

The door flung open as Soula bolted into the room dressed in her nightgown. "Child, what is wrong? Are you all right? I woke to go to the bathroom and heard you crying. Are you sick?" She sat beside Demitra and placed her hand on her forehead.

Demitra had brought this shame upon herself. All that mattered now was that she spare her family the disgrace of her actions. So she said the one thing she knew Soula would not question, the one thing she would understand.

"I miss Baba and my family. I want to go home."

Chapter Nineteen

New York

1921

"HURRY. THE BUS leaves in five minutes. If we miss this one, we'll have to wait an hour and miss our appointment at the church!" Pericles shouted as they ran toward the bus stop. "Come on!" He motioned for Maria to run faster.

They arrived just as the driver opened the doors and the passengers began to board.

Winded, Maria said nothing. She was hungry and hot and her legs trembled. She wanted nothing more than to fall on the ground and scream, to beat her chest and rip her clothing, but she would not allow him to see her like that.

On their last night together, as they clung to each other in bed, dreading the reality that would come with the sunrise, Mama had imparted only one piece of marital advice to Maria.

"Your husband should know you from the neck down, not from the neck up. From the neck up is yours, and yours alone. Your mind and your feelings are the only things that are truly yours in this life. Guard them wisely and carefully."

As she replayed Mama's words in her mind, Maria resolved not to allow him to see how scared she was, how nervous. She could not let him know she felt like a lamb going to slaughter. She would be strong, stoic, and brave. Like Iphigenia, she would face her fate with grace and her head held high.

"There you are!" a man shouted as he bounded up the steps and onto the bus. "I was wondering what was taking you so long." The man slid into the seat across the aisle from Pericles, then reached over and slapped him on the back several times.

"This is Maria," Pericles said as he leaned back in his seat.

When she looked up, Maria was struck with how familiar the man looked. She was certain she had seen him before. But how was that possible?

"I'm Tasso." He nodded in her direction. "It's nice to meet you."

Maria nodded politely, unsure of the proper response.

"Tasso will be our *koumbaro*," Pericles announced. "We work together in Milwaukee."

"How wonderful," Maria replied, attempting to sound engaged when all she wanted to do was go back and make sure Anna was all right.

Tasso pulled a crumpled pack of cigarettes from his pocket and handed one to Pericles as the bus pulled away. The men lit their cigarettes and leaned back in their seats, and Maria stared out the window, watching as the *Megali Hellas* faded from view.

"I mean, she was nothing like her photo at all." Tasso laughed as he spoke, picking an errant piece of tobacco from his tongue. "Talk about false advertising. I'm glad I escaped that one. Yours is pretty, actually." He nodded in Maria's direction.

"Well, you can always try again," Pericles said as he reached across Maria to flick the remnants of his cigarette out the window.

"And make this trip again? Only to be duped by some desperate father trying to unload his homely daughter? I don't think so." Tasso shook his head as he ran his fingers through his hair.

"What about the dowry?" Pericles asked.

"What about it? What about the time and money I spent to come here only to realize I had been scammed?"

Maria glanced over at him again. Something about this Tasso niggled at her. She was certain she had seen him before.

And suddenly, it came to her. *Tasso.* He'd said his name was Tasso, but that was the shortened version of his full name. The reality hit her in a surge of anger.

He was Anastasios, Anna's intended groom, and he had abandoned her on the dock because he thought she was not as pretty as her photo had promised.

Nauseated, Maria leaned out the window, gasping for air.

"Are you all right?" Pericles asked.

"Yes. I'm fine. Just a bit lightheaded," she said, forcing a smile, although she wanted to scream. She wanted to beat his chest and yell at him to go back, to force him to do the honorable thing. It was cruel and inhuman to abandon Anna, discarding her as if she were trash.

And yet, Maria was powerless to do anything beyond survive herself.

Chapter Twenty

Corfu, Greece

1953

JUST OVER A year since seeing Corfu for the first time, Demitra stood on the deck of the ferry to begin her journey back to Cephalonia, forever changed by her time there. She faced the open sea as the ferry pulled away from the port, turning her back on the vista she had fallen in love with. She could not stand to watch as her beloved Corfu and the life she had envisioned there with Aleko faded from view.

With her back pressed against the railing, Demitra held tight to the drawing Kiki had given her as they hugged in a tearful goodbye. It was a child's stick-figure drawing of the two of them holding hands, surrounded by hearts and flowers. A note was written in the corner, dictated to her mother by Kiki.

Don't burn this one. Keep it with you forever to remind you of me. I love you, Kiki

Demitra closed her eyes and pressed the drawing to her chest as the past week's events replayed in her mind.

He is a husband and a father. I am a fool. That was the mantra playing endlessly in her mind as she relived every touch, every caress, every moment he was beside her—and then the moment she learned it had all been a lie.

The tap on her arm startled her from her reminiscences.

"I'm sorry to bother you. Are you Demitra?" the young man in the ferry worker uniform asked.

"Yes," she replied, confusion on her face.

"Here," he said as he held a parcel out to her. "The gentleman asked me to give this to you."

"Gentleman?" She scanned the deck. There was no one else nearby except for a young mother and her children.

"Yes," the boy replied as he pointed back toward the harbor. "The gentleman on the dock. He asked me to give it to you once we left Corfu."

Demitra took the package and turned around to face the dock. She spotted him at once, leaning against his car, smoking a cigarette as he gazed at her.

Clutching the package in one hand, she reached out to grab the railing with the other, sea spray filling her lungs as she sucked her breath in sharply. She had not seen him since that day, a week ago on the plateia. She wanted nothing more than to cry and shout, *"How could you do this to me? Why did you do this to me? How could you be so cruel?"* Those words screamed in her head, even as others whispered, *I loved you. I really loved you.*

Broken, Demitra stared at him silently as the ferry carried her farther and farther away. When he was nearly out of view, he lifted his arm and waved a final goodbye.

She stayed there, rooted in place long after he was no more than a memory on the horizon, staring into the space where he had been. Finally, she turned her back against the railing again, a whirlpool of regret, anger, grief, and fear swirling inside her, threatening to pull her under again. And then she remembered.

"The gentleman asked me to give this to you."

She turned the parcel over in her hands. It was a small, square package wrapped in plain brown paper. For a moment she thought she might toss it into the sea. What good were gifts now? Even so, curiosity got the best of her and she slid her finger under the wrapping and ripped the paper away.

It was a book. A beautiful brown, leather-bound book embossed with gold lettering. She turned it over and looked at the cover, tracing her fingers over the title. *The Powerful and Magical Women of Myths.*

Flipping through the richly illustrated pages, Demitra recognized them one after the other. Medea. Helen. Electra. Medusa. The women who had consumed her imagination since she was a child. Something fell out of the book and fluttered to the ground. Demitra bent to pick it up.

It was a letter written in a familiar hand.

Dearest Demitra,

I never meant to hurt you, and I'm so deeply sorry. Every word I said to you I meant. Every moment we spent together was pure happiness, the happiest I've felt in my life.

I wanted to come back to Corfu and start a new life in the place I love with the woman I love. But I am bound to a woman whose greatest joy is to see me unhappy. Alexandra and I married when she got pregnant. I thought it was the right thing to do; I could not have been more wrong. All this time I thought my accomplishments and success would set me apart from my great-grandfather. All this time I imagined I had come such a long way. I now realize nothing has changed. Like him, I'm destined to play a role that others have cast me in, to live a life that is not my own.

I fought so hard and worked so hard to make something of myself, to find success and honor my family. It means nothing to me now. It means nothing if I can't share it all with you.

I'm so sorry. I never meant to hurt you.

You spent your childhood searching for the magic in the myths, Demitra, when you were the magic all along. Be the magic. Create magic and live the life of an artist.

You have an artist's soul and you will always have my heart.

With all my love,
Aleko

She sat with the letter in her hand, staring down at the page. How was it possible that he could simultaneously mend her heart just to break it all over again? Her hand formed a fist, and then she released it, not wanting to destroy the letter he had written with his own hand. His penmanship was crisp and beautiful, like him. So many thoughts swirled in her mind, yet one thing stood out above all.

She believed him.

She believed his words and his story. She knew in her core he had written the truth. And she understood now the very thing that perhaps drew them to each other, made them understand each other. As different as their worlds were, they were the same, each recognizing in the other what everyone else couldn't or wouldn't see in them. And for a few short months, they had believed it might be possible to be that version of themselves.

Part of her wished she had never read his letter, that she had tossed it into the sea when the boy first handed it to her. That would have been easier. It would have been easier to hate him.

To have had a glimpse of something beautiful, a taste of happiness, only to have it snatched away, was a cruelty unlike any other.

Thea Olga had been right. She had, for a few brief moments, experienced a pure and perfect love. And she was forever changed by it, understanding that it would never come again, because she was not who she was before.

part

three

Chapter Twenty-One

Cephalonia, Greece

1953

B ROKEN.

Demitra was broken, and from the very first sight as she stepped off the bus in Argostoli, Stella recognized it as well. But Stella did not bombard her with questions. She did not press her for answers. Stella merely allowed her space to grieve, running interference against Martha's insatiable appetite for gossip from Corfu and against Baba, whose impatience for his unmarried daughter seemed to grow by the day.

Nearly a week after Demitra arrived home, Stella heard her muffled sobs through the door. After a gentle knock, Demitra allowed her in. That night as she cried in Stella's arms, Demitra confided in her stepmother, sharing her story of the man she loved, the man she'd lost, and the dreams she feared would never be fulfilled.

"I love him, Stella," she cried. "All the things you talked about—about being a mother, having a child. I finally understood them. I finally felt them and wanted them. And for the first time in my life, I felt seen and understood. He told me I was beautiful, that I mattered. He told me I had talent, an artist's soul, and for a short while I believed it too."

"Oh, my sweet girl," Stella cooed as she stroked her hair and rocked her gently back and forth. "I'm so sorry. But you're wrong."

Demitra pulled away, the pain, grief, and now confusion so clearly visible in her eyes.

"You're wrong," Stella said again, her tone loving and comforting. "I see in you all the possibilities and all the dreams I never had for myself, that I never imagined possible for a girl, for a woman. God gave you a gift, Demitra. There's a reason he did. Aleko was not the only one who sees you for who you are. I see you too. I believe in you too."

From that day forward, Stella did everything in her power to help Demitra find the time and space to work on her art. Each morning, she woke earlier than usual, ensuring the house was clean and the meals prepared before taking Gerasimos to run errands or visit Martha so Demitra could work in peace. In the evenings, before Baba arrived home and she set supper on the table, Stella asked one thing of Demitra—to share with her the progress of her day so Stella could watch as Demitra breathed life into her subjects on the page.

"Oh, she's beautiful," Stella gushed as Demitra placed her pad on the table one night about a month after she had returned home. With the lightest touch, Stella traced her finger along the page, her eyes wide in wonder at the beauty before her.

"Amphitrite," Demitra said as she reveled in Stella's reaction. "I've been wanting to draw her for months now, and because of you I was finally able to."

In Demitra's hands Amphitrite's hair was long and wild, woven with seashells and coral and starfish. She sat on a golden throne in a crystal blue grotto, her gown, a living, breathing thing, the color of the sea itself. In Demitra's hands Amphitrite was not a timid nymph to be hidden away from the world by her lover. She was not a mistress, shy and afraid of how others might perceive her. No, this Amphitrite commanded the seas as she grew into her own power. And all around her, dolphins and seals jumped and frolicked to her delight as schools of fish swam by paying respects to the mistress she once was and the powerful goddess she had evolved into.

Demitra and Stella were both lost in thought at the beauty and power of Amphitrite. They did not hear Baba as he approached the house. When the door slammed closed behind him, Demitra quickly closed the pad and scurried to her room to put it away as Stella smiled and placed a whisky in his hand.

But it was too late. He had already seen enough.

THAT EVENING DEMITRA lay in bed reliving her time with Aleko. In the same childhood bed where night after night she had willed Mama to come to her, Demitra now conjured Aleko, rewriting the ending of their story in her dreams.

"Stop encouraging her!" Baba's raised voice and angry tone startled Demitra from that sacred space as she drifted somewhere between asleep and awake. From her bedroom Demitra heard Stella's footsteps pacing the floor as Baba slammed the whisky bottle on the table.

Demitra got up and stepped gingerly, not wanting the creaky floorboards to give her away as she pressed her ear to the door.

"Pericles, please, just give her time," Stella pleaded.

"She barely leaves her room, barely helps around the house. It's enough now, the way she walks around here like a sulking child." Baba's voice was loud, his words slurred.

"But she does help me. We are managing just fine. She needs a little time to settle back into life here. She'll find her place."

"And what place is that? I'm not like your father. I won't have the entire island laughing at me and my spinster daughter behind my back!" He spat as he slammed his drink on the table. "I never should have listened to you and your mother. She would have been married by now, a respectable wife and mother. I sent her to Corfu to help your family so she could learn how to cook, how to take care of a household and be useful so she could return home to fulfill her duties. But now she's even worse than before, skulking around and hovering over her coloring books like a sullen child."

"Oh, but, Pericles, it's not like that. She's a good girl, and she's talented. You should see the beautiful things she draws. Her talent is a gift—a gift from God." The words were barely out of Stella's mouth when Demitra heard a crash, as if Baba had thrown his glass across the room.

"God put women on this earth to be wives and mothers and take care of their families! Not to spend their time drawing ridiculous pictures. Do not insult me in this way ever again. I won't be made a mockery of—not now, not ever. Once the *panagiri* is over, we will find her a husband. I don't care if we have to sell everything in this house to come up with a dowry. I won't let that girl shame me anymore."

"Yes, Pericles," Stella replied. Demitra could hear the difference in her voice now; she sounded unsteady, shaken. Defeated.

Demitra gripped the doorknob, twisted, and pulled it open before shutting it again. She wanted to go to Stella, to make sure she was all right, but then thought better of it. What was once Baba's indifference toward her had clearly evolved into something else. She was a burden and an embarrassment to him, and over the years his frustrations had slowly simmered into loathing and then festered into rage.

"I see you too. I believe in you too," Stella had said the night Demitra cried in her arms. She'd known Stella only a few years, yet she saw and understood Demitra. How was it that Demitra had lived in the same house all her life with Baba, and he had never bothered to see her at all?

Chapter Twenty-Two

Cephalonia, Greece

1953

P ERICLES SAT IN his chair staring into the fire and draining the last of the whisky.

He was alone with his thoughts, with the demons that had tormented him since that day all those years ago.

Demitra had disappeared into her room as soon as the dishes were cleared from the table, as she had each night since her return. Stella lingered, attempting to calm his nerves, but that served only to anger him more. And then it had happened.

He could hear Stella's muffled whimpers coming from the bedroom. He poured himself another drink, holding the amber liquid to the firelight.

He had not meant to strike Stella. He had not intended to hurt her. If only she had listened. If only she had done as he'd instructed.

Where had he gone wrong? How had his quiet, timid child turned into this defiant young woman? He sucked the cigarette smoke into his lungs and then exhaled a thin stream. He knew the answer.

She was her mother's child.

Only once before had he raised his hand in anger toward a woman. That time he had intended to hurt her, the way she had hurt him.

The scene played out in his mind as he stared into the flames, as it had countless times since that night. It was more than twenty years ago, but he could still hear her crying. He had loved her, before his love turned to blind rage. He struck her once, and once was enough. She fell to the floor and then crawled on her hands and knees to cower in the corner.

He'd raged then; all the bitterness, anger, and disappointment he had swallowed for years boiled over.

She'd pleaded with him, begged for forgiveness, begged for mercy. But he offered neither. The floor was littered with debris—broken glass, dishes, everything within his reach he had smashed, demolished, destroyed—just like his marriage, just like his American Dream.

When nothing was left within reach for him to destroy, he took two steps toward her before the baby began to cry from the next room. *"Please, no,"* she'd pleaded, covering her head with her hands as her cries grew louder. Then his plan had formed. He would do the one thing that would wound her as deeply as she had wounded him.

Reaching down, he grabbed her hand and yanked the wedding ring from her finger. He glared at her and spat the last words he would ever speak to her.

"I should have left you on the dock. I should have let those men take you away. They would have saved me the trouble since you turned out to be a poutana anyway."

Her primal screams followed him out the door, down the street, and even now echoed in his ear incessantly, more than twenty years later.

Only when Stella's whimpers stopped, morphing into the rhythmic breathing of sleep, did he get up from his chair. He stepped gingerly into the room where she slept pressed against the wall, their son nestled beside her.

He pulled the closet open and rummaged through the hangers until he found what he was looking for. Running his fingers along the stitching, he located the tear in the lining and reached inside to pull out the envelope. He slipped his hand inside and took out the yellowed newspaper clipping, then returned the envelope to its place.

When he was back in his chair with a fresh glass of whisky, he unfolded the paper and stared down at the face he had not seen since he left America.

Among the dozens of ads for brides on the page, hers had been the face that made his heart stop as he noticed the fire in her eyes. Hers was the face that spoke to him, that whispered the names of their children in his ear, that inspired him to push himself harder to be successful, that made him want to be a better man.

Hers was the face that had broken his heart and made him do unspeakable things.

When he'd drained his glass, Pericles leaned over and dropped the paper into the fire, watching as the flames consumed the face he desperately wanted to erase from his memory, the face that had haunted him every day for the past twenty years.

But he closed his eyes, and there she was again, just as she was each time he tried to sleep. Her dark hair cascading to her waist, her cheeks flushed, and her eyes bright with fire, with anguish, and with accusation.

Chapter Twenty-Three

Cephalonia, Greece

1953

S HE DIDN'T WANT to face him. Only after she heard the door slam behind Baba the next morning did Demitra emerge from her room. Tucking her pad under her arm, she walked out into the yard and spotted Stella seated at the table under the olive tree shelling fava beans. The sound of Gerasimos's laughter filled the air as he ran and played between the clothes drying on the line.

"Good morning," Demitra said as she placed her pad on the table. "Can I help?" She did her best to sound cheerful, even as her stomach churned with the memory of Baba's tirade the night before.

"No, thank you," Stella said as she continued working, her head down as she focused on the task. "I'm almost done here."

Demitra inched closer. "Stella." She reached out and placed her hand on Stella's shoulder. Ever so gently, Demitra turned Stella toward her and gasped as they locked eyes.

"It's nothing," Stella said, lifting her hand to her face. "It's nothing, really," she said, her voice quivering. The bruise beneath her eye was deep purple, the eye itself red-tinged and swollen.

"Oh, Stella." Demitra's voice dripped with guilt and sorrow. "He hurt you. I'm so sorry. And it's all because of me. It's my fault. He's angry at me, not you."

"No. It was an accident, a flash of drunken anger. He didn't mean to hurt me."

Martha burst into the yard carrying a basket of freshly picked vegetables.

"Good morning! How is everyone today? Just look at what my garden produced. I tell you, these tomatoes are as big as my head and the sweetest you will ever taste . . ." She chattered on, only stopping when her eyes fell on Stella's face. She dropped the basket and was instantly upon her. "What happened? Are you all right?"

"Oh, it's nothing, Mama. I wasn't paying attention and walked into the door. I'm fine, just clumsy." She laughed as she looked at Demitra, a pleading expression on her face.

"Oh, Mama, these are gorgeous," Stella said. "They will be perfect stuffed with rice and mint. Demitra, you must take some to Olga when you go visit her. And make sure you say an extra prayer for us."

Demitra nodded silently, watching as Stella feigned excitement over the vegetables. In that moment Demitra decided she would not make her annual pilgrimage to visit Olga and the snakes for Panagia's day. She would call Olga and tell her she needed to stay here with Stella.

Since Demitra had returned from Corfu, she sensed a shift in the air. At first she thought she might be imagining it, that Baba's indifference had turned to hostility, but the bruise on Stella's face confirmed it. It was as if something long dormant had finally been unleashed. All her life, Baba had been restrained in his actions and emotions—detached, cold, indifferent. Never once had she feared him, never once had he raised his hand in anger to her. But something was different about him now. Anger filled him, simmering and threatening at all times, seething just under the surface.

And Demitra feared she was the cause of it.

Stella got to work cleaning the vegetables. This was all she wanted from life, all she knew—to serve her husband and family. Stella's joy derived from bringing joy to others. She had likely never known the freedom of racing down the road in a car with the windows down, the delight of sunbathing on the deck of a boat as the sea splashed her face, or the passion and pleasure of making love to a man who made her feel whole and alive.

Even though she had never existed beyond the stifling confines of the village or expressed interest in a life outside of the traditional norms, Stella had not judged Demitra for wanting more. Instead, she helped orchestrate Demitra's escape to Corfu. And then, when Demitra broke down and confessed she'd had an affair with a married man, Stella had not judged or chastised her; she had comforted her and held her close.

Stella looked up from peeling the vegetables to find Demitra watching her. She reached her hand out and placed it on Demitra's and squeezed tight. Perhaps Stella had never craved or asked for more because she never imagined anything more was possible, like a caged bird who had never known the beauty of flight.

DEMITRA WAS WAITING in the garden when Baba stumbled home from the kafeneio. She watched silently from the shadows, and he looked different to her. Once upon a time the sight of him staggering through the door would have sent tremors through her, causing her to worry if he would find the house clean enough, supper hot enough—to wonder if she had done enough to make him happy, to make him proud.

As she watched him stagger home now after spending the precious few drachmas he had to his name on drink, she felt something new and unexpected. He fumbled with the well, struggling to pull up the pail, and the sight of him still made her uneasy, but not as it had before. He was no longer larger than life. He was no longer someone to revere and fear. She was unsure if he had changed but certain that she had.

As she watched him, a drunken old man fumbling for a sip of water, she felt a swirl of emotions toward him—anger, frustration, and, perhaps most surprising of all, pity.

Regardless, she had waited up for him for a reason. She tamped down any empathy his pathetic state elicited and approached him, intent to do what she'd promised herself she would do. Intent on standing up for Stella the way Stella had stood up for her.

"What's wrong with you?" She seethed. "How could you do this?"

"Demitra." He squinted into the darkness. "Come here and help me with the pail. There's something wrong with it," he said as the rope slipped through his hands, sending the pail to the bottom of the well with a splash.

She took two steps closer and faced him, the well between them. "I said, what's wrong with you?" She raged but was mindful of keeping her voice down so she wouldn't wake Stella. "How dare you hit her. She doesn't deserve that."

"You don't know what you're talking about," he slurred as he pulled the pail up again and finally managed to take a drink.

"You hit her. You hurt her. How could you do that?"

He wiped his mouth with his sleeve. "Go to bed." He turned and walked toward the house.

She stood there as he walked away from her, disregarding her as he always had.

"Don't hurt her again. Please, promise me you won't hurt her again. She deserves better." But he was already gone, the door slamming behind him as her words echoed in the stillness of the night air. *We both deserve better.*

Leaning against the well as the cicada song filled the night air and a distant frog's croak kept time with her beating heart, Demitra felt the familiar frustration churning within. Yes, she had changed. She knew with every fiber of her being that she was not the same girl who had escaped to Corfu last year. Sometime between then and now, she had grown up, evolved, and managed to find her voice.

As she stood alone in the darkness, the bitter taste of Baba's disregard so fresh in her mouth, she wondered what was the point of finding her voice if no one was there to listen.

Chapter Twenty-Four

Cephalonia, Greece

1953

THE FOLLOWING MORNING, Demitra woke with a sense of urgency, knowing she needed to speak with Olga as soon as possible. Demitra waited over an hour as the messenger from the periptero ran to the monastery to tell Olga that Demitra needed her to call.

"Don't worry, dear," Areti assured her with a wave of her hands, bent and misshapen from arthritis. "I'll tell anyone who comes that the telephone is broken so your thea can reach you." She smiled a toothless smile, spittle crusting in the corner of her mouth.

"Demitra, what's wrong? Are you all right?" The nun's tone was frantic with worry when the call finally came through.

"Yes, Thea, I'm fine. I didn't mean to scare you."

Olga whispered a prayer of thanks. "What is it, child? The boy told me it was important that I call you right away."

The words poured out of her. "I can't come. I need to stay here with Stella. He hit her, Olga. She says it's nothing, but it's not nothing." Demitra spoke quietly, her back turned to the periptero. As kind and understanding as Areti always was, Demitra did not want her to hear the painful truth. It was hard enough to face the reality of what Baba had done without the scrutiny of village gossip.

"Your father has his demons, and they have haunted him for years. Do you know what happened?" Olga asked.

"He's changed since I came back from Corfu. He's so angry all the time. Part of me wishes I'd never come back; things would have been easier for Stella if I hadn't."

"Oh, Demitra. You are a comfort to Stella, just as you have always been a comfort to me. This is not your fault. Your father changed when your mother died. He's been different ever since he brought you home. It breaks my heart, but your father and Stella's story is not unique. I've cared for dozens of women who have come to the monastery seeking sanctuary, seeking safety. I pray it never happens again, that it was a mistake made in the moment, fueled by a bottle of whisky. Your father is troubled, we know this, but in my heart, I don't think he is like the other men I've seen, who take pleasure in hurting others. I pray I'm right. Stay there. Stay with Stella. I will pray for Pericles, for all of you."

"I'll come visit after Panagia's. I hate to miss the snakes. The times I've seen them with you are some of my happiest memories." Demitra turned then and locked eyes with Areti for a mere moment, catching a gentle, knowing expression on her face before Areti turned away to tend to other business.

"Oh, Demitra." Olga sighed, a deep, heavy sigh. "You are not the only one with news. I have something to tell you as well, my child."

THAT AFTERNOON, DEMITRA sat in her usual spot at the table in the yard, determined to make progress on her new drawing. But each time she put her pencil to paper, each time she attempted to bring life to Athena and the precious olive trees she gifted to the city of Athens, Demitra's mind wandered.

When Stella arrived home with Gerasimos, she finally closed her sketch pad.

Stella placed a glass of chamomile tea with honey beside Demitra as she sat across from her at the table.

"How was your day?" Stella asked, glancing at the closed pad.

"Not very productive, I'm afraid."

"And why is that?" Stella leaned closer, concerned. "Was it your father?" She glanced back toward the house.

"No. I haven't seen him all day. It's not him." She took a sip of her tea before continuing. "I spoke with Olga today, and she had some upsetting news."

Stella inched closer now. "Is she all right? Is she unwell?"

"No, Olga is fine. But she's worried. The snakes haven't come yet. It's four days from the Ascension and the snakes have not come yet."

Stella's face turned ashen. "Oh . . ." She looked off to the horizon, worry etched in every line on her face. "What does Olga think it means?"

"She's not certain. There was a tremor a few days ago, and the quake might have scared them away." Demitra paused, biting her lip. "Or at least, she hopes that might be the case. We still have a few more days, but I can't even think of it. She knew it was an omen last time. What could they possibly be warning us about now?"

Stella looked into the distance as she twisted her apron in her hands until it was knotted. Cicadas filled the silence with their summer chorus, and a donkey brayed in the distance.

After a few moments, Stella placed her hands on the table and sighed. "Olga's not the only one with news," she finally said as she stared into Demitra's eyes. "I have something to tell you as well." Her tone was measured, careful.

"What is it?"

"I saw Elena today."

"You saw her? Where? In town?" Demitra's eyes lit up with concern and curiosity. It had been more than a year since the last time she saw Elena, the pain of that day, and what Nektarios had done, still raw. She'd thought about Elena so many times since then, wondering if she was well, hoping she might catch a glimpse of her once more from the bluff, praying she might once again hear the sweet sound of her laughter on the breeze.

"I did more than see her, Demitra. I spoke with her. I went to see her, to take her food as I've been doing for months now. But this time was different. This time she let me in."

"She let you in?" Demitra's eyes widened.

"Yes. She let me in. I started going to her house soon after you left for Corfu. No one in town had seen her for ages, and I wondered if she was all right. It was like you told me when you tried to visit her; she was inside, but she never opened the door. She never responded. Never said a word. I began taking her food, leaving dishes outside the door for her. When I returned, the plates were empty, washed, and stacked. But she never spoke to me or acknowledged me or let me in." Stella paused. "Until today."

"What happened? How did you get her to open the door?"

"I stood outside the door like I always have and spoke to her. I offered her help. I offered her food. I even told her I know what it is to be hurt by someone you put your trust in. And then I told her about you, that you are back and that you are so talented. But that wasn't what did it, Demitra. That's not why she opened the door."

"What then?"

"I told her about Gerasimos. I just talked and talked and told her I have a son and that he's four years old and a jumble of energy and my greatest joy in life. That was when I heard her crying inside the house. And then the door opened."

"What did she say?" Demitra was breathless with anticipation.

"She stood there before me, tears streaming down her face. She was frail and so very thin, as if a gust of wind would knock her over. And she looked at me with those haunted eyes and she said, 'I had a child too.'" Stella's voice cracked.

"She has a child?" Demitra's mind was racing. "She had a baby? But when? Who is the father?"

Stella looked out toward the horizon and took a deep breath before continuing.

"No, Demitra. She said, 'I had a child too. Before they stole her from me.'"

Chapter Twenty-Five

Cephalonia, Greece

1952

THE PAIN CAME fast, faster than she'd anticipated. She walked, cradling her belly, until she could walk no more, her body splitting in two. The pain was so deep and low, reverberating through each fiber of her body. She leaned over, grabbing the edge of the table.

The pain subsided for a moment, but she knew it would return and quicker next time. She inched her way to the bed and managed to lay her head on her pillow just as the wave of pain wrecked her body again. She screamed, asking God to help her, to show mercy on her child. It was not its fault its mother was who she was.

"Dear God, where is the doctor? Why isn't he here?" It had been hours since she'd summoned the shepherd boy who lived just up the mountain and asked him to bring the doctor.

At last she heard the knock. The door opened before she could respond.

"Elena, it's Dr. Thomas. Lie back please. I'm going to examine you . . . It appears as if you are going to have a baby. And likely quite soon."

"Please, please help me. Please help my baby," she sobbed.

It took all of her strength, but Elena lifted her head to look at the doctor. She was crying now. She had been so scared and so alone these past several months. So many times she had been tempted to open the door for Stella. She, like her stepdaughter, Demitra, had shown her such kindness. But Elena was ashamed, so very ashamed. What right did she have to bring an innocent child into this world? She knew quite well what it was to have a mother who lay on her back for the entertainment of men. What kind of mother could she possibly be?

"It won't be long now," the doctor said as he examined her. "Take a few breaths in and out. And when I tell you, I want you to push."

The pressure came again, the pain radiating deep within her body so harsh she thought she might faint. And then, a primal urge. She knew what she needed to do before the doctor could speak the words.

"Now push," he commanded, but she was already pushing, using all of her strength.

She pushed five more times, hallucinating from the pain, feeling herself fading in and out of consciousness. She was no longer there; she was on the beach with her redheaded soldier. He held his hand out to her and they danced together on the sand as the gentle sea lapped at her ankles. And the girl was there too, Demitra. She was drawing them, a beautiful portrait, showing them so happy, smiling, dancing . . . and then the pain yanked her back from the beach, to her reality.

A primal scream filled the room. It took a moment before she realized it was her own.

"Push. One more push," the doctor commanded.

She screamed again, pushing with all the strength that remained in her body. Pain seared as her flesh stretched and tore.

In an instant it was over. The baby slipped out of her body and into the arms of the doctor.

She was panting, and time seemed to stand still. The room was silent.

The doctor was huddled over the baby, but she could see nothing but the back of its head.

Please, God, please. Why isn't my baby crying? Why is my child still silent?

All these months she'd hidden away in the house, she'd craved silence. And now she was desperate for a cry, a scream, anything to break the quiet.

And then she heard it. The room was filled with the most beautiful sound she had ever heard. The piercing wail of her child.

The doctor walked back over to where she lay in the bed amid the blood and tangled sheets and afterbirth and handed her the baby.

"You have a daughter," he said and placed the baby in her arms.

She was perfect. A tiny pink bundle with rosebud lips and full cheeks. As Elena looked down on her, it was as if her entire life fell into place. It did not matter who she was before, what she was before. Her life began now. She was born again, along with her daughter, the moment she took her first breath.

Elena touched her pink cheek, tracing her finger across her brow, down the tiny nose, and to her perfect lips. Instantly, she opened her mouth and began to suck. And Elena knew what she would do.

Once she got her strength back, she would leave Cephalonia and go home, back to Italy. The man in the employment office had been so wrong about her, but she had not realized it until this very moment. She was not who he had labeled her to be. She was not who he had destined her to be. She was none of those things. Perhaps she had been at one time, but not any longer.

She was Emanuella's mother.

She had a child and a duty and a responsibility and a reason to live. She would be a mother her daughter could depend on, a mother Emanuella could be proud of.

"You've lost a lot of blood," the doctor said as he placed his fingers on her wrist and fell silent, nodding as he counted. He then took the baby from her arms and placed her beside Elena on the bed. She felt lightheaded and weak but did not want to sleep, wanting only to gaze at her child, to watch her tiny chest rise and fall with each breath.

"You're weak," the doctor said. "I'm concerned you won't be able to do this alone, to take care of her in your condition."

"Stella. Please, Doctor, send for Stella. She told me to call on her if I ever needed her. She will help me. She'll come and she'll help me until I get my strength back."

"Very well, then," the doctor said as he closed his satchel. "I'll send for Stella."

She found herself drifting off to sleep, comforted by the thought that Emanuella was safe beside her and Stella would be there when she woke.

THE ROOM WAS dark and quiet when Elena opened her eyes. She blinked against the darkness, disoriented.

How is this possible? It was midmorning when she gave birth. How was it dark already? And why was the room so still and quiet?

She looked beside her at an empty space where Emanuella had been. She shot up, panic washing over her. Then she saw her, seated at the table, silhouetted against the orange glow of the fire.

"Thank you for coming," she said. "I'm so sorry to bother you. But you said to let you know if I need anything. And I do. I need help right now. But just until I get my strength back." She reached her arms out. "She must be hungry. Will you bring her to me, please?"

The woman stood and walked toward the bed, but the baby was not in her arms.

"Bring her to me, please," Elena repeated.

As she walked closer to the bed, the light from the fire illuminated her face. Elena blinked several times, not comprehending what she was seeing.

The woman before her was not Stella. It was Irene, Nektarios's wife.

She had never met the woman, but she had seen her before. Each time she passed the bakery, she had seen her there tending to customers. And there had been times, as Elena passed, that she could have sworn she felt the burning of Irene's gaze on her, just as she had felt the force of her husband's hands on her neck.

"Where is she?" Panic rose in Elena's voice. "Where is she? Please . . ." She shifted herself in the bed, swinging her legs over the side to stand, but as she tried, her legs gave out from under her and she had to grab the bed again to keep from falling.

Irene stood in place a couple of feet away, making no movement toward her, offering no help.

"Where is she?" Elena regained her balance, feeling her way from the bed along the wall.

"She's gone," Irene said, her voice without emotion, her arms crossed.

"What do you mean she's gone?" Elena was crying and tearing at her clothes and hair. "Give her to me. She's hungry. She needs her mother."

"She's gone. She died in her sleep, as newborns do sometimes." Her tone was flat, devoid of any emotion or sympathy.

"No. That's not true." Elena fell to her knees, her arms reaching out toward Irene, begging for the truth, begging for mercy, begging for the lies to stop.

"It's best that you accept it and pray to God for her soul, and for yours," Irene said as she took a step closer to Elena, who was writhing on the floor, howling as she tore at her hair and clothing.

A look of disgust crossed Irene's face.

"Do yourself a favor and leave this place. You don't belong here. You never did." Irene tossed a handful of drachmas on the table on her way to the door. "There's enough for passage back to Italy. It's best if you go. For all of us." She turned and looked at Elena one last time as if she were nothing more than a dead animal in the road.

"No!" Elena screamed. "Where is she? Where is my child? Dear God, help me, please. Where is my child?"

Irene did not answer her as she walked out the door. Elena convulsed in sobs as she watched the door close. She gasped for breath as she heaved uncontrollably. Then she curled up on the floor, her legs still stained from childbirth, her insides still raw and burning from where she had given life to her child.

Her child. Her daughter.

"No, no, no," she sobbed. Irene was right; there was nothing left for her.

There was nothing left *of* her.

Chapter Twenty-Six

Cephalonia, Greece

August 1953

Isn't there another way?" Demitra asked as she walked side by side with Stella along the dirt path into town. If they continued on this path, they would pass outside the bakery. Demitra's stomach clenched at the thought of seeing Niko and his parents.

"There is, but it's longer and not shaded, and I, for one, am tired and hot and have nothing to hide or be ashamed of, so we are taking the shorter, cooler path through town." Stella turned to face Demitra and slid her hand through Demitra's arm.

"I don't have the strength to face anyone," Demitra disclosed to Stella as they walked.

"Let me be your strength. Sometimes when we don't have enough, the ones who love us most will share theirs, and I'm feeling particularly strong today. Tomorrow, when it's my turn to have a moment and break down, you'll be strong enough for me." Stella pulled Demitra closer to her.

Up ahead, Gerasimos ran toward the beach where they spotted a group of boys playing on the sand.

"Mama, can I go play?" he turned and asked, his face flushed.

"Of course, my love. Just make sure you are home for lunch. When the sun is directly above the cliff, just above the beach and dunes, you know it's time to come home."

"Thank you, Mama," he said as he sprinted off toward the beach to join his friends.

Stella carried a long bamboo stick in her free hand, using it to tap the ground as they walked. She had explained long ago that the tapping noise kept snakes away.

"Does it worry you, what Olga said about the snakes?" Demitra asked. "Do you really think they could be warning us again? And about what?"

"To be honest, I can't bear to think of it, Demitra. This talk of omens and signs. How could we be punished further? Have we not been through enough?" Stella lifted her bamboo stick before tapping it back down with force. "Dear Lord, please let Panagia's snakes make their appearance, but please keep these snakes along our path hidden, at least while we are walking." She tapped the stick with more force. "Thank you." She winked to the heavens, then smiled at Demitra.

"Stella, you are a gift. I don't know what I did to deserve you in my life. You saved me when you married Baba, and you're saving me even now."

"I think we saved each other," Stella corrected and placed a kiss on Demitra's cheek as they approached town on their way to see Elena.

"Is that . . . ?" Demitra was confused as they continued toward the bakery. The sign out front read *Irene's Bakery and Rooms to Let*. Where there was once an empty patch of earth now stood four tidy bougainvillea-covered villas surrounding a swimming pool. Farther down the property, dozens of pine and cypress trees had been cut down, affording the villas an unobstructed view of the brilliant azure sea framed by the lush greenery of the island.

As they walked past, Demitra held her head high, smiling and laughing as Stella chattered about the weather and what she would make for dinner. Demitra made every effort to look straight ahead and not into the window or through the open door of the bakery.

It felt like forever, but soon they were beyond the bakery and Demitra finally exhaled. Then she had an unmistakable feeling of eyes staring into her back, tracking her as she walked.

"You feel it too, don't you?" Demitra asked, knowing Stella would understand.

"Yes. Yes, I do. Just keep walking," Stella said, then tipped her head back and laughed as if Demitra had said something uproariously funny.

Demitra turned to glance behind them and caught a glimpse of Irene slipping back into the bakery.

As they continued walking and made their way up the mountainside, a wave of memory washed over Demitra. She would never forget that day, the shock and pain of witnessing the cruelty that men are capable of.

I should have known then . . .

The house itself was as she remembered it, the small garden out back, the potted herbs at the front door, and the laundry drying on the line.

"It's been over a year since you've seen her, and she has been through so much. Be prepared. She looks different than she did then." Stella exhaled. "Everything's different now."

As they stepped up to the door, Stella glanced at Demitra. She gave a slight nod and a smile and then knocked.

"Elena, it's Stella. Demitra is here with me."

The sound of footsteps and shuffling came from within the house. And then the door opened. Demitra did her best to conceal her shock, internalizing to the best of her ability the grief that filled her, grateful Stella had prepared her. She forced a smile.

"Hi, Elena. It's so good to see you after all this time."

As Demitra gazed upon the woman before her, it was clear that the Elena she so fondly remembered no longer existed. There was nothing left of the beautiful young woman from the beach—her blonde hair, red lips, and smile a distant memory. The Elena of the bluff was lost, snuffed out by years of disappointment, disillusion, and the reality of how cruel people can be to one another. The Elena who stood across from Demitra was a broken woman, her hair brittle and hanging to her shoulders in limp wisps, her cheeks hollow, and her lips thin and scabbed.

Elena motioned for them to come in and take a seat at the table. Demitra glanced up to see both of the portraits were still tacked to the wall.

"You still have them," she said. "Your portraits."

"Yes." Even her voice, low and hoarse, held no memory of the Elena Demitra remembered, the lilting, rapid Italian now replaced with tentative Greek. "I never thanked you. I never told you what those pictures meant to me—what they mean to me."

"It was my pleasure. I remember being so moved by you, by how beautiful you were and how that beauty brought so much joy into the soldiers' lives—into my life."

"That girl is gone. What you captured was the last day she existed." Elena shook her head and glanced around the room as if she could see the ghosts of all those who'd hurt her, there, among them.

Stella reached her hand across the table and placed it on Elena's.

"You can tell her. You can tell Demitra your story. We'll do everything we can to help you."

Elena's face seemed to crumble before Demitra's eyes. The frail, broken woman was shattered beyond recognition. She closed her eyes again and breathed deeply in and out several times, as if gathering strength. When she opened her eyes again, she looked once more at Stella, who gave a slight nod.

"I had a daughter. Her name was Emanuella. And she was beautiful." Elena's lips were so pale, barely moving as she spoke.

"My baby was perfect. She was beautiful with pink cheeks and a strong cry. She was strong and she was alive." Elena closed her eyes, a faint smile finding its way to her lips as she conjured the image of her daughter.

"She slept peacefully beside me, there in the bed. I knew I was weak. I knew I needed help. I asked the doctor to send for Stella. Besides you, Stella is the only woman here to show me kindness. I knew I could trust her, that she would help me. When I woke, the doctor was gone and Irene was here, seated there in front of the fire." She glanced at Stella with a longing in her eyes.

"Irene told me my baby was dead. She said that sometimes newborns die. She said my daughter was gone."

It was one thing to lie about who the father of her own child was. It was another to hide the truth of her son's disability in order to secure him a wife. But to steal another woman's child, to lie to a mother about the death of her child? Demitra's mind was spinning. How could anyone be capable of such evil?

"And you don't believe her?" Demitra asked. She needed to hear Elena speak the words she already believed to be true.

Elena's response was instant. "No. I don't believe her. She's lying. My baby was not sick. My baby did not die. My baby was stolen."

Demitra digested this information, this cruelty.

"Elena, now that Niko is married, do you think . . . ?" Demitra weighed her words very carefully. "Could Irene have taken Emanuella to pass off as Niko and Tina's?"

Elena nodded slowly. "That's what I thought at first. That's what I prayed had happened. Nektarios is Emanuella's father, and I'm sure Irene knows it. I was so careful." A single tear left a slick path down her face. She made no effort to wipe it away. "For months I hoarded what supplies I might need, and I hid here on the mountain, not wanting to draw attention to myself or to the child growing in my belly. I thought that could protect us. But Irene knew. She knew about my child, just as she knew everything. There were times I could feel her there, outside the door. Sometimes even as I slept, even in the darkest hours of the night, I could feel her presence. I knew she was watching my house, watching me, knowing her husband's child was growing in my belly."

"Did you tell anyone? Did you go to the police?" Demitra asked.

Stella shook her head, answering for Elena. "What good would that have done? Who would believe her? Irene and Nektarios have fed the entire police department for years. Why would they believe Elena?"

Elena nodded in agreement. "At first I thought the same thing you did, that they would send Tina away and have her return with a child, claiming Emanuella as her own. But it's been a year now, and there is nothing. Tina is here, her belly flat, her arms empty. There is no sign of my child or any child." Elena's face crumpled, her tears forging wild paths down her face. "Where is my daughter? What did they do with my daughter?"

They sat in silence. No one had the answer. No one had the words to soothe Elena. It seemed impossible that such words could exist.

After a while, Elena broke the silence.

"I need to ask you something." She leaned in closer to Demitra as she wrung her hands.

"Yes. Of course. Anything," Demitra replied.

Elena glanced at the portraits tacked to the wall before turning her attention again to Demitra. "That day, the day you delivered the second portrait . . ." Elena's voice trailed off as she gathered her thoughts.

"Yes."

"That day, when you were here on my doorstep and slipped the picture under my door, did you see what Nektarios did to me? Did you see us through the window? Is that why you scribbled 'I'm so sorry' on the paper?"

The memories of that day came rushing back to Demitra. The confusion. The pain. Niko's warning, *"Don't let him see you."*

She nodded. "Yes. I did. I saw . . . I saw everything."

Elena closed her eyes, digesting the information as she brought her hands together in prayer. When she opened them again, her steely gaze focused on Demitra.

"I hated him, not for what he did to me but for what he did to that sweet boy. Niko didn't deserve to be treated that way. That kind young man deserved better. That was the moment I began to hate him. When I watched how he treated Niko. And then, when I saw your portrait under the door, I realized what it all meant— that it wasn't just Niko and me that monster hurt. He hurt you as well."

Outside the cicadas began their song, filling the stillness of the morning with the softest hum carried on the breeze, building steadily louder and stronger as if the entire mountainside were alive and vibrating with their chorus. As the song died down, Elena spoke again.

"That was the day . . ." She stared off into the empty space of painful memories. "That was the day I learned what hatred is. That was the day I should have killed him."

Chapter Twenty-Seven

Cephalonia, Greece

1953

D EMITRA SAT AT the table in Martha's kitchen tying the last of the oregano sprigs with twine. The kitchen was filled with the comforting aromas of freshly brewed coffee, bread baking in the hearth, and enough freshly picked oregano to last through the winter. They had been up since before dawn and in place on the mountain as the sun rose, painting the sky in sumptuous hues of pink and orange. Martha had burst into the house late the afternoon before, just after Demitra and Stella returned from Elena's, breathlessly ranting about the urgent need to pick the oregano after she'd noticed that some of the plants had already begun to flower.

"Oh, Demitra, thank you for your help this morning," Martha said as she placed a demitasse of coffee and a biscuit on the table before her. "The plants never flower this early, and I never would have noticed had my stubborn goat not wandered up the mountain yesterday. I bet Irene's too busy showing off her new bakery to even notice the flowers. Serves her right, and it's only fitting she'll have bitter oregano."

Demitra and Stella glanced at each other. They had not spoken a word of Elena's story to Martha, nor would they. It was one thing for Martha and Irene to have a lifelong rivalry about who was the better cook or whose oregano was more fragrant, but it was quite another to know that Irene was capable of something as insidious as stealing a newborn from its mother. Until they found a way to help Elena, Demitra and Stella agreed it was best to keep the information to themselves.

After she bundled and tied the last of the oregano, Demitra finished her coffee in one final sip. She tilted the cup this way and that, contemplating the grounds as the old women in the village did, wondering if it was possible that her fate could be revealed within the muddy sediment. But as she peered inside, Demitra saw nothing but sludge. She placed the cup in its saucer upside down, like she had seen some of the old widows do, hoping this might entice the grounds to reveal her fate.

Stella was at her side instantly, placing a knowing hand on her shoulder.

"What dress will you wear to the panagiri?" Martha asked as she set another biscuit on Demitra's plate.

"I think you should wear the blue," Stella responded. "You know how I love that color against your skin."

"I'm not going to the panagiri," Demitra blurted, bracing for what was sure to come next.

"What do you mean, you're not going?" Martha demanded as she untied her apron and tossed it on the table. "Why wouldn't you go? First your father locks himself away, drinking alone day and night instead of taking any time with his family, with his village, and now you?"

"I'm just not in a festive mood," Demitra replied as she picked up her cup and peered inside once more. Again, the grounds revealed nothing more than a muddy mess.

"You have to go. The whole village will be there," Martha chided as she waved her arms at Stella, encouraging her to chime in. Stella said nothing, averting her eyes and pretending to be consumed with sweeping the floor.

Before Martha could continue, Gerasimos came bounding through the door, a bundle of energy with a confused expression.

"What's wrong with the chickens today?" he asked. "They're so loud it made my ears hurt." He placed his hands over his ears and stuck out his tongue.

Martha gazed out the widow toward the coop. "Let me see what's going on over there. Why, just yesterday Sia's feral grandson scared my goat up the mountain. I'll beat his bottom if he's in there bothering my chickens. Keep an eye on that bread, Stella. You know you have a tendency to burn it." Martha pointed her wooden spoon toward the hearth before going outside to check on the chickens.

"Mama, can I go meet my friends at the beach, please?" Gerasimos asked as Stella slathered a piece of bread with a generous portion of honey.

"Of course, my love." Stella tousled his hair and handed him the treat, which he devoured in seconds.

Demitra stood, extending her hand to Gerasimos. "Come on, I'll walk with you. I'm going to head home and get some work done." She took his hand in hers. "Oh, that's sticky." She laughed.

"I see what you're doing." Stella narrowed her eyes. "Go ahead, make your escape before Mama comes back." She shooed them both out the door.

"You know me so well," Demitra called over her shoulder, laughing as she and Gerasimos made their escape.

They walked hand in hand down the dirt path, Demitra tapping with a bamboo stick to scare the snakes away.

"I'm learning the zeibekiko. Wanna see?" Gerasimos twirled around and around, slapping his foot and jumping in the air, showing off his skills before she could respond.

"Bravo!" Demitra clapped, cheering and whistling for him. "Bravo! You are a fine dancer, my brother. An excellent dancer." She tapped his nose with her finger, his bright brown eyes wide and shining.

"I'm going to dance at the panagiri. Will you throw money at me when I dance?"

She decided that despite wanting nothing more than to hide away alone, she would summon the strength to attend. After all, what were the stares and whispers of the village gossips compared to the delight of watching her little brother's performance?

"Gerasimos, I'm sure yours will be the best dance of the night and you'll make tons and tons of money. I remember watching Baba dance the zeibekiko the day he married your mama."

Gerasimos's eyes widened. "Do you think he'll come? Do you think he'll come and watch me dance? Or maybe he'll dance with me? That would be so much fun. Imagine all the money people will throw at us then!"

She stopped in the middle of the path, watching as her young brother's sweet face lit up with hopeful excitement. She was reminded then that she and Stella were not the only collateral damage of the war raging inside Baba, the demons that kept him from the simple joys of life, like playing with his son or taking the time to watch him dance.

"Look!" Gerasimos shouted as she spotted a gaggle of boys playing farther down the beach.

"Go on. Have fun. I'll see you at home." She shooed him off, watching as he sprinted toward his friends.

As she walked, droplets of perspiration formed on her brow and above her lip. Her blouse stuck to her uncomfortably and she could feel the wetness dripping down her back. She considered making a quick stop at the freshwater spring to have a drink and cool off, but then thought better of it. As tempting as a visit to the spring was, she would likely run into people she did not want to see and be asked questions she did not want to answer.

Above her, a large flock of birds flew over the pines and cypresses, their squawks echoing off the cliffs. For a moment the birds resembled a large black cloud, darkening the sky.

The road curved to the left just before the olive grove adjacent to their house. Even from the distance, she could see the flowers Stella had planted and tended with such meticulous care. The pots, bursting with color and fragrance, brought the garden and home to life. As she soaked in the beauty of the home Stella had transformed, Demitra thought of something she could do to bring a smile to Stella's face.

Her pace quickened as the image came to vivid life in her mind. She would draw the house and garden that Stella had infused with life and love since the moment she'd crossed the threshold on her wedding night. Each plant, flower, and bloom would come to life on the page, along with the ever-present laundry billowing on the breeze while Gerasimos laughed and played and ran between the fluttering sheets.

When she reached the house, Demitra dashed inside, eager to make the most of the quiet while she had the house to herself.

She grabbed her pad and pencils from her room and then went to the closet in search of an old cotton shift that would be much cooler and more comfortable in the oppressive August heat. She was in such a rush to change and get started that she carelessly tugged at the rack, sending several articles of clothing spilling to the ground. Exasperated, she gathered them all in her arms and hastily began hanging them and putting them back in their place.

As she picked up Baba's old coat from the floor, she noticed that the lining was torn and frayed. Demitra looked closer, running her finger along the seam. She could save Stella the trouble and mend it herself. As she was examining the tear, her fingers felt something in the lining. She dipped her hand inside and pulled out an envelope. Slipping her fingers inside, she felt a piece of paper and something hard and round.

Demitra choked with emotion as she held the object up to the light. It was a thin band of gold, a wedding ring. She regarded the ring as she traced her fingers along the smooth metal, at once delicate and impenetrable. *Mama's ring.* This was the ring that bound them together by God. This was the ring Mama wore as she cradled her baby in her arms, as she plaited Demitra's hair, as she held her tiny hand and wiped away her tears.

This was the ring Baba had slipped from her finger before her cold body was returned to the earth.

Why would he keep her ring hidden away, out of sight? Just as he'd kept his memories of Mama secreted away. She had asked him so many times in so many ways to share any small piece of Mama with her, anxious for any token or memory he might impart. But Baba never did. He kept his memories locked in the dark recesses of his mind, just as he'd kept her wedding band hidden in the lining of an old coat. Demitra held up her hand to the light and placed the ring on her own finger, regarding it in wonder, imagining what it looked like on Mama's hand.

She dipped her hand back in the envelope and pulled out a yellowed paper. It was torn with ragged edges.

Welcome to Our Parish

THURSDAY, MARCH 12, 8:00 P.M. CHURCH
HALL—MEETING OF AHEPA

Please join in fellowship for a meeting of the American Hellenic Educational Progressive Association. Since its formation in 1922 against the targeted racism, bigotry, and violence endured by Greek immigrants at the hands of the KKK, AHEPA has worked to uphold and promote the ideals of Hellenism while helping our brothers assimilate to American culture and society. With the recent uptick of KKK activity in the area targeting Greek-owned businesses, we hope you will join us as we unite to educate and discuss our plan of action.

Demitra scanned the page, confused as to why Baba would have this paper hidden. Although it was written in Greek, it appeared to be from an American church or newspaper, as she was unfamiliar with the words *AHEPA* and *KKK*.

She folded it up again to place it back in the coat when her eyes fell on the notice on the back of the page. Scanning the headline, she instantly felt disquieting flutters in her belly traveling up into her throat.

MONDAY, MARCH 16, FUNERAL OF MARIA
DIMITROPOULOS OF BLESSED MEMORY

It is with deep sorrow that we announce the passing of our sister Maria Dimitropoulos. Maria was a beloved member of our community and a devoted teacher at our Greek school. Maria's love for the youngest members of our community was legendary, as she spent hours teaching them the songs, stories, and games of her childhood in the mountains of Thessaly and instilling in our children a love for Greek language and culture. May her memory be a blessing.

Mama. This was Mama's funeral notice. Demitra stumbled back as she saw Mama's name written in black and white on the page. She had never held anything before that tied her to Mama in such a way. She lifted the paper to her cheek and then pulled it away, not wanting her tears to damage the words.

Mama was a teacher. A teacher of small children. She tried to imagine her singing to them and playing with them, sharing the songs and stories of her childhood. She imagined herself there with Mama and the other children as they sang and played. She had often wondered where Mama was born, where she had spent her childhood and how. *Thessaly.* Demitra closed her eyes and thought of Mama as a child, running and playing in the mountaintop villages of central Greece.

As she sat there, transfixed by her mother's name, the door sprang open. Startled, Demitra jumped to her feet, the paper still in her hand. She looked up to see Baba stomping into the house.

"Stella!" he shouted. "I need my other work pants. These have a tear and I can't spend the day painting the church with my ass hanging out of my pants." His tone dripped with annoyance.

"What's wrong with you?" he asked when his eyes landed on Demitra. "Why are you just standing there, and why is there a mess all over the floor?" He looked around the room. "Where's Stella?"

Demitra did not move.

He took a step toward her and then looked at the yellowed paper in her hand, then at his coat in a heap on the floor. She watched his expression change in a flash from annoyance to shock to anger.

Demitra held out the paper toward him. "What is this?"

"It's nothing that concerns you." His eyes narrowed.

"It's not nothing. This is about my mother's funeral." The paper quivered in her hand.

He snatched it away and his eyes fell on the gold band she wore on her finger. She watched as fresh rage erupted on his face.

"You have no business going through my things!" he yelled as he turned away from her, crumpling the paper and shoving it into his pocket.

She walked toward him, reached her hand out, and placed it on his shoulder. "Baba. Please."

He recoiled from her touch, shook her hand off his body, and walked away from her toward the door.

"Please, Baba. I need to know," she pleaded with him, her voice vibrating with emotion. Still he did not turn to face her.

"For my whole life you never wanted to talk about her, never shared her with me. I learned more about my mother from that old paper than I have from you. You can't just erase her like this. It won't make her go away. It won't make me go away." A storm of emotions unleashed in her then, frustration and anger simmering and boiling over. The idea that her mother's relics, the only things she had ever held, were hidden away from her in a dark closet all these years, released something unexpected in her.

"Why do you hate her?" Anger filled her voice as she cried, and she took a moment to wipe her eyes and nose with her sleeve. Her shoulders fell and her voice softened as she addressed him again, pain and longing steeped in every syllable. "Why do you hate *me*?"

As her tone transformed, a metamorphosis took place in Baba as well. Standing before her with his back to her, Baba appeared damaged, a relic of a man. Bones, sinew, and skin conjured to life with disappointment, regret, and rage, all saturated by a bottle of whisky.

"Please." Despite it all, she did not hate him. All she had ever wanted was for him to show her some kindness.

"You kept her from me my entire life. Please don't keep her from me now. What happened to her? Why did she die so young?"

"You have no idea . . . ," he began in a tone she did not recognize. This was not the bombastic man who'd raised her. This was a broken man. "You'll never understand. None of you will ever understand."

Demitra took a deep breath and walked toward him. "Then help me understand. I want to understand. I'm not a child any longer. I know how hard this has been for you. And I'm sorry. I'm sorry for what happened to her. I'm sorry you were left alone to raise me." She squeezed her eyes shut, but it did no good. The tears found their way. And then she said out loud what she had whispered into her pillow so many times, what she imagined he had thought countless times as well.

"I'm sorry I was ever born. I wish I was never born."

He turned to face her. She watched as her words seemed to hit with exacting precision. She watched as his face, typically emotionless and hard, dissolved into something she had never seen in him before.

"No. Don't say that. You were our miracle."

He took two steps toward her. "You were the greatest joy of our lives."

He was nearly beside her when the air filled with a deep churning noise. It sounded like thunder, but Demitra knew instinctively it was not.

She stumbled, the ground rising beneath her feet.

Nothing made sense. All around the sounds of cracking and popping filled the air as she struggled to keep her balance and the floor seemed to fall away and yet rise beneath her at the same time.

As the earth rocked and tilted, the house itself began to crumble. Noises came from all around, things snapping and breaking as if the earth were splitting open, readying to swallow her.

Oh dear God. It's an earthquake. The tremors. The snakes. This was the omen. We are going to die here, together, in this house.

Somehow she managed to keep her footing as the ground swayed and swelled again. Darkness was all around as the dirt and soot and dust filled the air, obscuring any daylight.

She heard a scream and a cry, not recognizing the sound of her own voice.

"Baba!" she cried again into the darkness.

She suddenly felt herself pushed back with a force unlike any she had ever known, and then Baba's voice pierced the rumbling.

"Aphrodite!" he shouted. "Aphrodite, no!" he screamed.

Demitra tried to maintain her balance, but it was impossible.

Was someone else there with them? Who was Aphrodite?

Before she could ask, she fell hard to the floor, pain reverberating through her body. She lay flat, but the floor was no longer a floor. The ground was now like the sea, alive and angry as it churned and roiled and shifted beneath her body, tossing her as if she were a feather floating on its surface.

"Baba!" she screamed into the darkness one last time as debris fell all around her, and then everything went black.

Chapter Twenty-Eight

ELENA HEARD THE roar when she was outside gathering figs. Like everyone across the island, across the Ionian, she had felt the earth tremble in the previous weeks, but somehow she knew that this was different.

The mountain itself seemed to be alive, coughing and sputtering as if waking from deep slumber, intent on expelling something from its lungs. The roar intensified and the earth tilted and shifted and rolled beneath her feet. She needed to brace herself, to grab something that would anchor her.

Frantic, she scoured the mountainside, and her eyes fell on an olive tree. She must get to the tree and wrap herself around its trunk, then pray its ancient wisdom would keep her rooted. She ran and pressed her body and cheek against the rough bark as she would a lover.

The tree wavered and rattled, but it did not break. It did not discard Elena or recoil from her embrace.

This is the end. This is how I will die.

The earth shrieked and bellowed, then another sound filled Elena's ears. Although her eyes were shut, an image came to her, as clear as if it were in front of her. Some might have called it a dream, others an omen or a vision, but for Elena, it was merely the truth.

Emanuella.

She heard the sound of her child crying, strong and full of life. She could see her, as clearly as the moment the doctor placed her in her arms—pink cheeks, dark inquisitive eyes. In that moment as she floated between this life and the next, Elena knew with certainty that her child was alive.

The earth continued to roar and tremble, and Elena knew she could not succumb. She would not give in. She would not let go of the life-giving tree.

All across Cephalonia, homes, buildings, roads, and mountain-sides crumbled, hundreds of people lost in the rubble, yet Elena felt reborn, infused with new purpose.

Dear God, please, please let me survive this, she prayed. *Please let me survive so I can find my baby. I know she's alive and I won't rest until I find her.*

And then the earth was still again.

Chapter Twenty-Nine

D O YOU THINK we have enough?" Stella asked as she scanned the table. After the last of the oregano was bundled and Demitra and Gerasimos went off together, Stella had gone to the garden to pick vegetables for briam, knowing that it was a favorite of Demitra's.

"Of course." Martha laughed. "She's one tiny girl. How much do you expect her to eat?"

"Did you hear that?" Stella lifted her head when she heard the rumble. A moment later there was no mistaking the sound as the ground trembled and the house shook.

"Mama, get out! We have to get out!" Stella jumped up from the table, grabbed Martha's hand, and began running to the door. The house tipped and tilted, tossing them across the room like rag dolls. Stella lost hold of her mother's hand. The floor seemed to rise up and drop suddenly, slamming both women to the ground where they slid across the room.

"Mama!" Stella shouted as she managed to gain her feet again and reached out for her mother. But Martha did not raise her hand toward her daughter. She did not answer to her name, and she did not open her eyes from where the force of her fall had slammed her head against the hearth.

"Mama, get up!" Stella shrieked.

She began stumbling toward Martha, inching along the wall as she struggled to keep her balance. The floor continued shifting and kicking like a wild horse intent on bucking her off. At last she managed to crawl to Martha, who lay still and silent.

Stella fell to her knees beside her mother, begging, praying. "Dear God, please help us. Please. Mama?"

Stella looked around, panicked. "Help! Please. Somebody, help!" Her cries were drowned out by the thunderous howls of the earth.

"Mama?" Stella touched her mother's head, then recoiled as she pulled her fingers away soaked with blood.

She stared at her hand in disbelief, then felt Martha's hand on her leg. Martha's eyes fluttered open as the blood pooling beneath her head grew, a crimson pool fanning out farther by the second.

"Mama. Let me help you. We have to go. We have to get out," Stella pleaded.

Martha's voice was a mere whisper. "Leave me, child. Leave me. Get out of the house."

"I can't leave you. I won't!" Stella yelled as she pulled and tugged, trying to force Martha to her feet.

But it was no use.

As the life drained from her, Martha used her last breaths to impart a final piece of wisdom to her daughter.

"Gerasimos needs you. Demitra needs you. Love them. Watch over them. I've lived my life. Leave me here. I love you, my beautiful girl, but our children need you more. Please, get out. Get out and be a mother to them."

It was nearly impossible to hear amid the thunderous chaos all around them. But Stella understood fully. As she had for her entire life, Stella knew that her mother's wisdom would guide her at this critical hour, just as it had throughout her life.

"Gerasimos!" His name escaped Stella's lips like a sob. The pool of blood grew larger under Martha's head. Her eyes were closed now.

I have to leave her. I have to get out. Gerasimos. Demitra.

"I love you, Mama," she whispered.

Then Stella pulled herself to standing, leaning her hands on the hearth to steady herself.

"Gerasimos." The earth continued to churn and shake. The house trembled as she stumbled toward the door.

"Gerasimos."

Then Stella screamed as the house pitched violently, daylight turned to night, and the walls and ceiling caved in all around her.

Chapter Thirty

NOTHING MADE SENSE.

It could have been mere moments or hours or days. Demitra did not know.

She was on her back. Her head pounded. Her body ached. Her chest burned as if sand had been poured down her throat.

Fear. She felt fear with every fiber of her being, but what she was afraid of, she wasn't certain.

The images came back to her in fractured moments. Mama's wedding ring on her finger. Mama's funeral announcement. Baba's anger. Baba's transformation before her very eyes.

"I'm sorry I was ever born. I wish I was never born."

"No. Don't say that. You were our miracle," he'd cried. And then as he walked toward her, the world shook all around them.

He had called a name, not her name but another name. *"Aphrodite!"* he shouted before running toward her and shoving her back just as the thunderous sound came again and everything went to black.

Aphrodite.

Who was Aphrodite?

An urge came then. She needed to open her eyes but was gripped with a sudden fear. She lifted her hand to her face, wiping away sand and dirt and grit and debris. At last her eyes opened, but as she lay there, Demitra looked up to see the sky, cloudless and brilliant blue. How was this possible? How was the sky inside the house? The world was upside down.

The earth had become the sea and the sky was now inside.

Surely I've died.

Surely she was in heaven where the rules of man no longer existed. She turned her head to the side, imagining Panagia's snakes might appear to crawl on her and tell her that everything would be all right.

But the snakes did not appear.

There was nothing but dirt and stones and debris. Slowly, she caught her breath and sat up. Around her, the house had fallen in on itself.

This was not heaven. This was her home in ruins.

Baba.

Searching her surroundings, she grew frantic. She screamed his name. "Baba! Baba!"

She crawled to her feet, careful as she stepped over what was once the floor of the house. But she could no longer see the floor. All around there was nothing but debris and rubble. There was nothing left but the shell of four walls.

"Baba!" she shouted, then spotted him a short distance from her. She struggled to keep her balance as she made her way to him.

She could see his face, covered in gray dust and dirt. His eyes were closed.

"Baba." She knelt beside him.

She placed her hand on his cheek. "Baba?" She shook him but there was no response. She scanned the length of his body, his slim frame visible beneath the tatters of his shirt. She placed her hand on his chest.

"Thank you, dear God. Thank you." She cried as she felt the gentle rise and fall of his breathing. She began clawing away the dirt and fragments that covered him.

"Baba, please wake up. It's me, Demitra," she said as she worked.

Then she saw it—a large wooden beam had fallen from the ceiling, pinning his legs. She leaned into it, using all of her might to push it away. Nothing. It would not budge. Again she tried, pulling and pushing and wrapping her fingers around the splintered wood. The beam would not move.

She looked up and around at what was left standing of the house, then remembered what had happened. She was standing below the beam just before the quake hit. That was when he ran to her and pushed her. Baba had pushed her out of the way of the falling beam.

Tears streamed down her cheeks.

"Help. Help!" she screamed, not recognizing the panic in her own voice.

"Baba. Please. Somebody, help me!" she cried as she scratched and clawed at the wood, but it was no use. No matter how hard she pulled and pushed, no matter how hard she cried and begged, Baba remained silent and still, trapped beneath the beam.

Chapter Thirty-One

THEY POURED INTO the harbor by the thousands that day, like the walking dead, covered in ash, soot, dirt, and blood. As the injured and displaced staggered into Argostoli, it was apparent that the destruction was massive, and the human casualties beyond comprehension.

Returning to Israel from their first ever training mission in the Mediterranean, the newly formed Israeli Navy answered the distress call and diverted their fleet to Cephalonia. As the first to reach the port of Argostoli, the fledgling Israeli naval officers found themselves in command of rescue operations, as maritime law dictated.

Among the officers that day was twenty-two-year-old Joseph Cohen, a Holocaust survivor from Thessaloniki. Joseph survived the horrors of Auschwitz only to be sent to a Cypriot refugee camp where he lived for two years before finally being allowed entry to Israel.

While the other officers set up command and established triage and a makeshift hospital near the port, Joseph and several other officers who spoke Greek were assigned to the outer villages where knowledge of the native language would come in handy.

Joseph and his partner, a young soldier from Jerusalem, made their way along the dirt roads and mountain paths, scouring the countryside for anyone in need. After several hours Joseph found himself on a bluff overlooking the sea. After scanning the beach below, he stopped for a sip of water from his canteen. He glanced down again as he brought the bottle to his mouth and stopped.

Below, near the edge of the cliffs, he spotted a figure. It appeared to be a young boy crouching on the sand.

"You, there!" he shouted. "Boy, are you all right?"

The boy did not respond. He did not look up or acknowledge Joseph.

"I'm going down there," Joseph said to his partner, who continued to scan the cliffs with his binoculars.

The bluff was littered with rocks and debris. There was no longer a clear path to the sea, so Joseph scaled the side of the hill carefully, each step sending earth and dirt tumbling to the beach below. Finally, he reached the sand.

"Hello." Joseph knelt before the boy. "My name is Joseph. What is your name?"

The boy did not look up. He did not respond. He sat there on the sand, hugging his knees and rocking back and forth. He looked to be about four or five years old.

"Are you hurt?" Joseph asked. "Can you tell me your name?"

The boy did not respond. He just continued staring out to sea.

"Won't you tell me your name, please?" Still the boy did not respond.

Joseph reached for his bag, digging through the medical supplies to find what he was looking for.

"Here," he said, unwrapping a lollipop. "It's strawberry. My favorite flavor. I hope you like strawberry."

At last the boy looked up, making eye contact. Silent still, he nodded, then accepted the lollipop and placed it in his mouth.

Joseph watched him silently for a few moments as life came back to his eyes.

"Will you tell me your name?"

"Gerasimos," he said, never removing the lollipop from his mouth.

"Are you hurt?"

He shook his head no.

"Will you come with me? I'd like to take you somewhere you will be safe, and we can get you a proper meal, as delicious as that lollipop is."

Gerasimos shook his head again.

"Can I ask why?" Joseph asked.

"I can't leave my friends. We're playing hide-and-seek."

Joseph scanned the beach up and down. "I know it must have been very scary. Are they still hiding? They can come out now." He looked across the beach again and shouted, "You are safe now!"

Gerasimos stared up at Joseph, tears brimming in his eyes. He removed the lollipop this time before he spoke.

"They were here," he said, pointing to the rock pile behind them and the towering cliff above. "They were here, hiding behind the rocks. It was my turn to find them, and I did. I saw them. I started running over to them, but then I heard the loud noise and then the mountain fell."

Chapter Thirty-Two

Please hold on, Baba. Please," Demitra begged as she gripped his hand and caressed his cheek. She had considered running into town to see if she could find and bring back help, but she could not bring herself to leave him, not now, not like this.

He had yet to open his eyes or speak. Even so, she stayed beside him, refusing to leave his side, talking to him, comforting him, and promising him help would come soon, hoping someone passing would hear her cries.

Hours passed, and no one came. No one responded to her pleas. No one arrived to save them.

Late morning spilled into evening, and she watched as the color drained from Baba's face. His skin, although covered in dust and soot, took on a gray pallor as well.

"Please, Panagia, please help us," she prayed. "Please, send someone to save us."

But no one came.

The earth trembled again in an aftershock that sent more debris tumbling to the ground around them. Baba moaned as the beam shifted, putting even more pressure on his legs. His lips began to turn blue.

Demitra could no longer wait for help to come. She could no longer afford to be passive, to believe someone would come to their rescue.

Martha's voice echoed in her ear. *"We are the power, Demitra. And we bring the magic and the love."*

She needed to find the power within herself to leave Baba and go find help. If she did not act now, she was certain Baba would not survive the night.

"I'll be back, Baba. I promise. I'm going to go up the road and see if I can find help. I won't leave you alone for long. I'll bring someone to help you," she said as she leaned closer and took his hand in hers, praying he could hear her.

As she moved to stand, she felt it. He squeezed her hand, holding on to her with what little strength was left in his broken body. She squeezed back gently and kissed his cheek. When she pulled away to stand and looked down on him again, a single tear forged a path on his soot-stained skin. She could not remember the last time they had held hands or the last time she had pressed her lips to his skin. She could not remember a time when she had ever seen him cry.

"I'll be back, Baba. Please, please wait for me." She sobbed as she spoke, wiping her eyes as she ran toward the road.

Less than an hour later, as dusk fell across the island, Israeli naval officers heard Demitra's cries for help. She held Baba's hand again as three men lifted the beam. He did not squeeze back this time. His color was grayer, his lips blue.

Demitra saw the full scope of the disaster as the Israelis carried Baba to the makeshift hospital they'd set up in the Argostoli port, their lanterns shining light on the decimated homes and buildings along the way. Everywhere she looked, houses and buildings were reduced to piles of rubble, ancient olive trees that had survived for generations had split open like walnuts, and majestic cypress trees had toppled like matchsticks. The earth itself seemed to have cracked apart, as if allowing Queen Persephone on her throne in Hades to gaze upon the earth and mourn the destruction.

At last they reached the port, and the Israelis carrying Baba shouted to another officer who motioned for them to place Baba on a stretcher near a table littered with medication and bandages. Demitra stood back, gnawing her knuckles and pacing frantically as she watched the doctor examine Baba.

"We will need to amputate. His legs are crushed, and it looks as if the wound is infected," the doctor explained through a translator. "The next twenty-four hours are vital; they will tell us if the infection has spread."

Amputate? And what then? Demitra wanted to ask questions, but the doctor was pulled away to tend to a woman who had gone into labor.

She sat beside Baba as the nurses cleaned and took care of him, replaying the morning in her mind. When the nurses cut away his pants and tossed them on the floor, Demitra bent down and took the paper from the pocket where Baba had shoved it during their argument. After scanning the page again, she folded it and placed it in the pocket of her dress.

She struggled to process what had happened and what would come next. She sat there, on the ground beside Baba, taking it all in, the injured all around her, those who had lost their lives, limbs, loved ones. And everywhere she looked, survivors were still covered in a gray layer of soot, shock written across their faces and in their eyes.

Demitra stood, anxious to run back to Stella, Martha, and Gerasimos and check on them now that Baba was in the hands of the doctors. She had been so consumed with freeing Baba that she hadn't realized their home was only one of thousands that collapsed during the quake. She had not comprehended the level of devastation across the island until now. She felt bile rising in her throat as panic coursed through her, and she prayed Stella, Martha, Gerasimos, and Olga were safe.

She turned to leave the medical tent and saw him—Gerasimos. He was there, walking into the tent, hand in hand with a young man in uniform.

"Gerasimos!" she shouted as she ran to him, then enveloped him in her arms. "Thank God you're safe!" She cried as he burrowed his face in her neck and hugged her back with all his might.

"Are you all right?" she asked as she eased him back and rubbed her hands up and down his arms and body.

He nodded and then leaned in to hug her again.

"We were playing," he whispered.

"Is he your son?" the soldier asked.

"My brother." Demitra stood, keeping a protective arm around Gerasimos. "You speak Greek?"

"Yes. I am Joseph from Thessaloniki," the man responded. "Your brother doesn't seem to be hurt." He paused, lowering his voice. "Not physically, anyway."

Demitra nodded in silent understanding.

"I found him on the beach."

"Yes. I left him there this morning. He was playing with his friends." She scanned the tent in search of Gerasimos's playmates.

"I'm so sorry. His friends. They . . ." Joseph shook his head rather than say the words.

Like the walls all around the island, Demitra's strong facade began to crumble. Up until that moment she'd had no choice but to be stoic and strong, knowing Baba's survival depended on it. But the thought of those children playing on the beach, that it so easily could have been Gerasimos—it was too much to bear. She turned her head away, and the tears came fast and hot.

Her mind flashed to Aleko. Once upon a time she might have pictured him beside her. In another lifetime she might have been able to lean on him for help and support. But he was lost to her too, like their beautiful island, like so many friends. And she was here alone to shoulder the burden of so much pain, so much responsibility.

"Thank you," she said to the soldier when she was able to catch her breath. "We have to go. We have to go find his mother." Her voice cracked with emotion. "*Our* mother."

Taking Gerasimos by the hand, she led them through the injured and displaced people, intending to take the path out of town, toward Martha's house.

"Demitra." The voice was gentle, as was the touch on her shoulder.

Demitra turned to find Areti standing beside her. The old woman's head was bandaged. Demitra leaped to embrace her.

"Are you all right?"

"Yes. I am. I was in the periptero when the quake happened. I managed to get out and was tossed to the ground, but thankfully I am all right." Areti's misshapen fingers clutched her cane as her eyes filled with tears.

"Thank God." Demitra smiled weakly. "I'm so sorry, but I have to go. I have to find Stella and Martha. I left them at Martha's house this morning. I need to go to them and make sure they're ok." She pulled Gerasimos and began to hurry away.

"Oh, Demitra," the old woman wailed. "I'm so sorry, Demitra. They loved you so much. Why, God? Why have you done this to us? How could you have taken them?" The old woman wept, shaking her head and raising her cane up toward the heavens.

"Wh-what do you mean?" The world was spinning, and Demitra did not know what Areti was referring to, nor did she want to know. She pulled Gerasimos closer, fearful of what the old woman might say next.

"Oh, Demitra, I'm so sorry. They loved you so. Gerasimos, sweet boy, to lose your mama and yia-yia like this . . ." The old woman keened, throwing her hands up to the heavens and clawing at her chest. "They're gone. My son went by the house to see if he could help, to make sure that they, that you all, were all right. Oh, Demitra, the house is gone, and it took them with it. They're gone. Stella and Martha are gone."

Demitra did not cry. She did not shout or scream. She pulled Gerasimos into her arms as the young boy began to cry. He burrowed his face into her shirt.

"Where is my mama?" he asked through his tears. "I want Mama. I want my mama. Please, let's go to her now. Where is my mama, Demitra?"

As she listened to the heartbreaking cries of her little brother, Demitra remembered quite well what it was to be young and in pain. She remembered the devastation of losing her own mother and the loneliness of her grief. As she enveloped Gerasimos in her arms, Demitra realized that her pain and her own desires were insignificant now. All that mattered, she held in her arms.

All that mattered was that she honor Stella by being the kind of mother to Gerasimos that Stella had been to her.

Chapter Thirty-Three

ELENA SPENT THE night outside under the stars, wondering if the earth would rattle again. When sunrise came, the haze of smoke and dust that had engulfed the island at last began to lift.

She had been too afraid to approach what was left of her house yesterday as aftershocks continued to jolt the island. But the earth had been quiet and still for several hours as Elena watched the heavens come to life with the sunrise piercing the darkness in streaks of gold and orange.

Gingerly, she stepped on the rubble, clearing stones and debris until her hands were raw and bloody. Finally, she spotted what she was looking for and eased it out of the rubble. The portrait Demitra had drawn of her with the Italian soldier was damaged and stained, but the image was still there. She was still there; proof that once upon a time, the girl in the picture had existed.

She wrapped the picture in a sheet that had been hanging on the line and placed it under the olive tree that had kept her safe during the quake.

Find Demitra and Stella. It was the one thing on her mind, the one thing she knew she needed to do. She prayed that their family was safe.

She stepped carefully as she made her way down the mountain. All around her branches, stones, and debris littered the path. As she walked farther, Elena was able to see more of the mountain. It seemed to be split in two with a large crack running all the way down and along the road toward town.

She navigated the crevice cautiously, taking the long road around rather than stepping over it. As she neared the base of the mountain, she heard a voice, faint and urgent. And distinct.

"Help me! Help me!" The voice came from the ravine on the other side of the road.

Elena approached the edge and gasped, blinking several times as her hands covered her mouth.

Is this real? Am I hallucinating?

Nektarios had fallen into the gulch beyond the olive grove. Just beyond the tree line, the earth pitched sharply, as if the mountain had been shorn off. Elena stood near the edge, looking down on him, adrenaline coursing through her as she grasped the reality of the situation, his situation. Nektarios was nearly ten feet below, wedged between the rocks on the cliff, which seemed to prevent him from falling farther down the serrated mountain.

His face erupted in relief as he spotted her. "Elena! Thank God. Help me! My leg. I can't move my leg. I fell and I think it's broken. I'm bleeding. Go get help. I need you to go for help."

She stood above him, staring down. His leg was gashed and grotesquely misshapen in the dirt. Blood was visible on his trousers.

"Elena. Help me!" His face was ashen.

Elena scanned the mountain. No one else was around.

"Where is she?" she asked.

"Elena, my shirt. Come tie it around my leg. The bleeding. We need to stop the bleeding."

"Where is she?" she asked again.

"Who? For the love of God, Elena . . ."

"Where is my child? Our child? You've known all along and so has your wife. Where is she?"

"Elena, I need help!"

"What did you do to my baby? It's one thing to hurt me, to treat me like I'm nothing. But to take my child, my daughter . . ." She began to walk away.

"Don't leave me! Please! Elena, you can't just leave me here!" His cries reverberated off the ravine.

"Where is my child?" She was screaming now. All of the fear and fury she had tamped down was simmering to the surface and boiling over. "What did your wife do? What did she do?"

"Elena, please, I don't know how much longer I can hold on. I'm slipping. The rocks are slipping."

"I know she's alive. Tell me what happened! Tell me or I'll walk away and leave you to the buzzards," she yelled at him as she began to walk away.

In an instant he responded, his voice raspy and desperate. "She's not dead. She's not."

Elena ran back to the edge. "Where is she? Tell me and I will go get you help. The harbor is filled with ships. I can go get them and bring them to help you, but only if you tell me the truth."

He tried to move, wincing in pain.

"Tell me!" She did not recognize her own voice, desperate rage coursing through her.

"It was Irene," he said as he winced in pain. "She saw you and she knew the child was mine. She knew. She heard about a man in Patra who works with an orphanage in Athens. He helps American families who want to have a child. He helps them adopt orphans."

"What does this have to do with my daughter? My child is not an orphan," she spat at him. "She has a mother! *I* am her mother." Elena sank to her knees at the edge of the ravine. "I am her mother!" she screamed.

"They take children to the orphanage, and they are adopted by American families."

"What are you saying? Tell me where she is! Where is my child?"

"They took her there, to Athens." He let out a long, low moan now. "To the orphanage. She was adopted by an American family."

Alive. Emanuella was alive.

She knew this in her bones, as if she could feel Emanuella's heartbeat.

The euphoria of this news was tempered with the truth of what had happened.

Adopted. Stolen. My baby was stolen from my arms and put into the arms of another woman, another mother. I have to find her. I will find her. Please, God, please help me find my baby.

She turned her attention again to Nektarios. "Why would you do this to me? I was going to leave. I told you I was leaving. I never spoke a word about the baby, or what you did to me—how much you hurt me. I kept your awful secrets, and you stole my child."

"Elena, please. I need help." Panic filled his voice.

"Why?" Her voice cracked with pain and emotion and the reality of what had been done to her. "Why would you do this?"

"The Italian investors backed out. They pulled their money out of the deal. We didn't have the money to finish the bakery expansion." He moaned a low, guttural moan, leaning his head back as his eyes closed. His breathing was low and rapid and yet he managed to continue. "Irene managed to get it. She managed to get the money."

"She sold my child." The words slipped out of her mouth. "She sold my child." She spoke louder now, each word punctuated with pain and horror and disbelief. "She sold my child to an

American family to pay for your hotel." She was wracked with sobs, trembling and shaking as if the island was hit with another aftershock.

Nektarios reached his arm up toward her, his eyes wild and unfocused, pleading. "Elena, please. I told you the truth. Now help me!" His head rolled back as he winced in pain.

She stood above the ravine, stepping closer to the edge and sending rocks and dirt cascading down on him.

"Please. I've lost a lot of blood." His voice cracked as he pleaded with her, reaching his arm up toward her again.

"And I've lost my *child*," she said. "I hate you. I will find my child. I will get her back. But you . . ." She inched closer to the edge, sending more dirt and stones raining down on him. "You . . ." She shook her head and said nothing more. She spat on him and then turned and walked away.

"No, please! Don't leave. Please! I'll die out here. Please, Elena!"

She continued walking toward town. As his voice grew fainter, her resolve grew stronger.

Mama will find you, my baby girl. I will not rest until I find you.

Chapter Thirty-Four

Demitra went to visit Elena at the bakery days after the quake, where she was working side by side with Niko to keep up with the demand to feed the thousands rendered homeless and destitute, as well as the international military brigade that arrived to help.

"Oh, Demitra. I'm so sorry. I'm so, so sorry." Elena wiped at the wetness in her eyes as a tear slid down Demitra's face untouched. "Stella was an angel on this earth, and I can only imagine her mother was the same. She loved you so very much." The women embraced as Demitra rested her head on Elena's shoulder.

"You look exhausted," Demitra said as they walked arm in arm from the bakery and sat in a patch of shade on the ground. Gerasimos stayed behind to help Niko knead a new batch of loaves.

"I am," Elena replied. "We all are. I don't think Niko has slept more than an hour a night. He is working day and night to feed the British, American, Israeli, and Greek soldiers who have come to help. He thanks them, each and every one of them, and has already learned most of their names."

"Is it true what happened to Nektarios? I overheard the nurses in the medical tent say the British found him in a ravine—after the animals did." Her mouth pinched as her brows furrowed.

Elena nodded and said nothing.

"How is Niko? It must have been so hard for him when he found his mother in the rubble of the storage shed."

"He dug her out himself, but it was too late. The bakery and the new hotel received barely any damage, while all of the older buildings turned to dust. I see how the guilt is eating away at him. He told me he should have been the one who went to the storage shed for more salt, but he was so busy, and he asked Irene to go . . ." Elena's voice drifted off as she looked out to the shimmering sea and horizon.

"I see him every morning in the medical tent, delivering bread to the doctors and nurses. The nurses tell me that sometimes he sits with my father, that they see him talking, even though Baba is sedated and barely conscious."

"Yes, he is a kind soul. Niko had nothing to do with what his parents did to me," Elena said as she fanned herself with a paper fan. "He had no idea what his mother was capable of. But he knows now. He knows everything."

"What will you do?" Demitra asked.

"I'm going to find my daughter. I don't know how, but I will. Niko asked me to stay and help him at the bakery, so I will. His wife left him just days before the quake. She went home to her parents, intent on getting a divorce." Her gaze darted around as she ensured no one could hear what she said next. "They never spent a night together as man and wife."

Demitra said nothing but gave a knowing nod.

"Niko said he would help me look for Emanuella. He has grown into a special young man. In many ways, he is childlike, but there is also a wisdom in him and a kindness not found in many men."

"I know you will find her," Demitra replied. "And I'll do everything in my power to help you." She looked out over the harbor

and raised her hand to shield her eyes as she watched more international aid ships arrive.

"What's this?" Elena asked, pursing her lips as she reached for
Demitra's hand. "Is there something you forgot to tell me?"

A nervous laugh escaped Demitra's lips. "It's not what you're
thinking." She squinted into the sun, her golden eyes ablaze. "It's
my mother's ring. I found it hidden in an old coat. And that's not
all I found." She pulled the crumpled paper from her pocket. "My
mother's death notice from a church. Baba kept it all these years.
She was a teacher in the Greek school."

"So that's where you get your gentleness and compassion."
Elena wrapped her arm around Demitra. "What do the doctors
say about your father?"

"He's in and out of consciousness. The infection seems to be
under control, but they say the next few days will be telling. Both
legs were crushed, and they had to amputate. They've been giving
him morphine pills for the pain, but he keeps asking for more. It's
the only time he speaks, to ask for more pills."

Elena nodded in understanding. "What about you? What happens next for you?"

"I don't know how we will manage, but we will somehow. That's
what we do, right? Figure out how to go on, somehow . . ." She
closed her eyes and exhaled, exhaustion and fear taking their toll.
She had barely eaten in days and sleep was an impossibility. Each
time she drifted off to a fitful slumber, she soon woke from night-
mares of Stella, Martha, and Baba trapped in the rubble. She
widened her eyes and exhaled, trying to shake the images from
her mind. "I'll have Baba and Gerasimos to look after. I'll be here
with them. With you."

"What about your family in Kerkyra? Is there anyone there
who can help you?" Elena asked.

Demitra shook her head. "No." She hung her head low and exhaled a long, slow breath. "I had a letter from them recently. They're moving to America. Sophia said it was unexpected, but Tino's family has a business opportunity for them. They're getting a fresh start in New York. I can't be a burden to them now."

Demitra paused then, considering what she might say next. In that moment she made the choice to confide in Elena, the way Elana had confided in her.

"There was someone in Kerkyra—a man I thought I could trust. A man I loved. His name was Aleko." She bit her lip, attempting to stop the swell of emotion that accompanied the sound of his name. "I believed in him. I believed we could be together, that the whispers and promises he made in the dark might actually come true. But he was married, Elena . . ." Her voice drifted off. "So, no. There's no one who can help me now."

"Hey." Elena reached out to touch her cheek. "It's all right. You put your faith in someone. You believed in the good in people. You did nothing wrong." Elena looked away toward the sea and into the distance, where she had once danced with handsome young soldiers and also believed the promises men whispered to her in the dark of night. "You fell in love, Demitra. It's not a sin to believe in love, to believe honesty and integrity exist."

Demitra followed Elena's gaze to the sea. She thought back to those days on the cliff, to the innocence and ignorance of her youth. She bit her lip, remembering it all, picturing it all, thinking of a life filled with laughter and love, that it was all possible.

"I once believed my life could be something meaningful, something significant. I believed I could make my own place in the world. And now look . . ." She bit her lip to keep from crying again, lifting her head toward the sky to keep the tears at bay, but it was no use. They came again, as they always did.

The women sat in silence after that, holding hands and leaning against each other, holding each other up as everything around them seemed to have crumbled. They'd met many years ago, from different faiths, different lives, different worlds. And now, after all the disappointments, heartbreaks, and loss, all they had left was each other and the knowledge that they were the same.

Chapter Thirty-Five

Hand in hand with Gerasimos, Demitra walked from the open field where they slept beside the other displaced villagers to the medical tent where Baba lay on a stretcher. He was pale, his eyes closed. It had taken all morning, but with Areti's help she was finally able to call the monastery and learn that Olga was safe.

Demitra sat next to her father and placed her hand on his. "Baba. Baba, I'm here," she said, resting her head on his arm. "Gerasimos and I are here. I spoke with Olga. She said she would pray for you."

There was no response or movement from Baba, just the slow rise and fall of his chest.

"How is he today?" Joseph asked as walked toward them. Gerasimos's eyes lit up at the sight of the Israeli soldier. Demitra sat up and turned to him.

"He's been more alert, waking several times a day, but he's not really speaking yet. He's in a lot of pain, despite the morphine. But the doctors say it looks like they caught the infection in time, and they think he'll be all right." She mustered a smile for Gerasimos's benefit.

The look on Joseph's face told her he saw through her facade.

"We are going to be all right, aren't we, Gerasimos? The worst is over and we will make a new life for ourselves. Every day we will honor and remember your mama and yia-yia, and every day we will make them proud." She bent to face Gerasimos and tapped his nose with her finger.

Gerasimos smiled at his sister.

"May their memory be a blessing," Joseph whispered.

She had promised herself she would no longer let Gerasimos see her cry. He was just a child and had already witnessed so much tragedy, so much devastation. She summoned all of her strength to keep the tears at bay, but it was no use. She turned her head away as she dabbed at her eyes with her finger, locking eyes with Joseph as she avoided Gerasimos's gaze.

"Gerasimos, the ball we played with yesterday is in my rucksack. It's just outside under the olive tree. Would you mind getting it for me, please?"

The boy nodded and headed outside to fetch the ball.

"How are you, really?" Joseph asked the moment they were alone.

"I'm managing as well as anyone else." She tried to summon a smile, but it was difficult without the incentive of Gerasimos's eyes on her.

"Thank you for all you've done, all you are doing. You've brought joy to Gerasimos when there was none to be found. You've saved us in more ways than you can imagine."

"I needed you as much as you needed me," Joseph said as he looked across the tent. "I left Israel more than a month ago, lost. I took the job with the navy because my mother and I need a roof over our heads and food on the table. During the entire training mission, I wondered what I was doing there. I felt like I didn't belong. Since arriving here, it makes sense. I understand who we are and what we need to do—who *I* am and what I need to do."

"And what is that?"

"I see your brother. I see all he has lived through and lost. And I see how the simple act of playing ball brings the smile back to his face. How even in the midst of this, he can still be a child. There are thousands of children in the immigration camps in Israel right now. I can do this for them. I can bring joy to their lives and smiles to their faces as they transition to their new lives."

Gerasimos ran back into the tent holding the ball. His cheeks were flushed and his face was plastered with a broad smile.

"Here," he said as he held the ball out to Joseph.

Joseph leaned over and tousled Gerasimos's hair. "Would you like to go outside and play?"

Gerasimos's eyes widened as he looked to Demitra for permission.

"Of course. Go," she said, then watched them walk off together into the afternoon sun.

Demitra remained in the chair beside Baba's cot, where she had kept vigil for the past several days. She was unsure if he could hear her in his morphine-induced slumber, but perhaps that made it easier. Seated beside him as he lay quiet and still, she was finally able to have the conversations with Baba that she'd never dared to dream of in the past, sharing her most intimate thoughts and dreams with him.

"I know it was hard for you, all those years alone," she said as she watched his chest rise and fall with each breath. "I know it was hard for you to raise me by yourself. It would have been easier for you to send me away, but you didn't. You kept me close, as close as you would allow me to be. I can't imagine how hard that must have been. And now I find myself scared too. I'm scared I'll never be enough for Gerasimos. I'll do my best to raise your son and make you and Stella proud. And I'll be here to take care of you. I won't leave you, Baba. Every day more boats arrive in the harbor to take people away. They're leaving by the hundreds, thousands. They say Cephalonia is dead, that there is nothing left for us here. But I won't leave. As long as you're here, I will take care of you, and I won't leave you."

Baba's eyes flew open, an unsettled, confused, and pained expression on his face. Then his gaze found Demitra's face and his eyes softened.

"Baba," she said, leaning closer so he could see her face. "I'm here."

He lifted his hand to her cheek and then closed his eyes again.

She leaned into his rough hand on her face, savoring the sensation of his touch. In her entire life, she could not remember a moment of shared intimacy like this.

"Baba? Can you hear me?"

He did not answer. The afternoon was silent and still, save for the rhythmic rattle of Baba's breathing punctuated by Gerasimos's squeals of delight as he played ball with the Israeli soldier along the beach.

Chapter Thirty-Six

Niko shuffled into the medical tent just before 5:00 a.m., shoulders hunched, eyes downcast as he carried the basket of fresh loaves. This had been his routine each day for the past week since the morning after the earthquake.

Amid the chaos and loss and fear, baking brought him peace and solace. Baking was dependable, certain. Each time he mixed the flour and yeast with water and placed the soft dough in the oven, a perfectly crusted loaf emerged. That was his only certainty, the only thing he knew he could control in his life.

As he had done each day since the quake, Niko made sure to deliver the day's first loaves to the injured and the doctors and nurses who tended to them with such care. All around the tent, men, women, and children lay on stretchers and makeshift beds, healing from physical and emotional wounds. Nurses prepared the day's medications and awaited the doctors' instructions.

"Thank you, Niko," a nurse said as he placed the basket of loaves at the nurses' station just beyond Pericles's stretcher.

"Will you sit with your friend again?" she asked as she portioned out the morning's pills. "He doesn't typically speak or even open his eyes for most people, not even for his daughter, only you. What a blessing you are." She leaned in to savor the scent of the warm loaves and smiled before setting off on her next task.

"Yes, I will sit with him," Niko said as he pulled a knife from his pocket. With meticulous care he cut into each loaf, dividing them into perfectly equal slices. Once he was finished, he walked over to Pericles's stretcher and sat down beside him.

"Good morning."

Pericles's bloodshot eyes slowly fluttered open. He turned his head slightly toward Niko.

"The sun will be up soon. I brought fresh loaves. They're still hot. Would you like some?" Niko asked.

"No. I don't want any." Pericles licked his lips.

"Would you like some water?" Niko asked.

"Yes. Water." Pericles's voice was a raspy whisper. Niko stood, carefully cradling Pericles's head as he held a cup of water to his lips.

"You're a good man, Niko," he said when Niko set the cup back down.

"My father told me I wasn't a man. I wasn't good enough or strong enough to be a man. I wasn't like him."

"Maybe it's a good thing that you're not like him." Pericles closed his eyes again.

Niko leaned over the stretcher, his face hovering inches above Pericles's.

"Are you sure? He told me I was the reason you sent Demitra away, that I wasn't man enough. He said it was my fault she left. He said I was an embarrassment."

"No."

"Are you sure?" he asked again as a tenuous smile crossed his lips. "Because he told me I should be ashamed of myself. He told me I'm no good. He's dead now. But that's what he told me."

"It's not your fault. None of it was your fault."

Niko beamed and repeated the words. "It's not my fault."

"You're more of a man than your father ever was." Pericles opened his eyes again and stared into Niko's. "And you are more of a man than I will ever be again." Pericles closed his eyes, wincing as a wave of pain shot through him. He grimaced, his hands squeezing into fists and a moan escaping his lips.

Outside the tent, dawn's first light appeared across the horizon. Niko watched as orange and pink streaked through the darkness. This new day would bring lines of hungry islanders to the bakery. More mouths to feed, more bread to bake. He could go to work and do the thing he was born to do, what he loved more than anything, and know his father was wrong. It was not his fault.

"I have to go." Niko stood, glancing down at Pericles, whose chest rose and fell with each shallow breath. "I'll be back tomorrow morning. I'll see you then." He walked out of the tent and toward the bakery, his chin held high, his gait steady and certain.

ARETI STOOD NEARBY, leaning on her cane and watching as Niko walked away. With the periptero damaged, she began and ended each day in the medical tent. The old woman proved to be a valuable asset to the doctors and nurses since she knew everyone's business across the village—who had a heart condition, which of the injured had family on the mainland where they could go to convalesce, and which victims were members of the same family and therefore should be buried together.

She stood quietly near the nurses' station as she had each morning, watching and listening as Niko sat beside Pericles. This morning had been different.

After years of sitting quietly in her periptero, watching and listening as people often received the best and worst news of their lives, Areti knew the importance of the conversation she'd overheard. The old woman inched forward until she was at Pericles's bedside.

She placed her hand on his shoulder, nudging him gently. "Pericles."

"Please, just let me die. Why won't you just let me die?" He gritted his teeth and then opened his eyes, surprise registering at the sight of the old woman. "I thought you were the nurse." Each word was steeped in defeat.

"I heard what you said to Niko." She leaned in close, both hands cradling the top of her cane. "You freed that boy from the dark shadow of his father. You set him free."

"I pray someone does the same for me. I've asked them to, but they won't listen to me. They won't let me die." Pain was etched into the deep crevices of his face. "All my life I ran from the memories, the demons that chased me. I ran and ran and never looked back. I can't run anymore, and I can't stand to be still. My demons have finally caught up with me. They are eating me alive. What kind of man needs tending from his daughter day and night like a child? What kind of life will that be for me, for her? I should have died in the rubble. I would have been better off. We all would have been better off."

The old woman said nothing as she regarded him, each moment and memory of her own life playing out before her. She remembered well the loneliness, frustration, and exhaustion of being confined to the house, of caring for her elderly, invalid husband, an angry and resentful man. She remembered praying day and night for God to take him, to end his suffering as well as her own. Only after he died and she found work in the tiny periptero had she felt any joy, any true sense of purpose to her life.

"I have spent years of my life watching people come and go from inside my little periptero on the square. I have watched Demitra grow up, and I see your beautiful girl. I see who and what she is. She deserves more than you gave her, more than I ever had. She deserves more than what's left for her here."

His eyes closed again as his face contorted with physical and emotional pain.

Areti said nothing more. Scanning the tent, she spotted the doctors and nurses meeting on the other side of the encampment. She shuffled over to the nurses' station, smiling as she leaned in to smell Niko's bread. She pulled a lace-trimmed handkerchief from her pocket and tipped a bottle of morphine pills onto the fabric along with a slice of bread, before closing her disease-ravaged fingers around the bundle.

She slowly made her way back to Pericles's bedside.

"What are you doing?" he asked as she placed her hand under his neck and guided him up.

She was an old, uneducated, lonely widow who had never held anything of value in her hands until that moment. Opening her palm, she revealed the pills, more than a dozen of them clustered together. As she gazed down on them, she understood the truth of what they were. Where others might see a pile of small white tablets, Areti saw Demitra's future, a chance to live a life that she, Stella, and Martha never could have dreamed of or even dared to imagine.

One by one she slipped the pills into Pericles's mouth before bringing the cup of water to his lips and then guiding his head back down to the cot.

part

four

Chapter Thirty-Seven

Milwaukee, Wisconsin

1925

MARIA WRAPPED HER shawl tighter around her shoulders, then stood to place another log in the stove. Just yesterday as she shopped for vegetables at the market downtown, she'd seen children skating on the frozen lake. She exhaled, shaking her head at the sight of her frozen breath, and reached for another blanket to drape across her shoulders.

Ten o'clock. She sighed as she walked over to the stove, lifting the lid on the pot. It had taken her more than an hour to peel the tiny pearl onions for the *stifado* and then another three hours of slow, careful simmering. She'd added just a touch of red wine vinegar to the tomatoes before sealing the lid to keep the aromas in like Mama used to do. Her stifado was perfect, just like the delicate rabbit stew Mama used to make in Karditsa for special occasions.

But now, ten hours after Pericles said he would be home, Maria's perfect stifado was dry and charred.

And she sat there alone in a freezing apartment. Again.

She sat in her usual spot, the chair by the window, and watched as the snow blanketed the street below. She was deathly afraid of slipping and falling in her condition, so she took a mental inventory to make sure she had enough food in the pantry to cobble together dinner tomorrow without needing to leave the house.

Her condition. She had no way of being certain, but she prayed that this time it was true. She prayed her child would not slip from her body before he even had a chance at life.

She was almost afraid to hope again, unsure if she could take another loss, afraid it might break her. If the loneliness didn't break her first.

The heavy stomp of boots and jingle of keys at the door brought her back from her contemplation. Pericles rushed inside, his cheeks red from the cold, his coat covered in a dusting of snow.

"It's a blizzard out there," he said as he slipped out of his coat and sat down at the table.

No mention of the hour. No mention of leaving her alone again. No asking how she was.

"It's coming down like a sheet of ice."

She placed her hands on her belly. *I won't be leaving this house for days.*

"Supper is dry and I fear scalded," she said as she placed the plate before him.

Pericles smiled up at her. "They called a meeting of AHEPA and I had to go. There was a diner in Chicago where the KKK threw a firebomb through the window and burned the place down. Thankfully no one was killed, but they're getting bolder, and they're starting to cause problems here."

"But I don't understand why. Why are they bothering with us?" Maria asked. "We don't bother with them."

"They don't like us. They never have. They think we're taking their jobs, their businesses. How am I taking their business when they won't serve Blacks? What do they care if I do?"

He shook his head and shoveled the stifado into his mouth. "It's good. It's still good."

"Pericles, is this safe? If they're as dangerous as you say, then maybe it's not smart to be here. Maybe we should go someplace else, someplace where you can work and not worry about these things." *Someplace where I might have someone to talk to.* She gnawed at her fingernails, which were bloody and bitten to the quick.

"Don't speak about things you know nothing about!" he shouted as he slammed his hand on the table, startling Maria, who jumped as a cry escaped her lips.

Shaking his head, Pericles put his fork down for a moment.

"I didn't mean to startle you. I told you what happened to me, to us, in Omaha in 1909. I made a vow I would never allow that to happen again. I worked for years to build my restaurant. We had a thriving, successful community, and then ruin. My friend Yianni was from Kalamata. He was so proud to be an American. That was all he wanted to be, American. He was trying to learn English so he could fit in, so he could get a better job. A young woman, a neighbor, offered to help him, to tutor him. She was helping him learn the language, nothing more.

"But Yianni was thrown in jail for apparently corrupting this nice white girl. Dirty Greek men had no business with nice, white American girls, was what they said. And arresting him was not enough. He was beaten badly, and he fought back. Yianni grabbed the officer's gun and shot him. That was when the mob came for us—the KKK, the men in white sheets. They came for our homes and businesses. They burned down everything we had. We lost it all."

He looked off into the distance, glassy-eyed, as if he could still see the men in white sheets, their arms raised as they held torches in the air, as they set fire to his American Dream.

"The worst part was that we believed them—I believed them. I believed I didn't belong. I believed I wasn't good enough, that maybe I did not deserve to call America my home. I wandered from job to job, and I slowly built a life again. I built a business again, then brought you here to build a life with me. And so, no.

I'm not going anywhere. I'm not leaving this time. I'm not running away. This time I will stay and face them. This time they will not win." He shoved the last forkful of food in his mouth and lifted his empty plate toward her.

Silently Maria stood and went to the stove to fetch another helping.

And what about me? She wondered if it was possible for him to hear the screaming inside her head. *I'm alone here in this icebox with no friends or family. What if something happens to you? What becomes of me then?* But she said nothing as she placed the plate before him.

When he was finished, he stood and reached for his coat again.

"You're going?" There was no masking the confusion and surprise in her voice.

"I have to. If they're targeting Greek businesses, I have to be there in case they come for ours." He grabbed the blanket from the chair. "I'll be back as soon as I can. It might be a few days." He kissed her cheek and was out the door in an instant.

ON THE THIRD day Maria woke in a pool of sweat, pain radiating from deep within, the bed soaked with another lost child.

When Pericles finally burst through the door on the fifth day, there were fresh linens on the bed, a pot of soup on the stove, and no mention of the child she had named Constantine.

Chapter Thirty-Eight

Bronx, New York

1953

S EE, GERASIMOS? THEY put up Christmas lights to welcome us to America." Demitra peered out the window of the car as Gerasimos sat perched on her lap while Tino drove through the streets and boulevards of the Bronx. "Have you ever seen anything so beautiful?" she asked, hugging him close.

Despite the frigid air, Gerasimos stuck his head out the window to take in the colors and majesty of the Bronx all dressed up and decorated for Christmas. Delicate strings of white lights canopied the streets while jolly plastic Santas and crimson-nosed Rudolphs kept watch on stoops and Christmas trees twinkled from behind curtained windows.

The moment they entered the apartment door, Soula was upon them.

"You're here! You're finally here! Let me see you." Soula barreled out of the kitchen, wiping her hands on her apron. "Come here, let me look at you. Oh, Demitra! Gerasimos. May their souls rest in paradise. I can't believe they're gone." She wailed and lifted her hands up toward the heavens. "Why, God? Why? My sister, my niece. Your father." She lurched forward and wrapped her arms around both Demitra and Gerasimos as she sang the mourner's lament in the tradition of the old island women.

"Mama, please," Sophia pleaded as she helped Tino into the apartment with Demitra's suitcase. "We're all in mourning, and we are all devastated, but the neighbors are going to call the police. Please, this is not Ipsos. They're going to think someone is being murdered in here."

"Well, my dream of growing old with my sister was murdered," Soula snapped as she continued to wail and wring her hands.

Tino shook his head and disappeared into the apartment while Soula's lamentation reverberated off the walls and down the corridor.

Kiki came in from the other room where Spiro was napping, a bright smile erupting on her face when she spotted Demitra. She rushed over and hugged her tight.

"Oh my goodness! Look how you've grown." Demitra scooped her into her arms. "Why, you've shot up several inches. How did that happen, my beautiful young lady?" Gerasimos inched closer to Demitra, eyeing Kiki suspiciously.

Demitra put her down and knelt to speak with Gerasimos, but before she could open her mouth, Kiki made the introductions herself.

"Hi, I'm your cousin Kiki. I'm sorry your mother is dead."

"Kiki!" Sophia shrieked, lunging across the room to grab her.

"Yes, she died and so did my baba and my yia-yia. A lot of people died," Gerasimos replied. "But there was a really nice soldier, and he gave me this ball." He pulled the ball from his jacket pocket.

"Do you want to see the Christmas tree?" Kiki asked. "We got a stocking for you, and don't worry. In the Bronx *Agios Vassilis* comes down the fire escape, not the chimney."

Hand in hand, the children went off to the living room to play ball and marvel at the tinsel-adorned tree. Soon the sound of their laughter and play echoed through the apartment.

Soula led the way to the kitchen and gestured for Demitra to sit as she busied herself at the stove and began plating the feta, olives, and salty taramosalata that served as appetizers for the elaborate meal she'd prepared. Sophia joined Demitra at the table.

"Thank you for letting us come stay with you." Demitra bit her lip as she spoke, emotions overwhelming her. "After the earthquake and the surgery, when the doctors told me Baba would survive, I resigned myself to staying, to taking care of him and raising Gerasimos at home, even though our home was no more than a pile of rubble. I knew I had to find a way to rebuild. But after Baba died . . . I didn't know what we would do, where we would go."

"You always have a home with us, always," Sophia said. "I never imagined this would be our home, but when Tino's cousin called and asked him to be his partner in the restaurant here, it was the fresh start we'd always wanted for our children. And for us." Sophia leaned closer and placed both hands on Demitra's. "You said he was recovering, that his death was unexpected. What happened?"

"I don't know, and I don't understand. I tried to make sense of it for days. Even the doctors and nurses seemed shocked when we found him. On his last morning, he opened his eyes and spoke—my friend Niko sat with him. They watched the sunrise together, and then he was gone."

"Oh, that poor man. To lose one wife and then another, and then his legs . . ." Soula wailed again as Sophia and Demitra exchanged knowing looks.

Then, as suddenly as it had begun, Soula's wailing stopped.

"What's this?" she shrieked and lunged across the table to lift Demitra's hand where Mama's ring glinted under the fluorescent kitchen light. Sophia's eyes flew wide open.

"It was my mother's ring." Demitra smiled. "I found it the day of the quake. My father hid it in a closet along with her death notice. I found it just before the quake, just before everything turned to rubble. I keep thinking how close I came to never knowing it existed, to never knowing he'd kept it. I keep wondering what else he hid from me that was lost forever. Maybe one day I'll go to Milwaukee and try to find the church. Maybe then I'll learn more about her . . . about the things that were too painful for him to tell me himself."

"Maybe I can help you." Sophia sat up straighter. "Once we get you settled, we can reach out to the archdiocese in Manhattan. I'm sure they can help us find out what church this is and where it is."

Soula snapped the dish towel from her shoulder and rubbed her hands with it furiously before tossing it on the table.

"That's enough from you two. You must stop this snooping around where your father didn't want you snooping. There must be a reason he never talked about what happened. There's a reason he hid that paper from you. No good will come of you disturbing the rest of the dead. Let him lie in peace. When you dig up skeletons, you disturb souls, and I won't have disturbed souls in my house.

"When you wrote to us, you said the day of the earthquake your father called out to someone, someone named Aphrodite. Don't you see?" Soula shook her head as she made the sign of the cross and brought her hands together in silent prayer. "Your father saw a ghost that day. Souls were disturbed and displaced, and I won't have you inviting them into my home. We've had enough bad luck without inviting ghosts from the past in to have their way with us. What's done is done. Let's hope it stays buried, where it belongs. It's a sin to disobey your father, even now, after his death. Especially now that he's dead."

Soula snapped the dish towel back in place over her shoulder and stomped back over to the stove.

Rolling her eyes, Sophia opened her mouth as if to challenge her mother.

"It's all right," Demitra whispered to her.

"Ignore her. She'll never change." Sophia glanced over her shoulder where Soula was pouring dried pasta into a pot of boiling water. She leaned in closer.

"Have you heard anything from Aleko? Did he ever reach out to you? I thought he might, after the earthquake."

It took all her strength to summon a weak smile. "No. I never heard from him. Nothing. I admit, I hoped he might somehow try to reach me. But he never did. He never even tried. At first it made me upset, angry even. But then I realized that maybe it's for the best. It's pointless to focus on the past and what might have been. I can't afford that right now. I have to focus on the here and now, and what's best for Gerasimos."

The clang of Soula fumbling at the stove startled Demitra.

"It's time to put this nonsense about the past to rest and start focusing on your future," she said as she tossed the pot lid on the counter. "You're not getting any younger, you know."

"She just got here, Mama." The familiar exasperated tone in Sophia's voice comforted Demitra. "Let the girl have a moment to settle."

Soula glared at her daughter over the steam rising from the pot. "I'm merely saying there are plenty of young men at the church here, and it would be good for Demitra to meet one and settle down with a house and a family of her own."

"Mama," Sophia chided. "Please, stop. She just got off the boat this morning. We can't be marrying her off already."

Demitra smiled warmly at Soula, remembering quite well that was the quickest and easiest way to defuse an argument with her. "No, it's all right. I understand and thank you, Thea, for your concern." She reached out and took Sophia's hand under the table, giving it a squeeze.

"Did your father leave you any money, at least?" Soula asked as she brought a spoon to her mouth, tasting the sauce with a gloating smile.

"Mama!" Sophia glared at her mother.

"No, my father had no money. None," Demitra said as she reached for an olive.

"But how did you manage the passage?" Sophia asked, her brows knotted in confusion.

The smile on Demitra's face was authentic as she remembered that amid all the devastation, something wonderfully unexpected had happened as well.

She sat up taller, infused with accomplishment and pride. "I sold a drawing."

Sophia clapped her hands in glee as Soula dropped the lid on the pot with a clang. "You sold a drawing?" Soula asked, "So you're an artist now?"

"Yes. I did. We met a soldier, a Jewish man from Thessaloniki who went to Israel after the war. He told me how much his mother missed Greece, and to thank him for being so kind to Gerasimos, I gave him a drawing of the port and the kafeneio to remind him and his mother of home. But he wouldn't take it as a gift. He told me that in his faith, there is a proverb that King Solomon wrote: 'He who hates gifts shall live.' He insisted on paying for the drawing."

A sheepish look crossed her face. "When I opened the envelope, I couldn't believe it. I told him it was too much, that surely he was overpaying. But he insisted." She smiled at the memory, at the kindness of the young soldier. "He told me we had helped him even more than he helped us, and he wanted to do a kindness for our family, a mitzvah, he called it."

"Ah, the Jews. It's no wonder. They're very good with money, you know." Soula shook her head as she plated the meal.

"Mama! Please, enough," Sophia shouted in exasperation.

"What?" Soula said indignantly as she brought the serving platter to the table. "Come on, let's eat. I've already changed my bra."

Chapter Thirty-Nine

Bronx, New York

1954

FOR THE NEXT year Demitra and Gerasimos settled into their new life in the Bronx. The apartment on Fordham Road was crowded and filled with laughter and love in the way Demitra dreamed of when she was a child. She and Gerasimos shared a small back bedroom, down the hall from Sophia and Tino, while Soula shared a room with Sophia's children. Soula's rattling snore was the first thing Demitra heard when she woke in the mornings and the last thing she heard before she fell asleep at night.

With Gerasimos enrolled in the local Greek-American school, it wasn't long before he was making great progress in English and helping Demitra with hers. He acclimated fairly quickly to his new school and language, yet Demitra sensed a heaviness about him.

At home she caught him sometimes sitting quietly alone, holding Joseph's ball as he stared off into space.

"Are you all right?" she asked one afternoon as he spent the better part of the time lying in his bed. "I miss them too. It's all right to miss them."

"I do miss them. I miss them very much," he said, turning to look at her, the brokenness in his expression gutting her. "I also miss the sea, Demitra. I miss our island, and I miss the sea."

She sat on the bed beside him then and stroked his hair the way she always did when he was sad or upset. "I do too, sweetheart, and we will go back one day. I promise you. How about we go to the beach this Sunday after church?"

He smiled and nodded.

The bus ride to Orchard Beach was crowded and hot. The water was mud-colored and the sand packed with boisterous groups of immigrants competing to see who could play their music the loudest. It was nothing like the pristine beaches of Cephalonia and the healing beauty of having the sea as their front yard.

UNLIKE OTHER NEWLY emigrated women in the community who stayed home to keep house and watch children, Demitra was insistent on finding a job and contributing to the household expenses.

"I'm so appreciative of everything you've done for us, but this is temporary. I want to save money to get our own place," she announced over dinner soon after they arrived from Greece.

"We can find a bigger apartment. Don't you worry. You won't need to live alone," Soula assured her each time Demitra brought up the subject. And each time, Sophia and Demitra exchanged knowing glances. Tino knew not to engage with Soula publicly, but he pulled Demitra aside and told her he had the perfect job for her.

Over time Demitra's English improved as she became more comfortable in her role as hostess and cashier at Tino's diner on Fordham Road, across the street from Alexander's Department Store. At first her English was limited to *hello* and *welcome* and *let me show you to your seat*. But soon she found herself conversing with the regular customers, learning how they liked their coffee and their eggs, and for the first time in her life, getting to know people who looked nothing like her.

The diner itself was small with counter seating and a few tables. Every day from the moment the doors opened at 6:00 a.m. to when they closed at 10:00 p.m., men and women of all backgrounds, ethnicities, and languages sat shoulder to shoulder as Tino, Demitra, and the staff of recent Greek immigrants served them American comfort food.

Despite working for family and with family, that tiny diner was where Demitra felt independence for the first time in her life. Each week, after putting aside enough money for Gerasimos's tuition and her share of the groceries, she walked down the street to the bank and handed her money to the teller. Then she stared at her passbook and marveled as her savings grew, along with her dream of one day having a home of her own.

She also grew quite fond of many of the diner's customers, welcoming them as old friends each time they walked through the door. Of all the customers-turned-friends that Demitra looked forward to seeing each day, April, a young wife and mother with two-year-old twins, made her face light up most, always having a smile for Demitra despite the exhaustion permanently etched on her face.

"Exactly how many jobs do you have?" Demitra asked with a laugh. "Do you ever sleep?"

"More than I can count, and sadly, no." April giggled as she hunched her shoulders up. "Some days I wonder how I'll manage, but then I tell myself that I have to. I have no choice but to manage. My great-grandparents were born in slavery," she explained. "My grandparents fled the South and came here, to New York. I'm raising my boys in the same building I grew up in, where I've lived my whole life, but I want more for my boys.

"I want to open the door and let them run and play outside. I want them to have fresh air and catch fireflies and feel grass under their feet. We're saving to buy a house in Long Island. Just another year or two, and I think we'll be ready," she told Demitra as she ate her usual breakfast of a cheese omelet and buttered toast. "Look at me, blathering on." April laughed as she looked at her watch. "I'd better hurry before I'm late for work. How much is that?"

Demitra waved her away. "This one is on me. Just promise you'll have me over when you buy that house."

"It's a deal." April said goodbye with a grateful hug before setting off to work.

As Demitra watched her go, a warmth washed over her with the knowledge that she had made her first friend in New York.

If only the same were true for Gerasimos.

Chapter Forty

My dearest Demitra,

I hope this letter finds you and Gerasimos well. I was so happy to receive your letter and to learn that you are safely settled in New York. I have news for you as well. I am a married man! Her name is Rebekah, and she is a beautiful woman with a beautiful soul. We met six months ago when Mama and I moved into our new apartment in Tel Aviv. She worked in the café on the corner, and I knew I was in love when I found myself drinking four coffees every day. I don't even like coffee! I cannot wait to take her to Greece one day, and we will be sure to visit Cephalonia as well. Until then, we enjoy the beautiful scene in your drawing, dreaming of the day we can sit at a café with you.

Please tell Gerasimos he has made a lasting impact on me and the entire country. Our program is now in every immigration center and camp across Israel. Each child who immigrates to Israel is cared for by our trained team with a focus on education and play. Every time I hear a child laugh and see a child playing, even as their parents navigate the challenges of setting up life in a new country, I thank God for bringing Gerasimos into my life. Together we are changing children's lives.

I am sending you love and well-wishes across the miles, and
I look forward to the day Gerasimos and I can play ball again,
and I can hear his sweet laughter with my own ears.

With love,
Joseph

D EMITRA! ARE YOU ready? It's time to leave," Soula shouted from the living room.

"Coming!" Demitra replied as she folded the letter and placed it in the top drawer of her dresser.

In addition to Joseph's marriage in Israel, the past year brought much news from Cephalonia. Olga had written to say that while rebuilding was moving along slowly, the islanders were up in arms over the construction.

The new buildings are said to be stronger, to withstand any
future quakes, but they are also horrifically ugly and hold none
of the charm and beauty of the old-town Venetian architecture.

Elena had gone even further in her letter, calling the new construction "an offense to the beauty that was Argostoli." She added that she and Niko were both well and that the bakery was thriving.

While there are not many villagers left to feed, those who
have come to help us rebuild have insatiable appetites. I thank
God every day for the gift of this gentle and kind young man.
Together, we are pooling our money and hired a lawyer to help
me find Emanuella. We know she was taken to Athens, to an
orphanage that was selling children to American families. I am
not alone, Demitra. We have heard that this has happened to
many mothers across the islands and mainland. I will not rest
until I find my child.

As Demitra closed the drawer, Soula's voice reverberated through the apartment. "Demitra! Are you coming?" Soula shouted again, each word soaked in annoyance.

"Mama, please." Sophia attempted to quiet her mother. "Of course she's coming. Tino just went to get the car. He's not even out front yet."

"Well, we can't be late. It's bad luck to get to a wedding after the bride. Besides, I told Stamatella we would be there. Her brother just came from Sparta, and he is in the market for a wife."

"Mama, you can't keep doing this!" Sophia shouted. Demitra reached them just as Soula turned her back on her daughter and stomped out the door.

The wedding was held at Zoodohos Peghe Church on Forest Avenue, which was the epicenter of the newly immigrated Greek-American community. The bride and groom emerged from the church after the ceremony to well-wishes and a shower of rice before the reception, held in the church basement. The bride, whose family was from the tiny island of Erikousa, was eighteen years old. Her husband, twenty-five, was from the neighboring island of Othoni. The pair had met at a recent church dance, which Soula reminded Demitra of no less than three times during the ceremony.

As the soulful strum of the bouzouki and shrill timbre of the clarinet filled the air, the bride and groom and their guests danced joyful *kalamatianos* and soulful zeibekikos in celebration of the new couple. Demitra spent the better part of the evening avoiding Stamatella's brother, whose facial posturing and exaggerated gesticulations reminded her more of a primitive mating ritual than a village dance.

All around her the women were coiffed and manicured to perfection, dressed in brightly colored silks and satins. Plunging necklines and cinched waists accentuated voluptuous figures dressed in adoring homage to their Hollywood idols—Marilyn Monroe, Elizabeth Taylor, and Sophia Loren. Audrey Hepburn gamines had no place among the church hall immigrants, where flaunting their newly acquired American wardrobes and figures was a competitive sport.

To Demitra it seemed as if there, in the windowless, paper-decoration-covered basement, drinking and dancing and celebrating with rare prime rib and a plastic-bride-and-groom-adorned wedding cake, each person was living the epitome of their American Dream. They were all of similar backgrounds and stories, and yet Demitra felt so out of place among the friends and family whose stories and experiences had, up to that point, all been so similar.

"AND WHAT WERE you doing last night that you look half asleep?" April asked when she strolled into the diner the next morning.

Demitra smiled at the sight of her and slid behind the counter to pour her coffee.

"Milk and three sugars, just the way you like it. We were at a wedding. It was nice but went very late." She leaned in and whispered, "And if Soula had her way, I'd be next. She keeps bringing around different men, thinking she's doing me a favor. But it's exhausting. I want no part of it."

"You don't want to get married?" April asked as she sipped her coffee.

"No." Adamance filled Demitra's tone. "My heart was broken a few years ago by a man I loved. He really hurt me, April. I don't know that I can see myself letting anyone else in right now, or maybe ever. Besides, I'm too worried about Gerasimos. Something is not right."

"He's still moping around?"

"Yes. I can't get him interested in anything. It's like he's lost his spark, his joy. I have to help him find it again. I moved us here to give him a better life, but I'm not so sure anymore. He tells me he misses home, but there's nothing left there to go back to. For him or for me."

"Come with us next weekend. John and I are taking the boys out to Fire Island. He'll drive and we'll take the ferry from Bayshore. John has been working with the contractors out there building some new homes. He said there's a beautiful beach and a lighthouse. Maybe a day at the beach will do Gerasimos some good."

"I think it might do us all some good," Demitra said as April paid for her breakfast before heading out the door.

Chapter Forty-One

Fire Island, New York

1955

Y OU'RE GOING WHERE? With who?" Soula made no attempt to hide her confusion or her irritation.

"I'm going to Fire Island with my friend April and her family."

"April? The *Mavri*?" Soula looked around the room to Tino and Sophia for support but found none.

"Yes, April is Black. And she's my friend, and Gerasimos and I are going to spend the day at the beach with her husband and children. It will be great for him to get out of the city, for both of us actually."

"Why are you going there with her?" Soula's tone dripped with annoyance laced with disgust. "There is a perfectly good beach here in the Bronx, and it's filled with our own people. Besides, people will talk if they see you with *Mavrous*."

"People will talk? What will they say? That I met a hard-working, lovely woman who cares about Gerasimos and me? That she worked two jobs and got her degree so she can support her family and save enough money to buy a house of her own and help her children get excellent educations? And while *they're* at it, maybe they'll learn a thing or two, because you and I both know that most of *them* can barely even write their names."

Demitra grabbed her bag and Gerasimos's hand and headed for the door.

Gerasimos was fairly quiet on the car ride to the ferry terminal on Bayshore. He answered politely when April and her husband, John, asked about school and who his favorite Yankees player was. When the twins began to fuss, he kept them occupied with a game of peekaboo and let them play with his prized possession—the ball Joseph had given him.

They boarded the ferry and sat up top, taking in the morning sun and the fresh, salty sea breeze. Gerasimos pressed against the railing as the ferry pulled out of its slip, leaning into the wind as it licked his face. The ride across the Great South Bay from the mainland to Fire Island took about thirty minutes, but as they stepped off the boat and onto the dock in the village of Saltaire, Demitra felt like they had been transported to another world.

"Well, what do you think?" John asked as he held the hands of his twins and led the way down the dock toward the beach.

"How is this New York?" Demitra asked, taking in the beauty of the place. All around them, the bay glistened as gulls soared above. The beach itself was narrow and pristine, bordered by a barrier of seagrass that swayed rhythmically in the breeze.

"There ya are, my friend!" The greeting came from a slight man with a boisterous voice and thick Irish brogue. "I almost didn't recognize you without your hard hat and work clothes. Is this what ya look like in real life? Why, a handsome devil ya are."

The man reached out and shook John's hand vigorously before patting him on the back several times.

"And who have ya here? Well, not only are ya handsome, but you're a lucky bastard as well. What a beautiful wife and children ya have." The man took off his hat and held his hand out, taking April's hand in his own and kissing it. "And who is this lovely here?" He extended his hand to Demitra, kissing hers as well.

"Ladies, meet my friend Patrick O'Brien," John announced. "The heart and soul of Saltaire and a master builder."

"Oh, well, thank ya, but I can't take credit for that. You and I both know Mr. Mike Coffey is the master builder of this island. I'm merely a lucky Irishman who came over from Cork five years ago and was smart enough to buy Mr. Coffey a few pints until he let me come work for him."

They walked with Patrick along the promenade where lovely wooden cottages and homes lined the bay, then continued moving farther inland, walking on quaint wooden-slatted boardwalks that served as streets. With no cars allowed on the island, except for emergency vehicles, the children were able to run ahead without a care as the adults followed behind.

"I'll leave ya here," Patrick said as they came to a house that was under construction. "You'll see my boys down on the beach. They're just a wee bit older than you." He tousled Gerasimos's hair. "Now that school's out, those boys will be running like wild horses up and down this island from the moment their eyes open in the morning to the moment their mother shouts for them to come home for bed."

"People live here year-round?" Demitra asked. "There's a school?"

"Well, we can't all be fancy weekenders, now, can we?" Patrick said with a laugh and wink. "There are a few of us that live here. The school's just a few miles down in Ocean Beach. My wife and I moved out here last year after the new school was built. It's a fine place to raise children. My wife and boys love it here, as do I. I mean, as long as the jobs and the drafts at the pub keep flowing." He winked again. "All right then, enjoy your day at the beach while the rest of us earn our keep." And with a tip of his cap, Patrick disappeared into one of the houses.

As they continued walking, Demitra stopped suddenly when they reached a marsh thick with reeds.

"Dear God." She jumped, startled as a deer and her fawn jumped from the brush and darted across the boardwalk. "You don't see that in the Bronx." She laughed.

"Unless it's a rat," April chimed in, dissolving both women into giggles.

As they walked to the top of the ramp leading to the beach, Demitra stopped and stared, breathless at the sight before her. The sand was a pale caramel color and dotted with only a few families spread out along the wide beach, unlike Orchard Beach where the families were packed in with barely inches between them.

The beach spanned endlessly to the left and right, as far as the eye could see. And before her, the ocean, brilliant blue and sparkling, was alive with waves that rose and fell along the shoreline, and where a gaggle of boys bodysurfed and dove and splashed, filling the air with their joyful laughter. She turned and looked to Gerasimos, whose face had exploded in wonder at the sight before him. It had been so long since she'd seen him like this, an image of unbridled delight.

"It's beautiful, isn't it?"

He nodded and then turned to her.

"Go on," she said before he had a chance to speak.

He raced down the ramp to the beach, kicking his shoes off as he went. If the sand was hot, he didn't notice, or he was moving too fast to feel it. He pulled off his shirt and tossed that, too, to the sand, before diving into the surf and emerging a moment later with a smile as bright as the midday sun. Soon after, one of the boys tossed a ball to Gerasimos, who tossed it back with perfect aim, which instantly cemented his place in their game as they waved him over to join in the fun.

Watching them play, Demitra marveled at how instantly taken with one another they were, accepting Gerasimos as one of the pack, as if they had been friends for years.

She, April, and John sat on a blanket and nibbled on their picnic lunch, watching the twins play in the sand and Gerasimos swim with his new friends. Demitra took it all in and realized that in that moment for the first time in as long as she could remember, she felt the tension in her body melt away.

"This is lovely, isn't it?" April asked as she kept a watchful eye on the twins.

"No," Demitra said as she lay back on her blanket, the sun on her face, the breeze in her hair, her ears filled with the happy squeals of children.

"It's not lovely. It's perfect."

1957

EVERYTHING CHANGED AFTER that first visit to Saltaire with April and John. It was as if the narrow barrier beach community opened a new world of possibility for both Demitra and Gerasimos.

Week after week, Soula pursed her lips and scowled when Demitra packed her bag with towels and a picnic lunch.

"You'll never find a husband at the rate you're going. There's a dance at the church tonight. Come with us. There are plenty of young men. You'll have your pick."

"Thea, I don't want my pick of men. I want to spend the day with my friends, sitting on the sand and watching Gerasimos play. I don't understand why you think I'm doing something wrong. He's the happiest he's been since the earthquake."

"He's a child. He'll grow up and out of it. Besides, people are talking. They're saying you spend all your time with the Mavrous."

Demitra bit her tongue to refrain from saying what she wanted to, which was, *"When did you go from being an uninformed busybody to a full-blown ignorant racist?"* Instead, she counted to three and said, "I'm not doing anything wrong, Thea. I made a friend and Gerasimos is happy. He's finally learned to smile again. I don't understand why that's a problem for you."

"And I don't understand why you can't stick to your own kind and just settle down like a normal girl with nice Greek friends like everybody else."

Despite Sophia and Tino's pleas to tune her out, it was becoming more and more difficult for Demitra to tolerate Soula's overbearing and heavy-handed judgment.

Each Sunday as they piled in the car with April and John and the twins, then boarded the ferry and crossed the Great South Bay bound for Fire Island, Demitra felt the stress and anxiety melt from her body.

One evening in mid-August as they watched the sun set on the bay while they waited for the ferry back to Bayshore after a perfect beach day, Gerasimos turned to Demitra.

"Do we really have to go back?" he asked, a wistful look in his eyes, melancholy in his tone. "Can't we just stay here?"

She looked around at the brilliant orange glow of the setting sun descending over the bay, the silver shimmer of the fading light dancing on the water's surface, and the familiar fishermen who greeted them each week when they arrived in the morning and then patiently showed Gerasimos their catch in the evening. Demitra opened her mouth to respond but stopped herself.

Why can't we just stay here?

She glanced all around her at the island that had grown to mean so much to them both. And then she remembered a recent conversation with Patrick after they were invited for coffee at his home.

"Our boys have grown quite fond of that young lad of yours, and my wife loved having ya for coffee last week. Let me know if ya ever decide to leave the city. I'd be sure to find ya a good deal on a home out here." They had both laughed at the time, repeating the phrase "wishful thinking" as she boarded the ferry and waved goodbye.

But Demitra was not laughing now.

"Demitra." Gerasimos moaned as he tugged at her skirt. "Why do we have to go back? Can't we just stay here?"

She looked down at him then, at his sun-kissed olive skin and bright eyes, his hair streaked with caramel by the sun.

"Yes, my sweetheart. We can stay here. And we will."

BETWEEN HER SAVINGS from working at the diner the past four years and the mortgage Tino cosigned and helped her secure with the bank, Demitra had just enough to purchase a small bungalow on Bay Promenade with a lovely deck and windows facing the water. It was the offseason with little work to be found on the island after the summer residents had gone, but Demitra had budgeted carefully and had just enough money to last through the winter. Patrick and John both assured her there would be plenty of work for her during the summer season, so she planned to spend the next few months doing what she loved best: doting on Gerasimos, enjoying the unspoiled beauty of the island, and rediscovering her passion for drawing.

The house itself was tiny, with a kitchen, small living room, and two bedrooms. Patrick helped her gather some furniture, since he knew which summer residents were moving or redecorating and had no further use for the odd chair, table, or bed. As for the walls of her little beach cottage, that was where her own art, the collection growing month by month, found a home.

Each morning after seeing Gerasimos off on the bus, Demitra made herself a cup of coffee and sat in her favorite spot, outside on the deck overlooking the water. It had been so long since she'd had the luxury of time alone, time to lose herself in her own thoughts and imagination. She savored every moment, treasured every opportunity for solitude, observing her new morning ritual out on the deck, drinking in the beauty and tranquility surrounding her, watching as does and their spotted fawns feasted on the shrubs and flowers along the shoreline and the gulls shrieked and dove into the sea to fetch their morning meal.

When the last drop of bitter Greek coffee was drained, Demitra peered into her cup, wondering if today might be the day her fate would be revealed. With one hand she twirled her cup this way and that, trying to make sense of the muddy grounds. But each day was the same as before; no images appeared in the cup, no road map for her future, no secrets untangled. Unlike before, the realization filled Demitra with a new sense of pride and purpose, serving as confirmation that her story and her future were in no one's hands but her own.

As she set her cup aside, Demitra took her most valued possession in her hands. Caressing and stroking the soft leather as one might a lover, she closed her eyes and pressed her cheek to the book Aleko had given her, imagining what might have been if only they'd been given a chance. She traced the golden letters on the cover with her finger, *The Powerful and Magical Women of Myths*. This book, these women, that man, were the embodiment of everything that inspired and haunted her.

Just yesterday she had finally finished her drawing of Persephone. In Demitra's interpretation Persephone was not a distraught maiden, her fate sealed by six pomegranate seeds. In Demitra's hands Persephone was the queen of the underworld, seated on her throne, ruling side by side with Hades, persuading him to allow heartbroken Orpheus a chance to resurrect his love. In Demitra's hands Persephone was more than a motherless daughter; she was a woman who had grown into her own mind, her own power, and her own place in the world.

With her easel set up before her, her pencils lined up on the table, and the serenity of the morning light dancing on the water's surface, Demitra picked up a black thin-tipped pencil and tingled with the excitement and anticipation of a blank new page.

Starting with the woman's eyes, large and bright, Demitra began to draw the goddess who had consumed her thoughts since she first made the decision to leave the familiarity of the Bronx and move to the unspoiled beauty of Fire Island.

With feathery, delicate strokes Demitra slowly brought her to life: Artemis, goddess of the hunt. There was more to Artemis than her skill with her bow and arrow. Demitra had been drawn to Apollo's twin for her fierce independence and refusal to marry, choosing instead to live alone in the forest where she danced and hunted with her closest friends, the woodland nymphs.

Artemis was in many ways a study in contradictions. She was the goddess of the hunt and yet a staunch defender of animals. She was a virgin, having vowed never to marry, and yet she was also the goddess of childbirth. And despite being the protectress of children, Artemis was the one who called for the sacrifice of Agamemnon's daughter, Iphigenia, in retribution for the king's hubris.

Demitra worked on her drawing for the better part of the morning, not noticing that lunchtime had come and gone. Only when she heard Patrick's joyful greeting did she look up and realize what time it was.

"Well look here, Margaret. Did ya know we have an artist among us?" Something about Patrick's voice, his joyful tone and deep brogue, brought a smile to Demitra's face each time she was in his presence. With blue saucer eyes, a hearty laugh, and a quick smile, Patrick's wife, Margaret, had quickly become a trusted and valued friend.

"Hello there." Demitra stood and arched her back, stretching toward the cloudless blue sky. "The day got away from me."

"What have we here?" Margaret asked and leaned in to have a look at the drawing as she placed a plate of homemade soda bread on the table. "She's quite something, isn't she?"

"Yes. Artemis. My current muse," Demitra replied as she reached over to break off a corner of the bread. "Oh, you know this is my favorite," she said before popping it into her mouth.

"And don't think I came empty-handed, as my wife here plies you with gifts. Look what arrived today on the ferry," Patrick said as he pulled a folded newspaper from his back pocket and slapped it on the table. "One of our workers lives in Astoria. He said he would bring the paper out here for you."

"Oh, Patrick. Thank you!" Demitra squealed. It was the *Ethnikos Kirikas*, the Greek-language newspaper and daily chronicle of Greek and Greek-American news that she had read every day in the Bronx. "I could kiss you." She wrapped her arms around him and planted a kiss on his cheek.

"Careful there, the wife is likely to get jealous." He raised his eyebrow.

"No, not likely at all." Margaret laughed and shook her head. "But I am likely to have a cup of coffee if you're making it."

Demitra made a fresh pot, and they sat on the deck enjoying their coffee in the afternoon sun, filling each other in on the latest news and comings and goings on the island.

"Have you spoken to April recently?" Patrick asked.

"No. It's been a few days, but I'm hoping they'll come out this weekend."

"I hope so too. They could use a bit of a break. John came by yesterday, and he was angry and upset. I imagine April is the same."

"Why? What happened?" Demitra put down her coffee.

"There was a house they wanted in Levittown. Lovely home with a yard on a quiet street. They said it was perfect. The owners were an older couple who wanted to sell, but there were other . . . 'complications.' The bank declined the mortgage."

"That doesn't make sense." Demitra struggled to understand. "They have good jobs. Good credit."

"My dear, there is a lot about our new country that we love, but there is also a lot that does not make sense." Patrick harrumphed.

"But they're American . . ."

"Yes," Margaret added with a knowing sigh. "And apparently even for Americans the streets are paved with gold for some, and for others, there are many unfortunate detours."

Demitra made a mental note to call April later that evening. This all made no sense to her. April had told her about the discrimination her grandparents faced in the South and how they chose to come to New York where a hardworking Black couple could make a good life for themselves and educate their children. How and why could they be denied a mortgage?

"We should get going." Patrick stood to leave. "I have to sort out an open house for this weekend in Fair Harbor. The house is lovely, but even with the furniture we brought in, it looks cold and sterile, like an empty shell. The real estate agent says homes sell for higher prices when they look lived in." He placed his cap on his head.

"Let me show you something." Demitra stood and ushered them inside. "You can borrow these, if you like." Demitra pointed to the art she had recently framed and hung. "You're welcome to some or all. It's the least I could do. This is Persephone. And this is Amphitrite. And over here, this is Daphne."

Demitra stopped beneath the picture of Daphne, watching as Patrick and Margaret regarded the drawing, a smile developing on each of their faces as they studied the beautiful nymph brought to exquisite and careful life. In Demitra's hands Daphne was not the frightened nymph depicted in other works of art. She was not the girl who called out for her father to save her. Instead, she was a young woman who knew what she wanted and what she did not. In Demitra's hands Daphne's shoulders were straight, her head held high, chin tilted toward the heavens and a serene smile on her face. In Demitra's hands the moment the nymph's legs turned to the bark of a tree and her hands sprouted branches and leaves was the moment she took control of her life. This Daphne was not a woman running from a life she did not want; instead, she was firmly rooted in the life she chose for herself.

"This one," Margaret said as she pointed to Daphne with a knowing smile.

"Yes. She'll do nicely." Patrick nodded in appreciation as he took a step closer to Daphne. "That's an excellent idea. Fair Harbor is an artist's community filled with writers and journalists. They'll love this. Thank you, Demitra," he said before taking the framed drawing off the wall. He regarded it closely. "Nice to meet you, beautiful lady. Let's hope you bring us a wee bit of luck." With that he tucked it under his arm and walked toward the door.

Chapter Forty-Two

Fire Island, New York

1959

D APHNE DID INDEED bring Patrick luck.

The open house was a success, with a Manhattan couple falling in love with the property—and the drawing of Daphne. They made an offer on both the house and the drawing that very afternoon. He was a playwright, and she a theater critic for the *Village Voice*. Soon after they moved in, a neighbor at one of their dinner parties took notice of Daphne and asked about the artist.

The next day that neighbor walked over to Bay Promenade and made an offer for Persephone. Within weeks Demitra had developed quite a following among the art-loving community of Fire Island. A goddess drawn by the resident Greek artist quickly became the most coveted acquisition of the season.

Watching as interest in Demitra's art surged over the next two summers, the proud owner of Daphne was no fool, seizing the opportunity to drive up the value of the drawing he'd purchased for a song.

In June of 1959 the headline of the *Village Voice* profile of Demitra declared her "The Greek Goddess of the Art World." The article detailed how the beautiful, exotic artist had fled earthquake-ravaged Cephalonia for New York, where she was disrupting the art community with her pencil interpretations of the extraordinary women of myth.

"I mean, I've always known you were a disruptor." April laughed when they finally caught up by telephone.

"Ha! The only thing I've ever disrupted is Soula's peace." Demitra laughed. "I finally broke down and decided to get an agent. Her name is Stephanie, and she said she'll help me open doors I've never even dreamed of. She also asked me to stop selling directly to whoever shows up at my house, like—what did she call it?—oh yes, a garage sale." This dissolved them both into laughter.

"How is Gerasimos taking all this news? What does he think of your newfound celebrity?"

"He couldn't care less, to be honest. He's just so happy to be outside playing with his friends. He's doing well in school also. Oh, and he's going by Jerry now, by the way. He says he'll always be Gerasimos, but he asked if it would be all right to use a more American name at school."

"What did you say when he asked that? Is it all right with you?"

"I said yes, of course. Unlike Soula, I'm not afraid of diluting our Greek identity. It's not like a sock; it's not something that's easily lost. It's who we are, who we'll always be. And listen to this: once the *Village Voice* article hit, I got a call from the Greek paper. They did a story on me too. And you know, after being such a bitter disappointment to Soula for so long, she now tells everyone I'm her favorite niece and that I'm like her daughter. I think she's trying to drive up the price on the drawing I did of her restaurant in Ipsos." Demitra laughed again, twirling the phone cord in her hand. "Enough about me. What's going on with the house? I'm almost afraid to ask. Is it done?"

"Yes. Thank God. I can't believe how long this has all taken, but we finally signed the contract on the house in North Amityville. It's so beautiful. I can't wait for you to come see it. And, Demitra, the yard is big and beautiful, and the neighbors are families with children. The boys will be so happy there. After what happened in

Levittown, I was so discouraged. But I think in the end this is a better fit for us. I just wish it hadn't happened the way it did.

"I was so angry when we lost Levittown, and I wanted to fight, to *make* them give me that house. But then I realized I didn't want to raise my children in a neighborhood where the people wouldn't throw their arms around us to welcome us. Our lawyer said if we took them to court, we would win, that the initial contracts the residents signed forbidding them from selling to nonwhite families were not constitutional. But what's the point of all that if I have to worry about the safety of my children every time they walk out of the house? What's the point of having neighbors if every time they see my children, they look at them and think they don't belong? How could I live next to people who would not look after my house and children as if they were their own?"

"Oh, April. I'm so sorry you had to go through this. You and your family deserve only the best. Anyone would be so lucky to have you as their neighbor. I'd give anything to have you next door to me. It's just not right. It's infuriating, actually. But this new house sounds perfect. I know you'll be happy there," Demitra said as she poured a cup of coffee. "Let me know when you're settled, and I'll come over. I've got to run for now. I have some work to get done before Gerasi—I mean Jerry—comes home."

She hung up the phone and took her coffee outside to the deck and sat at the table, gazing out across the bay. The morning sunrise had revealed clear, bright skies when she took her beach walk earlier, but now dark gray clouds appeared over the mainland and bay.

I guess I'll be working inside later today.

She opened the Greek newspaper. In their first meeting, her agent, Stephanie, had suggested they curate a show of more obscure, yet fascinating women of myth. Demitra had borrowed several books from the Saltaire Library and planned to spend the afternoon researching possible new subjects. But first she wanted to enjoy her coffee with the Greek paper on the deck before the storm set in. She brought the cup to her lips and took a sip as she scanned the headlines.

KING PAUL AND QUEEN FREDERICA GREETED BY THE POPE AT THE VATICAN

EDDIE FISHER MARRIES ELIZABETH TAYLOR HOURS AFTER HIS DIVORCE FROM DEBBIE REYNOLDS

NEW YORK LAWYER INDICTED IN ILLEGAL GREEK ADOPTIONS PROBE

Demitra put her coffee down and read the headline again.

NEW YORK LAWYER INDICTED IN ILLEGAL GREEK ADOPTIONS PROBE

Her heart raced as she began to read. The article went on to explain that a Brooklyn attorney had been arrested for receiving payments to illegally place Greek children with American families.

Mr. Michael Niaxos was charged, along with three other defendants, with operating a black market of Greek children for American families who were not properly vetted and paid thousands to choose their adoptive children from photographs Mr. Niaxos provided. Many of the children were from the Saint Helen Orphanage in Athens, where they were placed illegally, some stolen from their families. There have been reports of children being sold to families who had previously been denied by sanctioned U.S. adoption agencies or deemed unfit for adoption by U.S. adoption laws. After children were placed with their new families, there were no protocols in place for follow-up visits to assess the children's home environment and no welfare checks. It is believed that Mr. Niaxos personally placed more than fifty children in homes here in the New York area.

Demitra felt nauseated and unsteady on her feet as she stood and took a few breaths to steady herself. The skies above were dark and ominous. She heard a distant clap of thunder as the bay seemed to have turned from blue to black. She went inside and picked up the phone to call Cephalonia, grateful Niko had recently installed a telephone in the bakery.

It was late afternoon in Greece, and Elena would likely still be at the bakery cleaning up from the day and making preparations for the morning. The phone rang five times before she answered.

"Elena, it's Demitra."

"Well, hello to the famous artist. I haven't spoken to you in weeks. I figured you're much too busy giving interviews to check in on your old friends."

"Elena, I have to tell you something. There's a story in the papers here. A Greek-American lawyer was arrested for selling babies here in New York."

Elena gasped.

"It says there are at least fifty adoptions that they know of. The children were taken from an orphanage in Athens. The last time we spoke, you said your lawyer tracked Emanuella to an orphanage in Athens. Do you remember which one?"

"Yes. Yes, of course I do. He even went there. Niko paid for him to go, but the records are sealed. They won't allow us to access any records or speak to anyone. We've tried everything, but they won't help us."

"Elena, what's the name of the orphanage?"

"It was Saint Helen in Athens, near Erythro Stavro. Near the hospital."

Demitra inhaled sharply, grasping the table to steady herself, her voice quivering with emotion.

"Elena, that's it. That's the orphanage. He placed children from Saint Helen with families here in New York."

The sounds of Elena's soft whimpers filled Demitra's ear. And then there was silence.

"Elena? Did you hear me?" Demitra asked as she twirled the phone cord around her finger. "Elena, are you there?"

But Elena did not answer.

HEMPSTEAD, NEW YORK

"Are you sure about this? Are you sure this is the right thing to do?" John asked as he opened the car door for Demitra. She slid onto the bench seat beside April and reached over to give her a warm hug.

"No. But I know it's something I need to do."

"How did you get the address anyway?" April asked. "You never told me."

"Patrick's cousin is a police detective who works in the courts. Patrick asked him if he knew anything about the adoptions and told him about Elena and what happened to her. Then this angel of a man somehow got his hands on the file. All the information is correct—her name, her birthday. It says her mother was a prostitute who died in childbirth. It's her. She was adopted by a family that had three sons and wanted a daughter." She paused, looking out the window. "So they bought one."

"Oh dear God." April sighed.

"There were no systems, no screening, nothing. All that mattered was that the families were Greek and that they could pay in cash. Patrick's cousin said some of these children were handed over to abusive parents. The problem is that the adoptions were legal in Greece, so the charges against Niaxos, the attorney, were dropped. There's nothing anyone can do to help get the children out of these homes unless abuse is reported. Here's the address," Demitra said, handing John a piece of paper. "They live in Hempstead."

"Ok," John said, pulling out a Rand McNally map of Nassau County and studying it for a few moments.

"Thank you for doing this. For driving me. I promised Elena I would go, just to try to catch a glimpse of her. From there, who knows? We can try, somehow, to get her back, to prove she was stolen and the adoption was illegal. But Elena can't wait any longer. She wants to know that she's all right, that her daughter is safe." The emotions once again overwhelmed Demitra as they had so many times in the past few months as she tried helping Elena navigate this horrific situation.

"We've got you." April reached over and grabbed Demitra's hand. "Let's go. Let's go find your friend's child."

It was nearly 11:00 a.m. by the time they found the home on Stewart Lane in Hempstead. The lawns were manicured and the street was quiet, lined with neat split-level and colonial homes with brick and aluminum siding. The home at the address she'd been given was redbrick with neatly pruned shrubbery and four carved jack-o'-lanterns on the porch.

John parked a little farther down the street, affording them a perfect view of the house. For nearly two hours they waited and watched as neighbors came and went. The driveway was empty and the curtains drawn. It appeared as if no one was home.

"It's Sunday, so they likely went to church," Demitra said. "If that's the case, if they come home after services, they'll probably be back around twelve thirty or one."

They waited in the car with the windows rolled up. April was singing along to "To Know Him Is to Love Him" by the Teddy Bears on the radio when her serenade was interrupted by John shushing her and pointing to the house, then turning down the radio.

A black Buick drove down the street and turned into the driveway.

They each held their breath and sat up straighter as they stared out the window.

The car doors opened, and the mother and father stepped out. They looked to be in their midforties. She was portly with jet-black hair cut just past her chin and teased and sprayed into a flip. Her thick waist was cinched with a wide black leather belt, and she wore a pale blue twinset and pearls. He wore a brown suit with a tie, his belly hanging generously over his trousers.

The back door of the car opened, and the children streamed out. Three boys, who appeared to range in age from about ten to twelve. They, too, were well dressed in slacks and collared shirts.

Then a young girl exited. She looked to be about seven or eight, the age Emanuella would be now. She wore a pale blue dress with pearl buttons. Her hair was light brown and cinched in French braids tied with white ribbons.

Demitra raised her hand to her mouth as she watched the girl, emotions rising quickly. She had never laid eyes on this child before, but Demitra felt the familiarity in her bones. The girl was tall and slim with lithe, lean limbs and an upturned nose, like Elena.

As the father stood on the front porch and opened the door, a large German shepherd raced outside and jumped him, licking his face before running out to the lawn and zooming in circles to the delight of everyone. The girl picked up a ball and threw it across the grass, and the dog raced after it and brought it back to her, dropping it at her feet before attacking her with kisses all over her face. That sent her into a fit of giggles as her parents and siblings watched, laughing and holding their bellies until they doubled over.

"Darling!" the mother shouted. "Remember Yia-yia and Papou are coming for dinner later. I'm making your favorite—pastichio with créme caramel for dessert. Please make sure you get your homework done before they arrive. And don't forget you have ballet tomorrow. Let's make sure you pack your leotard and shoes. We don't want a repeat of last week." She shook her head and laughed, even as she feigned anger and wagged her finger in reprimand.

"Yes, Mama." The girl skipped over to the woman and planted a kiss on her cheek before going inside. The dog followed closely behind and then the woman.

Once the door closed, Demitra turned to April and John. They all seemed to exhale simultaneously. No one spoke for a moment.

"It was her. It was Emanuella," Demitra whispered as she wrung her hands. "I know it. She looks like her mother. She moves like her mother." She exhaled a long, deep breath before turning her gaze out the window again toward the house. "She is her mother's daughter."

Everyone was silent, digesting what they'd just witnessed, digesting the significance of it all.

John finally broke the silence. "We can stay longer. We're in no rush," he said as his hands gripped the steering wheel. "April's mother is with the boys. We can stay as late as we need to." He turned to Demitra with softness in his eyes. "As late as you want to."

Demitra smiled at him in appreciation and turned her gaze back out the widow to the house. "No. I think we've seen all we need to see." She swallowed and looked straight ahead while grabbing and squeezing April's hand. "Let's go home."

Later that evening when Demitra called, Elena answered on the first ring.

Cephalonia, Greece

SHE HAD ALREADY cleaned the counters, portioned the flour for the next day, and swept the floor twice. Everything else was clean, so Elena paced back and forth as she stared at the phone mounted on the wall, willing it to ring.

"Nothing?" Niko asked as he came in from the storage room, a sack of flour draped across his shoulder.

"No. She promised she would call as soon as she had news." Elena glanced at the clock on the wall again. It was nearly midnight. "Please, don't let me keep you. You should go to bed. It's late." She walked over to Niko and wiped a dusting of flour from his shoulder.

"No, that's all right. I'll wait with you," he said with a yawn as he went back into the storage room.

She turned then to the display case, grabbed a cloth, and wiped down the glass, even though she had done so nearly four hours before when the bakery closed for the day.

The jingling of the telephone startled her, despite the fact she had been waiting on the call for hours.

"Hello?" she answered breathlessly.

"Elena, it's me." The words poured out of Demitra's mouth in rapid succession. "I saw her, Elena . . . I saw her. I know it's her. We found Emanuella."

Elena sank to the floor, still holding the phone to her ear.

"Tell me," she said with a whimper. She glanced up to find Niko watching from the doorway. She nodded at him, her eyes filled with tears. He shuffled over and sat on the floor beside her, his head leaning back on the counter.

Demitra shared everything in exacting detail. From the tidy brick home to the mother's cherubic appearance to the way Emanuella squealed with delight in her Sunday best as she played with the family's dog on the front lawn, her braids bouncing behind her.

"She's tall and so beautiful," Demitra reported. "And she takes ballet."

Elena let out a wistful sigh. "My daughter, a ballerina . . ." Her voice trembled with emotion as she imagined Emanuella gliding across the floor to a beautiful symphony, a vision in pale pink tights and a tutu, elegant and refined.

"There has to be a way to get the records from the adoption agency," Demitra was saying. "They lied. They falsified the documents to say she was an orphan. Now that we know where she is, we can have your lawyer reach out to them, to explain." Elena could hear the nervous tapping of Demitra's fingernails on the counter as she finished formulating a plan. "We'll hire an attorney here in New York too. I have some money from my drawings. It's not much, but it's enough for a start. I'll ask Patrick to help; he'll help us find—"

"Did she look happy?" Elena asked.

"She skipped over and kissed her mother. She squealed with delight as she played with her dog."

"She did."

"Did she look well cared for?"

"Her pretty French braids and ribbons trailed in the air as she played. She wore a pearl-buttoned sweater to keep the early fall chill at bay."

"Yes, she did. She's beautiful. You have a beautiful daughter, Elena. And I know if we hire an attorney here in New York—"

"No." Elena interrupted Demitra's orchestrations, her voice soft but resolute.

"I'm sorry, what? There's something wrong with the phone. I can barely hear you." Elena heard Demitra tapping the receiver in frustration. "There's interference with the line. I didn't hear what you said."

Elena waited a moment, trying to regulate her breathing, trying to regulate her thoughts. Finally, she spoke again, her voice stronger.

"I said no. It's done, Demitra. Thank you. But it's finished now."

"I don't understand. What's finished?" Demitra's voice rose an octave. "I'm confused. We found her. Elena, we found Emanuella."

"All I wanted was for my child to have a chance at a better life, a good life." Elena tried to conceal her crying, but her sobs filled the air and the time and space between them. She struggled to catch her breath, and when she spoke again, her words were stuttered.

"I wanted t-to be the one to t-teach her, to w-watch her grow up. I wanted m-my hand to be the one she reached for when she wanted assurance, m-my bed the one she crawled into when she was afraid at night. I always d-dreamed she would be my best friend. I knew she could be my best friend." Elena paused, conjuring the scenes in her mind as she had so many times before. She took a deep breath.

"But I can't be that for her, Demitra. Not now. I can't be her best friend or her anything. Me, a poor prostitute with a painful, sordid past and no future. My daughter has a chance at a life I could not even dare to dream of. My daughter, a ballerina . . ." A guttural moan escaped her lips as she struggled to compose herself again, to finish what she was intent on saying out loud.

"I love my child more than anything, Demitra. I gave her life and held her in my arms for a beautiful moment, and then she was gone, ripped away from me, and my heart was ripped out with her. I always dreamed of finding her, of holding her again, of telling her how I never stopped searching for her, how I never stopped loving her . . . but it's finished now."

"Elena, what are you saying?"

"I'll always be her mother. But I won't take her away from her new family, from her new mother. They are her future, Demitra. Not me. What future can I offer her? I'm not a smart woman. I'm not an educated woman, but what I lack in book learning, I make up for in my capacity to love. And I love her more than I ever thought possible. I love her more than she'll ever know."

Overwhelmed with emotion and consumed with pain but also resolve, Elena closed her eyes, imagining the moment she'd held her daughter in her arms, picturing her delicate, angelic face. The face she knew she would never see again.

"I am her mother, and I love her enough to know that I have to let her go." Elena dropped the telephone receiver and fell to the floor, broken.

Niko said nothing. He picked up the telephone, stood, and placed it back in its cradle. Then he stayed there for a moment as she lay on the floor, her body convulsing in sobs. He sat back down next to her, inching closer until there was no distance left between them. Without lifting her head, Elena reached her hand out to him. He took it in his, holding it silently as she wept beside him.

Chapter Forty-Three

Milwaukee, Wisconsin

1929

Seven inches of snow fell in Milwaukee on December 18, 1929, the day Maria's prayers were answered and she finally gave birth to a healthy baby girl.

"I'd like to name her after my mother, if that's all right, to keep a little bit of home with me here," she said from the hospital bed where she was propped up against a backdrop of pillows, exhausted after thirty-six hours of labor.

"You can name her anything you like," Pericles said as he cradled their daughter in his arms, walking around the hospital room in circles and gazing at her in wonder.

Four days later Maria waited for Pericles in the vestibule of the hospital, the bitter wind slicing through her thin coat as she nestled her daughter in her arms.

She blinked several times, unsure if the vision before her could be real as Pericles pulled up to the hospital in a black Buick, honking the horn, a smile unfurled on his face.

"What in the world?" She gazed up at him as he guided her carefully from the hospital entrance to the front seat of the car, the baby swaddled in layers of homemade crochet blankets and held tightly to her chest.

"The roads are a mess. I couldn't trust a taxi in this weather, not for my girls. I borrowed Tasso's car," he said as he smiled at her and peeled back the blanket to plant a kiss on his daughter's cheek.

The drive home was treacherous as the snow and ice rendered many of the roads slick and others impassable. Pericles focused intently on the road and gripped the steering wheel, his knuckles turning white as Maria sang and cooed to the baby.

The surprises did not end with the car ride home.

"What . . . ?" Maria's face crumpled with emotion when she opened the apartment door and saw a small, decorated Christmas tree in the corner.

"I couldn't have our daughter go without a tree for her first Christmas. I thought you might like it too," he said.

"Oh, I do. I like it very much. Thank you," she said as she bounced the baby in her arms.

"I brought you some soup from the restaurant. It's on the stove."

She sat down at the kitchen table and peeled back the blanket from the baby's face. It was cold and drafty in the apartment, so she made certain to keep the baby swaddled and held close to her chest. As she looked around at the tree, Pericles warming her soup on the stove, and their perfect daughter in her arms, Maria felt a swell of emotion. Perhaps she'd been wrong. Maybe now that they had a daughter and he had a reason to come home, they could finally be a family. Maybe she could find happiness with this man in this drafty apartment in this strange, bustling city.

She looked up at him, gratitude in her eyes as he placed the hot soup before her. She shifted the baby into the nook of her arm and slowly brought the spoon to her mouth. She had never tasted anything so perfect and satisfying before.

She had not yet finished her soup when he grabbed his coat and headed for the door.

"Where are you going?" she asked as the baby began to cry. She put the spoon down and unbuttoned her blouse, bringing the baby to her breast.

"I have to get to the restaurant. We've been busier than ever. The storm shut down the rail lines, and many of the workers can't get home to their families for Christmas, so we've been feeding them. And . . . there's been another incident. I thought the weather might keep the white mob away from us, at least for a little bit, but this was plastered on the door overnight." He pulled a paper from his pocket and placed it on the table. "It says 'Shut Down the Dirty Greeks.'" He shook his head. "A Christmas gift from the Klan to us."

There was nothing about her that did not scream in pain at that moment. Her nipples were on fire from the newness of nursing a tiny, ravenous child, her insides were stretched and torn from birth, and her emotions were raw from the euphoria of at last becoming a mother, and now the devastation of being abandoned. Again.

"But I'm still weak. I'm not sure I can care for her myself. Can't you stay? Even for a little while?"

"Don't be silly," he said as he buttoned his coat and wrapped his scarf around his neck. "You'll be fine. You have food and water, and I'll be home in a few days. In the village women went to the fields the day after giving birth. All you have to do is sit here in your own home with the child we prayed for. Now you have it all, everything you could ever ask for. It's all right here." He snatched the paper from the table and shoved it into his pocket before walking out the door.

For the next four days, the baby did not stop crying. For the next four days, neither did she.

He walked through the door on Christmas Eve smelling of stale whisky and cigars.

"I'm home!" he shouted. "What's for supper? I'm starving."

part

five

Chapter Forty-Four

Soho, New York

1970

A TOAST!" STEPHANIE RAISED her glass of champagne into the air. "To the darling of the art world. Today, we celebrate you, Demitra. What you have accomplished is unprecedented. Not only have you made the international art community stand up and take notice, but you have also captured our imaginations with your masterful, evocative, and emotional storytelling.

"When I was first told about Demitra and her art, I must admit I was skeptical. Pencil drawings, really?" Stephanie twisted her lips and knotted her brow, which made the crowd erupt in laughter.

"But then I saw the magic of her storytelling, the lessons in grace and love and courage that permeate each piece, and I knew there was something very special here. Now, in celebration of this carefully curated collection, let's celebrate the first of what promises to be many shows by our favorite Greek goddess of the art world."

"To Demitra!" Everyone in the gallery raised a glass in her honor. The Soho gallery was packed to capacity with friends, family, and art lovers for the opening of the exhibit, titled "Behind the Myth." In the center of the gallery placed on a glass table was a beautiful vase of white roses. The note attached read, "With love, Elena and Niko." Even Jerry was in attendance, having arrived that afternoon on the train from his studies at Georgetown.

"Thank you." Demitra tried to hold back her tears, but it was no use. She shook with disquieting anxiety and had argued with Stephanie about the need for her to make any sort of remarks. But Stephanie insisted, so Demitra prayed for strength and took a deep sip of champagne before stepping into the center of the room to speak.

"Thank you, Stephanie, for believing in my work, and in me. Thank you all for coming tonight. In keeping with the themes I love to explore, all the women you see here today are strong, inspirational, and layered. You might look at them and think you know their narrative—or who history, tradition, or mythology tells you they are, anyway. But as with most women, what you see on the surface is only part of the story. What she allows you to see and who she really is are often very different. I hope you'll take some time to get to know these fascinating women, to unlock their mysteries, to look deeper, to learn and be inspired by the lessons they impart, even today. And remember that boring women rarely make history or great art. Thank you, everyone, for coming."

"Bravo! To Demitra!" April shouted over the crowd as she raised her glass. Everyone else followed suit, cheering and clapping wildly.

"To Demitra!" the chorus cheered as they toasted her.

Raising her champagne glass in gratitude, Demitra wove her way through the crowd to find her friends and family gathered in a corner of the exhibit.

"She's beautiful and fierce, this one," Margaret said as she gestured to the drawing before them. Patrick raised his glass in agreement. "'Cassandra,'" Margaret said as she read the plaque adjacent to the frame.

"Yes. Cassandra was very beautiful, as you can see." The nervousness in her speech seemed to melt away, and Demitra felt a glow from within as she discussed her work with her friends. "Apollo fell in love with Cassandra and gave her the gift of prophecy as a way to entice her to be his lover. I mean, who could refuse a god and the gift of prophecy, right?

"But Cassandra did refuse. She was not interested in becoming the god's lover, so he was furious, as you can imagine. Apollo wanted to punish her, so, while Cassandra could see the future, Apollo made sure no one would ever believe her. The woman who was praised and adored and worshiped for her beauty was ultimately punished for it as well. She spoke the truth; she warned the Trojans about the Trojan Horse. When they refused to believe her, she tried to burn it down herself to save them. But instead of being called a hero, she was vilified for speaking the truth."

April opened her mouth to ask a question but was interrupted by the booming sound of Soula's voice.

"My famous niece! I knew it the minute you drew my taverna. I told everyone you would be a famous artist, and now, look at you. We are all so proud of you!" she exclaimed, throwing her arms around Demitra. "Even when we were in Ipsos, I saw something special in her. I knew she would be a success," Soula gloated as she put her arm out to stop a passing waiter, taking not one but three caviar canapés in her hand.

All around the gallery the room was filled with excited chatter as critics and patrons appraised each drawing to universally positive responses and reviews. For all the fanfare and despite Stephanie's directive to "work the room," after a single hasty lap, Demitra found herself hiding in the corner again.

"Demitra," Stephanie called as she made her way over with a tall, bald gentleman in tow. "I'd like you to meet Phillip. He's with the American School of Classical Studies in Athens. Phillip was just telling me about a visiting artist program they sponsor."

"Yes. I've been an admirer of your work since I saw you profiled on the news years ago," Phillip said. "It's been inspiring to watch the progression of your work, especially as a Greek woman of a certain generation. As we all know, culturally and socially, women of our age were compartmentalized. The mother, the wife, the daughter, but not often as an artist, let alone an astute, independent businesswoman."

Demitra nodded and smiled in acknowledgment. "That is a very generous way of putting it."

"Yes. When I met Demitra she was selling her work literally off the walls of her home to anyone who walked over and rang her bell." Stephanie laughed.

"Well, it's obvious much has changed since then." Phillip gestured around the crowded gallery. "One of your earlier works in particular caught my attention. Persephone. I loved the play of color and your subtle yet very powerful use of symbolism."

"Thank you. That's kind of you to say." Demitra felt her face flush, uneasy as always when she was complimented in such a way. She turned the focus again to the work, gaining her bearings and confidence with each word. "Persephone was one of my favorites as well. Growing up without a mother myself, it was meaningful for me to highlight her evolution, her transformation from victim to queen, and all that entails."

"Yes, exactly." Phillip nodded knowingly. "We are working on a program to help introduce the classics to a wider audience, to highlight the timeless nature of the lessons in these stories, in these women, and how they relate to the women's rights movement today. There's a relevance here that speaks to a younger, modern audience. But as we all know, the lesson is only as powerful and impactful as the delivery, and the one who delivers it." He reached out, taking a glass of champagne from a passing waiter.

"I was hoping you might accept an invitation to present your work at the American School of Classical Studies this summer. It's quite prestigious, if I do say so myself. We'd love to have you if you'll join us."

The swell of emotion in her throat prevented Demitra from speaking. Instead, she merely bit her lip to keep from crying and nodded, whispering, "Yes."

THE MOMENT STEPHANIE explained that the show had been a success beyond her wildest dreams and the collection had sold out in the first week, Demitra knew exactly how she wanted to celebrate.

She had never drawn a self-portrait before, but she spent the next week perfecting an image of herself, head tilted back on board a boat at sea, hair blowing in the wind, sunglasses on, and a giant smile on her face as she hoisted a cocktail in the air.

She made copies of the drawing and wrote a letter that read,

> *Please do me the honor of being my guest as we sail the Ionian islands together. These islands are my home and mean so much to me, as do you.*

She sent copies of the portrait and letter to April and John, Patrick and Margaret, Sophia and Tino, and even Joseph and Rebekah in Israel. She also sent the invitation to Elena and Niko, understanding that they were not likely to leave the bakery for a sailing trip, but it was important to her that they knew they were included.

They were an unlikely pair, the former prostitute and the eccentric, childlike baker. But theirs was a beautiful partnership that blossomed over the years, like siblings who had found in each other what they had been craving their entire lives— companionship and friendship without judgment or prejudice.

Demitra knew Soula was offended at first when she was not included, but she gifted her with a drawing that was sure to fetch thousands if Soula ever decided to sell it, and the scowl on her face turned to a smile.

"Is it all right if I bring Genevieve?" Jerry asked tentatively, not sure how Demitra might take his request. It was one thing to know he was spending each night with his girlfriend at school, but quite another to have them sleeping together under Demitra's watch. Demitra had yet to meet Genevieve, but there was a lightness about Jerry since they met, an ever-present smile on his face and a proud glint in his eyes at the mention of her name, or as he detailed her involvement as organizer of the Law Students for Women's Rights protests at Georgetown.

Demitra did not hesitate. "Of course she can come. I can't wait to meet her."

As they boarded the plane that would take them to Athens, where she would speak at the opening night of her exhibit at the American School of Classical Studies, Demitra looked around her at the friends and family who would be joining her on this adventure. They had each enriched her life in ways she had not anticipated and shown her the true meaning of friendship. And yet, a sadness washed over her as she noticed something she had not before. She was with all the people she adored most in the world, each one excitedly chatting as they took their seats, holding hands, and leaning in for a kiss as the plane prepared for takeoff.

And yet, for all the joy and camaraderie surrounding her, Demitra was the only one without a hand to hold, without a lover's ear to whisper into, or a shoulder beside her to rest her head on.

As Demitra prepared for the most significant accomplishment in her life and career, surrounded by the people she loved most in the world, she had never felt more incomplete or alone.

Chapter Forty-Five

Greece

1970

THE PRESENTATION AT the American School of Classical Studies was a huge success with a standing room only crowd and a collection of Demitra's latest works on display.

Demitra was at the podium, midspeech, when Joseph and Rebekah arrived, having come straight from the airport when their flight from Israel landed. She could not help but pause for a moment, watching as Gerasimos spotted Joseph and ran to the back of the room to throw his arms around the older man. Tears welled in her eyes as this time it was Gerasimos who pulled a ball from his pocket and handed it to a beaming Joseph.

From Athens the group flew to Corfu where they prayed beside Saint Spyridon, asking him to watch over their loved ones as the saint watched over his beloved island. They enjoyed a perfect dinner along the Liston as the sun set over Garitsa Bay and the swallows sang and soared through the sky with their frenzied orchestrations.

The next morning they boarded the charter and sailed around the verdant island, stopping in Sidari at the famed cliffs of the Canal D'Amour.

"Legend has it that those who swim the narrow canal and reach the open sea together will have an everlasting love, one that defies all obstacles and odds," Tino announced before he took Sophia's hand in his, and they jumped into the sea. Demitra watched as each of the couples leaped from the boat into the water and swam the length of the canal together. She was waiting with towels as they climbed back on board, laughing and celebrating as they toasted to the legend and each other.

"To love!" Patrick exclaimed, hoisting his glass in the air as he pulled Margaret in for a kiss.

"To love!" everyone shouted as they toasted.

Demitra did her best not to lose herself in the moment, celebrating the joy of her dearest friends. Yet she could not shake the melancholy that washed over her as she remembered what it felt like to be wrapped in a lover's arms, here among these very cliffs and beaches.

From northern Corfu they sailed south, passing the old town seawall and fortress that had welcomed and entranced Demitra when she'd first arrived on the island so many years before. They passed the southern tip of Corfu, and just as they entered the open water between Paxos and Corfu, Demitra opened her mouth to share the myth of how Antipaxos was formed. But then she thought better of it, feeling the need to sail in silence instead.

As the captain docked in Gaios for the group to disembark and have lunch, Demitra was swept away in an unrelenting flood of memories. The port, desolate and deserted the last time she was here, was now dotted with patrons and bustling tavernas. Deeply tanned, bikini-clad foreigners feasted on local delicacies and hoisted beers in the air, shouting yiamas, as white-haired yia-yias sat sipping their coffees beside grizzled old men fidgeting worry beads between their fingers.

Although it was busier than she remembered, the port had not changed much since Demitra strolled the harbor with Aleko.

Brightly whitewashed storefronts lined the promenade overlooking the port where peeling and weathered fishing boats bobbed beside gleaming yachts.

The group continued a bit farther into the harbor, and Demitra stopped when she saw the sign. *Stamatis.*

"I was here years ago," she said. "The owners were the loveliest couple. This is the spot." She took her seat, trying to hold tight to the happy memories and will away the persistent, relentless sadness that always seemed to follow her.

Lunch was heavenly as they feasted on freshly grilled fish, calamari, Greek salad, and an assortment of dips and pita. All around them the port was alive with the laughter and chatter of friends and the cheerful sound of the clinking of glasses, followed by joyful shouts of "Yiamas!"

"Are you well?" Sophia leaned close while the others were distracted, placing her hand on Demitra's cheek. "You look a bit pale."

"Yes. I'm good. Haunted by old ghosts, but that's not always a bad thing, is it?"

Sophia squeezed her leg and offered a sad smile, understanding at once.

When the bill came, Joseph jumped up this time, insisting the meal was on him. It had become a daily tradition among the group, the post-meal argument over who paid the bill. The drama had become a highlight of the trip with loud pronouncements, feigned arguments, and the use of sneaky tactics like bribing the waiters, a source of endless entertainment and laughs.

Since Joseph had secured the bill, raising it over his head in victory, Demitra excused herself to go to the restroom. Once inside the taverna she turned to their waiter, who was wiping down glasses and placing them behind the bar.

"Excuse me. I was here years ago and met the owner, Stamatis, and his wife. They were the loveliest people. Did you know them?"

"Yes." The waiter smiled broadly beneath his bushy mustache. "Stamatis was my theo. He and my thea Polixeni both passed away years ago. I'm so glad you remember them fondly. I'm Stamatis also, so you see, I didn't even have to change the sign." He smiled, a gold tooth glinting in the afternoon light.

"I'm so sorry to hear they've passed. They left quite an impression on me."

"Yes. It's been about ten years now. Thea Polixeni went first and then Theo Stamatis, just six months after. I think he lost his will to live without her."

Demitra nodded knowingly. "They were a beautiful couple. I loved meeting them. We had the most wonderful meal, and they even took us to see their house and garden. Oh, it was so beautiful."

"Well then, you must come see it now as well. They sold the land years ago. I think it was a difficult decision, but they couldn't care for it any longer. It's still the prettiest spot on the island, just beautiful. It was the first large-scale hotel built on Paxos. Well, only ten rooms, but still large by our standards. They did a beautiful job with it, and even though the land was sold, our family still lives in our ancestral home on the property." He finished with the glasses and took off his apron. "I'm done with my shift and running up to the house if you'd like to come see it."

Demitra thought for a moment. Part of her wanted to lock those memories away, to forget about that idyllic day and her naive dream that like Stamatis and Polixeni, she and Aleko would grow old together. But there was also something that tugged at her, the need to see the place where she had spent some of the happiest moments of her life, back when she believed in love, back when she believed in promises that were whispered in the dark.

"I'd love to come," she said before running outside to the table where everyone was preparing to explore Gaios for the afternoon and do some shopping in the town's artisan shops.

"I'm just running a quick errand with my friend here. I knew his family years ago. He's taking me up to their home to have a quick look. You know how nostalgic I can be."

She laughed then and caught Sophia and Tino exchange worried glances. Demitra waved away their worry with a smile and a swat of her hand.

"Enjoy the town. I'll meet you later back on the boat." She could feel Sophia's and Tino's eyes on her as she walked away.

The car ride up the mountain to the house was just as she remembered it with beautiful flowers and the ancient olive orchard shading the drive up the cliff. The entrance to the compound was even more lush and picturesque than she remembered. In addition to the cluster of homes, which had been restored, on the edge of the bluff overlooking the sea a new building stood. It was a marvel of modern architecture, made of steel and wood and glass, and yet a tribute to the island's rustic history with stone, wood, and old-world touches throughout.

"It's something, isn't it?" Stamatis said. "Go have a look. I can drive you back down in a bit. I'll come find you if you like."

Two extraordinary gardenia bushes lined the path to the entrance, their flowers pristine, white, and as large as her hand, their sweet scent perfuming the air.

She followed the stone path into the main building, which was stark white with soaring ceilings and an impeccable view of the sea glistening in the afternoon light. In the center of the room was a large fireplace, open on both sides, towering to the ceiling and set all around with pale stones. The effect of the massive hearth with the sea beyond was staggering.

She walked around to the other side to get a closer view but stopped suddenly and blinked a few times to make sure she was not hallucinating. She walked closer, gazing up at her, biting her lip until the metallic taste of blood was in her mouth.

This was not a dream. This was real. And she was here. In Paxos.

Amphitrite.

Demitra's own Amphitrite.

Demitra stood beside the fireplace, mouth agape, her skin erupting in goose bumps. There she was, Demitra's drawing of Amphitrite. Here, commanding the room as she stared out from above the exquisite fireplace. Amphitrite's eyes glowed; her gown fanned out with the current as it became one with the sea, as the dolphins and fish and sea creatures adored their queen.

She laughed out loud now at the insanity of this coincidence. A London collector had purchased the drawing years ago. How had she ended up here? Perhaps this was the collector's property? Perhaps he sold Amphitrite when the value of Demitra's works skyrocketed. Taking a moment to gather her thoughts, she turned toward the interior of the hotel, where the bar and reception area were located.

As she walked toward the bar, something caught her eye in the distance. She walked quickly toward it, her stomach doing flips with each step.

Cassandra.

And there, above the reception area, were Io and Selene, two drawings from her previous exhibit.

Each of these pieces had been sold either through auction or privately during her exhibits. How was it possible that they all ended up here? Was this a curated exhibit of her work without her knowledge?

"Excuse me." She was breathless as she approached the reception desk. "Excuse me, what can you tell me about those pieces, please? The artwork in the hotel. Do you know how they came to be here? Were they purchased for the hotel, or are they on loan?"

The clerk was friendly but clueless. "I can certainly ask about them for you. The owner is here. Would you have a seat, please? I'll be right back."

She stumbled toward the couch near the fireplace and took a seat. Her hands were trembling with nervous, excited energy as she placed them on her lap, attempting to steady them.

Her scattered thoughts were interrupted by the efficient *click-clack* of heels on the marble floor.

"May I help you?" a voice asked.

Demitra looked up, her skin once again covered in gooseflesh as she locked eyes with the woman. It had been seventeen years since she last saw her, but she remembered the moment as if it were yesterday. The striking child with olive skin, green eyes, and unruly blonde curls whose beauty had taken Demitra's breath away.

Standing before Demitra now, she had grown into an elegant young woman, her eyes lined in black kohl and her hair styled in waves cascading to her waist. Even after all these years, there was no mistaking her.

"Flora." Although she spoke the name out loud, the sound of it stunned her.

It was clear by the shocked expression on the woman's face, the way she shifted her weight from one foot to the other, that Flora knew who she was as well.

Aleko's daughter opened her mouth to speak. "Demitra. It's you."

Chapter Forty-Six

Paxos, Greece

1970

"PLEASE, NOT HERE," Flora said as she glanced around the room to the handful of employees and guests going about their business. "Come into my office, please." Flora ushered Demitra across the hall and into a sun-drenched room containing a massive desk.

Demitra was trembling, and there was no hiding her shock or her agitation as she sat in a large wingback chair. Flora sat across from her behind the desk and folded her hands atop the oiled wood surface.

"You know who I am?" Demitra asked, flustered.

"Yes, I do," Flora replied, a picture of calm and poise.

"How?" Demitra asked. "How do you know who I am? How is my work here, in the hotel that you own?" She tried to remain composed, but her voice cracked with emotion.

"The hotel my father owned and built."

"Your . . . father?" There was no masking the pain in Demitra's voice. "But how? Please, I need to know."

Flora regarded her for a moment. Her mouth was tight, her eyes focused on Demitra. She glanced out the window toward the sea in the distance as if collecting her thoughts. And then she spoke. It was not what Demitra expected to hear.

"My father loved you."

So many years later, so much loss, so much heartbreak. She could not understand how and why these words could still eviscerate her the way they did.

"Countless times I've thought of you, pictured you, wondered what I might say if I was ever to see you, but no matter how many times I've thought of this moment, dreamed of this moment"—a nervous laugh escaped Flora's lips—"no words seem adequate."

With her perfectly tailored dress, elegant shoes, and tasteful makeup, Flora was the epitome of sophistication. And, like her father, she bore kindness in her eyes, a sadness permeating them in the most unexpected way.

"My father was a good man, and he loved you," she said plainly.

"Was?" The word was no more than a murmur on her lips.

Flora nodded. "A motorcycle accident on Corfu nearly eight years ago."

Demitra closed her eyes, uncertain which hurt more, hearing that he was gone, that he had still loved her, or that he had a wife and a child all those years before.

"My parents' marriage was not a happy one. My mother was not easy, and that's a kind way of putting it. She was unwell. She *is* unwell. She can be cruel and selfish. She always has been. At first, they fought all the time, and then my father stopped fighting. He told me there was no point in fighting, that he just wanted peace, for me to live in peace." She shook her head as if she could see the memories like a movie reel in her mind.

"When I was little, my father wanted us to move from London to Corfu, but she wouldn't hear of it. Mama had friends in London, or that was what she called them anyway. Men, lovers—a revolving door of lovers. In London no one noticed, and no one cared, least of all my father.

"When he returned from Corfu, he was different, so different. There was a joy and a lightness about him. She was too busy to notice at first, but I did. I was little, but I remember how happy he was when he came back. I saw the difference in him right away. And then he asked her for a divorce, saying he needed to be on Corfu, that his life was on Corfu.

"She didn't care. She had long stopped being his wife, and he, her husband. The plan was for me to go back and forth between them, and they would each live their lives. And it was finished. Their marriage was finished."

Demitra's eyes widened as she tilted her head up to the ceiling. When she glanced at Flora again, a single tear slid down her cheek. Flora pushed a box of tissues across the desk.

"I was there when the phone rang, when she got the call. A real estate agent on Corfu said the apartment on the Liston was available, that the paperwork was being drawn up. He assured her there was nothing to worry about, that the seller had no problem waiting however long it took for the wedding to take place, and while it was not the norm, the deed would indeed be drawn up with both names—my father's, Aleko, and his wife's, Demitra."

A primal moan escaped Demitra's lips, her face contorting with emotion.

"That was when everything changed. That was when I learned the truth about who and what my mother is. That was when we boarded a flight to Corfu."

Demitra could picture the scene as if it were playing out before her. She could feel her heart break again, just as it had that evening when she first laid eyes on Flora and her mother.

"I heard them arguing, then screaming. I heard him telling her he wanted a divorce, that he'd met someone, someone kind and good, someone he loved. She didn't want him. She didn't love him. But she didn't want him to love anyone else either. So she refused. She refused to divorce him, and she denied my father the happiness he deserved, with you.

"He could have tried still, petitioned the courts and the church to dissolve the marriage. But she held something over him, the one thing he loved more than life itself: me. He knew she would make my life miserable if he left. That she would use me to get back at him, that she would stop at nothing to hurt us both. So he stayed. And he lost the only chance at happiness he ever had, the only woman he ever loved. He lost you."

Demitra brought her hands to her mouth and closed her eyes.

"I remember sitting with him at home, having coffee one morning before school, when he saw the article about you in the paper. He lit up as he told me you were an old friend who was very special to him. He told me all about you and your story, that you had lost your mother, lost everything, and then built a life and a career with your own talent and determination.

"I was here the day he hung Amphitrite. I remember how he stayed for hours after, staring up at her. After he died, when I was sorting through his things, I found a letter. He hired someone to check on you after the earthquake, to make sure you were alive, to make sure you weren't hurt. And that was when I knew. I knew you were more than an artist he admired. You were the one he loved."

The room was spinning as Demitra struggled to compose herself. She sat silently, her head and shoulders slumped forward, as if she were unable to bear their weight. She understood even then that no matter how much he had encouraged her to follow her dreams and to dictate her own story, he was unable to do the same. All those years, all those times she'd cried herself to sleep, wondering if he ever thought of her, if he could love her still, now she knew. She finally knew.

Flora stood and walked around to the other side of the desk. She folded her arms and knelt before Demitra.

"When I realized who you were, what you were, I realized then what Amphitrite meant to my father and why. I would see him here, in this hotel he built and loved, and I would watch him sitting there, staring at Amphitrite for hours. My father was lonely for so many years." Flora's voice cracked with raw emotion. "After my father died, I bought Cassandra and Io and Selene. I brought them here so Amphitrite would not be alone. I thought that in some way, it would make him happy to know she wasn't alone."

Demitra reached her hand out, taking Aleko's daughter's hand in her own. They stayed there in silence for quite some time, the artist and the daughter, mourning the man who had loved them both.

IT WAS NEARLY sunset by the time Demitra returned to the boat. As she climbed on board, everyone was gathered on deck, sharing a cocktail and stories of their day.

"How was your afternoon?" Sophia asked, searching her eyes.

Demitra bit her lip, smiling at Sophia, who leaned closer, placing her head on Demitra's shoulder.

As they made their way out of the harbor, the sun began its slow descent, painting the sky and sea in jeweled tones.

Demitra had wondered so many times over the years how and why their story ended the way it did, why he never tried to find her, why he never fought harder to be by her side. And now she understood. He was a good man, a man of honor and integrity. In the end he did what parents do, and he chose his daughter's happiness over his own.

"Hey," Demitra said, pouring a glass of wine. "I have another story to tell you all. And it just might be my most favorite myth of all." Everyone gathered close. "This, my friends, is the story of Amphitrite."

Demitra inhaled deeply and began. "The great god Poseidon spotted the nymph Amphitrite dancing, and he fell instantly in love. Poseidon was married, and Amphitrite knew this, so she wanted nothing to do with the brash, handsome god. But over time, with patience and persistence and with the sincerity of his love for her, Poseidon won her over, and Amphitrite agreed to be his.

"The god was so happy, he took his trident and pierced it into the southern tip of Corfu, breaking off two pieces of land, and these became Paxos and Antipaxos. There in the blue grotto caves of Paxos, Poseidon kept Amphitrite hidden from the jealous gods and his wife. It was a place where they could be together always and celebrate their love. Theirs was a beautiful life and love. Together, the god of the sea and the nymph created dolphins and sea lions and every type of fish and sea life you can imagine, filling the world with wondrous creatures born of their love.

"Over time, their love never faded, but the other gods grew jealous, as gods often did, and they learned about Poseidon's happiness, despite his efforts to keep Amphitrite safe and hidden. The gods spread rumors and warned Amphitrite that her lover was unfaithful. So one day, a brokenhearted Amphitrite swam away from the safety of her lover's arms and the beautiful home he'd created for her.

"Time went on and Amphitrite's heart never mended, and neither did Poseidon's. Night after night, as she drifted off to sleep, Amphitrite dreamed of her one true love, never knowing that night after night he did the same. But even though their love did not have a happy ending, and their time together was not nearly enough, Amphitrite was grateful for the life they had shared and the time they had together.

"Every day, as she looked around her at the magnificent and loyal dolphins, at the silly seals and otters, and at the extraordinary beauty of sea coral and the oysters' precious gifts of pearls, she knew that despite the pain she felt, it had been worth it. It had all been worth it. Because however brief it was, their love was true. And she knew that together, they had created magic, and the world was a more beautiful place because of their love."

"Beautiful. How beautiful, Demitra." Everyone cheered and lifted their glasses toward her.

She stood then, turning away from her friends and family, watching as the silhouette of Paxos disappeared into the horizon.

Cephalonia, Greece

"THERE YOU ARE!" Elena ran to her and literally lifted Demitra into her arms as she hugged her and welcomed her home.

"It's so nice to see you after all this time. Welcome back." Niko kept his distance, lifting his hand in a slight wave.

Joseph and Jerry smiled at each other as they stepped off the gangplank and onto the dock in Cephalonia.

"It looks slightly different, doesn't it?" Jerry smiled as they made their way down the picturesque promenade that lined the harbor. Where once there had been medical tents and piles of rubble and supplies, there were now freshly paved promenades and palm trees swaying in the breeze.

From the port they walked to the bakery, where Demitra was amazed at the sight before her. Together, Elena and Niko had built an extraordinary complex, a thriving bakery and restaurant with guest cottages that had become the heart and soul of the town.

As they walked arm in arm, Demitra leaned into Elena. "It's amazing what you've done. Each time I come back, it's even more beautiful than before."

"Wait till you see your old house. You won't even recognize it." Elena beamed. "We built you a studio in the yard. The windows are huge. I know how important light is to you."

"I can't begin to thank you enough. I have an exhibit next year in Chicago. I'm thinking I might come back in the fall and stay for a few months. I could use some fresh inspiration. Jerry is graduating and he'll be going off to conquer the world." She laughed as she glanced at Jerry, who had his arm draped around Genevieve as he walked. "It would be nice to come back and stay for a bit, to spend time with you."

"Nothing would make me happier." Elena smiled broadly. "We all need our roots, don't we, Demitra?"

"Yes," Demitra said as she threaded her arm through Elena's and pulled her even closer. "But that's the thing about roots, isn't it? There are the ones that are visible to us and the ones that are hidden from sight. One is no more important than the other, Elena. They both sustain us. They both give life and connect us to the people and places that mean the most."

"Yes." Elena nodded. "Yes, they do."

Surrounded by the friends and family who meant everything to her, Demitra spent an idyllic week back home, eating glorious food, swimming in the sea, and making a pilgrimage to pray beside Saint Gerasimos. As mid-August approached, there was one last thing she needed to do before heading back to New York.

"Snakes? Really?" Margaret and April said in unison as the bus pulled up to the church.

"Yes, snakes," Demitra said. She led the way along the road adjacent to the church. "My aunt was a nun at the monastery here. She was my favorite person in the world, my safe harbor in my most difficult times. She passed away about ten years ago, but I swear she still watches over me. She taught me about the snakes, not to fear them, how their appearance was an omen of good things to come. And if they came to you, if they let you pick them up, that was the greatest blessing."

While on this trip, they had prayed beside two mummified saints, dove from craggy cliffs into the sea, were spit on by old widows claiming it was good luck, and feasted on grilled lambs' intestines without a moment's hesitation. But now, as Demitra led the way into the church to see Panagia's snakes, not everyone was convinced it was a good idea.

Patrick was the first to speak up. "This is another legend, right? Like Poseidon and the caves? There are not really snakes in there, right?" he asked with a chuckle, attempting to make light of the situation.

"Patrick!" Margaret scolded with a swat of her hand. "You, who are named for the saint who drove the snakes from Ireland. Come on, man, are you really nervous about making a few new friends?" She winked and took him by the hand and led him inside.

They walked through the arched doors of the church, where dozens of worshipers had already assembled, waiting for the divine liturgy to begin. There were whispers in the crowd that the snakes had been spotted earlier in the week, but they had yet to make their appearance that morning. Demitra lit a candle, placing it into the sand-filled trough and making the sign of the cross as she bent down to kiss the icon of Panagia.

They all stood in the church, shoulder to shoulder, taking in the wonder of the place, when Sophia nudged Demitra. "Look," she said, pointing to the other side of the church where Jerry stood beside Genevieve.

Demitra watched as Jerry looked down at the ground, a startled expression on his face. Demitra followed his eyes to see that a snake, slim and dark gray with a white cross visible on its face, slithered across the floor and onto Jerry's foot. He stood statue-still as he watched the snake contort its body and wrap itself across his shoe and ankle. His startled eyes quickly turned to shock. He then lifted his gaze and frantically scanned the crowd, stopping when he spotted his sister. Raising his hands and pointing down at his feet, Jerry's expression was one of fear as he stared into Demitra's eyes.

Demitra grinned and mouthed the words "*It's ok,*" which instantly calmed Jerry. He nodded at her, then glanced at Genevieve before bending down and picking up the snake.

A hush fell over the church as the priest continued the service, his voice booming as he saw the snake on the young man's arm.

As she watched him now, the broken little boy she had raised with all the tenderness and love that had been missing from her own childhood, she marveled at the young man he had become. She prayed that Stella could see her boy now, that she could share in the moment and know that her child, the miracle child she had prayed so hard for, was indeed blessed.

part

six

Chapter Forty-Seven

Milwaukee, Wisconsin

1933

Oh little bunny, little bunny, you naughty thing, you are going
to get a spanking. Hopping around in a stranger's orchard,
stop digging those holes.
Don't wrinkle your cute little nose at me.
Don't wiggle those bunny ears.
You are as beautiful as a lovely drawing.

APHRODITE ERUPTED IN squeals as Maria sang the nursery rhyme for the tenth time that morning. It was the same song her own mother sang countless times as she made bunny ears with her hands and chased Maria and her sister, Paraskevi, across the wildflower fields on the mountainside. Maria sat on the drafty floor of the fifth-floor Milwaukee walk-up as her own daughter hopped along and clapped inside the cramped apartment.

"All right, sweetheart, come here," Maria said as she brushed her hair and straightened her bow. Glancing up at the clock, she realized they needed to get moving or they would be late. She grabbed the tray from the stove with one hand and took Aphrodite's hand in the other.

The streets outside were crowded with revelers as the municipal society prepared for the Fourth of July parade. Although she had lived in Milwaukee for more than ten years, this was the first year

Maria intended to attend the parade and fireworks. After arriving on the *Megali Hellas*, she'd experienced the first seven years in America as lonely and isolating. Maria had rarely left the apartment, and when she did, it was typically only for grocery shopping, church on Sunday, and her weekly English lesson with the old schoolteacher down the hall.

For the longest time, there was no joy in her life, nothing and no one to celebrate as she sat day after day alone in the apartment, praying for companionship, praying for a child. Since the arrival of her beautiful Aphrodite, Maria celebrated each day as a gift and approached everything with fresh eyes and excitement.

"Hello!" she shouted as she walked through the door of Pericles's diner, greeting the staff and patrons alike.

"Baba, Baba." Aphrodite spotted her baba behind the counter and ran into his arms.

Pericles bent to scoop her up as an annoyed look crossed his face.

"I heard it was America's birthday." Maria smiled and placed the tray of *loukoumades* on the counter. "In Karditsa when it is someone's birthday, we make loukoumades." She smiled as she pulled back the wrapping on the tray, revealing a pile of golden fried dough balls dripping with honey.

At 11:00 a.m., it was too late for breakfast and too early for lunch. The diner was far less crowded than usual with a handful of patrons scattered between the counter and tables. Maria smiled at each and every one of the men, marveling how here in her husband's restaurant, whites and Blacks and Italians and Germans and Greeks all worked together and ate side by side. She was proud of him for this and intended to tell him so, until he once again managed to suck the last remnant of goodwill from her.

"Oh, what have we here?" Tasso popped a loukoumadae into his mouth as he grabbed a fresh spatula and headed to the kitchen where he commanded the grill, churning out American comfort food like burgers, meatloaf, and grilled cheese expertly and efficiently.

"Maria, would you do me a favor, please, and come over to teach Lamprini how you get these so fluffy?" He laughed as he dropped a burger patty on the grill. "Hers are like lead."

"Yes. Of course." She feigned a smile, regarding him carefully as she always had since the day they'd first met. Tasso's wife, Lamprini, seemed like a nice girl. But after the despicable way he'd abandoned Anna that day on the dock, Demitra always eyed him suspiciously, keeping him and his wife at arm's length.

"What are you doing here?" Pericles hissed in her ear.

"I brought you a surprise for the Fourth of July. I thought you might like it." As moody and short as he was lately, his reaction was not the welcome she'd anticipated. This was hurtful, even for him. "At church on Sunday, Father mentioned that it was America's birthday, so I thought I might surprise you with loukoumades. Aphrodite helped me make them."

"It was so fun, Baba," she chirped as her little fingers grabbed a sticky ball from the tray.

"You shouldn't be here," he snapped. "I'm busy, and this is no place for a child. They're boycotting Greek restaurants up and down the city. The last thing I need is to draw more attention to us. You should go. I don't want you here. It's not safe."

She'd felt the sting of his words many times over the years, but this was different. She had resigned herself to the fact that he was married to the restaurant, that his sacrifices were so they could have a better life, so he could provide for their family. But Pericles's resolve and purpose had changed in surprising ways, beyond merely chasing his American Dream. Maria had watched as his rare smiles and kind gestures slowly disappeared over the years. His ambition evolved from passion to obsession. He seemed to believe that making a success of himself now would negate the humiliation of being run out of Omaha.

As little as Maria understood his drive for success, one thing was clear as she packed up her tray and started toward the door. This was the last time she and her child would ever step foot in the restaurant. This was the last time she would make an effort and extend warmth or affection toward her husband. This was the last time she would see him for anything other than what he was—a man who valued his pride and financial success more than his family.

"I thought we were staying for lunch, Mama." Aphrodite tugged at her sleeve as they walked out the door and down the street.

As she turned her attention to Aphrodite, the tray in her hands tilted, threatening to spill the loukoumades.

"Hold on there. Let me help you." The voice and hands came from behind, steadying the tray.

"Thank you," Maria said as she regained her bearings. She looked up to see that her savior was a young man she recognized from the diner. He was one of the young Italian men who were eating at the counter.

"Zeppoles." He smiled, pointing to the tray. "That's what we call them."

"Loukoumades." She smiled, holding tight to Aphrodite. "Thank you. You saved me and my zeppoles."

"Well, it's the least I could do. I saw you back there at the restaurant. That's your husband?"

"Yes. And this is my daughter, Aphrodite." She swung her arm back and forth, dissolving Aphrodite into a fit of giggles.

"Well, your husband makes the best burgers in town. I'm in law school, and time and money are really tight. I think my friends and I would starve without him."

She nodded politely as she continued to walk.

"Forgive me if I'm being too bold. He makes a great burger, but he's an ass of a husband. I heard the way he spoke to you, and I'm sorry."

She stopped, shocked. Her mouth a tight line, her brow furrowed, she regarded him silently, unsure of what to say.

"I'm sorry, but it's true. He's an ass." A sheepish grin erupted on his face as he hunched his shoulders.

Maria's response was a surprise to both of them.

"Oh my goodness." She burst out laughing, almost losing control of the tray again.

"Here. Let me carry this for you." He smiled at her, taking the tray in his hands as they walked.

"I'm Anthony," he said, nodding politely.

That night, she joined him to watch the fireworks from the room of a building in the Italian neighborhood, across the street from the Blessed Virgin of Pompeii Church, where she knew no one would recognize her. And that night, as Aphrodite was delighted and distracted by the bursts of light from above, Anthony leaned in and kissed Maria for the first time.

Maria leaned closer and kissed him back.

Chapter Forty-Eight

Chicago, Illinois

1975

A s she looked out over the crowd gathered to welcome her to the Hellenic Cultural Center in Chicago, Demitra marveled at how many people had come to hear her speak and witness the unveiling of her new exhibit.

As much as she preferred to lose herself in the quiet solitude of her work and never quite overcame her apprehension of public speaking, something about this collection instilled Demitra with peace, pride, and a newfound confidence.

"This exhibit is a departure for me," Demitra began. "I was raised by a single father. Often, he did not know what to make of me, nor I of him. He was so devastated by my mother's death that he didn't speak of her. He couldn't speak of her. I had no memories of my own—of my mother, of my early childhood, of the magic that exists between mothers and daughters.

"So I turned to myths to fill in those missing pieces of my childhood, crafting my own made-up memories, the wishful pining of a lonely child. I imagined my mother was a goddess, an ethereal, powerful creature. I dreamed of her each night. She came to me in my dreams to console me, to comfort me, to tuck me in, and to hold me in her arms. I was only a child when she died, and as hard as I tried, as much as I concentrated, I could not remember what she looked like.

"Maybe that's why I've been so obsessed with women's faces since then. I've always searched for the stories in the faces all around me, the crinkle of the eyes, the curve of a smile, the laugh lines . . . the worry lines. I went back home to Cephalonia recently, and I finally stood still long enough to look around me. And that was when I saw them. I saw the wisdom and the beauty in the faces all around me, in the women who had loved me and made me laugh and comforted me and sustained me.

"This collection is a testament and a tribute to them, to the myth and the magic that exists in each one of them, in each of us. These are the women who live the simplest lives, who've never held anything of value in their hands, and yet there is no end to the richness of their lives. There is no end to the abundance of love they give, the love they are capable of. And that, my friends, is the most powerful magic of all."

As she looked around at the room that was packed to capacity, Demitra was in awe. She had given dozens of presentations by then. She had spoken to and shared her work with countless people across Greece and the United States, and achieved endless accolades and acclaim. Yet she had never experienced what she saw as she looked out from the podium that day. Row after row, person after person, she watched as women and men, young and old, dabbed at their eyes and nodded their heads, clearly touched by her words, by her art.

She waited as the crowd clapped, jumping to their feet in support. The swell of emotion was overwhelming, and she took a moment to gather her composure, gesturing from the podium to the gallery, where the collection was hung and displayed.

"Over here, this is my friend Elena. She's had a hard life, a life filled with disappointment and pain, yet her capacity for love is boundless. And here, this is my aunt, Olga. Olga was a woman of deep faith, a woman whose gentle soul touched everyone she met and who never let me forget that to love someone is the godliest of gifts. And this . . . this is Stella, my stepmother. Stella showed me kindness when I no longer believed in its existence. These are the heroines of our time. These are the Penelopes and Persephones of today. Their stories are not written in books; they are not taught in schools. But they should be. They should be studied and learned from and emulated. These are the goddesses of our time. Thank you."

THE LINE TO meet Demitra wound down the corridor. She stood beside her work, taking the time to greet everyone and thank them for coming. After nearly two hours of greeting guests and well-wishers who shared with her how moved they were by this collection, it appeared her night was winding down at last. She was helping herself to a much-needed glass of wine when she spotted Grace, the cultural center's director, chatting with a man beneath the picture of Elena.

"I see you've met my friend." Demitra smiled as she reached them and raised her glass to Elena's portrait and then to Grace and the man beside her. He was slim-built and tall with a mop of chestnut curls. A brilliant smile peeked out from beneath a salt-and-pepper mustache and beard.

"Congratulations, Demitra. The exhibit is extraordinary. I don't think there was a dry eye in the house. I kept picturing my own yia-yia, dressed in her widow's black and head scarf, standing over the stove as she told me stories about life in the village." Grace sighed as she turned to the man beside her.

"I'd like you to meet my friend George. He and his family have been tireless supporters of the center since we opened our doors. He's on our board and spearheading fundraising efforts. Our dream is to one day open a museum of Hellenic culture, history, and heritage."

"Congratulations on your exhibit." George raised his glass to her. "It's truly lovely. And I believe the museum is more than just a dream. I think we can make it a reality. We are nothing if not tenacious, wouldn't you agree?" he asked, smiling at Demitra.

"We are tenacious indeed," she agreed, smiling back at him.

"Grace tells me you're living in New York," he said.

"Excuse me," Grace said before walking away to greet someone.

"Yes. When I came from Cephalonia, I moved in with family in the Bronx, like everyone does. Like good Greek girls are expected to do."

He laughed. "I know exactly what you mean."

"It was a bit much for me. My brother and I both missed the serenity of Cephalonia—and the sea. So I did the unthinkable. I went to work and saved money and bought my own house. We moved to Fire Island. It's quiet and beautiful and perfect for us. What about you?"

"Quite a trailblazer you are." He lifted his glass again in admiration. "I've lived in Chicago for about twenty years now. I own a restaurant just down the street—Greek man who owns a Greek diner, married to his restaurant, no time for a life. Not as original as your story, I'm afraid."

It was her turn to laugh.

"I love Chicago, I do, but I also miss the quiet of home sometimes. Luckily, home for me is a lot closer than Cephalonia. My father is from Evia, so being on the water was important to him. Every time I go back to Greece I'm reminded of how hard it must have been to leave and come here with nothing. He built our house with his own two hands right on the shores of Lake Michigan. Milwaukee is only a two-hour drive, so I get the best of both worlds."

"Milwaukee?" Demitra reached for another glass of wine from a passing waiter. "That's where I was born."

"Really?"

"Yes. My father never really talked about it, so I don't know much other than my mother was a teacher in the Greek school. She died in 1933, when I was three, and that's when he took me back to Cephalonia. My cousin and I tried to write to the archdiocese years ago to see if they could help me in some way, but we never found anything."

"There's more than one Greek church in Milwaukee, and I imagine records from that time are difficult to find, at best. But my father has lived in Milwaukee since he came over in 1910, and you know the way we Greeks are, especially back then. They kept to their own and they all seemed to know one another or were connected in some way.

"When my mother died, I think every Greek in the Midwest came to the funeral. It's still a tight-knit community, which is why I feel so strongly about the museum." He paused a moment, seeming uncertain, then tapped on his glass with his finger.

"I'm going home tomorrow, to visit my father. You're more than welcome to come with me, to see the town where you were born, maybe see the church where your mother taught Greek school, and to meet an old man who loves nothing more than to talk about the old days and his friends in AHEPA. At the very least he can tell you what it was like for them at that time. From what he's told me, it was not an easy time for anyone."

Demitra regarded him, hesitant for a moment. Under any other circumstances she would never get in a car with a man she had only just met for a two-hour drive—or any drive for that matter. But this man was not a stranger, not really. He was on the board of the Hellenic Center and was a well-respected member of the community. Perhaps even more than that, this man had given her the first glimmer of hope in a very long time that some connection to her mother might still be within reach.

"Yes," she said. "I would love to go to Milwaukee and meet your father."

Chapter Forty-Nine

Milwaukee, Wisconsin

1975

G EORGE HAD HOT coffee and fresh donuts waiting in the car when he picked her up at nine the following morning. To Demitra's delight, the glove compartment was packed with the latest Greek 8-track tapes, including her favorite singer, Marinella.

They were likely a spectacle to other cars passing on the freeway, but neither seemed to care. Windows rolled down, hair blowing in the wind, they sang out loud as Marinella found love, lost love, and lamented about her one true love.

"I can't sing to save my life." Demitra laughed and shook her head.

"You have a beautiful voice." He smiled as his hand tapped the steering wheel in time to the music.

Once they reached Milwaukee, George drove to Annunciation Church.

"Excuse me, can you help me with an old funeral record, please?" Demitra asked the silver-haired secretary in the church office. "I'm trying to find information on my mother. She was buried here in 1933. Her name was Maria Dimitropoulos, and she was a Greek schoolteacher."

After the secretary sorted through the records, the response was no different than the letters from the archdiocese years ago.

"I'm sorry, but we have no record of that funeral here."

It was the same a few miles down the road at the Church of Saints Constantine and Helen.

"I'm sorry, but that record does not exist here."

After all this time and all these years and all this frustration, Demitra felt she should have known better than to allow herself to hope. She did her best to tamp down her disappointment as George popped another 8-track into the tape player, no doubt attempting to lighten her mood.

"Did you notice how there are two Greek churches literally within a few miles of each other? My father told me that when he first moved to Milwaukee, there was only one church, Annunciation. But then, just as the political turmoil in Greece boiled over, things got heated here as well with the congregation splitting. Greeks who supported the monarchy left to build their own church. How's that for separation of church and state and brotherhood of man?" George shook his head and smiled.

"We are nothing if not dramatic." Demitra laughed, fully cognizant and appreciative of the effort he was making to temper her disappointment. "And what did he do, your father?"

"Oh, he's a royalist all the way and never afraid to speak his mind. Trust me, you'll see for yourself soon enough." His smile widened as he drove along Lake Shore Road, overlooking the glistening shore of Lake Michigan. "We're just a bit farther down the road," he said, tapping his finger on the steering wheel as Marinella sang about another lost love.

"Baba!" George called as he turned the key in the door. "Baba, I'm here, and I brought Demitra, the artist I told you about."

They found him in the living room with the game on the television and the Greek newspaper in his lap.

"Welcome, welcome! I'm Tasso." He stood to greet her. Although his hair and mustache were white with age, he carried himself with unbridled energy.

"See, what did I tell you?" George winked as he pointed to a framed photo of exiled King Constantine and Queen Anne-Marie on the coffee table.

"I've heard about the famous Greek artist from New York," Tasso said. "What an honor to have you in my home."

"No, the honor is all mine," Demitra replied. "It was so kind of George to bring me here and show me around the city. I was born here, but unfortunately this is my first time visiting."

"Well then, welcome home." Tasso's face erupted in a broad smile as he gestured around to the wood-paneled living room. "So where is your family now? And why did they leave our beautiful city?" he asked as he sat back down, motioning for Demitra to do the same. She and George sat on the couch.

She explained the story again, telling him about her mother's death and her father's silence and secrets.

"I see. It was a hard time for us back then. It wasn't like today. We were the outsiders, the foreigners with our strange language, customs, and food." He sighed deeply. "And in many ways, we were unwanted."

"My father was closed off and very private. I always wondered what life was like for him here, why he returned to Greece after Mama died. I guess it makes sense now. It couldn't have been easy for him, but he never talked about it. He never talked about her," she said, stealing a glance at George. "I was hoping to find something of my mother on this visit. We went to both churches already, but they said there's no funeral record for Maria Dimitropoulos in 1933."

The old man sucked in his breath sharply, his mouth falling open as he jolted forward.

George and Demitra looked at each other and then back to Tasso, confusion and surprise on both of their faces. In an instant George was at his father's side.

"Demitra, pardon my manners. It's just that . . ." Tasso shook his head, his mouth twisting as the lines on his face appeared to grow deeper. "You said your mother's name is Maria? Maria Dimitropoulos?"

"Yes."

"And your mother died in Milwaukee?"

"Yes. She died in 1933." Demitra's eyes widened with hope. Each word out of her mouth, each detail she shared, a piece of the puzzle she had long ago given up hope of ever solving. But now this kind old man could quite possibly hold the missing pieces. "That's the year my father, Pericles, took me home—"

"To Cephalonia." The old man finished her thought.

"Yes . . ." Her eyes narrowed as her heart raced and she tried to understand what was happening.

Tasso leaned back, shaking his head.

"Baba? Are you all right?" George sprinted to fetch a glass of water. "Here, Baba. Have a drink. Please."

"I knew them." The glass trembled in the old man's hands. "I . . . I . . . I knew your parents."

"You knew them?" Her face erupted in a shocked smile. "You really knew them?" She had dreamed of such a moment for so long. Finally, someone who could shed light on the mystery Baba held so tightly. Someone who had also heard her mother's laugh, the same beautiful laugh that lingered in her ears even after all these years.

Unlike the joy and excitement she felt, the old man looked to be in distress, as if the memories of long-lost friends unearthed something raw and painful from his own past.

"When you dig up skeletons, you disturb souls."

"Yes. I knew your father, and your mother. I knew them both. And I knew you. I remember you, this beautiful little girl. You were everything to her, her entire world."

His words comforted and eviscerated her simultaneously. *I was her entire world.*

He paused then, and his eyes glazed over with emotion as he leaned closer to her.

"But your mother didn't die when you were a little girl. She was very much alive when your father—"

Demitra recoiled, pulling back as if he had physically assaulted her.

He closed his eyes and exhaled, anguish in his expression when he opened them again and looked at her.

She leaned forward again. "What are you saying?"

He sighed, tenderness and pain existing simultaneously in his eyes before the words spilled out. "It's the truth. I was there. I lived it with them, with her."

"But I don't understand. My father told me she died. He took me home where he could raise me himself. My mother died when I was three."

He shook his head as she spoke. "No. Your mother was very much alive when your father took you back to Cephalonia. Your father took you back to Greece to punish her, to hurt her."

She looked to George for understanding and clarity, but he wore a shocked expression.

"He changed your name. Your name was not Demitra. Your mother named you Aphrodite, after her own mother. He changed your name so she couldn't find you."

Aphrodite. The name Baba called out as the house fell around them. A chill ran through her. It was not a phantom he saw that day. It was her. It was the ghost of the child he had once loved. The ghost of her mother's daughter.

"Every word is true. I wish it were not, but it is," Tasso continued, gripping the armrest of the couch. "We all made mistakes. We all hurt others. Those were different times, and I can't explain why he, or any of us, did what we did.

"What I can tell you is that your mother loved you. Her name was Maria and she loved you with all her heart, and she never stopped loving you. She never stopped praying that one day you would be reunited."

Chapter Fifty

Milwaukee, Wisconsin

1933

Pericles was seated at the table waiting for her when she walked through the door just after 4:00 p.m.

"You startled me," she said when she saw him there. "Aphrodite, go wash your hands and then we'll make supper."

"Where were you?" His tone was ice.

"Where was I?" Her legs felt shaky and she reached for the counter to steady herself, even as she summoned her strength to put a smile on her face. "I was out with Aphrodite, doing some shopping."

"But you don't have any packages." He stood and took three steps toward her.

She inched away from him without realizing she was doing so.

"Yes." She concentrated on her smile, on her breathing. She could not afford to make a mistake. "I went to the Turkish market, and nothing was fresh. I should have known better than to go to him. Tomorrow I'll go to the Cypriot down the road. His tomatoes are always the sweetest . . ." She turned her back to him and began pulling cans from the pantry, praying he did not notice her hands shaking.

"Where is he?" he growled.

"Where is who?" she asked, trying to keep her tone even, keeping her back to him.

"Where is your dirty Italian?" he hissed as he grabbed her shoulder and yanked her around to face him.

His face was crimson. The rage in his eyes froze the blood in her veins. She stared at him, focusing on staying upright, focusing on breathing. "I . . . I don't know what you—"

"Don't lie to me!" he seethed. "How long did you think you could sneak around? How long did you think it would take before I found out you've been screwing a greasy Italian?"

The slap to her face was hard, precise. Her head snapped sharply from the force of it, her body crumpling to the ground in a heap. She felt the heat of his handprint on her cheek and the metallic taste of blood in her mouth.

"Please . . . no," she cried as she crawled on her hands and knees to the corner, desperate to get away from him. All around her came the sounds of glass smashing, plates breaking, shrapnel flying everywhere as he tore through the apartment, destroying everything in his path.

From the other room, she could hear Aphrodite crying.

"Mama? What's wrong?"

"No!" she shrieked. "Aphrodite, be a good girl. Stay inside. Mama will be there in a moment. Please. Close the door and stay inside."

Obedient as always, Aphrodite closed the bedroom door as Pericles continued to tear through the apartment.

"Do you know what it is to work my fingers to the bone day and night to provide for you? And do you know what it is to be a laughingstock, to hear the filthy Italians sitting at my counter, at my restaurant, pointing at me, laughing at me, because my wife is screwing one of them?" He lifted a pile of dishes and threw them to the ground, daggerlike porcelain shards flying everywhere.

She cowered in the corner, covering her head, sobbing now.

"No, please . . . It's not like that."

"It's not like what?" he spat at her, towering over her. Reaching down, he grabbed her hand and yanked the wedding ring from her finger. He glared at her, spitting at her the last words she would ever hear him say. "I should have left you on the dock. I should have let those men take you away. They would have saved me the trouble since you turned out to be a poutana anyway."

He turned toward the door but then stopped when he heard Aphrodite crying from the next room.

"Mama? Mama. I want Mama."

"It's all right, sweetheart. Mama will be right there. Mama loves you. Mama loves you more than anything."

He paused before opening the door. In that moment Maria realized the cruelty he was capable of. She struggled to her feet as he turned to face her again.

"No!" she screamed. "No! No!" she howled as he wordlessly pushed her back to the ground and threw open the bedroom door, then lifted a crying Aphrodite into his arms and stormed out of the apartment.

Chapter Fifty-One

Milwaukee, Wisconsin

1975

DEMITRA, GEORGE, AND Tasso sat in the kitchen huddled together over thick, bitter coffee and the mistakes of the past.

"Your mother was quite lonely." Tasso gazed into the dark liquid in his cup as if he could see the past playing out before him.

"It was not an easy time, as you can imagine. Maria didn't know the language at first. She didn't know the culture, and she didn't have any friends or family. There were very few Greek women here at the time, which was why your father and I chose picture brides. Marrying an American or another immigrant was not an option. It simply wasn't done." He brought the cup to his lips, his hands trembling slightly.

"There was an ever-present sadness about Maria. I can see that now. Pericles and I were too busy with our own troubles to notice hers. That was what was expected of us. Of all of us. The men worked and the women took care of the home and children, waiting for us to come home. There was no 'How was your day?' or 'Are you happy?' like I see on the American television shows now.

"Your father and I ran a small restaurant, and we worked hard to make it a success. Many shops would not serve Black people at that time, and others would only provide food for takeout. Your father insisted that we serve them, that we treat them as we would want to be treated ourselves. We both knew what it was to be an outsider, to be vilified for not being white enough. And your father knew what it was to be hunted by the men in white sheets.

"We ran a good business, a fair business, until the white mob noticed, and they began to threaten us, to target us. Your father gave everything he had to that restaurant. He survived the boy-cotts, the graffiti, the broken windows, the times they attempted to set fire to the building with us inside."

Tasso shook his head at the memory, then looked up, his tired eyes boring into Demitra's.

"Your father worked day and night, around the clock, sleeping there for days at a time. 'They can't win this time,' he said to me again and again. 'I need to be a man my wife and daughter can be proud of. I can't let them win.'" Tassos's head hung to his chest.

"And it worked. It worked. 'The dumb, stubborn Greek,' as they called him, protected that restaurant with everything he had and eventually the mob moved on to another target, and he was ready to be a husband and a father again. But by then it was too late. All he wanted was to win, and in doing so, he lost it all."

Demitra gnawed on her knuckles as she listened, seeming to lean closer with each word out of Tasso's mouth, drawn to the painful truth like a magnet.

"Your mother was alive when he left, when he took you back to Cephalonia. I wrote letters for her, countless letters. She could not read or write, so I wrote for her. But how do you translate the desperate cries of a mother to the page? Tell me how you reduce a mother's broken heart to mere words?"

Demitra covered her face with her hands, shaking her head back and forth. It was only when she stopped, when she lifted her eyes to meet Tasso's again, that the old man continued with his story.

"He wrote me back only a few times. He said he burned my letters."

"He burned your letters?" She could see herself, a small child gripping a pencil in her hand, drawing crooked hearts and stick figures, and placing them to burn in the fire. She had not been the first to do so. She had watched him do the same.

"Yes. He moved away from his childhood village, and he changed your name so she would never find him, so she would never find *you*. Every few months he would go back to the village and collect my letters. And every few months I would get a letter back, warning Maria not to try to find him, that she would never find you. She knew he took you back to Cephalonia, but she felt helpless, afraid of what he might do if she dared to follow. And how could she anyway? She knew there was nothing she could do, no way to bring you back. Who would help her? She had no one. The shame and hopelessness ate her alive, day by day, bit by bit. She never stopped praying, but beyond that, there was nothing she could do."

Tasso explained that after Baba disappeared with her, Mama spiraled in her grief. Abandoned by her husband, then eventually by her lover. Tasso took pity on her and gave her a job in the restaurant where she worked day and night, never giving up hope that she might one day find her Aphrodite.

"You were her entire life. The dream that she might see you again one day was the only thing that kept her alive. She hated herself for what she'd done, and she never forgave herself. But she was so lonely, Demitra, and she found someone who promised to love her, to stand beside her, until the novelty wore off, and then she was alone again. She found some solace in the church, and she loved the children, singing to them, playing with them. But they were not you."

"When did she die? How?" Demitra asked, her voice cracking with emotion. Tasso reached out his hand and placed it on hers.

"She died in 1948. There was a terrible flu outbreak and she developed pneumonia." The old man shook his head. "But to be honest with you, I think she was tired—tired and alone. I think she simply lost her will to live."

Demitra sucked her breath in sharply as she looked from Tasso to George. "In 1948? That was the year Baba got married. All those years I wondered why. Why then?"

"That was the last letter I sent him—her funeral announcement—to tell him she was gone. That's why you haven't been able to find anything about her funeral. It was in 1948, not 1933."

Demitra nodded quietly, playing it all back in her mind, overwhelmed with sadness, compassion, and grief. For both of them. For all of them.

All this time, all these years, she had imagined her story was one of a young child who lost and grieved her mother. Sitting there in a faded kitchen, mired in the painful memories of an old man, Demitra understood the truth of her own family's myth.

All of them—Mama, Baba, and even herself—were grieving what they once had, what they had loved so dearly, and in the end, what they had lost.

IT WAS 2:00 a.m. when George dropped her off at a nearby hotel with a promise to pick her up in the morning to continue mining Tasso's memories. She didn't even bother to slip out of her clothing; she didn't have the strength. Demitra rolled over and looked at the clock.

It was morning in Cephalonia.

Elena answered on the third ring. "It's me. Elena, I have to tell you something. My father took me from her. I was stolen from my mother too."

Despite the prohibitive expense of a transatlantic call, they stayed on the phone for more than an hour as Demitra wept and explained to Elena what she had learned.

"I knew he was troubled, but this? How could he have done this?" Demitra asked as she sobbed into the telephone.

"It's amazing the things we can be capable of sometimes." Elena's voice was calm, soothing Demitra through the phone. "Our ability to love, to forgive, or to hate and hurt. There is no way to fully understand the primal urges that can come over us, the horrors we can be capable of. Don't try to make sense of it, because you won't. You can't. Don't dwell on your father's ability to hurt. Instead, focus on your mother's ability to love. She never stopped loving you. She never stopped looking for you. And I know, I know with every fiber of my being that she is with you, that she watches over you and read every letter you sent to her and heard every prayer. Now, please, go to sleep. You'll be drawing until you're eighty to pay for this call alone."

As she hung up the phone, Demitra lay in bed, but sleep was an impossibility. She tossed and turned until dawn's first light bled through the hotel drapes.

Finally, she drifted off, dreaming of Mama for the first time in years. And just like when she was a child, Mama appeared to her, opening her arms as if to embrace her. An image came to Demitra, an image of mother and daughter sitting on the floor, playing together and laughing as the sweet timbre of Mama's laughter filled the air. In the distance the faint melody of a childhood song played as Mama made animal puppets with her fingers and Demitra squealed with delight, racing into her mother's arms.

❁

WHEN SHE WOKE later that morning, Demitra could think of only one thing—returning to Tasso and George. There were so many questions she wanted to ask, so many things she had not thought to say. It was overwhelming and exhausting, and her mind raced with countless thoughts.

"Good morning," George said as she slipped into the car beside him. "Did you sleep?"

"Not at all."

"I think you'll need this then." He smiled as he handed her a large cup of coffee.

Leaning back in her seat as she took her first sip, Demitra closed her eyes and smiled as the hot liquid worked to revive her.

George glanced at her as he drove. "I'm so sorry about all of this. My father is racked with guilt. He feels terrible."

"But why would he feel guilty? He didn't do anything. He helped my mother when no one else would."

"Yes, but his guilt ate away at him. He was supposed to have a picture bride too, like your mother. He went with your father to meet them in New York in 1921, but he didn't think she was pretty enough, and he left her there on the dock. That decision has haunted him every day of his life. He knows he ruined that girl's life. He knows things would have been so different if only your mother had had a friend, companionship, instead of being brought here alone to make a life with a man she didn't know. I can't imagine what it was like for her, for them. They called them 'picture brides,' but let's call it what it was—human trafficking. Many of them were just children." He exhaled and slapped at the steering wheel.

She watched him as he drove, compassion etched in his face.

She had not noticed his eyes last night, how they creased in the corners, how they glinted when he smiled. She had not noticed his smile, slightly lopsided, the chipped tooth that peeked out from beneath his mustache.

"Thank you for everything, George. I mean that. For your patience and your kindness."

"You don't have to thank me. I just wish I could do more to help you. To help both of you."

She glanced out the window as the shoreline of Lake Michigan shimmered in the distance, savoring each sip of coffee, anxious and eager to discover what today's revelations might bring.

"WELL, GOOD MORNING to you both." Tasso was already seated at the kitchen table when they arrived at the house.

"Good morning." She greeted him with a hug and a kiss on each cheek. "I still don't know what to think. But I'm grateful to you, for your honesty, and for showing such kindness to my mother."

"She was a good woman, and she deserved better," Tasso said. "I have something for you. I tore up the house this morning, but I found it." He placed his hand inside the breast pocket of his jacket and pulled out a yellowed paper. It looked like an old newspaper clipping.

"Here," Tasso said as he placed the paper on the counter. Demitra and George leaned in to get a closer look.

"You look like her," Tasso said. "Your beautiful smile, your dark curls." Emotion rose in his voice. "This is the picture bride ad that your father answered. This is your mother."

Breathless, Demitra brought her hands to her face and then placed them on the counter on each side of the paper. George leaned in, placing his hand ever so gently on her back. Her eyes welled with tears, blurring her vision, but none of that mattered. Demitra looked down and, for the first time since she was a child, since the day she was ripped away, gazed upon the beautiful face of her mother.

"Oh . . ." She cried softly as she drank her in. "Mama." The dark curls, the cupid's bow lips, and a faraway expression on her face.

"She was barely eighteen in this picture, barely more than a child. Her father lied to her. He told her this photo was a present for her mother in Karditsa, a gift, a surprise." The words seemed to exhaust Tasso and he wiped his brow with a handkerchief he pulled from his breast pocket.

"Look," George said as he placed his finger on the yellowed page, tracing the fine features of Maria's face. He smiled down at Demitra. "You have the same eyes. You can see it, even here in black and white. You have the same firelight in your eyes."

Chapter Fifty-Two

Greece

1980

H<small>E NUDGED HER</small> awake gently as the plane touched down. "Demitra, we're here."

As her eyes fluttered open, Demitra lifted her head from his shoulder, where she had fallen asleep after the plane took off from London.

"I can't believe I slept the whole time." She placed her hand on his leg and squeezed. "I'm anxious about the reviews. Do you think we'll hear soon? Stephanie said she would call as soon as she heard."

George stroked her cheek. "You have nothing to worry about. Everyone was raving at the gallery. I stood next to a writer for the *Herald Tribune* and she was going on and on about your brilliant marriage of social commentary and art."

"Really?" She sat up straighter as she rubbed the sleep from her eyes.

"Yes, really. I mean, who could curate a show about the child trafficking of Greek picture brides in the early 1900s and have the international art community and the entire Greek-American diaspora celebrate the exhibit?" He smiled. "My wife, that's who." He pulled her in for a kiss. "When did you say Jerry and Genevieve arrive? Sorry, I know you told me, but my brain is scrambled with these final permit applications for the museum groundbreaking."

"Tuesday. They had to wait until after Stella's ballet recital." She looked out the window as the plane taxied to the gate, the arid hills of Athens welcoming them in the distance.

The drive north took nearly five hours, winding from the congested streets of Athens, along the Aegean Coast and then snaking up the serpentine mountain roads of Thessaly. As they neared their destination, Demitra fidgeted in her seat, her foot tapping incessantly.

"Is this really happening? Can this really be happening?" she asked.

"You asked me the same thing when I asked you to marry me, when your last exhibit broke a record at auction, and when the *New York Times* celebrated you as"—he smiled mischievously as he tapped his finger to his temple—"what was the exact verbiage? Oh yes, 'an artist who uses her gift to lend voice to her muses, the forgotten and voiceless women of Greek history.'" He laughed. "So yes, this is really happening."

"I wish your father was here with us."

"All he wanted was to hold on long enough to see us married. And he did. He told me it was the happiest day of his life and he could go peacefully now. None of this ever would have happened without him, so I have to believe that in some way, he is still here with us." He brought her hand to his lips and kissed it softly.

"Look." George reached over, pointing just down the road. "There it is."

Her throat constricted with emotion as her eyes fell upon the sign.

KARDITSA 10 KILOMETERS

At last, after what seemed like an eternity, they pulled into a beautiful village square with a handful of pristine tavernas nestled by glorious flower-covered mountains all around.

Demitra let out an audible sigh as he turned off the engine. She waited in her seat, breathing deeply, trying to calm her nerves as George walked around and opened her door. She took his hand and stood there, overwhelmed with conflicting emotions of joy, sadness, achievement, and loss.

"She said on the phone to meet in the square by the fresh spring fountain," Demitra said, her eyes darting around. "She said they would be waiting at the café next door."

As she scanned the square, Demitra locked eyes with her, instantly feeling the spark of connection. Although this was their first time meeting, a peaceful familiarity washed over her. She knew at once what it was, what she had prayed for all those years as a lonely child. Here in this place, in the presence of this old woman, she felt a sense of belonging.

Demitra walked briskly ahead, and George dropped her hand. She stopped and turned to him, uncertainty on her face.

"Go. You've been waiting your whole life for this. Go ahead. I'll be right here, where I will always be. For you, and with you."

She nodded and smiled at him. Untethered, Demitra sprinted toward her, emotions radiating like the heat of the summer sun above.

"It's you," the old woman said. "It's you. I could tell it was you even with my old, tired eyes. You look like her. Dear Lord, you look just like her." Tears flowed down her cheeks, disappearing into the deep lines on her face, which, like words on a page, told the story of a lifetime of sorrow and loss. "My sister's child. My beautiful sister's child." Paraskevi cried as she enveloped Demitra into her arms.

"Oh, Thea, I'm finally here. I'm finally home." Demitra buried her face into the fabric of her aunt's dress, overcome by the scent of mountain air and lavender water.

They stayed like that for quite some time, the illiterate provincial spinster and the internationally celebrated artist, weeping as they clung to each other while the clear, cold mountain water rushed from its spout, just as it had decades before when two scared young sisters held tight to each other at this very spot.

At last Paraskevi was the first to pull away. "Let me look at you. Let me see you." Then the old woman's face crumpled with emotion anew. "Oh my," she whispered, her hand trembling as she brought it to her lips.

Demitra inched closer, her artist's eye digesting the visceral change in the old woman. "What is it?"

"You look like your mother, but you have my mother's face as well, your yia-yia, Aphrodite. She was never the same after your mother was sent away. She's been gone for nearly fifty years now, but to see you here, it's like she's here with us. I see her in you, in your eyes, in your smile, and most importantly, I feel her in your spirit. I lost them both, my sister and then my mother, and now it's as if we are at last together again. And it's because of you. It's all because of you. Oh, Aph—" The old woman stopped then, embarrassment written across her face.

"It's all right, Thea. It's the name my mother gave me. It's who I am. Please, my name is Aphrodite. Call me Aphrodite."

Epilogue

Cephalonia, Greece

1980

S HE IS BEAUTY personified.

Goddess of lust, passion, procreation, sensuality, and love. Protectress of prostitutes.

Celebrated through the centuries in pristine marble and on rich-hued canvas.

Worshiped and summoned in soft moans and urgent whispers, piercing the otherwise silent night.

But there is more to her story, and to her. She is more than history dares to remember. And now, as the visions in her dreams slowly call to her, stirring her awake, her namesake, the artist, remembers as well. She is one of the few who are unfazed by her origins, unafraid to look beyond the superficial to the beginning of the story, of how she came to be, of who she really is.

Long ago, before the gods existed on Olympus, Ouranos, the heavens, took Gaia, the earth, as his wife. The marriage of heaven and earth produced monstrous children, like the one-eyed cyclops and the hundred-handed Hecatoncheires. Ouranos understood and feared the power of his offspring and hid them away, deep in Tartarus where they could not overthrow him.

But Mother Gaia did not see in them what her husband saw. They were her children. She loved them and could not bear to be apart from them.

For the love of her children, Gaia convinced her son Cronos to take vengeance on his father—to cut off Ouranos's testicles with a saw-toothed sickle and toss them into the sea. The sea roiled and churned, transforming into foam. And from the frothing sea emerged the personification of beauty and love.

Aphrodite.

She woke as if from a fever dream, blinking into the night as the moon's gray light bled through the slats on the shutters, casting haunting silhouettes across the room. She was certain she'd heard her name, whispered from somewhere between the shadows. As she stared into the darkened room, all she could hear was the frenzied beating of her heart and the rhythmic breathing of her husband sleeping beside her.

She closed her eyes and heard it once more.

Aphrodite.

The room was filled with the golden light of midmorning when she heard her name again.

"Aphrodite." George stood behind her, placed his hands on her shoulders, and gazed down upon the easel where she had been working for hours.

"Yes." She placed her hand on his, a serpentine smile unfurling on her face.

"She's beautiful," he said. "You gave her your hair and your eyes."

"We have a lot in common. More than I ever imagined."

And she was beautiful, with her dark torrent of curls cascading down her back, surging and spilling into the sea like a wedding veil trailing behind her. Her eyes were saucerlike and dark, illuminated from within as if a fire burned inside her.

Her face tilted up to catch the light of her father, Ouranos. He was complicated, a swirl of storm clouds and broody turbulence. And yet, he loved her in his own way, the only way he was capable of. Ouranos commanded the dark clouds to part, allowing a sliver of light to shine down on her, illuminating his daughter in his essence.

Aphrodite emerged from the sea-foam, her slick olive skin awash in her father's ethereal light, a serene look on her rosebud lips. And although she was born of water and the heavens, there in the distance, watching over her, was the earth.

Gaia was alive with the wisdom and strength of the ancient olive trees, rooting her to Aphrodite, despite the time and space and distance between them. Across the lush mountains and fields, blankets of pale blue forget-me-nots danced on the breeze. Gaia's eyes were awash with the life-giving gift of fresh mountain water, flowing freely in pride and in sorrow as she watched Aphrodite emerge, then immediately be summoned away from her. Gaia whispered a prayer, carried on the wings of Zephyr across the land and ocean, for the child she loved with all her heart but whom she would never truly know.

Despite the distance between them, and the poets and artists who erased her from the story, Gaia understood that she was and would always be Aphrodite's mother. The tangle of tiny blue flowers woven into Aphrodite's hair would always be a testament of their bond and proof that sometimes only after the experience of pain, longing, and sorrow can love exist in its truest and most beautiful form.

"She's magnificent," George said as he inched closer. "Is she for your next show?"

"No," she said as she stood and kissed the lips of the man she loved. "She's for you. She couldn't be for anyone but you."

Author's Note

On the surface, Demitra and I may seem to have little in common.

She, a 1950s Greek woman struggling to find her voice at a time when women were valued not for their intellect and creativity, but for their dowries and virtue. Me, a modern-day Greek-American journalist whose family encouraged and supported my career.

But despite the outward differences of our lives, Demitra and I are indeed kindred spirits. I, like Demitra, found my voice, and in many ways salvation, through art.

When my children were little, I was the quintessential stressed out working mom. Each morning when the alarm blared at 5 a.m., I felt I had already failed the day before I even got out of bed. Between my obligations at home and at work, I was giving away every bit of myself until there was nothing left of me, or for me.

And then it happened, the assignment that would change my life. In 2005, my children were two and four and I was in the weeds of working motherhood when, in my day job as a producer with *extra*, I was sent to interview a young woman who had just won *American Idol.* Her name—you might have heard of her—Carrie Underwood.

I remember watching and listening as Carrie, glowing with joy and bursting with pride, explained what it felt like to live her dream of becoming a performer. She was standing before me, both feet firmly planted in the green room of the television studio where we were chatting, and yet she seemed to levitate. And in that moment, I realized what was missing from my own life and what I desperately wanted and needed. I wanted to know what *that* felt like. I wanted to know what it felt like to chase and achieve my own dream, to be buoyed by pride and accomplishment.

As a journalist I had spent my entire career telling other people's stories. I realized then, that it was time to find my own. That was the day I decided I would sit down and attempt to achieve my dream of becoming an author.

I began setting my alarm an hour earlier, waking at 4 a.m. and carving out time to write before making the kid's lunches, tackling the morning chaos, and heading off to work. Soon I no longer needed to set the alarm because the characters I created would wake me, eager for me to go downstairs and put on the coffee so they could tell me their stories. It took several years of writing and editing, and then the additional years of brutal rejections. Yes, there were tears (quite a few). In 2014 my first novel, *When The Cypress Whispers*, was published. And now in 2024, ten years later, my fourth book, *Daughter of Ruins*, has been published and found its way to your hands. BTW, I hope you liked it and thank you so much for the support!

There were so many times along this journey when friends and family would look at me as if I were insane. They could not understand how actually depriving myself of sleep, declining countless invitations and hiding away alone in my writer's cave for months at a time, while continuing to juggle my responsibilities at work and at home, could possibly be the answer to my physical and mental exhaustion. But it was. And it is.

There's a line in *Daughter of Ruins* that describes Demitra as "an artist who uses her gift to lend voice to her muses, the forgotten and voiceless women of Greek history." Demitra and I are of difference times and experiences, but we aspire to the same goal.

As a daughter of Greek immigrants, it has been my greatest honor and joy to write stories inspired by the women of my family and the extraordinary Greek women who forged a path before us. Each of my books highlights little known stories of these often-illiterate women who lived humble yet extraordinary lives. *When The Cypress Whispers* and *Something Beautiful Happened* tell the story of my own yia-yia and the brave yia-yias who defied the Nazis during WW2 to save their Jewish friends. In *Where The Wandering Ends*, I write of the provincial mothers who sacrificed everything, even their own lives, so their children might survive the brutal Greek Civil War. And now with *Daughter of Ruins*, it was so important to me to shed light on the difficulties faced by early Greek immigrants to the US, struggling to make a life in a strange culture and country. I was shocked and saddened when I learned of the young Greek picture brides, so many impoverished young girls, ripped from their families and homes and forced into marriage with strangers. For generations, countless intelligent women were told time and again, that their voices should not be heard, that their opinions did not matter, and that their place, and worth, were confined to the kitchen and bedroom. These women, their stories, and lessons they impart on us today, are culturally and historically significant. And yes, they do matter.

My children are older now, and while I no longer need to make their lunches and sent them off to school, the characters in my head still often nudge me awake before sunrise, eager for me to put on the coffee so they can tell me their stories.

Like Demitra, it brings me great joy and immeasurable honor to give voice to these once voiceless women whose sacrifices and struggles paved the way for generations of women like me to chase and accomplish our goals.

Like Carrie, I now know what it feels like to live my dream. And you know what, it's even more wonderful and rewarding than I ever imagined.

Acknowledgments

My deepest gratitude and endless thanks to my miracle worker of an editor, Becky Monds. Becky, I don't know what sorcery you invoked to help wrestle this story out of me, but you should find a way to bottle and sell that stuff. Thank you for your patience, even when I told you my word count was literally twice what it should have been, and when I was freaking out about delivering the manuscript while knee deep in Travis Kelce/Taylor Swift Super Bowl coverage. Collaborating with you has been a gift and one of the most rewarding experiences of my career.

Endless thanks to the entire team at Harper Muse Books, Amanda Bostic, Margaret Kercher, Savannah Breedlove, Taylor Ward, and Nekasha Pratt. So much gratitude for my publicists, Bridgette Maney and Kristin Dwyer. What a privilege it has been to be your friend for all these years, what an honor to now also be your client. And to Maria Karamitsos, aka, windy City Greek, a tireless advocate for Greek-American authors.

My deepest appreciation to Tina Manatos and Matina Kololis-Psyhogeos and Ada Polla for your support, kind words and encouragement through the years.

To my brilliant agents, Ali Kominski and Jan Miller, thank you for believing in me and my stories and championing me every step of the way. To Lacey Lynch, you are an inspiration.

To Nena Madonia, thank you for taking a chance on me so many years ago. Your wise words resonate each and every day.

To my Extra family, thank you for the years of support, especially Theresa Coffino and Jeremy Spiegel. Special thanks to Marie Hickey, the greatest friend, colleague, boss and beta reader a girl could have. And to Nicki Fertile, forever the cheerleader and sister of my dreams.

Cheers to the friends who have been by my side through it all, and who don't blink an eye when I disappear into my writing cave for months at a time. Bonnie Bernstein, Jen Cohn, Albert Lewitinn, Adrianna Nionakis, Olga Makrias, Karen Kelly. Thank you for being there with a coffee, glass of wine and most importantly, your friendship, when I emerge again. To my brilliant beta readers, Denise Sheehan, Michelle Tween and Grace Manessis. And to Gigi and SW Howard, thank you again for sharing your beautiful home, my favorite writer's retreat.

I am nothing without my family and nothing matters without my family. So much love

For my Corfu crew, Frousha, George, Alexia, Anna, Alex, Patty, Nico and Noli.

To my children, Christiana and Nico, you both amaze me every day with your kindness, compassion, strength and passion. From my little peanuts to extraordinary and driven young adults, you make my mama heart burst with pride.

To my mom, Kiki, the heart and soul of our family and the epicenter of all that is good.

To my best friend and partner, my husband, Dave. As Demitra says to George, this book could not be for anyone but you. Thank you for your endless support, love, laughter and for the beautiful family and life we built. Now let's go travel the world and come home to our kids and Teagie.

And to you, dear readers. Thank you for embracing me and my stories and for allowing us into your hearts and homes.

Discussion Questions

1. What does the title *Daughter of Ruins* mean to you? How does Demitra's life reflect this title? In what way are Elena and Maria also daughters of Ruins?

2. While their journeys are different, how are Demitra, Elena, and Maria's dreams and struggles to live authentic and meaningful lives, similar? How do cultural and generational factors stand in their way? In what ways do you think women still struggle for their voices to be heard in patriarchal societies today?

3. The snakes of Panagia play an important role in Cephalonia's history and culture. Only twice in modern history have the snakes failed to appear. What happened in these instances? Do you believe that the disappearance of Panagia's snakes was an omen?

4. The Myth of Amphitrite has special significance to Demitra and Aleko. How does the myth of Amphitrite and Poseidon reflect and foreshadow their relationship?

5. Even though women in the US were unable to secure mortgages alone until 1974 (!), Demitra is able to purchase her

Fire Island home with the help of Tino, a recent immigrant. Meanwhile, April's family, who were descended from slaves and lived in the US for several generations, was denied a mortgage and prevented from buying a home in Levittown. Were you familiar with the disparity here, the red line laws and racist real estate provisions that prevented Black families from securing mortgages and accruing generational wealth?

6. While many in the U.S. are familiar with the history of the Japanese picture brides, history has mostly forgotten the thousands of Greek picture brides who came to the US in the early 1900s. What are your thoughts on this practice? In addition to the loneliness faced by Maria, what other difficulties did these young women face?

7. Despite the poverty, lack of education and opportunities that the women had, Martha tells Demitra, *"Men think they hold the power, but we are the power, Demitra. And we bring the magic and the love."* In what ways do Martha's words ring true?

8. There is a resounding theme of mothers, and in Aleko's case, fathers, sacrificing for their children's happiness and futures. How and why do the parents of *Daughter of Ruins* sacrifice themselves for their children? In what way do you recall your parents sacrificing for you, and if you are a parent, when and how have you put the happiness and needs of your own children before your own?

9. The American Hellenic Educational Progressive Association, AHEPA, was formed in Atlanta in 1922 to help Greek Immigrants organize and assimilate in response to violent

attacks by the KKK targeting Greeks and their businesses. Were you aware of the discrimination and racism faced by the Greek immigrants by the KKK and of the targeted attacks against them like the Omaha Greek Town Riot of 1909?

10. In Yvette's author's note, she shares how, like Demitra, she found purpose and in many ways, salvation, through art. Yvette explains how writing helped her find fulfilment and a sense of self in the most difficult moments of working motherhood. What do you do for yourself to help boost your confidence and find fulfillment? Why is finding and carving out a sense of self very important?

About the Author

Photo by Connie Fernandez

YVETTE MANESSIS CORPORON is an internationally bestselling author and Emmy Award–winning producer. To date, her books have been translated into sixteen languages. A first-generation Greek-American with deep family roots on Corfu, Yvette studied classical civilization and journalism at New York University. She lives in New York with her husband and two children and she spends her spare time reading, running, and trying to get into yoga.

Visit her online at yvettecorporon.com
INSTAGRAM: @yvettecorporon
X: @YvetteNY
FACEBOOK: @YvetteManessisCorporonAuthor

LOOKING FOR MORE GREAT READS? LOOK NO FURTHER!

HARPER MUSE

Illuminating minds and captivating hearts through story.

Visit us online to learn more:
harpermuse.com

Or scan the below code and sign up to receive email updates on new releases, giveaways, book deals, and more:

@harpermusebooks

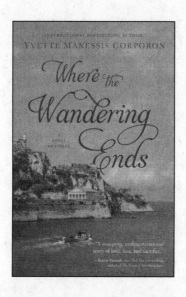